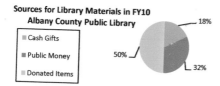

FIRST MURDER IN ADVENT

OTHER FIVE STAR TITLES BY SHARON WILDWIND:

Some Welcome Home

FIRST MURDER IN ADVENT

AN ELIZABETH PEPPERHAWK/
AVIVAH ROSEN MYSTERY

SHARON WILDWIND

FIVE STAR

An imprint of Thomson Gale, a part of The Thomson Corporation

THOMSON

GALE

Detroit • New York • San Francisco • New Haven, Conn. • Waterville, Maine • London

THOMSON
GALE

Set in 11 pt. Plantin.

LIBRARY OF CONGRESS CATALOGING-IN-PUBLICATION DATA

Wildwind, Sharon Grant.
  First murder in Advent : an Elizabeth Pepperhawk/Avivah Rosen mystery / Sharon Wildwind. — 1st ed.
    p. cm.
  ISBN 1-59414-527-X (alk. paper)
  1. Nurses—Fiction. 2. Military police—Fiction. 3. Convents—Fiction. 4. Research institutes—Fiction. I. Title.
PR9199.4.W542F57 2006
813'.6—dc22   2006018307

U.S. Hardcover:
ISBN 13: 978-1-59414-527-8
ISBN 10: 1-59414-527-X

First Edition. First Printing: October 2006.

Published in 2006 in conjunction with Tekno Books and Ed Gorman.

Printed in the United States of America on permanent paper
10 9 8 7 6 5 4 3 2 1

To the instructors and class advisors of the Medical Field Service School, now the AMEDD Center and School, Fort Sam Houston, Texas. You always expected us to be—without reference and without error—outstanding nurses and officers.

And to my classmates in Army Medical Service Officer Basic Course 6-8-C20 (ANC-AMSC), Class #2, 25 August to 26 September 1969. We survived the madness.

ACKNOWLEDGMENTS

Thanksgiving to God for His gift of writing, and for the memory of friends.

It was quite a trip back, trying to recapture the feelings of my first heady days as a civilian. Loads of people accompanied me on that trip. Thanks to:

Gene Moser and Noonie Fortin, both U.S. Army, retired, and Ivan Van Laningham, who helped refresh my military memories.

Major David Bill supplied information about Darby's alma mater, Georgia Military Academy.

Dr. Ronald Craig confirmed where Avivah went to military police school. Dr. William Atwater and Steven Klein gave me information on military weapons.

Jill Grundfest, Ellen Brodsky, Alvin Abram, and Rabbi Lawrence Pinsker helped me keep Avivah on the best path.

Father David A. Godleski, S.J.; Vocation Director; Chicago Province of the Society of Jesus, did the same for Father Ron.

Margery Flax and G. Miki Hayden told me about Central Park in the 1970s. I'm sorry I had to delete the park scene; you'd given me wonderful details to work with.

Lauretta Allen, Carolyn Haines, and I shared a giggle over southern relatives and family trees.

Janet Benrey, my agent, waited patiently until I finished yet another draft. She was, as always, terrific.

Acknowledgments

Thanks once more to my editor, Bill Crider, and to Five Star for allowing Pepper, Avivah, and Benny to continue their journey back to civilian life.

My wonderful husband, Ken, read every draft and managed, sort of, to keep them straight. He also, casually, one day mentioned a pervasive flaw in my sentence structure that I had completely overlooked. Thanks, friend.

And finally one correction. After *Some Welcome Home* was published, Jack Ward, retired U.S. Army master sergeant, pointed out that I'd made a mistake in naming a military post. It's Fort Leonard Wood, Missouri, not Fort Leonard Woods, as I'd written. Thanks, Master Sergeant.

INTRODUCTION

At least in my day, entering the Army was more complicated than leaving it.

Becoming a military nurse involved a six-week course at the Medical Field Service School, Fort Sam Houston, Texas. As a newly minted second lieutenant, I baked in the Texas sun as I tried to absorb the intricacies of Army staff organization, military leadership, the Code of Military Justice, compass and map reading, management of battlefield causalities, how to give and receive salutes, and a number of other courses that seemed, at the time, esoteric and unfathomable.

Three years later, all I had to do to become a civilian again was sign papers and take possession of a manila envelope, which contained veterans' benefits information. The only advice or counseling I received was to never, ever lose my DD-214, that piece of paper which proved I'd been a soldier.

Vietnam was never a popular war; few wars are. When we Vietnam veterans became civilians again, other people— sometimes our own relatives—didn't know what to do with us. They were afraid that drug use, rampant in the military, combined with our military training would unleash the demons, and that we would become violent killers, loose in their own suburbs.

A non-veteran friend asked me to "talk some sense" into another woman veteran he knew. She had been so stigmatized by her community that she had broken all contact with her family. She was terrified to apply for a job because her prospective employer would discover that her last nursing job had been with the Army. We met only on the telephone. She refused to see me in person, and asked me not to call again.

Vietnam veterans were denied medical care, insurance, housing, and jobs. They were spit upon, insulted, and beaten. They were asked to leave military clubs, and denied membership in some veterans' organizations for the first confusing days.

I was denied membership in a national veterans' organization, not because I was a Vietnam veteran, but because I was a woman. Their refusal letter stated, "It is our national policy not to admit women members." This organization was not the American Legion. Unlike Benny and many other veterans, I always had positive experiences with Legionnaires.

A noted psychologist, announcing plans for one of the first studies on post–traumatic stress syndrome, said that there were no plans to include women in the study because "there were too few of them to matter and, anyway, women handle stress better than men, so they are unlikely to have any lasting effects from Vietnam."

Being a female veteran was particularly isolating. Not only were we subject to the same prejudices as male veterans, but additional ones stemming from gender. During the late 1960s and early 1970s, when most of us came out of the military, we could not use our G.I. house loan without getting a man to co-sign the mortgage. Even if a woman was a Vietnam veteran, her credit rating came from her father or her husband.

It was a long journey home, and it began in those first heady days after we took off the uniform, tried to remember civilian vocabulary, and headed back to the world, back to the block, to get on with our lives.

CHAPTER 1

Sunday, 26 November 1972
Womack Army Hospital
Fort Bragg, North Carolina

Ward Six-A was almost deserted. Every orthopedic patient who could walk, limp, or wheel was home for Thanksgiving. The few who remained, mostly guys in traction, fueled by self-pity and boredom, spent the weekend playing increasingly unfunny practical jokes. Sunday morning, Captain Elizabeth Pepperhawk phoned the hospital's Red Cross recreation room and squawked, "Help!"

Now almost everyone had been moved, in their beds, to the Red Cross room for movies and ice cream sundaes. Nurses and corpsmen went with them, leaving Captain Pepperhawk to babysit one patient. Not that he got much of her attention. She had too much paperwork to finish and too little time to do it.

Her phone rang.

"Go away," she grumbled.

The phone kept ringing. She rooted unsuccessfully for it among forms, patient charts, and three-ring binders, which littered her small desk. Afraid her caller would hang up, she yanked on the cord. A heavy black phone rose like a whale, scattering papers. She caught the receiver before it tumbled to the tile floor. "Womack Army Hospital, Ward Six-A, Captain Pepperhawk."

"Pepper, it's Benny."

11

She looked at a photograph tacked to her small bulletin board: a round-faced, stocky man in a green beret. Benjamin Kirkpatrick: ex–Special Forces first sergeant, ex-housemate, now a civilian. She missed him.

"The police caught the guy who vandalized my father's store."

Benny's homecoming had divided his parents' tiny farming community, led to school yard and parking lot fights, and had ministers preaching on both sides. On Halloween, someone spray painted anti-Vietnam slogans on his dad's hardware store. Benny figured his dad was lucky it had been paint, not gasoline and a match.

"The police caught the guy who vandalized my father's store."

Pepper knew Benny's moods almost as well as she did her own. From the sound of his voice, he was either in trouble or in pain, and he didn't admit easily to either one. She stopped tidying her desk and sat down in a creaky, Army-issue chair. "And?"

"It was our next-door neighbor. Damn it, Pepper, he's fucking known me since I was four years old."

Four-year-olds grew up. Went to Vietnam. Got escorted out of the local American Legion by the sergeant-at-arms, because a few World War II veterans didn't want any reminder, as Kenny Rogers put it, of "that old crazy Asian war."

"How's Lorraine taking all this?"

"Scared. So are her boys. Randall is acting like a tough guy who will take on all comers, but Mark is wetting the bed again."

Randall was eleven; Mark, five. Their dad, Benny's best friend, had been listed as Missing in Action/Presumed Dead for four years. Pepper had difficulty coining an easy term to describe Lorraine. Woman-in-limbo was at least shorter than woman-who-would-marry-Benny-in-a-heartbeat-if-she-knew-for-certain-her-first-husband-was-dead.

Benny had spent a decade practicing deadly skills. Pushed too far, he would use those skills in ways civilians wouldn't appreciate. He wouldn't kill, but he would surely make life unpleasant for his neighbors.

What Pepper wanted to say to Benny was, Get out of Missouri. Put Lorraine and her boys in your car, right this minute, and drive back here. Don't put yourself or them in any more danger. What she said instead was, "I'm sorry. How are your parents?"

"Mom is spitting nails. She and her cronies are talking protest marches down Main Street. My dad says he'll petition all the way to national headquarters, if he has to, to make sure Vietnam veterans are welcome in any Legion."

"What are you going to do?"

There was a pause. "I don't suppose you've seen today's *New York Times*?"

The *New York Times* was not a hot item in the sandy back reaches of Fort Bragg. Pepper chuckled. "You supposed right."

Another pause, even longer. "We're not hurt, but Avivah and I were involved in a gun battle in Central Park yesterday afternoon."

Pepper took the receiver away from her ear and stared at it. She considered a possibility that Benny was flat-on-his-ass drunk at three P.M., but Benny never lost control like that. He wouldn't joke about a gun battle, especially one that included her best friend, Military Police Captain Avivah Rosen. Blood drained to Pepper's toes. She put the receiver back to her ear. "You what?"

"Avivah witnessed a robbery in progress and went after the thief. I went after her. We sort of chased down this guy and captured him."

"Sort of?"

"Well okay, we chased him down and held him until police arrived. He had a gun. He fired a few shots, but fortunately, no one was hurt. The story made front page news."

Avivah was stationed at Fort Dix, New Jersey, a stone's throw from New York City, but Missouri was a long way from Central Park. "What are you doing in New York City?"

"It's a long story."

Pepper leaned back in her chair. Nothing was more important to her than a blow-by-blow account of whatever fiasco Benny and Avivah had stumbled into. Only after she savored every detail could she be furious or impressed, depending on circumstances. "I have loads of time, Benny."

"I don't. There's a cab coming for me in a few minutes."

Pepper grabbed a pencil and pushed papers aside, looking for scrap paper. A binder fell to the floor. Pepper ignored the paper waterfall sliding over green-and-black tiles. "I want to talk to Avivah. Is she back at Fort Dix?"

"She's on emergency medical leave."

Pepper's stomach tightened. If Benny hadn't already assured her that no one was hurt, she'd be certain Avivah was lying in a hospital. There had to be more Benny wasn't telling her.

"She can't talk to you. We had to sedate her and hide her from reporters."

Avivah was brassy enough to take down a thief, but Pepper could not imagine her allowing anyone, even Benny, to drug and sequester her. Avivah hated taking even an aspirin. Something was terribly, terribly wrong. "We?"

"Avivah and I had lunch yesterday with an old friend of hers. He was with us in Central Park. While the police were cuffing our guy, a *New York Times* reporter showed up. As soon as he told Avivah he worked for a newspaper, she went ape-shit. Hysterical. I thought she would kill him. I've never seen her like that. Her friend made arrangements for her to stay with someone who could protect her from reporters."

Pepper hoped this stranger was very good at protection. Women Vietnam veterans weren't that common. Reporters would go crazy over a woman veteran who'd been in a front-page shootout.

"You promise me that Avivah is safe?"

"Yes."

"Swear it on your beret."

Benny's beret was the most sacred thing he owned. She would believe even his most outlandish story if he swore it on his beret.

"For Christ's sakes, Pepper."

"Swear it."

"I swear, on my honor as a Green Beret, that Avivah is safe and well cared for."

Pepper looked at her bulletin board again. She ran her finger over a photograph of Avivah, wishing somehow her friend could magically feel her concern. "I'm still clearing post, and the new owners don't take possession of Lorraine's house until late Thursday. Friday morning, I'll be on the first plane for New York. Meet me at the airport."

"We won't be here. Avivah and I are flying out of New York this evening. Avivah's friend knows a place where reporters will never look for her. It's pretty close to you. Do you know where Crossnore, North Carolina, is?"

Pepper thought she'd driven through Crossnore once, on her way to visit her aunt in Tennessee. "Vaguely. I'll find a map."

"We'll be at the Convent of the Visitation of the Blessed Virgin Mary."

A convent. Oh, shit. Pepper had attended convent school for twelve years, but hadn't been to Mass or confession since Vietnam. No lapsed Catholic belonged at a convent. Okay, for Avivah's sake she'd go there, but she wasn't going to like it.

Benny asked, "Do you want directions? I don't want you to get lost."

"If Crossnore is as tiny as I remember, even I couldn't get

lost there. I'll stop at a gas station and ask for directions."

"See you Friday. Got to go. My cab is here." He hung up.

Pepper worked thumbtacks carefully out of several photographs. Benny's formal portrait in his beret. Pepper, Avivah, and Benny clowning around with a hose, washing Pepper's car. Avivah, wearing a flack jacket and helmet, standing beside a military police jeep in Long Bien. Benny, Avivah, and herself hanging off a streetcar in San Francisco. Happier times. Almost happier times.

San Francisco still worried her. They met Avivah's freedom bird, the plane that brought her home from Vietnam, and spent three days together. In spite of feeling giddy that they had all survived tours in Vietnam, Pepper never once saw her friend smile. She hoped it was fatigue and jet lag, something that regular meals and sleep would cure, but deep down, even then, she'd suspected there was more to it.

Benny pegged it right away. "I've seen too many guys come back from 'Nam carrying heavy emotional baggage. Avivah's changed. She's in trouble."

Pepper tried everything: long-distance phone calls, silly cards, serious cards, long letters, little presents, but Avivah kept her distance. She'd talk about her new assignment as logistics officer for the military police dog school; comment on weather; update Pepper on her various family members; but she would not—absolutely not—say one word about Vietnam. Now she had gone chasing a thief in Central Park. Bad times all around. Okay, no more nice guy. She and Benny would find a way to force Avivah to tell them what was wrong. They owed it to her, as her friends, to be concerned about her.

Pepper walked back into her six-bay ward. Weak winter sunlight slanted through large windows, making bright patterns on the linoleum floor. All was ordered and quiet. Iron-framed beds stood in precise rows, spreads taught, white pillows aligned exactly on each bed. The radiator clanked as it pumped out heat.

Her one patient, who liked privacy more than movies, lay with his casted leg propped on pillows. He had a bowl of grapes on his over-bed table and an issue of *Analog*. He looked up. "Afternoon, Captain. Nice uniform."

Pepper laughed as she looked down at her sweatpants and faded T-shirt that said "University of Mississippi School of Nursing." She wasn't, officially, at work. Head nurses didn't work Sunday afternoons, but Ward Six-A had become as much of a home for her as Lorraine's house, which she and Benny had shared after Lorraine moved to Missouri. She pulled up a chair and sat beside his bed. "Thanks. You're from western North Carolina, aren't you?"

"Newland, up in Avery county."

"Is that near Crossnore?"

"Shoot, Crossnore is about four miles away."

She tried to remember the convent's complicated name. "Do you know how to get to the Convent of the Visitation of the Blessed Virgin Mary?"

"Visiting Sisters? Sure, you go up the mountain about three miles from the gas station, and turn right. But directions won't do you any good."

"Why not?"

"The convent's closed."

Pepper sat up straighter. "Closed? Like for Thanksgiving?"

"No, ma'am, I mean closed forever. The nuns ran a girl's orphanage for a long time, but they shut their doors last June. My mom told me about it. Some group is going to turn it into a conference center."

"You're sure?"

He frowned. "Pretty sure. If you'll wheel a phone over here, I'll call Mom and ask her."

"That's okay. Don't bother."

He turned as much as he could manage with his bulky cast. "How come you're interested in the Visiting Sisters?"

"I thought a couple of friends of mine would be staying there this week. I guess I misunderstood them."

"Guess you did."

She got up. "Can I get you anything?"

He held up his magazine, turned to a story by Joe Haldeman. "Nope. Me and this Bill Mandella character are doing just fine."

Pepper started back for the nurses' station.

"Captain."

She turned. "Yes."

"We're going to miss you."

Her throat tightened. "I'll miss you, too. You behave for this new head nurse; you hear me."

"Yes, ma'am, always."

In a pig's eye, Pepper thought, as she walked back to her office. They would test the new head nurse, just as they tested her. Most of her patients had seen and done things she couldn't even imagine, despite having done her year in Vietnam. You couldn't fool them. You had to be honest with them. The last year and a half had been a bumpy ride at times, but she'd worked hard to earn their trust and respect. Whatever came next for her, she was proud to take that feeling with her.

She picked up the phone in the nurses' station. "I'd like information for Crossnore, North Carolina."

There was an unlisted phone number for the convent. How odd that a convent would be unlisted. Maybe there was just a caretaker there.

Pepper was sure of one thing: Benny attracted trouble like a magnet. He had no more control over it than he did his receding hairline. A sensible person would run away from Benny, but then, as Avivah was fond of saying, no one could ever accuse Elizabeth Pepperhawk of having any sense at all.

CHAPTER 2

Friday, 1 December 1972
Crossnore, North Carolina

The gas station attendant, a skinny teenager with "Toby" embroidered on his high school sports jacket, eyed snow pelting at Pepper's U-haul. "Going far?"

She'd spent enough vacations in Tennessee to know that Smoky Mountain people did what they could to take care of one another. Toby wanted to know whether she was a stranger, passing through, or if she had a connection to someone he knew. She pulled a pen and piece of paper from her glove box. "Going to see the Visiting Sisters. Can you draw me a map of how to get to their convent?"

He shook a few drops of gasoline into the snow, and, with a clank, hung the nozzle. "Visiting a student?"

Thank goodness she'd had the patient from Newland. If she'd said "yes," no telling where Toby's map might have led her. "The orphanage closed in June. I'm visiting one of the nuns." She desperately hoped there were still nuns in residence.

"Seems kind of funny she didn't give you directions."

At least now she knew there were still nuns at the convent. She felt better about Benny and Avivah having come here. All convents had a Sister Mary Something. She waved at the U-Haul. "Sister Mary gave me directions, but I packed them by mistake. I have no idea which box they are in."

"So Sister Mary Rachel expects you?"

Pepper didn't know. Benny must have told someone to expect her. "I promised I'd be there by supper."

He sketched a winding line and a few landmarks. "Sorry about questioning you, but with the women up there all by themselves, we don't like strangers bothering them. I'll call ahead and tell Sister Mary Rachel you're on your way."

Pepper accepted his hand-drawn map, grateful that she'd passed Toby's test. She was sure of one thing: If Toby thought the women were alone, he had no idea that Benny was there. Hiding Avivah must have worked. "Sure. Thanks."

He tapped on her window frame. "You drive careful now, you hear. If this snow gets any worse that road will be real slick and these rental vans are top-heavy."

As she pulled onto the road, Pepper glanced at her dashboard clock. Fifteen-thirty hours. Three-thirty, she corrected herself. She was on civilian time now, and she had to use civilian vocabulary. Last night at midnight, as she slept in a motel halfway between Fort Bragg and Crossnore, she'd become, for the first time in four years, plain Elizabeth Ann Pepperhawk. Registered Nurse, Bachelor of Nursing, she added hastily, feeling a need to have some qualifiers still attached to her name. Like a diver coming up from a great depth, it would be smart to make this transition in slow steps or she'd risk getting the bends.

It would be dark in an hour. Toby's map didn't give a clue how far she still had to drive. Pepper shivered as she realized she might not finish her journey before nightfall. Still, there was no turning back. Not only did Benny expect her before supper, but now, thanks to Toby, Sister Mary Rachel did, too. It never paid to worry a nun.

She didn't see one other car on the road. When snow hit, mountain people stoked their fireplaces and woodstoves and waited for better weather. A small patch of ice, taken too fast, could send a car plummeting down a mountain. She wished

Toby hadn't reminded her that her van was top-heavy. Pepper shifted into low gear. "I can do anything. I've been to Vietnam."

It had been a standard joke in the officers' club every time someone got a shitty assignment or was faced with too much work. I can do anything. I've been to Vietnam.

Within a mile, she would have turned back if she could. Her neck and shoulders burned from fighting the wheel and, on each curve, her tires slid for a few seconds. Waves of adrenaline surged through her. As they said in Vietnam, nothing like a little excitement to brighten your day.

Coming here in a U-Haul had been stupid, but Benny's phone call had thrown her into a tailspin. She'd already sold her car. When she ran out of time to arrange for a moving company to pack and store her belongings, the U-haul was her only option. She never imagined that she would be going up a winding mountain road, at dusk, in a blizzard. Great planning, Pepperhawk.

Wiper blades scraped across her frozen windshield. When she used the washer, liquid froze immediately, cracking into a Jack Frost pattern that obscured her view. She kicked the defroster up as high as it would go, and a dime-sized hole thawed just in time to let her see enough to keep from driving off the mountain.

Trembling, she kept her eyes on the road and one hand on the steering wheel as she fumbled for her thermos. As she worked off the plug, hot liquid dribbled down, making her cab reek of strong coffee and expensive brandy. She singed her lips and tongue sipping straight from the thermos, but enough fiery liquid ran down her throat. In five minutes, she relaxed and managed to cap the bottle one-handed.

Benny should have picked any other place besides a convent to hide Avivah. Pepper toyed with the idea of looking a nun straight in the eye and saying, "Yes, I went to convent school for twelve years, but what I saw in Vietnam kicked my faith out of me."

She could never pull it off. It would be *Yes, sister. No, sister. Thank you, sister.* She'd be lucky not to curtsey. Ursuline nuns at her high school expected their students to curtsey.

Keeping her van almost against a rock wall, she negotiated a particularly slippery curve. Pepper adjusted her defroster, which by now had cleared the windshield and moved on to roasting her fingers.

She could be home by Christmas. Yeah, right. She wasn't going back to Biloxi this Christmas or any other, except for weddings, graduations, and funerals.

Eighteen months ago, at home on leave after Vietnam, her mother still cleaned up after her, made her bed, and left notes pinned to her pillow. "Don't leave your bed in a mess. Your future husband will expect a tidy house."

Her favorite shorts and T-shirts disappeared. "I threw them away, dear. They were so ragged; I couldn't bear to look at them. You have to dress properly if you expect the right young men to notice you."

The right young men had already noticed her, even if she wore fatigues and combat boots. Her own voice drifted back to her. "Come on, stay with me. Focus right here on my face. Stay with me. Just a few more minutes until we get you to surgery."

No, going home to live was absolutely out.

Taking a deep breath and leaning over the steering wheel, she strained to see through rapidly falling snow. Her headlights picked up two granite pillars. One had a brass plaque: "Visitation Convent."

Pepper turned into the drive, and her heart pounded as her van almost skidded into the ditch. As she fought the steering wheel with both hands, her thermos fell out of her lap and rolled away. Pepper looked toward heaven. "All right. I get it. I promise to behave around the nuns."

She drove at a slow pace, just fast enough to keep going forward. On her left a small stone house was barely visible. It looked deserted. Must have been some sort of guardhouse. Gatehouse, she corrected herself again. Civilian vocabulary.

The road cut through deep forest. Snow partially obscured one set of fresh tire tracks. She was relieved to see that at least one other car had traveled this road not so long ago. Another sign that she'd find people here. Pepper drove around a small curve. The forest opened into a large clearing. Mouth open, she gaped at the gloomy stone building, partially obscured by falling snow.

Nothing prepared her for a monstrous three-story building, constructed of the same grey mountain granite as those entrance pillars. An impressive center staircase led to main doors, which had etched glass covered by white, pleated curtains. At intervals, peaked dormers capped the grey, slate roof. To the convent's right a tall wall enclosed something, probably a garden.

Pepper parked where she hoped, under the snow, lay a graveled turnaround, and not a prized lawn. She couldn't see any lights, or any other cars, which might have made the tracks she saw on the road. This convent looked as deserted as the gatehouse.

Unbidden and unwelcome, Major Darby Baxter's soft Georgia accent floated through her head. He had stood under a tree, protected from harsh Texas sun, and instructed her basic class, who sat on bleachers. "When you encounter an unexpected situation, remove yourself as far as possible from danger. Secure yourself and think out your options. Worst case? Best case? Survival scenario?" Secure yourself. Pepper reached over and locked the van's door.

Her breath came in short, painful gulps. If there was one thing she didn't need right now, it was an ex-boyfriend giving her advice. Or maybe that was just what she needed: advice—not her boyfriend.

Think. Best case was that someone was here, in a room that she couldn't see from where she parked. Worst case: those car tracks went out instead of in. There had been an emergency: Benny, Avivah, and the nuns left in a hurry to take someone to a hospital. She was all alone, in the dark, in freezing weather, in front of a completely isolated convent. No one in the world, except Benny and a teenaged gas attendant, knew she was here. A crazed mountain ax-murderer could kill her, bury her body on the mountain, and no one would ever have a clue what had happened to her.

Building a survival scenario was better than focusing on that possibility. No way she was going back to Crossnore. Driving at night, in this weather, was too dangerous. She had enough clothes and blankets that she could survive. She might be hungry, she might be cold, but she wasn't going to die.

She scanned the building, willing some small light to appear. A shadow stood in a round-topped tall window, on the third floor, just under a massive cross. Pepper's chest constricted. Someone watched her. Trying to forget all the scary movies she'd seen, she sank back and tried to make herself invisible. When she'd watched for five minutes, and the shadow hadn't moved, she laughed. It wasn't a person, it was a statue, probably Mary or the Sacred Heart of Jesus.

A door opened, spilling warm, golden light on fresh snow. A thin, tiny woman, in a traditional black habit, trudged unsteadily toward the garden's wooden door.

Relief flooded through Pepper. Best case scenario after all. "Thank you, Lord," Pepper muttered. Her words sounded strange. It had been a long time since she thanked the Lord for anything. Must be the atmosphere.

She looked again at the nun. No one that thin should be out

in a snowstorm. Pepper unlocked her door and got out. Cold air smelled clean and wonderful after being cooped up. Pepper inhaled deeply as she pulled her jacket hood over her head and closed her zipper. She waved. "Sister . . . Sister."

Pepper noticed that the nun wore no coat or gloves. She fumbled, barehanded, with a black iron clasp, not noticing the padlock above her head.

Pepper stepped beside her and gently put her hands over cold fingers. "Sister?"

The woman looked to be in her fifties, maybe early sixties. The stiff band that supported her wimple made a crease in her forehead. She had a thin, wizened face that was part child, part old woman, and completely vacant. Dementia. Why had anyone allowed her to be alone in this deserted place?

People with dementia often feared strangers. Hoping to avoid a panic reaction, Pepper carefully linked her arm through the nun's thin one. "It's very cold, sister. We will go inside and warm up."

The convent's side door turned on well-oiled hinges. Pepper and her charge stepped into an anteroom. Winter and rubber boots lined a shoe rack. Black coats and cloaks hung over them. A sturdy mahogany holder held umbrellas and walking sticks.

Pepper released the sister's arm long enough to throw a door bolt, placed she noticed, like the garden's padlock, too high for the sister to reach. Taking her companion's arm again, she stepped into a warm corridor, where ubiquitous Catholic-institution cream walls made her feel as if she'd never left her Ursuline Academy. "Hello? Anyone here?"

Smells hit her. Damp clothes. Chalk dust. Incense. Prayer books. Soap and disinfectant. Hot, rich convent food. A Catholic Convent—capital letters. Pepper's knees almost buckled under memories. In a meek voice, she tried again. "Hello?"

A woman in her mid-forties, wearing a black skirt, white

blouse, black jacket with a silver cross pinned to it, and modified, shortened wimple, came out of a doorway. She wiped her hands on a dish towel. "I'm Sister Mary Rachel. You must be the person Toby phoned about."

She did not have to say she was the sister-in-charge. Pepper could still recognize one. Why would the administrator be in the kitchen?

Pepper propelled her charge forward, as if the frail nun would provide a barrier between her and Sister Mary Rachel. "I found her outside, without a coat."

Sister Mary Rachel turned and called into the room she had just left, "Helen, come here, please."

An older woman, dressed in white cotton uniform, apron, and thick hairnet, entered the hall.

"Sister Valentina was outside." Her tone conveyed, "I'm disappointed in you, and you will do better."

The hard set of the woman's stocky face said she had no intentions of being bullied. Not now, not ever. Pepper envied her strength. The woman put her arm protectively around Sister Valentina. "Oh, mein Gott. Come, sister. Hot chocolate and toast are ready. We go in kitchen and get warm." Without a single glance back, they disappeared.

Sister Mary Rachel gave Pepper a long up-and-down look. Pepper remembered she wore jeans and swallowed hard. Wearing any kind of pants was forbidden in convent school. She was sure to get detention.

"And you are?"

"I'm sorry, sister. Elizabeth Pepperhawk." She didn't add that most people called her Pepper. The less Sister Mary Rachel knew her the better.

"Mr. Kirkpatrick's guest. You are expected. I believe that he is in the visitors' lounge. Go out the door you came in, around to the far end, and back in a door marked 'Visitors' Entrance.'

I'll send Sister Angelus to show you to your room."

Pepper knew there had to be a way down a long, warm corridor rather than through night and cold. Sister Mary Rachel wasn't about to let her use it.

Offer up the discomfort for the most deserving soul in purgatory. Pepper wondered if she could bargain with God, offer it up instead for a soldier in danger in Vietnam. The ones in danger were never far from her thoughts.

"I'm parked in front. Shall I leave my van there?"

"There's a garage on the other side of this building."

"I'm driving a U-Haul. I'm not sure it will fit in a garage."

"Then park beside it." Pepper recognized a tone identical to the one her high school science teacher used. "Use your brains, girls. That's why God gave them to you."

Pepper smoothed her hands down her jeans, as if that movement could hide what they were. "I'm sorry about the way I'm dressed, sister. I didn't think. I won't wear jeans again." Her mind raced though what clothes she'd packed in her suitcase: far too many pairs of pants.

With a tone that suggested her world had already gone to hell in a handbasket, the sister said, "There are no longer any students here. Wear what you wish, but please remember that alcohol is not permitted here."

Pepper tried to smell her clothes, without letting the sister know what she was doing. She didn't smell that bad. It was useless to argue that she'd only had one small drink. Well, okay, maybe two or three. "I will leave the brandy in my van."

"See that you do. Supper is at six," Sister Mary Rachel announced with a finality that conveyed, barring Christ's second coming, don't be late. It never paid to buck convent routine.

Pepper went out into the cold night, proud of herself. She'd stopped herself before she curtsied.

CHAPTER 3

Pepper still wished Benny had chosen anywhere but a convent, and she certainly wasn't going to tell anyone she was a lapsed Catholic, but it *was* nice to be inside. Baking odors hung in the air; dessert would be a sensory overload. Who could ask for more than caramelized sugar and a warm bed?

She had seen a dozen convents, not only her own, but ones she'd visited for retreats, debate tournaments, and intramural sports. This one had the standard, ubiquitous photo beside its visitors' entrance: a nun and ten girls, dressed in identical clothing, standing on the front porch of a large house. No doubt that was the original convent building.

Familiarity plucked at her flannel shirt like a malicious elf. "You're safe here," he whispered. "It's warm, and they will feed you." Travelers had reacted this way to nunneries for two thousand years. Not that Pepper believed the elf any more. Safety and warmth were, at most, transitory gifts. Let someone start a war, drop bombs, set Claymores, and safety evaporated.

Pepper found a tiny, windowless cloakroom beside the visitors' entrance. Eight coats filled the hooks, over eight sets of footwear, and the damp wool miasma made her feel claustrophobic. A man, with his back to her, bent over a coat, and took something from a pocket.

Pepper cleared her throat. He jumped and spun around to face her. His hand moved discreetly into his own pants pocket.

He was in his late thirties or early forties, with a lean body and stylishly cut black hair. Dressed in a fine linen shirt, grey cashmere sweater, and pleated wool slacks, he looked like a successful novelist or a senior accountant for a huge company. He pushed black-framed glasses up his nose and peered at her. "Miss Pepperhawk, I presume?" He had a New York accent.

Pepper stepped back. She didn't like a stranger knowing her name. "You have the advantage of me, sir."

He held out his hand, but she didn't take it, which seemed to offend him. "Gary Dormuth. Avivah stayed with me last weekend."

He didn't match Pepper's image of Avivah's protector. She'd expected someone older, powerful, and rich. "Just what are you doing here, Mr. Dormuth?"

"I flew down from New York with Avivah."

"Why? Did she need an escort because your tame doctor sedated her to the gills?"

When he stood erect, he towered over Pepper's five-foot-four frame. "Not at all. I wanted to come with her. She wanted me to come."

They faced one another; his brown eyes locked on hers. She'd made a mistake when she assumed Gary Dormuth wasn't powerful. He was a debater's nightmare, an opponent with immutable drive to confront, argue, and win. She had been an adequate debater, but when confronted with an opponent such as Gary, she mentally curled up and mewed like a kitten.

That was before she'd been an United States Army officer. Right now she was tired and worried about Avivah. She didn't feel like curling up. "Do you make it a habit of rifling coat pockets?"

His shoulders tensed. She'd scored a hit.

He took out a key ring, which held two keys and a rental car tag. "We rented a car at the airport. Even in a convent, it's a bad idea to leave car keys unattended."

why are we on earth as God's creatures."

She'd met answering a question with a question before. Her high school debate coach had been a Jesuit. Jesuits—members of the Society of Jesus, founded by a Spanish soldier, Saint Ignatius Loyola—had reputations as rigorous thinkers.

e set her cup and saucer on the small table beside her. "e a Jesuit, aren't you?"

grinned again. "I see you've met at least one of Ignatius' before. Guilty as charged. And I'm here, in this parlor, b flew down from New York with Avivah. She needed a s and this was the safest place I could think of."

d been eight coats in the coatroom. How many other own down from New York with Avivah because she needed protection? She was about to ask hey had rented a car or chartered a bus, when d the corridor.

Four men entered, single file: an older man ew cut; a very tall, disheveled man; and a in a black suit and tie. She barely had time re the fourth man entered. Suddenly dizzy, eady herself by gripping the cool marble- chair. Breath left her body completely.

d straight at her. Too well trained to al- o change, he hesitated for the blink of etime. Mister Military himself came axter. Six feet tall, curly blond hair, ect poster child for Special Forces, r . . . date? Far more than that. or lack of trying on Darby's part. d in front of her chair, and gave rgia accent she'd missed since d, "You must be our eagerly vid Barton." He pronounced

Her old debate skills kicked in. She analyzed his statements. Rented a car: probably true. Bad idea to leave keys unattended: known to be true. He was looking for those keys: unsubstantiated assumption. She had no proof that keys were what he removed from someone's coat or that the keys he held belonged to his rental car. But he was oh, so smooth. She'd let it ride for now, but she wasn't prepared to trust Gary Dormuth one inch.

"Visitors' parlor is the first door on your left. Benny is there, but Avivah isn't. She worried so much about you driving on icy roads that I suggested she lie down."

Pepper already suspected Gary Dormuth bent truth and argument to his will, but was he now outright lying? Avivah wasn't a worrywart. Pepper couldn't see her taking to her bed with an attack of the vapors just because Pepper was driving in a little snow. "Who put you in charge of her?"

"I put myself in charge, and she hasn't complained. I take some small pride in making this past week easier, and safer, for her."

Pepper pressed her lips together to keep from saying something she'd regret later if he turned out to be Avivah's old and beloved friend. She'd always given Avivah credit for better taste in friends. "Is she all right?"

"I've only known her six days, but, in my opinion, insomnia, hysteria, and crying jags are far from all right."

Avivah was a tough cop. She wasn't a person who had hysterics or cried easily. Stunned, Pepper sat down hard on a tiny bench. "You can't be serious?"

"I wish I weren't."

Pepper knew one thing now. Gary Dormuth couldn't be Avivah's old and trusted friend. He just said he'd only known her six days. "How did you meet her?"

"I was with her and Benny when they made their spectacular capture in Central Park. Avivah fell into a pond tackling the thief. Her clothes were soaked and the temperature near freezing. My apartment was only a few blocks from the park, so we took her there to clean up. She stayed."

Yes, but had she stayed of her own will after Gary and Benny had her sedated? If Gary was right about hysteria and crying jags, Pepper conceded that they might have done the right thing to call a doctor. Whether she liked Gary or not, he had cared for Avivah. "Thank you for protecting her."

He smiled. "Protecting her isn't easy, is it?"

"No. She's stubborn and likes to take care of herself."

"I've noticed." He opened a heavy door, through which Pepper saw a long, dark corridor.

"My brother was a marine. He died in the A Shau Valley. I never thought I'd have anything to do with any Vietnam veteran, but Avivah proved me wrong. I like her, and I think she likes me. So, Miss Pepperhawk, don't go building conspiracies where none exist." For effect, he jingled keys in his pocket.

The heavy door glided shut behind him.

Contrary to what Sister Mary Rachel and Gary Dormuth said, Benny was not in the visitors' parlor. An auburn-haired, bearded priest, dressed in a cassock, sat there reading a book. He stood as Pepper entered, marking his place with his finger. "I'm Father Ronald Lincoln. You must be Pepper. Avivah told me all about you."

First Gary, now Father Lincoln. What had Avivah said about her? Did *all* include her current lack of attendance at Mass and confession? She was in no mood for counseling, proselytizing, or a lecture, the only responses she expected from a priest.

He put his book down, moved a second chair closer to the fire, and pointed to a linen-covered table, which held coffee and tea. "Benny said he would be back shortly. May I get you something to drink?"

Pepper sat gingerly on the chair's edge. "Coffee with milk and sugar, please."

He prepared coffee for both of them.

"Thank you, Father Lincoln."

He stretched his long legs out toward the fire, and wed away her honorific. "If you must be formal, Father Ron, what my nieces and nephews call me. Otherwise, j Ron."

"I'm afraid Avivah never told me about *you.*"

"No? I'm disappointed. As one of her dearesc sumed my name was constantly on her lips." twinkle in his eye. She chortled, and settled b She certainly liked Ron better than she like

Ron smiled. "That's better. When you though your pet had been run over."

"I had an encounter with Gary Do

"Sounds like that boardgame: room, with an attitude."

"You know him?"

"I've known Gary several him a chance to warm up t question, Avivah and I m We marched together in went a baptism of fire

Police used fire rights demonstrati Pepper felt a hint he understood make a black in it. "If yo Ron st expressi why am I h each syllable of the name distinctly, as if to make sure she heard them correctly.

Darby Baxter—David Barton. He hadn't even changed his initials when he concocted a false identity. Why was a Special Forces intelligence officer here, under an assumed name? She knew what he was trying to tell her. Behave and don't blow my cover. As if she would. She prided herself on being too good an officer.

Pepper knew one thing for certain. Unless he'd met her recently, Darby had never, in his entire life, laid eyes on Avivah Rosen. No way he could be here because he thought she needed protection. Whatever was going on here was more than one woman hiding out from reporters.

She'd been right not to believe that malicious elf. If Darby were here, she had unwittingly stumbled into something dark and dangerous.

Benny once told her that she was a threat to national security. "You let a guy drown in your big, brown eyes and he tells you things he shouldn't. Thank God you know how to keep your mouth shut."

She hoped Darby/David had packed water wings. He was about to drown, and, with any luck, he'd tell her everything she wanted to know about his being here. Pepper extended her hand, and let her voice slip into her Sunday-best Mississippi vowels. "How do you do, Mister Barton. I'd be so pleased if you called me Pepper."

He took her hand, stopping short of kissing it. "Permit me to introduce you to my friends."

Darby escorted her to a man in his mid-fifties, who had a brown-and-grey military haircut. "Sir, it is my honor to present Miss Elizabeth Pepperhawk. Miss Pepperhawk, General William Pocock-Nesbitt."

General. That explained why he'd been first through the door.

He expected to be in charge. He offered a dry hand. "I'm retired, but everyone still calls me General Bill."

Something about the man irritated her. Pepper had met a few other ex-officers who took unfair advantage of having been a soldier, long after they became civilians. She hadn't liked it when they traded on memories of past accomplishments. She and General Bill probably weren't going to be buddies.

David moved her to a tall, cavernous man, who gave her a weak handshake and looked at the carpet as he mumbled, "Thomas Hackmann."

Seeing him close-up, Pepper suspected the slight tremor in Mr. Hackmann's hands and face were a side effect of taking psychiatric medications. General Bill hardly seemed likely to be comfortable around a trembling psychiatric patient. The world got curiouser and curiouser.

The third man was precise and dapper, with well-groomed, shoe-polish black hair and beard. He held out a manicured hand. "Dr. Saint-Mathias."

Maybe he accompanied Thomas Hackmann. Being in an isolated convent with a patient who required constant medical supervision didn't thrill her. "A physician?"

"Ph.D. in military history. Louisiana State University."

Okay, counting Gary Dormuth, she'd met a possible thief, a priest with a sense of humor, an undercover military intelligence officer, a puffed-up retired general, a psychiatric patient, and a military historian. None of whom, other than Ron and Gary, had any reason Pepper could discern for being here. Perhaps she really had slid into a ditch on that last curve and now lay at the bottom of a ravine, dying of hypothermia and hallucinating. It was as good an explanation as any for her feeling of complete disorientation.

Benny chose that moment to appear. At Fort Bragg, when out of uniform, he'd worn cutoff shorts and brightly-colored tropical shirts. Seeing him in tan, polyester shirt and slacks, with his black hair long enough to reach his ears took getting used to. He looked too—Pepper struggled for a word—too civilian. This wasn't how she wanted her hero to look.

He grinned at her. "I see you finally got here. Still snowing?"

"Like crazy."

"I won't ask how your trip was. My old nerves can't take any more strain."

His old nerves were only five years older than hers were and they'd already stood up to a lot of strain.

He gave her a hug, and she settled into his warmth. She'd missed him so much. He really was the same old Benny, different clothes, but a great hugger.

Darby and Benny knew one another. Benny was even less likely to blow a fellow soldier's cover, but he must have an opinion about Darby's fake identity. Pepper was dying to ask him what it was.

Behind her, Pepper heard asthmatic breathing. A nun's habit swished. She turned.

A chubby, older nun, dressed in an enveloping, traditional black habit, stood at the doorway. She wheezed as if she'd just finished strenuous exercise. Every man who was seated, except General Bill, rose to their feet.

"Good evening. Take your seats, gentlemen. I am Sister Angelus. Because of our unexpected guests, we did not prepare enough sleeping spaces for men."

So General Bill and his party arrived without notice. That accounted for the partially covered tracks on the road and for Sister Mary Rachel cooking. They were converting supper for five into dishes that would serve nine. A loaves-and-fishes meal.

"Father and Mr. Kirkpatrick are in our priest's suite. Everyone else will make do with dormitory accommodations on the second floor. That space has been shut down for some time.

We will turn on the heat, but I doubt that those rooms will be comfortable before tomorrow."

Pepper recognized the sister's unspoken message: you won't complain.

Pepper took Darby's arm, and added extra southern charm to her voice. "Mr. Barton, I left my suitcase in my van. Would you mind walking out with me to get it?"

He bowed again. "I'd be honored."

Benny removed Pepper's hand from Darby's arm. "Mr. Barton, why don't you help sister hurry the heat along. I'll go with Pepper."

Both men glared at each other.

Ron clapped his hand on Darby's shoulder, "I'll come with you, and pray over their furnace."

Pepper waited until she and Benny were well out of the building, on the way to her van, before she exploded. "What kind of a goddamn circus is this? What the fuck is Darby up to?"

"Gee, Pepper, how pleasant to hear you haven't lost your Vietnam vocabulary."

She glowered at him. "Who are those men?"

"Governing board of the Saratoga Patriotic Foundation."

"Which is what, and why are they here?"

"According to Ron, they're a private military think tank. This is their convent."

Pepper stopped, almost slipping in wet snow. "Pardon me, but what claim does a military think tank—which does what, by the way—have on a Catholic convent?"

Benny's brow furrowed. "Get Ron to tell you about it. It's complicated. As for what a military think tank does, I guess they think . . . about the military."

"Meaning you don't know either."

"Haven't a clue what this group does. They showed up, unexpected and uninvited, a couple of hours ago. William—call me General Bill—Pocock-Nesbitt says they are here to inspect before they take possession next month. I think not."

"You don't like him?"

Benny shivered, moving from foot to foot, his hands jammed deep in his pockets. "No I don't; I gather you don't either; Sister Angelus sounds like she doesn't like him. None of God's children like General Bill." He held out his hand. "Give me your keys, before we freeze to death."

Sliding onto the frozen seat, he started the motor, and turned the heater to high, then waved his hand in front of his face. "Jesus, Pepper, it smells like a distillery in here."

They closed their doors at the same instant; two pressure changes colliding with one another. Pepper's ears hurt.

Benny held out his hand. "Give it to me."

She pulled out her thermos. "Just a little hot toddy. You know, like Saint Bernards carry."

He shook it, unscrewed its silver top and sniffed. Metal ridges grated against one another as he slowly closed the thermos. "Give me your word that you won't drink and drive again."

She bounced as she huffed back against her frozen seat, folded her arms, and stared straight ahead. "You mean my word as an officer and a gentleman? Well, as of midnight last night, I'm neither of those any more."

The Congressional Commissioning Act made no provision for women. Four years ago, by order of Congress, she'd been made an officer and a gentleman.

She leaned her head against cold metal. Encased in boots and thick socks, her toes curled in embarrassment for being caught at something as stupid as having open alcohol in a vehicle. "You're right, Benny. I won't drink and drive again. Why is Darby with this Saratoga Patriotic thingy?"

"I don't know, and I don't care. Neither do you."

"Yes, I do."

Benny cocked his head. "You never told me why you two broke up."

Pepper traced a line in the condensation their breaths made on her window. When she saw her line turning into a heart, she balled her hand into a fist and erased it. Beads of water rolled down the glass. She lowered her head and, with a dry throat, managed, "Sex. He wanted it. I didn't. He persisted. It got tiresome. I told him to take a hike. End of story."

End of late-night phone calls, and romantic presents.

Benny sat up straighter. "How hard did he persist?"

"If you mean, did he try to force his attentions on me, no. Let's just say he brought strong arguments to bear. That Georgia accent of his can be very enticing."

Benny threw back his head and laughed.

"It's not funny. Do you know how hard it is to say 'no' these days, especially when Darby has his hands . . . Never mind."

"I warned you that even for a Green Beret, Major Baxter had a reputation as a ladies' man. He's one of those men women fall all over. Your saying 'no' must have come as quite a shock to him."

"Even when we were dating, you never told me how well you knew him."

"Our paths crossed occasionally, but I knew him mostly by reputation."

"Which is?"

"He volunteers."

He volunteers: damning judgment from an enlisted man about an officer. Soldiers died when they served under an officer who volunteered too much.

In frustration, Pepper beat her fist on her seat. "If you'll just leave me alone with him for five minutes, I know I can find out why he's here."

Benny put his hand over her fist. "I know you can. That's

what worries me. Do you remember that last piece of paper you signed before leaving the Army?"

"Where I swore I wouldn't divulge any classified information I learned on active duty?"

"That one. For your own good, file Major Darby Baxter, aka David Barton, or whatever he calls himself this time, under *classified information*. You have no *right* to know. You have no *need* to know. In *my* heart, you will always be an officer and a gentleman, and I expect you to behave like one. Give me your word that you will leave Baxter alone."

A woman's screams, muffled by cold, snow-encrusted air, stopped Pepper from making a promise she had no intention of keeping.

CHAPTER 4

Fish and broccoli odors permeated the small museum room. Only an empty stomach kept Avivah Rosen from vomiting.

Gary Dormuth lay facedown on the polished wood floor. The thin wire used to garrote him had been barely long enough. It lay completely buried in the flesh around his neck. Two small wooden pegs—handles to prevent the wire from cutting his killer's fingers—lay twisted together just under his right ear.

At least she'd stopped screaming. Good police officers didn't scream when they found a body, but then, she'd stopped being a good police officer a long time ago. Perhaps there was a special dispensation for screaming when discovering a lover's body. Her fingers gripped the varnished door frame so hard they cramped. No matter how much she wanted to run, her body refused to cooperate.

Avivah looked at a massive display case, which held two mannequins, one dressed in a school uniform and the other in an old-fashioned religious habit. At a second, shattered glass case. At glass shards, old schoolbooks, letters, and papers, scattered over the body. At framed black-and-white photographs, and a kneeling bench in one corner next to a white-and-yellow papal flag. At anything but Gary, because if she looked at him, she'd rush to him, pry the wire from his neck, hold him to comfort him as he'd held her. He was beyond comfort.

A sound of people running came from all directions. David Barton pushed past her. He squatted beside Gary, trying to find a pulse. Glass crunched as Ron knelt at Gary's head and raised his hand in benediction. "Sister Angelus, bring me anointing oil."

Avivah wanted to yell, "Stop! You're contaminating a crime scene." Nothing made it past her lips except a whimper.

Pepper pushed by her, knelt across from David, and said, "Help me with CPR."

When had Pepper arrived?

David's hand reached out to stop her before she could turn the body over. "Don't bother. Garroting crushes the windpipe. You'll never get air in."

Avivah sensed Benny standing beside her. He cupped his palm around her chin, and turned her head, so that she had to look into his green eyes. "I'm giving you an order. You're a trained military police officer. You have to tell us what to do. We depend on you."

Give it up, Benny, she wanted to say. They both knew the same drill: emotional first aid for a battle-fatigued soldier. Get his attention. Give him an order. Keep him occupied. It didn't matter that Benny was an ex-sergeant, and she was a captain. When someone came apart in combat, trust mattered more than rank. Something deep within Avivah creaked as it moved, like a wheel rusted in place for a long time.

She had no legal authority anywhere except on a military post, and too close a personal connection to the victim, but she set both of those things aside. Evidence had to be preserved, and she knew how to do that. She found her voice, dry and cracked though it sounded. "Pepper, you and David leave. Now."

David helped Pepper stand. Broken glass stuck to their pants.

"Ron, you too, as soon as you've finished."

"Good girl." Benny whispered in her ear. He stood behind her, his body a barrier between her and everyone else. She was grateful for his protection. Giving the first order had been hard, but now they came easier. Avivah turned. "Sister Mary Rachel, call the sheriff."

Sister Mary Rachel softly hurried away.

"Is there a key for this door?"

Sister Angelus reached inside her voluminous habit and brought out a key ring. She worked off one key and handed it to Avivah.

Ron finished anointing Gary. As he came past Avivah, he laid his hand on her shoulder, and, with that simple solace from an old and close friend, she had to fight to keep from crying. No one, except Gary, had comforted her in months.

She pulled the door shut, locked it, and turned. Pepper, Benny, Ron, General Bill, David Barton, Thomas Hackmann, Dr. Saint-Mathias, Sister Angelus, another nun she hadn't met yet, and two older women, dressed as kitchen workers stood in a circle around her. That she didn't recognize three women after being here five days frightened Avivah. How many other people lurked in the shadows? She turned to Sister Angelus. "Is there anyone else in the convent who's not here?"

The sister shook her head. "We're all here, except for Sister Mary Rachel."

Avivah ordered, "Everyone stay together until the sheriff arrives. How far does he have to come?"

"It's only seven miles to Newland. That's where his office is, but with this snow, it will take him longer than usual to get here."

"How much longer?"

Before the sister answered, every light went out. Rooms lined both sides of this corridor, so there were no windows. They were in complete darkness. People bumped into one another as they milled around. Male voices cursed. A high-pitched keening filled the air. That sound made hair on Avivah's neck stand up.

She dropped the key in her bra. No matter what else happened, it was her job to make sure no one entered the museum.

Zippo lighters clicked, a sound, that for Avivah, was as unique as the crack of an AK-47. She knew both sounds too well. She smelled lighter fluid, and remembered Permanent Overseas Replacement School, a week of orientation classes that everyone headed for Vietnam had to take.

Guys figured lighting one cigarette on guard duty couldn't be that dangerous. To show them how wrong they were, a soldier stood on the stage of a completely dark auditorium, opened his Zippo and lit his cigarette. His face became a perfect target. Then a recorded sniper's rifle fired, and his lighter went out. Silence had been absolute.

Avivah had thought she would forever associate Zippo lighters with that profound silence. She was wrong. The image she knew she would carry instead was three yellow flares in this dark convent hall. Three male faces—General Bill, Benny, and David Barton—shown in small spots of light. The keening noise dropped to a whimper, very much like she herself had made earlier.

Avivah grabbed Sister Angelus, practically shaking her. "Where's your fuse box?"

A voice came from down the hall. "It's not a fuse."

Everyone turned. Sister Mary Rachel carried a lit candle in each hand. The men closed their lighters.

"All outside lights are dark, too, and they aren't on our fuse box. Electricity is off. I expect ice brought down power lines." The sister gave a candle to one of her kitchen helpers. "Patience, you and Helen take Sister Valentina to the chapel. Light some candles, sing hymns with her, and lead her through her evening office."

Avivah took the candle. "No. I want everyone to stay together."

Pepper put her hand on Avivah's shoulder and said in a low

voice. "Sister Valentina has dementia. She's almost hysterical right now; that was her making that horrible noise. Being with people she trusts, and a familiar routine may calm her."

Avivah looked at the nun, who was still making guttural noises and pacing in tiny, nervous circles. Leave it to Pepper to know a stranger's medical condition. She motioned for Pepper and Sister Mary Rachel to step a few feet away, and whispered to them, "Is Sister Valentina dangerous? I mean, is there any chance that she killed Gary?" Her voice caught when she said his name.

Sister Mary Rachel shook her head. "Not a chance. She's a lost soul who doesn't understand what goes on around her. The only time she becomes uncontrollable is when we try to take her away from this convent. Even then, all she does is hold to whatever she can grab, and scream."

Pepper said, "She's like a little bird. I can put my fingers around her wrist. Garroting requires strong arms. Hers would have snapped."

Avivah had to concede that this tiny woman wasn't a good suspect. She handed her candle back to the kitchen help. "All right, take her, but you three stay there together until I send someone to get you."

Looking like a reversed Oreo cookie of white, black, white, they guided Sister Valentina away.

Avivah asked Sister Mary Rachel, "How long before the sheriff arrives?"

"He isn't coming. 'Hello' was all I got out before my phone went dead. I didn't even have a chance to say who was calling."

General Bill insinuated himself into their conversation. "You must have a fallback position, such as the sheriff sending a deputy to check on you in bad weather."

Sister Mary Rachel smiled. "I'm afraid things are different here. People rely on their own strengths in an emergency."

Responsibility flooded through Avivah like a wave, so heavy on her shoulders that she could hardly stand. She wanted to run again, but there was no escape. The Central Park chase had depleted what little reserve strength she'd been husbanding for months. Benny and Ron had been kind, but it had been Gary's attention that had saved her mental health. Finding him dead shattered the energy she'd managed to salvage. She pressed her lips together to keep from crying and turned to Pepper. Her voice waivered. "I don't know what to do."

Pepper put her arm around Avivah's waist. "Everyone has had a shock. Let's go back to the visitors' parlor. We need to stay warm. There's a fire there. Perhaps, sister, we might eat?"

There were general protests of not being hungry.

Sister Mary Rachel raised her hand in a placating gesture. "Miss Pepperhawk is right. We must stay together and care for one other. It seems that fish and broccoli were a bad choice; I, for one, find these food smells disturbing. Sister Angelus, just soup, bread, and cheese. Perhaps some fruit."

Buoyed by Pepper's arm around her, Avivah found strength for a small protest. "She shouldn't go off alone. There's safety in numbers."

Benny stepped forward. "I'll go with sister."

She hadn't realized before what an ideal suspect Benny made. Once, at Fort Bragg, she'd asked him about garroting. Using a piece of wire from his toolbox and two scraps of wood for handles, he'd decapitated a four-inch salami with one, swift motion.

Murder required motive. For the life of her, she couldn't think of a single reason for Benny to kill Gary. Avivah decided to play the odds that he'd have even less reason to attack a nun. "All right, Benny, go with sister."

Their candlelit procession looked positively medieval. All it needed was a Gregorian chant soundtrack. When they reached the visitors' parlor, Sister Mary Rachel moved about, taking candles and candlesticks from a chest and lighting the candles. Avivah collapsed in a chair in front of the fireplace. Pepper took a chair opposite her. No one suggested they relinquish the best chairs.

Thomas Hackmann went to the coffee table, poured a glass of water, drank it, and poured a second glass, which he brought with him to a chair. General Bill drummed his fingers on the sofa arm. Dr. Saint-Mathias not only took time to prepare himself a cup of coffee, but helped himself to several cookies as well. Apparently murder made him hungry. Ron took a set of black beads from his pocket, made a sign of the cross, and threaded beads, one-by-one, through his fingers.

David Barton took a chair in the farthest corner. He sat in shadow, facing the entrance, with walls protecting his back. Finding that protected spot in a room became second nature for anyone who had been in Vietnam. Avivah recognized the same compulsion in herself.

Mr. Barton had introduced himself as a science teacher and recruiter for Georgia Military Academy. She'd assumed his military bearing came from setting an example for cadets. Now she knew better. How long ago had he been to Vietnam, and did he know how to garrote?

Benny and Sister Angelus appeared with a wheeled cart filled with a soup tureen, bowls, bread, cheese, and apples. Benny filled a soup bowl and handed it to Avivah. "Mushroom soup."

At least it wasn't tomato. Though Gary had not bled, Avivah didn't think she could face a bowl of red liquid just now. She gratefully wrapped her fingers around warm china. Bland, hot soup might placate her protesting stomach.

As shock wore off, a hollow pain filled her chest. She knew—really knew—only three people here: Pepper, Benny, and Ron. As much as the idea hurt, Benny was on her suspect list until he proved an alibi. How had it become *her* list all of a sudden? Because there wasn't anyone else who could take charge of a murder investigation.

She could trust Pepper. Avivah had never met a worse candidate for murderer. It would be better, for now, not to confide in Ron. Not that she believed he could kill any more than Pepper could, but he and Sister Angelus were brother and sister. Ron did like to gossip. Anything Avivah told him might find its way to Sister Angelus, and from there, who knew?

She and Pepper could be trusted; nine suspects couldn't. Sister Valentina was lost in her own private world. If Gary's death wasn't an isolated, premeditated killing, everyone could be in danger. There were too many people to watch and too much empty convent space for Avivah and Pepper to protect everyone. Bitterness rose within her. She knew all too well what losing a battle felt like, and she had no desire to go through it again. She ran her hand wearily over her face.

For now, wind and snow prevented their killer from escaping. It would even be a blessing if he did try to escape. At least she would know who he was. He or she, she corrected herself, but deep inside she knew men were better suspects.

General Bill set down his bowl. "Sister, if you'll show me where your backup generator is, I'll start it."

Sister Mary Rachel folded her hands in her lap. "We don't have a generator."

Pepper contributed, "Mountain folk pride themselves on being self-reliant. When power goes out, people use fireplaces and woodstoves."

Sister Mary Rachel looked appraisingly at her. "You seem to know quite a bit about mountain customs."

"I have an aunt and uncle in Bat Harbor, Tennessee."

The sister said to General Bill, "What Miss Pepperhawk says is true. Appalachian culture values self-reliance. Our girls learned very quickly to take care of themselves in all kinds of weather."

She made it sound like earning Girl Scout badges.

General Bill looked peeved. "What's so damn self-reliant about not having a fucking generator?"

David Barton was on his feet, his hands balled into fists. Blood suffused his face, outlining his blond eyebrows, like two white caterpillars against his darkened skin. "There are women, including nuns, present, sir. I'll thank you to keep a civil tongue."

Avivah expected him to issue a dueling challenge, "My seconds will speak with your seconds," but all that happened was that the two men glared at one another.

Being without electricity did raise several interesting questions Avivah hadn't considered before. "Sister, what heats this convent?"

"A fuel oil furnace, fed by an electric pump. The building will be freezing by morning. We have, thankfully, a large supply of candles, several flashlights, and a woodstove for cooking, so we will have light and hot food. But our water pump is also electric, so running water and toilets won't work. We'll use honey buckets." She said the latter with particular relish, as if, could she make life more difficult for General Bill and his buddies, she'd do just that.

Avivah—who'd spent summers at camp—knew realities of hauling water, keeping fires, and living without plumbing. "When the electricity went out, how did your students keep warm?"

"Several rooms have fireplaces, plus our kitchen woodstove. We divided our girls into groups and kept them in those rooms. We had some grand times during storms," she finished, almost wistfully.

Avivah would have never guessed that a no-nonsense woman like Sister Mary Rachel could be wistful about anything.

Pepper asked, "What would you have done in case of a medical emergency?"

Good question, thought Avivah.

"If we had something our school nurse couldn't handle—thank the Lord we never did—our plan was to have a nun ski or snowshoe over to the next valley to get help. There is a well-marked ski trail."

While everyone else had eaten an austere supper, Dr. Saint-Mathias had helped himself, repeatedly, to food. He dabbed carefully at his mustache and mouth with his napkin. "We have cars. One of us can drive down the mountain to secure assistance."

The sister disagreed. "Unless you favor plummeting into a gorge, I wouldn't advise that. On these winding roads, all it takes is one patch of ice, sometimes no bigger than a few inches wide, to send a car sliding out of control."

Dr. Saint-Mathias paled. "I see."

Thomas Hackmann stood, trembling as if he were a nervous child forced to recite in front of a class. He spoke slowly, in a rehearsed way. "I grew up in Minnesota. I skied almost as soon as I could walk. I'll go for help."

Avivah had to admit she didn't favor Tom Hackmann for the top of her suspect list. Garroting took cold-blooded resolve. Thomas looked too nervous, but she knew well enough that killers didn't always look tough.

General Bill also stood, a slow uncoiling, which reminded Avivah of a snake. He patted Hackmann's back. "That's terrific, Tom. Thank you for volunteering. Very noble of you."

Father Ron spoke up. "I don't think Avivah wants anyone going off by himself."

Avivah didn't want anything. She had no authority here. There wasn't a thing she could do to stop General Bill from sending Thomas on a rescue mission.

General Bill stiffened. "Correct me if I'm wrong, but as a military police officer, Captain Rosen has no authority in a civilian situation."

She regretted having told him her rank. He made it sound as though she'd gotten her captain's bars out of a Cracker Jack box.

"Come on, Tom, let's go with Sister Angelus, and find a pair of skis that fit you."

Everyone watched them leave. David Barton waited until they were out of earshot, then said simply, "Thomas earned the Congressional Medal of Honor at Chosen." He let his words hang in the air without explanation.

Chosen Reservoir had been fought in snow and bitterly cold weather. That answered Avivah's question about why General Bill wanted Thomas on his board of directors. He traded on Thomas' glory. "Thomas Hackmann, Congressional Medal of Honor, Korea" looked great on a list of Saratoga Patriotic Foundation board members. He was about to trade on that glory again. "Saratoga Patriotic Foundation Board Member in Heroic Rescue" would make a fine headline for a fund-raising brochure.

Avivah glanced around and saw, in Pepper, Benny, and David Barton, a reflection of the way she felt. They all wanted to close ranks, protect Thomas not only because he'd been a soldier, but because he'd earned the highest honor their country could bestow. No soldier took that lightly. That common look confirmed her suspicion that Barton had, some time recently, been a soldier.

Someone must go with Thomas. He wasn't healthy enough to battle snow and cold.

Benny and David said in unison, "I'll go with him."

Her two prime suspects wanted to leave. Would she let them? What was needed here was a command decision. As much as taking charge was the last thing she wanted to do, she had to make a choice. Better a devil she knew.

"Benny, you go."

CHAPTER 5

Having been given a mission, Benny resembled a perpetual-motion machine. He waxed skis, checked bindings, and assured himself that Thomas had proper outdoor clothing. He gave Helen, the cook, precise instructions about how much food and coffee they needed, and how to pack it. Sister Mary Rachel shared an old topographical map with him, which pleased him. He loved maps.

Pepper understood Benny's frantic devotion to duty. After months of unemployment, living with his parents, and enduring animosity from former friends, he was important again. She thought it pathetic that both Thomas and Benny had to put themselves at risk to feel important. Understanding what drove them didn't relieve her anxiety. She assigned herself a mission, too, one she hoped would help Benny: find out more about Thomas Hackmann's medical problems.

General Bill hovered around Thomas, arm around his shoulder, whispering encouragement. After an hour of careful maneuvering, Pepper managed to be alone with Thomas in the visitors' parlor.

"Do you have your medicines with you? I'm a nurse and nurses worry about things like that."

Thomas, his eyes bright with excitement, showed no surprise that she knew he took medication. Chronically ill people often accepted that nurses knew things like that.

He took four bottles out of his pocket. "I've taken everything today, except my bedtime pills. Should I leave my medicines here? I don't want to lose them."

Pepper read the labels, and stopped herself before she said "Oh, shit" out loud. He was on huge doses of two psychotropic medications, plus a tranquilizer and a sleeping pill, all issued by a Florida Veterans Administration hospital. She gave them back to him. "You've taken these a long time?"

"Twenty years."

She had a good idea of why they had been prescribed, but she wanted to see what he would say. "Do you mind if I ask what they are for?"

He looked at the floor, and mumbled, "Manic-depression, anxiety, and chronic insomnia." Mental illness still carried a stigma. His voice became shriller, and his hands curled into fists. "But I'm all right, really I am, as long as I take my pills on time. I can do this. You don't have to worry. I can do this."

That she might be able to stop him from being a hero terrified him. Damn General Bill for filling his head with dreams of glory. Some psychiatric patients, pushed to their limit, struck out with incredible speed and strength. Pepper was afraid that Thomas would hurt her if he lost control. She backed away. From the look in Thomas' eyes she realized that had been the wrong thing to do.

Instead of striking out at her, tears coursed down Thomas' cheeks. "It was a good idea to let Mr. Kirkpatrick run things. I'm not as organized as he is, but please, please don't take this away from me."

For all of his pomposity, General Bill had known what Thomas needed more than she had. Pepper suddenly saw things from Thomas' point of view. He'd volunteered to ski for help, something he took pride in knowing how to do, and they'd saddled him with an unrequested partner, who immediately took over responsibility for every detail. She'd resent it, too, if people thought she needed keepers to manage for her.

"I'm so sorry. We never intended to take this away from you."

Thomas sucked in a wet breath and ran the back of his hand over his eyes. "It's okay if I go, then?"

"It's very okay."

Pepper remembered a story about an Alaskan nurse who pinned a bag of desperately needed medicine to her slip so she wouldn't lose it. "Take your pills with you. You might not get back here until tomorrow. You were right to be concerned that they might fall out of your pocket. Maybe, instead, Sister Angelus could find a little bag you can wear around your neck, under your coat."

Thomas said he liked that idea. After he went to find the sister, Pepper went looking for Benny. He was standing outside, studying falling snow. He had a glass of milk in one hand and a sandwich in the other. Both were untouched.

Benny never ate before a mission. He always had the best of intentions. He'd studied what foods he should eat for stamina and quick energy, and conscientiously prepared them, always convinced that this time his stomach would quiet down enough that he could eat. It never did. It was a little detail Pepper had forgotten now that they lived half a continent apart.

Her heart filled with a familiar compassion. For all his tough-guy stance, there were moments Benny appreciated a little tender, loving care. He didn't notice when she took the sandwich and milk from him.

She said, "I just talked to Thomas. He's a walking psychiatric text: manic-depression, clinical anxiety, and chronic insomnia."

"Tell it to me in English."

"He's a piss-poor choice for a rescue mission, but General Bill has him so worked up about being a hero, there's no way to stop him. I just thought you should know he's not a healthy man."

"I agree with you. Going out tonight is a bad idea, but it's too late to hold Thomas back. Don't worry, pretty lady. I've led patrols before with guys who weren't healthy. Old mother-hen Kirkpatrick almost always gets them through."

Only Benny and Darby ever called her "pretty lady." Being called that always left a little kink in her heart. She wasn't bad looking, but she knew both of them weren't referring to physical beauty, and she valued being their kind of pretty lady above all else.

Benny asked, "I suppose he takes medicine?"

"Four kinds. He shouldn't take his bedtime pills until you get somewhere warm where you can sleep. He'll be carrying pill containers in a bag around his neck. Follow directions on the labels. Would it help if I went with you?"

Benny laughed. "When have you ever cross-country skied?"

"Never."

"I thought so. Growing up in Biloxi didn't lend itself to winter sports, did it?"

"No."

He leaned over and gave her a peck on the cheek. "Thanks for offering, but we'll be okay. All we have to do is follow the ski trail. Sister Mary Rachel says we can see houses from the top of the ridge. We pick a house, ski to it, and they send for help."

When they left, Pepper waved and waved until they were mere specks. There was nothing more she could do for those two men, but everyone else needed a place to sleep. She went to find Sister Angelus, to see what she could do to help with accommodations.

It was almost eight o'clock when Avivah unlocked the museum door, stepped inside, and locked herself in. Gary's body was a dark shape on the floor. A popular Simon and Garfunkle song played through her head. Darkness *could* be an old friend.

Glass crunched under her shoes. She'd had to improvise her crime scene garb: linen dish towels and plastic bags for shoe covers. A new pair of rubber kitchen gloves for her hands. An Instamatic camera and flash cubes borrowed from Sister Angelus. Her own flashlight. Still, it would be enough to make a record of the crime scene, without compromising evidence.

She couldn't risk waiting for the sheriff. Even if she had the only door key, their killer might find a way to break in and destroy evidence. Better police officers than her had let murderers slip through their fingers because of compromised crime scenes. If she could help it, Gary's killer wasn't going to slip away.

Looking down at his body, she whispered. "I owe you this, and a lot more."

He'd sheltered her, made sure she had food, held her, made love to her, and protected her from police and reporters. Just before they'd left his apartment to catch their plane, he'd brought home two large hanging bags. An expensive red wool dress was in one, a matching coat in another. He said, "There are reporters downstairs. I don't know how they found me, but they did."

Her heart had immediately responded as if it were a trip hammer. Gary put his arms around her and rubbed her back. "We need a diversion. You're tall enough to be a model. Let's use that to your advantage."

After she dressed, he opened a flat velvet case and took out a string of pearls. One of her aunts had a particular fascination with pearls. Avivah could recognize good ones when she saw them.

Gary put them around her neck. "Turn around."

She put her hand to her throat, holding the strand in place. "I don't think this is a good idea."

He fastened the clasp. "Details are very important. A loan

only. They belonged to my grandmother. Now, lets see if this bit of costuming works."

Gary walked her straight to the bevy of reporters, gave her a wink, patted her arm and said, "Excuse me a moment, darling."

They mobbed him with questions about Avivah, while she stood there, trying to look as if she were a simple bauble for Dormuth's arm. Once they were in his car, Gary said, "It never occurred to them that you could be a military police officer. They were looking for someone with a butch haircut, mustache, and combat boots."

At least he'd already taken his pearls back. She would make sure whoever packed his things got them back to his family. "I owe you," she whispered again.

Shivering, she decided—all things considered—she liked bodies cold rather than hot. Less mess. Less smell. At least the food odors had mercifully dissipated.

Would this frigid room stay cold enough to preserve Gary's body? She shined her flashlight on a geometrically patterned stained-glass window. If she opened that window an inch, outside air would turn this room into a walk-in freezer, at least until the blizzard stopped. No telling what damage blowing snow or a gust of wind could do to evidence, to say nothing of small wild creatures who could squeeze through an inch-wide space. No open windows.

Taking a deep breath, she passed her flashlight beam slowly over his body. His eyeglasses were missing. Perhaps they were under his body, but she wasn't going to move his body. She saw no signs of a fight. Someone had come up behind him, thrown the garrote over his head and pulled.

Her gloved fingers opened the cold skin folds at his neck. Scratch marks told her he'd clawed at his throat, trying to free himself, suffocating from a crushed windpipe. She refused to allow herself to speculate on how long it took him to die.

She played her light over the walls, where blank spots, with faint grime outlines, showed spaces where large photographs had hung. Eight large frames stood with their top edges resting against the wall. She examined them carefully, disturbing them as little as possible. The heavy frames had wooden pegs driven into them, with thick strands of wire—just like around Gary's neck—strung between. One frame had empty holes where the pegs should be.

That argued for a spur-of-the-moment killing. The killer hadn't brought a weapon with him, or if he had, hadn't used what he brought. It would have been a moment's work to pull out loose pegs. That meant Gary was comfortable enough to turn his back on his killer.

Snow made the windows translucent. Now that her night vision had adjusted, she had enough light to see without a flashlight. She turned it off, and let it dangle from a strap on her wrist. In the dark, she framed several shots in the camera's viewfinder, closing her eyes each time she pressed the shutter. Partly she wanted to keep her night vision, but mostly, she had no desire to see Gary's body in sharp, strobe-like details. She already had one dead man's face etched in her memory.

She squatted, took out a small notebook, and wrote a inventory of each item she saw. Perhaps Sister Mary Rachel could tell her if anything was missing. Papers, books, and other objects were on top of Gary's body. The killer had smashed the glass case after Gary was already dead.

Only when tears dripped on her notebook did Avivah realize she was sobbing. She rocked back into a sitting position. Damn. Not here, not now! At least she was alone in a locked room.

Blind, dumb luck of being alone when crying jags hit had already saved her military career a few times in the past year. One day, when her luck ran out, she'd break down in public. The military's double standard would finish her career.

A male officer might take medical leave and a transfer, but a hysterical female officer would have two choices. A medical discharge, labeling her "unfit for service because of a mental health condition," or a non-prejudicial discharge, which was a fancy way of saying she wasn't good officer material. In either case, no civilian police force would hire her.

A month ago, when uncontrollable crying terrified her, she'd consulted a civilian doctor in New York City. Carefully concealing her military connection, she'd used the name and address of a deceased great-aunt. After an expensive, and thorough examination, her doctor said there was nothing physically wrong with her. She must have a hormone imbalance. He wrote out a prescription for six months of birth-control pills. The unfilled prescription was still in her purse.

In spite of her best intentions, Avivah felt herself sink again into all-too-familiar self-recriminations. She should never have gone to Vietnam. Benny had been right when he said it was no place for a woman, only she'd been too stubborn to listen to him.

She rolled, and pressed her back into a corner as she curled into a fetal position. What she was unprepared for was a presence that filled her, like comforting water rising from her ankles to her head. Her body filled with warmth, and a feeling closer to hope than anything she'd known since her first month in Vietnam.

Someone knocked on the door. Sister Mary Rachel's voice called, "Captain Rosen, are you in there? Are you all right?"

Half an hour later, sitting in Sister Mary Rachel's office, Avivah accepted a second cup of tea.

The nun, dressed in a grey quilted robe and night cap, asked, "Can I get you anything else?"

Making excuses for her behavior had become a pattern. "No, thank you. I apologize for the state you found me in. I had several immunizations last week, and I must be having a reaction."

The sister pursed her lips, and remained silent. Avivah had never lied to a nun before. It made her uncomfortable, though she bet, not as uncomfortable as it would have made Pepper. She was also curious about how Sister Mary Rachel had managed to show up precisely when she did. "Why did you come to look for me?"

The sister took exquisite care to set the tea pot on her desk, then sat in a large leather chair across from Avivah. "Do you believe in miracles?"

"Religious miracles?"

"Events which have no worldly explanation, coupled with an intercession for a spiritual intervention."

Avivah knew a whole body of Jewish mystical tradition existed, but she had no idea what it contained. "I don't know. I've never witnessed anything like that."

"Members of our order bore witness, at this convent, to something exactly like that."

After taking hundreds of witnesses' statements, Avivah was suspicious of eyewitness accounts. "Were you one of them?"

The sister chuckled. "I wasn't born until four years later, but there are extensive records."

"What was it, some kind of apparition like what supposedly happened at Lourdes?" She hoped the sister wouldn't be offended that she was skeptical about Jesus' mother visiting earth.

The sister's mouth made a little moue. So she was offended. "In 1922, one of our orphans was critically ill with pneumonia. The doctor said death was imminent. Several hours later, our infirmarian fell asleep, cradling the dying infant in her arms, and praying to Sister Elizabeth Rose."

"Who?"

"The nun who founded this convent. Near dawn, the infir-

CHAPTER 6

r decided that waiting alone in the visitors' parlor for
Angelus had been a bad idea. She listened for sounds of
people in the building, but thick walls and massive
re made ideal sound baffles. She heard only the wind

ing logs hissed at her; *you are trapped with a killer.* She
self that Gary's death had to be a fluke, an old score,
d nothing to do with her or with being at this convent.
ke. Someone tried to take his head off with a piece of
hand went to her own throat in a protective gesture.
ed her throat the way it was.
up and stirred the fire. It needed doing anyway, she
f, and had nothing to do with the comforting feel of
poker in her hand. She also probably shouldn't have
Angelus how many rooms this building contained.
happier not knowing. Keeping track of everyone
ty-five bedrooms, eight communal bathrooms,
an infirmary, priest's suite, offices, kitchen, two
ng rooms, chapel, sacristy, servants' quarters, nuns'
huge corridors would be like herding cats.
d when Sister Angelus appeared. She really had to
her nerves.
nnounced, "You and Miss Rosen will sleep in the
r. It has a fireplace. I have asked our other guests
ds in there for you. Men will sleep in the priest's

marian awoke with a strong sense of someone beside her. A figure in a habit took the baby from her arms. The figure said, 'God heard your prayers. This is His special child. Sleep now while I watch over her.' A few hours later, the doctor examined a healthy infant, without a trace of illness. A miracle had happened."

Avivah thought immediately of an alternative explanation: a country practitioner misdiagnosed the child's condition.

"Our order hoped her recovery might be the first miracle credited to Sister Elizabeth Rose. That was not to be." She folded her hands in her lap. "Our Mother Superior permits us to make intercession to Sister Elizabeth Rose, even though she is not yet a saint. I did that tonight. As I was doing so, a strange feeling filled me. I felt compelled, almost bodily carried, to knock on the museum door and call your name."

Avivah shivered. Psychic manifestations, if they existed, were safer left to rabbis schooled in the Cabbala and other esoteric traditions. Ghost stories and fairy tales—really stories about ultimate good and evil—were no place for amateurs. Better to discuss something concrete. Avivah dug in her pocket for her notebook. "This is a list of everything I saw on the museum floor. Can you tell me if anything is missing?"

Sister Mary Rachel put on a pair of reading glasses. "I don't see a portable writing desk listed."

"What does it look like?"

With her hands, the sister indicated a size like a large telephone directory. "About this long, by this wide, dark wood, with a hinged leather-covered top, and a thin drawer for papers."

Avivah had seen nothing like that. She was fairly certain it couldn't have been concealed under Gary's body without making a noticeable hump. "Was it valuable?"

"Only to us. It belonged to Ermengarde Hackmann, the

widow who, in 1865, provided land, and the original house for our convent."

"Hackmann? As in Thomas Hackmann?"

"His great-great-grandmother. It's her fault that the Saratoga Patriotic Foundation was able to rent this convent."

Avivah was confused. "You did say 1865, not 1965?"

"Yes."

"How could a woman who lived over a hundred years ago have anything to do with the Saratoga Patriotic Foundation?"

"About a year and a half ago, while researching his book, Dr. Saint-Mathias uncovered Ermengarde Hackmann's will. Thomas may be her only direct male descendent. If so, he owns this convent and land."

Avivah saw right away where this led. "I thought you said that Mrs. Hackmann gave the land to your order."

"We always assumed she had, but in fact, she may have granted us the *use* of land. There's a difference in law. Eighteen-sixty-five was a time of great upheaval. Land records were in chaos. Either Sister Elizabeth never recorded the deed or there was no deed. After all the investigation we've done, I've concluded the latter."

"Could that missing deed have been in Ermengarde's writing desk?"

"We thought of that. Sister Angelus supervised a local cabinetmaker, who took that desk apart, cleaned it, and restored it. When he finished, there wasn't so much as an undiscovered piece of lint."

Sister Mary Rachel stood and began to gather tea things on a tray. "Don't mistake me. I have nothing against Mr. Hackmann personally, and if this land belongs to him, he should have it, but I do believe he's being manipulated."

"By whom, to do what?"

"By William Pocock-Nesbitt, to take possession of this

convent, and give it to the Saratoga Patriotic Foun[

"You don't like General Bill?"

"I don't like this peaceful place being turned o[that realizes personal gain from war. I am not against the military or people like you, who [their country, but I do object to using d[patriotism for personal gain."

"If Thomas owns this property, why is the [Foundation renting it?"

"Not to speak ill of the dead, but I hold [directly responsible for that. Mother Super[ing council decided—rightly in my op[orphanage long before Dr. Saint-Mathias [ness. We have much more modern build[our girls."

Avivah looked at the dancing shado[especially by candlelight."

"It was a Victorian institution, an i[to grow up." She sighed. "Until ow[Mother Superior could have chosen [or have a temporary tenant in [persisted in pointing out advantag[cupation."

Avivah's hand went to her n[rested. "Mr. Dormuth had a flai[

"He certainly did."

Persuasiveness didn't seer[murder. "With Gary dead, wil[

"Oh, yes. All parties sign[murder anyone—God forg[would go after William Po[pray very hard that the kil[rive soon, I fear we will en[

suite, though I'm sorry to say some of them will have to sleep on the floor."

She didn't sound sorry at all.

No, Pepper decided, splitting up wouldn't do at all. Surely, Avivah planned to mount a guard, and to do that, everyone had to sleep in the same room. Pepper wished she knew where Avivah had gotten to; probably in conference with Sister Mary Rachel.

She pushed herself out of her warm chair. A few hours ago, she'd been afraid she'd curtsey to nuns; now, with hardly a butterfly in her stomach, she was about to confront Sister Angelus with a plan the sister would hate. Funny how murder changed priorities. "Where is the biggest room with a fireplace?"

"Third floor."

"Show it to me, please."

Reluctantly, the sister took her to the top floor, and opened a door into a huge, cold room. It had tall windows, a wide-plank wooden floor, two fireplaces, more than enough sleeping space for everyone and one door, easy to guard. Pepper recognized a good deal when she saw it.

The sister said, "This was our old nursery. We converted it into an arts-and-crafts room."

That explained scarred tables dotted with paint and glue, and lingering turpentine odor.

"This is perfect." Pepper made an attempt to sound diplomatic. "Thank you for suggesting the other arrangements, but everyone will sleep in this room instead."

Sister Angelus drew herself to her full height, which didn't look menacing in someone as short and round as she was. "Not in this convent, they won't."

"Sorry, sister, I know men and women sleeping in the same room offends you, but there's safety in numbers. I, for one, will feel a lot better if everyone is together in one room. That includes you, the other nuns, Patience, and Helen." She looked up. "We may be able to hang curtains between men's and women's sides."

"Your morals are between you and God, but I will not permit you to corrupt Patience and Helen. They will sleep with us, in the nuns' quarters. I strongly recommend you perform an examination of conscience before you sleep tonight."

As she strode away her wooden rosary beads clacked like a flock of angry sparrows.

An examination of conscience, a review of sins since her last confession, was the last thing Pepper planned to do. Her list was too long and contained far more important sins than suggesting men and women stay safe by sleeping in the same room. She went to find people for a work party.

Under General Bill's tutelage—he was obviously one of those officers who believed rank conferred a privilege of not working—Darby, Dr. Saint-Mathias, and Ron moved furniture, swept and mopped the floor, hung makeshift dividing curtains, hauled firewood up three flights of stairs, and lit fires in both fireplaces. Darby found two large galvanized tubs, which he placed on both hearths. To the tubs he carried endless buckets of water. Not only would they have warmed water for washing, but moisture eased the dry, stuffy air. For that kindness alone, Darby was almost back in her good graces.

Pepper walked over to a tall window, and peered through bare oak branches, which pressed against the glass. Snow rounded everything to soft mounds and bent evergreens into distorted arcs. If they weren't miles from help, housing a killer, she might even think the view beautiful.

"Stay safe, Benny." It was as close as she could come to prayer, even in a convent.

She leaned her forehead against cold glass. What would make everyone safe, including her, was to catch Gary's murderer.

Means were dead obvious: a garrote. She smiled. Black humor puns came so much easier after a few years in the Army.

Deciding who had opportunity required those tedious timetables that frustrated her in books. Let the sheriff take care of determining opportunity. Motive interested her most. Who hated Gary enough to kill him? And that other Latin thing, which lawyers always talked about. *Cui bono?* Who profited? Hate and profit were great motives for murder.

General Bill strode into the room, rubbing his hands as if warming them in front of an imaginary fire. Darby, Dr. Saint-Mathias, and Ron flanked him, looking exactly like an inspection party of military VIPs.

For a moment, Pepper was back in Qui Nhon. When a general entered, ward staff came to attention. She automatically pulled her body and head erect, eyes straight ahead and focused on nothing, hands exactly aligned along her pants seams, and thumbs tucked into her curled fingers. Old habits died hard. Except Qui Nhon had been two years ago, and she would never go back there. She was a civilian now, and she never had to stand at attention again. She uncoiled her hands and forced herself to slouch. It had been a long time since she slouched.

General Bill jollied the troops along, as he'd been doing for a couple of hours. "Let's make one last foray, gentlemen, to ensure we have more than enough firewood."

Ron, already red-faced and sweating, quoted Shakespeare's *Henry V* under his breath. "Close the wall up with our English dead." Darby just sighed.

It was Dr. Saint-Mathias who broke ranks. Bits of tree bark covered his previously impeccable black suit, and his tie hung at an odd angle. He picked up a folded bedsheet. "I'm sure Miss Pepperhawk could use help here."

General Bill pushed his lips together in a tight line. "All right, Yancy." He turned and slapped Darby and Ron on their backs, a hale-fellow-well-met gesture, showing he valued their company more than someone who preferred to make beds. "Come on men, let's attack that woodpile."

Spare me, Pepper thought.

The professor took time for a toilet, using some of their precious warm water and not, Pepper noted, bothering to replace it. Fifteen minutes later, he examined himself in a mirror flanked on either side by candles. He gave his lapels one final tweak, and took a thin flask from his back pocket. "Care for some?"

"No thanks. I'm not much of a drinker."

"Is that why you arrived smelling like a distillery?"

They eyed one another across the unmade bed.

"I had one drink."

Dr. Saint-Mathias shrugged as if what she did didn't matter to him, took a drink, and capped his flask.

Pepper spread sheets over the bare mattress. "My second cousins, the Guilettes, come from Lafayette. Perhaps you know them?"

He smoothed his side of the sheet. "There are dozens of Guilettes in Lafayette, and I don't care to know any of them. I was born and raised in New Orleans."

Plain and simple, Dr. Saint-Mathias lied. Pepper had gone to school with girls from New Orleans, Lafayette, and tiny Cajun communities, like Jeanerette and Mamou. She recognized different accents. No matter how much he protested, Dr. Saint-Mathias came from bayou country.

She knew where his reticence to admit his origins came from. To be a French-speaking Cajun was to be judged poor, stupid, and uneducated, to be vulnerable to practical jokes and snide comments from, well, girls like Pepper. Harassing "coon-asses" at school wasn't a memory she cherished.

Thomas was a psychiatric patient, Dr. Saint-Mathias ashamed of his origins, and Darby undoubtedly up to no good. It didn't surprise her that a blowhard like General Bill surrounded himself with damaged men. In the land of the blind, a one-eyed man was king.

Truth to tell, she wasn't above using Dr. Saint-Mathias to her own ends. If she were going to find a motive for murder, she might as well start by finding out what he thought about Gary. She smiled at him. "Do you have a specialty in history?"

"The Civil War."

There was no need to ask whose civil war. *Res ipsa loquitur.* In the South, the thing spoke for itself.

"I always found Lookout Mountain fascinating. A battle in the clouds."

He shook a pillow into its case. "Ulysses S. Grant wrote, 'The Battle of Lookout Mountain is one of the romances of the war. There was no such battle and no action even worthy to be called a battle on Lookout Mountain. It is all poetry.'"

Battles as poetry. Pepper understood that. Many things she'd done in Vietnam moved with a rhythm that seemed, in retrospect, poetic.

He asked, hopefully, almost shyly, "Perhaps you've read my book? *The Third Brother: Stay-at-Home Soldiers in the American Civil War.* Louisiana State University Press. 1970."

"I'm afraid not."

"I'll send you a copy. I'm working on a sequel. *One Came Home, One Stayed Behind: Reintegration of Third Brothers in Post–Civil War America.*"

At least she'd gotten him talking, even if what he said made little sense, and gave her no clue about motivations for murder. "What does 'third brother' mean?"

"It's a term I coined. From that folk song." He sang in a reedy, off-key voice, "Two—oo brothers on their way, two—oo brothers on their way, One wore blue, one wore grey, as they marched along the way, fife and drum began to play." Mercifully, he stopped singing. "My thesis is there was a third brother, one who stayed at home, who though reviled as a coward and a shirker, contributed significantly to war effort."

He veered into a lecture about food production, local militia, carters, road maintenance, and population security. Clearly the topic obsessed him. Pepper tried to think of a way to recapture this conversation and turn it back to Gary's death.

"Certainly we have a prime example, here in Crossnore, of reintegration difficulties faced by third brothers."

She feared he might sing again. Better to keep him talking, even if it weren't about Gary. "What happened in Crossnore?"

He perched on a corner of the partially-made bed. "A young man, Lucas Hackmann, did not enlist."

"Hackmann? As in Thomas Hackmann?"

"His great-great-uncle. As I was saying, Lucas chose to remain at home, and that decision resulted in the most dire consequences. Unfortunately, my research has not yet documented his motivation for remaining at home. Five common motives for avoiding conscription or enlistment included . . . "

He was dangerously close to full lecture mode again. Pepper heard herself slipping into her most southern accent. "I'm dying to hear what happened to Lucas."

"Oh, he was stabbed to death in the fall of 1864." Dr. Saint-Mathias said it offhandedly, as if he described Lucas stepping out to buy a loaf of bread. "Several returned veterans took umbrage with him for not putting on a uniform. After an altercation in a bar—really, just a shack where liquor was served—the owner threw them out. The men waylaid Lucas on his way home and killed him. My thesis is that he was just as much a war casualty as anyone who died in battle, and I hope to show that in my upcoming book."

He droned on again about historical theory. He just didn't get it. To him, the hate, anger, and resentment that drove those weary veterans to kill Lucas were academic exercises. Dr. Saint-Mathias had no clue what those men had gone through or how they felt, and no capacity to understand. Pepper wondered what cockeyed theories academics would have a hundred years from now about people who went to Vietnam, and people who didn't. At least now she knew how to phrase her question about Gary. She interrupted him. "Doctor, from a theoretical point of view, who do you think killed Gary Dormuth?"

"Someone who thought the Saratoga Patriotic Foundation would be better off without him."

"I don't get the connection."

"Gary was our employee."

Pepper hoped she didn't look as startled as she felt. What kind of mare's nest had Avivah stumbled into?

There was a noise at the top of the stairs. Pepper turned. Ron arrived, carrying a large load of firewood. He puffed noisily. "Give me a hand, Pepper, before I drop this."

She went to him and rescued wood before it fell. He said to her. "You look pale. Are you all right?"

She nodded in Dr. Saint-Mathias' direction, and whispered in Ron's ear. "Did you know the Saratoga Patriotic Foundation employed Gary?"

He whispered back, "Yes."

From across the room, Dr. Saint-Mathias said, "Surely, Miss Pepperhawk, you could find a more private spot to have father hear your confession."

Ron pursed his lips and quoted again from *Henry V*, "And gentlemen in England now a-bed / Shall think themselves accurs'd they were not here, / And hold their manhoods cheap whiles any speaks / That fought with us upon Saint Crispin's day." Father Ron might be a civilian, but he thought like a soldier, and he didn't much care for Dr. Saint-Mathias. For a priest, there was a disturbing amount of malice in his eyes.

Just after midnight, Pepper stood outside the nursery door, staring out a window. Snow still fell. If Thomas and Benny had made it to a working telephone, shouldn't help have arrived? It was only seven miles to Newland. She didn't want to think about the possibility that Benny and Thomas wouldn't be able to get through at all. Whatever was happening out there, she felt helpless enough because she couldn't do a thing about it.

It had been years since she'd done a night shift and her body, already tired and sore from packing and moving, her emotions stretched by a week of goodbyes, rebelled. She desperately wanted sleep. Come on, she cajoled herself; this is for Avivah.

Avivah screaming, clutching a door frame, saying she had no idea what to do next didn't bode well. Benny was right: Avivah was in trouble.

Pepper knew a lot about death. If someone bled or broke his leg or came down with an esoteric disease, like cholera, she knew exactly what to do. She had no clue what to do with a killer. Murder was Avivah's work and no matter what else happened, Pepper had to keep Avivah from falling apart until the sheriff arrived. If Gary's death wasn't isolated and pre-planned, they could all end up dead in their beds.

Someone stirred. Feet slapped across the wooden floor in a familiar cadence. She and Darby never shared a bed, but on weekends when they managed to meet halfway between Fort Benning, Georgia, and Fort Bragg, North Carolina, they'd had separate beds in the same motel room. She knew who was awake even before he slipped his arms around her.

Did a murderer hold her? She didn't have to ask him whether he knew how to garrote. Darby knew enough dark skills to kill her six ways from Sunday. With a little catch in her breath, she allowed herself to sink into the coveted warmth of his body.

She'd missed him.

He rested his chin on her head. "Can't sleep?"

"I'm standing guard so no one runs off. Avivah will take over at two." She looked at her watch. "I'm worried about Benny and Thomas. They've been gone almost five hours. Maybe we should get up a search party."

"Kirkpatrick can take care of himself." He lowered his voice. "Does Avivah know about me?"

"She knows I dated someone, and that we broke up. She doesn't know you are that someone."

It seemed to satisfy him. His body relaxed. Warm breaths tickled her ear. "You have no idea what you did to me tonight, pretty lady, when you hit a brace for the general."

Hit a brace was military-speak for coming to attention. She turned to face him. "What are you talking about?"

His eyes were dark and smoky. He turned her toward the nursery. "What does that look like to you?"

She studied the double row of iron bed frames with a desk halfway in the middle of the row. Unconsciously, and unintentionally, she'd recreated a ward layout from Qui Nhon, or it could have been any Army field hospital. Nightingale wards had been a standard in U.S. Army hospitals for over a hundred years.

"Seeing you standing at attention in the middle of a Nightingale ward took me places I haven't been in years."

Pepper hung her head. Darby had done two tours in Vietnam. Hard tours, particularly his second one, which he never talked about. She had no idea how deep his bottom-feeding memories were, and not knowing bothered her. Had she, inadvertently, stirred up something better left alone? "I didn't do it on purpose."

"I didn't say you did. We watched you, you know."

"I know."

He didn't mean that he, personally, had watched her. She and Darby had been in Vietnam at different times and, she suspected from references he made, in different places. He meant that soldier-patients in open wards watched nurses. Darby had two Purple Hearts and two interesting scars, a long scar down his left leg, and a through-and-through gunshot to his right shoulder—small entry wound on his chest, large exit wound on his back. He'd been facing the enemy when shot. He never talked about those wounds, either.

He asked, "What did being watched feel like?"

"Like being on stage. Sometimes it felt good, as though we were a little bit of home. Sometimes it was scary. They expected so much from us, things we couldn't deliver, like getting them sent to a convalescent unit instead of back to the field. More than once I had to hide in our supply room to get a few minutes of privacy."

He kissed the top of her head. "Comes with the territory."

Benny said the same thing when he talked about flashbacks. She wasn't sure if Darby referred to his reaction to her, as he put it, "hitting a brace," or to what she'd just told him about being watched. Probably both.

Did you kill Gary? Those four words filled her mouth, but her tongue wouldn't push them out. Darby Baxter fascinated her from the day they met. To her way of thinking, he was *the* consummate officer. Dating him had only made her infatuation worse. They'd recognized in one another a need for danger and mystery, as well as heroism. He didn't talk about Vietnam, or his wounds, not because she wouldn't understand, but because he used information in the way a chef used rare spices, doling it out in small bits, flavoring their conversations, and always leaving her wanting more.

For reasons they'd never talked about, and she never dared examine too closely because they frightened her, he thought she was as much a heroine as she thought him a hero. They had each other's measure too well. No matter how he answered her question, Pepper would know the truth, and right now not knowing was better. She asked instead, "How well did you know Gary Dormuth?"

"I met him at a Saratoga Patriotic Foundation board meeting."

"What are you doing mixed up with this bunch of over-the-hill Boy Scouts?"

"I'm not mixed up with them. Yet. My name comes up for a vote at their next meeting."

Pepper pulled away and faced him. "Why are you doing this?"

"I can't talk about it."

Of course he couldn't. In Darby's universe there were two kinds of people: those with adequate security clearance, and those without. It was as Benny said, she had neither need nor right to know.

"How well did you know Gary?"

"We had drinks, exchanged lies. Typical guy stuff."

"Could any of those lies have led to murder?"

"Not on my part. Trust me, my mission here has nothing to do with Dormuth."

Mission. He'd as good as admitted he wasn't here paying a social call. There was so much about Darby she still didn't know.

Pepper looked down at the clunky gold West Point ring on his right hand. Darby valued that ring, and what it stood for, above everything. Getting him to swear on his ring was like asking Benny to swear on his beret, only between Darby and her, swearing on the ring felt different, more like kids, decoder rings, and secret clubs in tree houses. "Swear on your ring."

He hesitated. With great deliberation he took it off, placed it on her palm, and curled his left hand over both the warm ring and her fingers. "I swear on this ring and on every West Point tradition that I hold sacred that I'm here for a personal reason, which has nothing to do with Gary Dormuth, the Army, Special Forces, or military intelligence."

She noticed he hadn't sworn that he hadn't killed Gary. She hadn't expected him to be outright honest. She asked him, "Where does the Army think you are right now?"

"On leave."

Darby faced the window. He suddenly straightened up and said, "Shit." He grabbed his ring out of her hand, shoved it on his finger, and ran for the staircase.

Pepper whirled around. Two figures crossed the open space in front of the convent. Benny carried Thomas. In a heartbeat, Pepper raced after Darby. When she reached the visitors' entrance door, Darby had it unlocked.

She'd been wrong. Benny wasn't carrying Thomas. It was the other way around. Covered with snow, Thomas staggered inside; an unconscious Benny slung over his shoulder in a fireman's carry.

Pepper kneeled beside Benny's still body and frantically groped for a pulse. It was strong, but very, very slow. Thank You, Lord. She looked at Thomas. "What happened?"

"I had to knock him out. He wanted to leave me, so I'd die in the snow. He's your killer."

CHAPTER 7

Darby slung Benny over his shoulder and carried him upstairs. A few paces behind him, Pepper guided a shaking, incoherent Thomas toward the third floor. She wasn't too steady herself. Benny couldn't have killed Gary. What motive did he have to kill a man he barely knew?

Pepper halted abruptly on the first landing, jostling Thomas into the bannister. How did she know Benny barely knew Gary? He'd never told her why he'd been in New York City. Benny, as a soldier and housemate, she understood like a brother; Benny, as a civilian, was a stranger. A shiver ran through her. He *could* be their killer.

When they trooped through the dormitory, everyone woke up. Amid a cacophony of voices, Pepper led Thomas to a chair. Curtains, fashioned out of bedsheets and safety pins, hung on a piece of clothesline across the room's far end. This created a little alcove, providing privacy for her and Avivah. She threw back those curtains. Avivah, her black hair tousled around her face, sat up in bed.

"Oh hell, is that Benny? What happened?"

"I'll explain later. Go find Sister Mary Rachel. See if she has a first aid kit."

While Avivah fumbled for her robe, Pepper pulled back covers on her unused bed. Springs bounced as Darby deposited his burden. Benny might be only five-foot-eight, but he was solid and none of it fat.

Pepper lit a single, tall candle, and pulled the curtains closed again. Bare water-oak branches threw patterned shadows across the curtains, giving the small space a macabre feeling. With practiced efficiency, Darby removed Benny's boots and socks, then unbuckled his belt. When he opened Benny's shirt and saw his burn scars, his pause was almost imperceptible, unless you were watching for it, as Pepper was. His face had a neutral, comes-with-the-territory expression, which pleased her. Too many people reacted to Benny's burns with disgust or pity. Benny tolerated neither.

He whispered, "What happened?"

She knew he didn't mean tonight. "His team was careless; they didn't clear an adequate perimeter around an A-camp. Benny went out, during a Viet Cong attack, to burn their perimeter and deny the enemy the ground. His flamethrower backfired."

Avivah came back with Sister Mary Rachel, Sister Angelus, a first aid kit, and an antiquated stethoscope.

Pepper shooed everyone out. Thin sheets did nothing to mute the noise of half a dozen people talking at once. She yelled, "Take it somewhere else. I can't hear myself think."

Conversation paused, then there were noises of people trying to be quiet as they moved away.

Pepper put hard stethoscope pieces in her ears and the heavy, Bakelite bell on Benny's chest. Her own heart raced, and she had to listen carefully to pick out his slow, even heartbeat. If Vietnam had taught her to do one thing it was to make a rapid, accurate assessment. But, unlike Qui Nhon, she had no doctor to call for backup, and that scared the piss out of her. Benny's life was on her shoulders.

Never again, would she travel without a stethoscope, blood pressure cuff, and anything else she might need for a proper examination. Being unequipped was like a long-distance runner competing in Olympic tryouts in borrowed shoes.

Avivah pushed aside the curtain. "How is he?"

"Breathing."

Avivah sat on her rumpled bed and asked no more questions.

A little later Pepper completed her examination, stood back, and watched Benny for a full minute. "It doesn't fit."

"What doesn't?"

"The classic signs of severe brain damage are profound unconsciousness, slow heartbeat, deep respirations, and a widening pulse point. I can't measure his pulse point without a blood pressure cuff, but he certainly has the other three signs and a sizable bump on the back of his head. So my assessment says head injury, but when I stand back and look at him, that conclusion doesn't look right."

"Nurses' instinct?"

"Something like that."

"Your instinct I trust. If not brain injury—thank the Almighty—why is he unconscious?"

Pepper held Benny's hand. As long as he was vulnerable, his safety was her sacred trust. "That's the frustrating part. I can't think of anything fitting this pattern." She turned him on his side and hyperextended his neck to open his airway and keep him from choking if he vomited. "There's nothing more I can do for him right now, except keep an eye on him. Do you want to question Thomas?"

"You know what a good-cop, bad-cop routine is?"

"Is that like in the movies, when one officer pretends to be friendly, the other plays hardball."

"Close enough. I'll be good cop."

Pepper wasn't sure she knew how to act like a police officer. "If I'm bad cop, do I have to have an attitude?"

"Your attitude is you don't like Thomas, you don't trust him, and everything that happened to Benny is his fault."

"Aw, Avivah, I hate to be mean, especially to Thomas. It's like kicking a puppy."

"Fine then, we'll climb back into our beds, pull the covers over our heads, and wait to see whether we're all alive come morning. Gary is dead, and Benny knocked senseless. Hasn't any of that sunk in yet?" Avivah ran her fingertips lightly over Benny's forearm. "Sorry, Pepper. That was uncalled for."

Pepper tried to not allow hurt feelings to get the better of her. "Could I play bad nurse instead? I have models for that."

"If bad nurse works, do it."

Thomas sat in a chair, just outside the dormitory door, with two nuns fussing over him. No one else was around, though Pepper could hear faint conversation coming up the stairwell. Thomas didn't look to be in any shape for company.

He'd washed and put on pajamas, but he still trembled and looked in no better shape than he had when he arrived. Playing bad nurse wasn't going to be all that easy, but Pepper steeled herself to do it.

Avivah and Pepper stood on either side and helped him up. Pepper said, "Come on, Thomas, let's get you into bed."

Once they were inside the dormitory, Avivah turned, and said to the nuns. "Sorry, we need privacy." She closed the door and locked it, leaving both sisters with their noses pressed against the glass, like children at a shop window.

Pepper said, "Damn, you've got balls. I've never locked a door on nuns before."

"You can return the favor next time my aunts are on a rampage. Ever faced a squad of lifetime Hadassah members intent on righting a wrong?"

"Can't say I have."

"God should preserve you."

Avivah looked longingly at her comfortable bed. Benny's arrival interrupted the first deep sleep she'd had in months. It couldn't have been real sleep, more likely exhaustion and depression, she told herself.

Thomas looked at Benny's still figure as he sat on Avivah's bed. "Did he say anything?"

He wasn't worried about Benny's injuries, just if he'd said anything. Avivah hoisted Thomas' legs into the bed. "I, for one, won't put much trust in anything he'll say."

Pepper took a deep breath. "Benny won't say anything useful or truthful any time soon. He may be in a coma. He may never wake up."

Thomas' face darkened. "He won't wake up?"

Avivah sat in a chair. "Of course he will wake up. But, Miss Pepperhawk needs to know exactly what happened to him, so she can help him."

Pepper muttered, "As if anything could help him now."

Avivah clenched her teeth and glowered at her. *Don't overplay it, Pepper, or he'll never talk.* "You left here about seven-thirty. What happened next?"

"We were okay for a while. The trail was marked." Thomas' chin dropped to his chest. He muttered, "Just like Chosin. We were out there so long. It was so cold."

Avivah couldn't afford a twenty-two-year-old detour to Korea. She had to hear his story before Benny woke up to contradict him. "It was cold. You walked a long time."

"Benny left the trail. He said he'd studied a map and knew a short cut."

Benny had studied Sister Mary Rachel's topographical map a long time. "Was it a short cut?"

"It didn't feel like one. I told him it felt as though we were going back toward the convent, not away from it. He ignored me. Finally, we came out on the road. I knew that wasn't where we should be because there were no houses, just rocks and trees. Benny said it was time to stop and build a fire, so we could warm up and drink something hot."

Pepper asked, "Benny, a trained soldier, picked a vulnerable spot beside a road to build a fire? Avivah, does that make any sense to you?"

Her voice had just the right amount of incredulity in it. Avivah suppressed a smile. Her friend made a decent bad-cop after all.

Thomas faltered. "A little ways away. In trees where no one could see us."

He was lying through his teeth. Avivah leaned forward and nodded as if she were in sympathy with him. "What happened after you built a fire?"

"We drank coffee and ate. He told me how he'd killed Gary, and how I was in his way, and this was as far as I went because he couldn't afford any loose ends."

It sounded like bad dialog in a B-grade movie. Benny didn't talk like that.

"When I bent over my pack, he attacked me with a rock. We fought. I took the rock away from him and hit him." Thomas moved from trembling to shaking hard. The iron bed rattled. "I didn't mean to do it; it was him or us. There was blood in the snow. He would get us killed. None of us wanted to die. I had to do it."

Pepper stepped between Avivah and Thomas. "That's enough for now."

Thomas' story was a complete fabrication. Benny was a trained killer, and he'd never been one to waste time or energy. If he'd wanted Thomas dead, he would have killed him, without saying a word, fifteen minutes after they left the convent. How far would Thomas go to spin out his tale? "Just one more question. Did Benny say why he killed Gary?"

"Yes."

"Why?"

"You should know."

"I don't know. I'm relying on you to tell me."

"Mr. Kirkpatrick killed Gary because he raped you. He did it because he had to protect you."

Avivah felt dizzy and disoriented. She and Gary had fallen into bed together out of mutual need. Nothing came close to rape. Besides, Benny didn't know about them, at least she assumed he didn't. Even if he had thought Gary raped her, he would have been more likely to meet Gary behind the convent for a conversation with fists. Then he would have phoned the police and had him charged. Benny might be a soldier, but he was eminently practical as well. If there were a legal recourse, he'd take it.

If Thomas told half-truths, then where did he get the true half? How had he had any inkling that she and Gary were lovers? Yesterday afternoon, after the Saratoga Patriotic Foundation arrived, she'd seen how General Bill patronized Thomas. He talked around him, as if he weren't present in the room. She wouldn't put it past General Bill to speculate about her relationship with Gary. Thomas wove what he'd heard the general say into his attack-on-the-mountain story.

In Vietnam, Avivah had endured enough rumors about her sex life. She thought she'd put all that behind her, but even a remote innuendo, from a distressed man, made her feel dirty. She desperately hoped Benny hadn't also been listening in when General Bill held forth. Benny was the one person she couldn't afford to be interested in her sexual partners. If he did, he might start digging, then everything that happened to her in Long Bien would inevitably work its way to the surface. When that happened, she might as well be dead.

Pepper worked a small bag from around Thomas' neck. "It's all right, Thomas. You did what you had to do. No one can do any better than that." She opened his bag, shook some pills into her hand and helped him take them with water, then tucked covers around him. "I'm going to ask one of the sisters to stay with you. You're warm and safe now, and no one is ever going to ask you any more questions about what happened in the snow."

Like hell they weren't, Avivah thought. Just wait until the sheriff gets here.

It took a while to find everyone, get them back to bed, and station Sister Mary Rachel to watch the two men. Pepper was everywhere, giving directions in tight, clipped sentences that left no mistake about what she wanted and when. Avivah recognized Pepper's behavior as her automaton reaction, the one where she'd seen Pepper take refuge when the world got too scary. She's terrified, Avivah thought. She thinks Gary raped me, and Benny killed him in retribution. Once, she said to Pepper. "What Thomas said didn't happen."

Pepper snapped back, "Of course it happened," and pushed her way past Avivah toward the next thing on her private agenda.

At last, she and Pepper were alone in a deserted classroom. Pepper spread a clean, white towel over the teacher's desk, and emptied one of Thomas' pill bottles. She counted, put pills back in the container and repeated her routine three times. "Taking into account when Thomas filled these prescriptions and how many pills remain, three medicines are correct. Four Secobarbital are missing. My guess is that Benny is sedated to within an inch of his life. His symptoms fit Secobarbital overdose."

"Secobarbital is a sleeping pill, isn't it?"

"Big time sleeping pill. Not only puts you to sleep, but depresses respiration and circulation. How's this for a scenario? Benny and Thomas stop to rest. Thomas gives Benny a cup of coffee, laced with Secobarbital. Fifteen minutes later Benny topples over and hits his head on a tree root or a rock."

"I believe that a lot more than Thomas besting Benny in hand-to-hand combat."

"If Thomas had left him out there, Benny would be dead of hypothermia by now. Thank God he couldn't afford another body on his conscience."

Adrenaline surged through Avivah. "Are you telling me Thomas is our killer?"

"Thomas is *a* killer, but I don't know whether he's *our* killer. Chosin happened in snow and bitterly cold weather, just like tonight. That's where Thomas saw blood in the snow."

Avivah leaned back against the teacher's desk and folded her arms over her chest. "So?"

Pepper wandered, picked up a small sliver of forgotten chalk and made random marks on the blackboard. "I spent a lot of time in Vietnam listening to patients tell stories. Guys reveal a lot about combat between the lines. Thomas said, 'It was him or us. He was going to get us killed. We didn't want to die.' Plural, not singular.

"I think twenty-two years ago, someone panicked. Thomas picked up a rock and killed him. What are you willing to bet that when we get a copy of his Medal of Honor citation, it says he carried a dead soldier back to U.S. lines? That's what saved Benny's life. Thomas couldn't leave the body of the man he killed to be captured by Chinese troops, and he couldn't leave Benny to die."

So Thomas, too, had killed a fellow soldier. A sudden pain squeezed down so hard in Avivah's chest that she thought she was having a heart attack. She wanted to tell Pepper about Long Bien, but her mouth denied her the words; her lungs refused to put any breath behind them. What came out instead, what must sound to Pepper like a complete non sequitur, was, "You wouldn't believe Central Park. It's not the way I remember it. Graffiti everywhere, and unsavory people hanging around.

Most people won't go there after dark. We were there in the middle of the afternoon. I saw a violent robbery in broad daylight."

Pepper put down her chalk and stared. "When the thief started shooting, didn't it occur to you that running after him wasn't a good idea?"

"When a guy is puking all over you, doesn't it occur to you that being a nurse isn't a good idea?"

Pepper laughed. "No, it occurs to me that I should do something to stop him from puking. I get your point."

"The guy I chased was a veteran, a druggie living on the street. Gary said there are a lot of them. They sleep in doorways and they scrounge for food in garbage cans. Why the hell isn't the Veterans Administration doing something for them?"

Pepper threw the chalk fragment across the room. "You know the answer to that as well as I do. Because we're losing. American soldiers aren't supposed to lose. We've disappointed a lot of people. And, those wackos—who just happen to be Vietnam veterans—who take a high-powered rifle up a tower and start shooting, scare the hell out of them. Civilians are afraid of us." She sat down in a straight-backed teacher's chair, and stared at her hands in her lap. "You know, going into the Army was a whole lot more fun than coming out of it is proving to be." She paused. "Is Benny in or out as a suspect?"

Avivah sat on the floor. It felt good to sit in a corner, her back protected on two sides by sturdy walls. Nothing could sneak up on her. Although she didn't believe a word of Thomas' story, if Benny had gotten the wrong end of the stick, thought Gary had hurt her—maybe, just maybe—it would have been enough to push him into murder. Benny had been under a lot of stress lately. She put aside personal feelings and answered as a police officer. "In."

"Much as I hate to admit it, I agree. I just wish I knew why he was in New York City in the first place."

"That was my doing."

"He came to see you?"

"Not exactly. Lorraine phoned me a few weeks ago. She said Benny was impossible to live with, and asked whether I had any ideas how to get him out of his funk."

Four years ago, Lorraine Fulford's husband, Benny's best friend, had gone missing-in-action, presumed dead in Vietnam. Having lost one husband to combat, she refused to marry Benny as long as he was on active duty. Benny resigned from the Army because that's what Lorraine wanted, but his becoming a civilian hadn't improved their relationship. She still refused to become engaged to him.

Pepper made a face. "Pretty soon, Lorraine will have to either fish or cut bait."

"I agree. I told her about Ron's Catholic men's retreats at his theologate. She convinced Benny to come up for Thanksgiving week. The retreat ended Friday. Benny and Ron met me in New York City for lunch on Saturday. Ron asked me whether I minded if Gary joined us, that he and Gary had some business to discuss after lunch."

"So you and Benny met Gary only last Saturday?"

"Yes."

"And Gary didn't . . . I mean, you never, he never . . . ?"

Her innocence rankled Avivah. A twenty-five-year-old nurse with a college education and an officer's commission should be able to mention sex without blushing. "Yes, we went to bed together. By mutual consent. There was no rape."

"You only knew this guy six days. When was there time for all this to happen?"

"The first time was last Saturday night."

Pepper pressed her palms to her temples. "You went to bed

with a man you'd only known a few hours? Avivah, how could you!"

"It's not like I'm under the age of consent."

"There are diseases." She pronounced each word slowly, with a heavy southern accent. "Di-sea-ses" got a full three syllables. Pepper's eyes grew round. She whispered, "You didn't do it *here* did you?"

"Well, not in *this* classroom, we didn't. Grow up, Pepper. There's been a sexual revolution, or haven't you noticed?"

"Noticed? I've spent the last six months on my own personal barricade. Darby showing up here hasn't exactly . . ." Pepper clapped her hand over her mouth.

Avivah leaned back into her protected space. Darby Baxter. David Barton. Her first thought when she'd met David had been how much Pepper would like him. She should have guessed. She even knew exactly what Darby looked like; Pepper's letters had been painstakingly descriptive. That she hadn't recognized him was another sign she was losing her street-cop smarts. "What is he doing here, under an assumed name?"

"I haven't a clue. He insists he's on leave, and that being here has nothing to do with Gary."

"You believe him?"

Her friend looked truly miserable. "He promised on his West Point ring. I hate to say this, but I think you should put him on your suspect list, too."

Avivah didn't bother to tell Pepper that she already had done that.

Pepper looked thoughtful. "We can eliminate Patience, Helen, and Sister Valentina."

Avivah had already eliminated Sister Valentina on physical and mental grounds. "Why eliminate Patience and Helen?"

"Lack of motive. They wouldn't gain anything by Gary's death. This convent closed months ago. Even if the Saratoga

Patriotic Foundation never rented it, both women were already out of a job, or likelier, considering how old they look, in line for a pension."

Avivah asked, "Why not eliminate Sister Mary Rachel and Sister Angelus as well, or does orientation to convent life include garroting?"

"No, they specialize in psychological warfare."

Avivah couldn't tell whether Pepper were joking or not.

Pepper continued, "We don't know anything about them. Maybe they haven't been nuns all their adult lives. For all we know, during World War II, they could have been members of Wild Bill Donovan's Office of Strategic Services. OSS operatives certainly knew how to garrote. And, when Sister Angelus came to tell us about the sleeping arrangements, she was out of breath, as if she'd just done something physically hard."

Pepper was right. They knew far too little about almost everyone here. Seven suspects: Darby, Benny, General Bill, Thomas, Dr. Saint-Mathias, Sister Angelus, and Sister Mary Rachel. Eight suspects, she added ruthlessly. If she put Benny on the list, she had to put Ron Lincoln there, too.

Pepper asked, sounding hopeful, "If the sheriff isn't coming, are you going to conduct an investigation?"

Their guttering candle threw shadows on the ugly walls. Hemingway's clean, well-lighted place was one thing, but this convent was more like the Castle of Otranto. A few days of candlelight, cold rooms, and nuns' habits swishing down corridors would be enough to send anyone, including herself, over the edge. She could only imagine what it might do to someone who was unbalanced enough to kill. A smart, patient killer would wait, bide his or her time, and play the odds. In her experience killers were rarely smart or patient.

"Away from a military post, I have absolutely no authority to conduct an investigation. I can't compel suspects to answer questions. The only way to find Gary's killer is to get the sheriff here soon. Thomas said the trail was well marked and easy to follow, but if I ski for help, you'll be here alone."

Pepper took a new candle out of her pants pocket, and lit it from the dying flame. Her hand trembled. "What alone? I've got enough people here to rewrite 'The Twelve Days of Christmas.' " She sang, "Three Catholic nuns, several former soldiers, one ex-boyfriend, and a Jesuit in a pine tree."

"I wish you'd stop acting as if my leaving you here with a killer is a joke. It isn't to me."

Pepper plucked at a piece of hardened wax. "It isn't to me, either, but I figure laughing is better than screaming in terror. I don't suppose you brought your service revolver with you?"

Leaving Pepper with a .45 automatic pistol was almost more frightening than leaving her unprotected. Pepper wasn't good around weapons. Not that Avivah had a weapon to leave with her. Her Army-issue pistol was locked in a military police arms locker in New Jersey. "I don't suppose I did."

Pepper nodded and squared her shoulders, like an officer prepared for inspection. Her voice didn't waiver. "You go. We'll all be here when you get back."

The unasked question hung between them. Would all of them still be alive when she got back?

CHAPTER 8

Before dawn Saturday morning, a ragged group, led by Sister Angelus carrying a tall altar candle, dragged itself to the chapel. Pepper's eyes stung, and her body moved with the sluggishness of having been awake all night. She would have gladly gone to bed, but she'd promised Avivah she'd watch everyone.

At least she felt better than Benny looked. As soon as he woke up enough to swallow, she'd encouraged him to drink massive amounts of water. By morning, his kidneys had pumped most of the Seconal out of his bloodstream. He was awake, and on his feet, but if she remembered her drug book correctly, Seconal left a horribly hung-over feeling. As she watched Benny drift slowly down the hall, occasionally bouncing off a wall, she concluded her book was probably right.

Thomas looked scared. He kept glancing surreptitiously at Benny, as if waiting for him to unravel his carefully told tale. Pepper thought that, given a chance, Thomas would run, though where he could possibly run *to* she'd didn't know.

On one of their bathroom trips, she and Benny had talked. It had consisted mostly of Pepper talking and Benny grunting in agreement. He didn't remember very much: a stop for coffee and food, feeling dizzy a few minutes afterwards, then nothing until he woke up. She'd told him that Avivah had planted a seed with Thomas that Benny wouldn't remember anything, and that was the way he was to play it until Avivah got back. She'd left out her surmise about what had happened in Korea.

People filed past her. Finally she stood alone, just outside the carved door, and watched the worshipers kneel. Three nuns, Patience, and Helen, occupied the first pew on the right. Wrapped in identical, voluminous black cloaks with hoods, they looked like five harpies. Thomas, Darby, Dr. Saint-Mathias, and Benny sat on the left side of the chapel.

Briefly, she considered joining them, then decided against it. In Vietnam, for the first time in her life, there had been no parents, no Ursuline nuns, no Sodality of Mary, no Catholic Youth Organization, no Newman Club. The Church excused her from attending Sunday Mass if no priest were present, and absolved her from days of fast and abstinence because she was in a war zone. Without church authority, family, and peer pressure, something snapped like a dry stick. She wasn't sure what, but she knew her relationship with the Catholic Church had irrevocably broken. She wasn't sure yet whether she'd broken with God, too. She pulled the door almost shut, leaving just enough of a gap that she could keep an eye on everyone.

Other than being without sleep for over twenty-four hours, Pepper was pleased with herself. She'd managed to push enough fluids into Benny, while not disturbing Thomas' sleep. And she'd watched everyone to make sure no one left and followed Avivah. Of course, she hadn't been able to watch the harpies, but since they'd all appeared for Mass that seemed to have worked out all right.

Pepper looked at her watch. Avivah had been away long enough to reach help. All Pepper had to do was stay awake until reinforcements arrived. Then she could sleep.

Sister Mary Rachel's gloved hand reached for a brass bell in front of her. She rang it sharply three times before stilling its sound by placing it on a velvet pillow. Everyone stood. Benny looked up as if startled and wobbled to his feet out of sync from everyone else.

Father Lincoln, wearing a long white alb and black chasuble—his hands hidden mandarin-like inside wide sleeves—entered from a side door. He bowed and turned toward his miniscule congregation.. His words made little white puffs in cold air. "A requiem mass for repose of Gary Dormuth's soul."

As the priest ascended the altar steps, everyone knelt.

"In the name of the Father, and of the Son, and of the Holy Ghost. I will go up to the altar of God."

Respondents answered. "To God the joys of my youth."

"Our help is in the name of the Lord."

Trapped in a familiar pattern, Pepper murmured, "Who made heaven and earth."

Behind her, a lighter flipped open, and she smelled cigar smoke. She turned. General Bill, dressed in a parka with his hood pulled up, lit a large cigar and flipped his lighter closed. His words came out surrounded by cherry-smelling smoke. "My smoking lamp is lit."

Pepper didn't bother pointing out the "No Smoking Anywhere in the Convent" sign posted just above his head. William Pocock-Nesbitt wrote his own rules.

He waved his cigar in Benny's general direction. "Your boy okay?"

The door made a heavy clunk as Pepper closed it. For the next twenty or thirty minutes, she didn't have to watch everyone. They weren't going anywhere, except to communion, and she didn't want cigar smoke drifting into the chapel. "Benny isn't my boy."

General Bill puffed his cigar. "I didn't see your friend in there, but then I can't imagine a Jewess attending to all that Popery nonsense."

Only Sister Mary Rachel knew Avivah had gone for help. If anyone else asked, Pepper would say she was asleep in nun's quarters and not to be disturbed under any circumstances. She shoved her hands deep into her coat pockets and strode away from the anti-Semitism in how he said "Jewess."

General Bill followed her. "You're an Army nurse."

Darby. He must have blown her cover. One thing Pepper didn't want was any common ground with this cigar-smoking bigot. She tried to make her military service sound unimportant and distant. "Was, past tense. Water under the bridge."

"You girls do a wonderful job. I always knew my boys were in good hands."

He hadn't been remotely friendly toward her before. Why was he trying to worm his way into her good graces? Was it a military thing, or with everyone else at Mass, did he just want to talk to someone?

Pepper gritted her teeth. "What boys would those be?"

He pulled himself up to his full height and puffed out his chest. "Artillery. I went in as a shave-tailed lieutenant after Pearl Harbor, and came out a brigadier general twenty-five years later. Artillery all the way."

Pepper's radar went on. She did quick calculations. If he joined in 1942, twenty-five years would have been 1967, when Vietnam escalated and the military desperately needed experienced senior officers. One-star generals with only twenty-five years service didn't voluntarily retire in 1967.

General Bill patted his chest. "Wanted to go for thirty years, of course, but my docs told me this old ticker couldn't stand the strain."

It didn't wash. Her gut feeling—nurses' intuition—told her he hadn't retired for medical reasons. A cardiac condition made great cover. She remembered how he avoided any real work last night. A supposed heart condition garnered sympathy, and gave him an acceptable excuse for not exerting himself. She was curious to see what happened if she played along with his charade. "That's too bad. You must be terribly disappointed."

his misogyny and bigotry, Pepper inched as far away from him as she could toward her end of the bench.

"Hackmann's widow pawned her bastard grandson off on the nuns—my guess is she was too ashamed to raise him herself—gave them use of this land and a house as a sop to her conscience, moved to Raleigh, remarried, and started a second family." He poked Pepper's chest, hard, with his index finger. "Use of land, mind you, use, not a deed."

She grabbed the offending finger and pushed it aside.

"Fast forward a hundred years. Dr. Saint-Mathias is mucking around in old records. He comes across the old lady's will. I quote, 'I will the property he grew up on to my grandson, Lucas Hackmann or, if he be deceased, to his direct male descendants.' End of quote. She'd kept quiet about this grandson; her second family didn't know he or her daughter ever existed. Lucas Hackmann was also her dead son's name, and her family figured, in old age, she'd forgotten he was dead and meant to write 'to my son, Lucas Hackmann.'"

Pepper put it together. "This is the property Lucas Hackmann grew up on, and Thomas Hackmann is a direct male descendent."

General Bill beamed. "Not *a* descendent, little lady, he and his father are *the only* direct male descendants. Mr. Hackmann Senior is real interested in proving their ownership of this property. A future for Thomas, as it were, so he'll always be taken care of."

"Your Saratoga Patriotic Foundation will make sure he has that future?"

"Holding money in trust for him, making sure his needs are met is the least we can do for a Medal of Honor winner."

She wondered if General Bill would have been so eager to provide for Thomas if he'd been just a psychiatric patient instead of a war hero. Once they got out of here, she would ask her lawyer-uncle how to make sure Thomas' interests were really served.

"The convent was already up for sale. Once I realized what we had in Thomas, I applied for an injunction against them being able to sell it, which the judge granted. The Visitation Order can't do anything with this building until a court decides ownership. Can't sell it, must keep it in good repair, and no one else had the faintest interest in renting it."

"Is that where Gary Dormuth came in?"

General Bill ground his cigar out in a china bowl that stood on a table next to his end of the bench. "Those nuns put up more of a fight than I thought they would. It was a close thing. Gary pushed and pushed until he brokered us a sweet rental deal. God rest him; he was one hell of a fighter. He grabbed these nuns by their tits and wouldn't let go."

Sister Mary Rachel's voice boomed. "There is no smoking in this convent!"

Illicit smoking had been *de rigueur* in school. Reflex brought Pepper to her feet. She looked around for a place to ditch her cigarette, before she realized she didn't have one.

The sister bore down on them. Yards of brocaded cloth swished after her, an enraged raven in full attack. "You will get rid of that disgusting cigar butt and wash that bowl. Present yourself, with a clean bowl, if you expect breakfast."

Pepper seated herself at one of two massive refractory tables, and tried, unsuccessfully, to picture both tables filled with nuns, dressed in old-fashioned habits. Even in its heyday, she couldn't imagine twenty-four sisters in this out-of-the-way place.

No, nuns would have had a private dining room. She looked around. Still did. That's why none of them sat at this table. Lay teachers, secretaries, laundry workers, housekeepers, handymen, and groundskeepers would have eaten here. Their meals would have been filled with the gossip, backbiting, and infighting that happened in any closed group. This morning her group barely filled one half of one table, and they were silent.

She inhaled the wonderful smells of scrambled eggs, biscuits, grits, sausage patties, sawmill gravy, and coffee. They might be trapped in an isolated building, without electricity, and a killer among them, but Helen still understood comfort food.

General Bill—grudgingly admitted to breakfast after he produced a clean china bowl—Dr. Saint-Mathias, Thomas, and Darby occupied the far side of the table; Father Ron, herself, and Benny, the near side. Helen hovered, ready to serve once Father Ron said grace.

Ron bowed his head. "Bless us, O Lord, and these Thy gifts, which we are about to receive, from Thy bounty, through Christ, Our Lord. Amen." He looked up. "Helen, you may serve now."

Filled plates quickly appeared in front of everyone.

Thomas stared at his plate. He began to move one hand around the other, as if he were washing them. His words came out in a tumble. "I'm sorry, Mr. Kirkpatrick. About last night, I mean. I'm really, really sorry."

Benny looked at him. "It's okay, Tom. I know you did what had to be done. I'm just grateful to be here. Go on, now, and eat your breakfast." He picked up his own fork, made an unsuccessful attempt to spear some eggs, dropped the fork, and rested his head in his hands.

Pepper, her mouth full, asked, "Number ten day?"

"Number ten-thou won't even cover it."

"You want more aspirin?"

"Just go away and let me die in peace."

"No can do, G.I."

General Bill watched with an amused smile. "I see you haven't forgotten military jargon, Miss Pepperhawk. You can't have been out of the Army all that long."

Pepper became very interested in her food. "Long enough."

"From my point of view, I'm glad I got out when I did. The military isn't what it once was. The Army is going to hell in a handbasket."

Darby laid down his fork and sat back in his chair. "What is your point, sir?"

His laid-back posture and half-lidded eyes didn't fool Pepper. Anger radiated from Darby like steam rising from asphalt in July.

General Bill considered. "Let's just say the military has become a little too colorful for my tastes, if you get my meaning."

Beside her, Pepper felt Ron's body tense. They had both gotten his meaning. In spades. She chided herself for using that word, even in her head. Her ward master at Fort Bragg, whom she liked and respected, had been black.

Medical condition, her eye. General Bill's only heart problem was that his heart wasn't big enough to include soldiers who weren't white males. Despite putting on a brave public face about an equal, integrated Army, racial tensions—some more overt than others—flourished. Smart soldiers, both black and white, calculated just how far they could go without bringing discipline down on their heads. To be asked to resign his commission over race issues, General Bill would have had to have acted blatantly, outrageously bigoted, and to have continued his behavior after his superiors ordered him to stop it. Was he that dumb or just that angry?

Benny looked as if he had pulled himself as far awake as he could. "You mean we should go back to segregated, but equal, units."

General Bill said, "It worked."

There hadn't been anything equal or workable about segregated military units.

Benny echoed Pepper's thoughts. "It did not work."

Darby interrupted, "If you'll pardon me, Mister Kirkpatrick, I think he has a point."

Pepper turned. She'd never asked Darby about his racial politics. In truth, she hadn't wanted to know. She'd always assumed that, since he was a good ole boy, born and raised in Macon, Georgia, that they were on opposite sides of the integration question. It was easier not knowing for certain that Darby was a bigot.

General Bill's eyes glittered. "So, Mr. Barton, you favor segregated units?"

Pepper saw a look pass between Darby and Benny. She got their drift and had a hard time holding back her grin. She'd wished all morning that someone would take General Bill down a peg or two. Major Darby Baxter was about to do it for her.

Darby said, "Absolutely. I think every soldier, from private to general, should be required to take a competency test. People who have necessary sensitivity to understand and defend truth, honor, and an American way of life should be put into separate battalions and given the honor of going into battle as the vanguard."

General Bill's military crew cut bristled. "I know what color that battalion would be."

Darby drew himself up to where he was almost sitting at attention. "It would be the color of courage, sir. As a man I admire very much said, 'Willing to die, if God and my country think I have done my duty.' "

Dr. Saint-Mathias chuckled. "Good old Jimmy Stuart."

General Bill's face clouded. He looked lost. "From *The Lone Eagle*, right?"

Dr. Saint-Mathias had a small bit of sausage stuck in his beard and biscuit crumbs decorated his usually impeccable black suit. "No. Mister Barton just quoted a minor Confederate officer. No one of any consequence."

The longer she looked at Dr. Saint-Mathias, the more Pepper realized he was, if not drunk, already past squiffy, and it was only eight o'clock. She was also certain Doctor Saint-Mathias was having General Bill on.

Jimmy Stewart. She worried his name around in her mind, like a dog playing with a ball. When she listened to the name instead of visualizing it, she got it. Not Jimmy Stewart, actor, but James Ewell Brown Stuart, major general, Army of Northern Virginia. The romantic, plume-hatted Confederate cavalry officer that some southern women still swooned over. It had never dawned on her before that he might actually have been an outstanding soldier. Darby would admire no less. She'd have to ask Dr. Saint-Mathias to recommend a biography about J.E.B. Stuart. Now, however, did not look like a good time.

General Bill was in full sail. "The Army expects illiterate coons and spicks to understand a hundred-and-five millimeter gun-howitzer. Hell, half of them don't speak English. What kind of an army is that, I ask you?"

Ron steepled his fingers. "Is that why you plan to turn these convent lands into your own private artillery range? So men worthy of the guns can learn to handle them?"

Behind her, Helen dropped a plate. Pepper's breath caught. Matters of mutual interest, research, and historical documentation be damned; General Bill really did plan to start his own Army and, somehow, Ron had uncovered his secret.

General Bill never missed a beat. "Hell, yes. Recruiters are having a hard time getting the right sort of people, what with being attacked on campuses, and recruiting offices set on fire. There are many good American men out there who'd jump at the chance to be in artillery, if somebody took time to show them what it was all about. I intend to do that. Give them some gun practice. Once a real artillery man knows the sound and smell of the big guns, he never forgets it."

Neither, thought Pepper, did people on the receiving end. She looked from face to face. Ron knew about the general's private plans. If Benny was privy to the secret, it was probably because Ron told him. Darby's face was bland and closed. Darby, bland and closed, wasn't something Pepper liked to contemplate. It meant he was as mad as hell. She felt relieved there weren't any dueling pistols here. Dr. Saint-Mathias looked more titillated than horrified. She couldn't tell whether he had known. Thomas Hackmann just looked stunned. Pepper was willing to bet that General Bill hadn't told any of his board members that he intended to turn acres of lush mountain land into a no-mans land, stripped and pitted by artillery fire.

Cold fury filled Ron's face. "Gary's brother died from *friendly* artillery fire. You didn't know that, did you?"

"It wouldn't have mattered to me if I had known. His brother was a marine. It was his God-given right, as an American fighting man, to risk his life."

In one fluid motion, Pepper stood, pulled back her hand, and slapped General Bill's face. The sound and feel of her hand meeting his flesh felt truly satisfying. She walked away, shoulders back and her head high.

Once the door closed behind her and she was safely in the hall, Pepper shivered. The atmosphere had changed. Hate and mistrust now surrounded that breakfast table. Nothing sacred or secular in this convent could protect them from what Ron's revelation just unleashed. From now on, it was her own back she had to watch. Hurry, Avivah, she prayed. Hurry back with help.

CHAPTER 9

After breakfast, Sister Mary Rachel hurried everyone outside to collect more firewood. Snow had stopped, for now. The best analogy Pepper could think of was being in the eye of a hurricane. She was a lot more familiar with hurricanes than blizzards. Only an occasional, errant flake stuck to her coat, but just wait. Huge, pewter-colored clouds boiled across the northwestern sky. Even coming from a snow-deprived childhood, Pepper could guess that a lot more snow was coming.

Today everyone worked, including General Bill. Women collected fallen wood; men emptied the woodpile, carrying every log inside against the eventuality of another night without heat. So far, Pepper had managed to avoid General Bill by making sure she carried wood in as he came out, and vice versa. She knew she couldn't avoid him forever, and she had no idea what she'd say to him. All she knew for certain was that she wasn't going to apologize.

Pepper's teeth worried at a small piece of dry skin on her bottom lip. Could his secret artillery range be motive enough for Gary's death? Was Ron in danger for having told that secret? What would she do if the weather closed in again before Avivah made it back? Someone else might die if she wasn't watchful, but Pepper knew she couldn't stay awake much longer. Who did she trust enough to turn to for watchkeeping?

If Ron were in danger, he couldn't watch himself. Darby, Benny, Thomas, Dr. Saint-Mathias, and General Bill were all on her suspect list, or sick, or both. That left only nuns. She had to admit she'd never met a stupid nun. Rigid, opinionated, even persnickety, but never stupid.

A flock of cardinals chattered around a cluster of empty bird feeders. Pepper trudged toward them, glad for a task that didn't require much energy. "Aw, pretties, is everyone too busy wood-gathering to pay attention to you?"

She brushed away snow from amorphous mounds. One turned out to be a wooden bin with a hinged top. Pepper opened it and peered inside. Birdseed. Taking a scoop, she filled feeders. "Here y'all go. Your mess hall is open."

Sister Mary Rachel, her arms filled with small branches, passed by and chuckled, not unkindly. "Saint Pepper of Assisi."

Pepper tossed her scoop back and closed the lid. " 'Consider the ravens: They do not sow or reap, they have no storeroom or barn; yet God feeds them. And how much more valuable you are than birds!' Luke 12:24."

"I was under an impression you'd distanced yourself from religion."

"It's this atmosphere."

Puffing, the sister set her branches down and sat on a bench made out of cut logs. "Catholic school for how many years?"

She'd grown to respect, or at least not fear, the sister. If Pepper could assure herself that the nun wasn't likely to know how to use a garrote, Sister Mary Rachel would be her least likely suspect and her first choice to take over guard duties. "Twelve years convent school with the Ursulines in Biloxi."

It was obvious from the sister's face that she had heard of Ursuline's strictness. "In some ways, that's unfortunate. Too much of anything can cause a person to lose perspective. Did you ever think you might have a vocation?"

Pepper sat beside her. "Every Catholic girl thinks that at some point. A cloistered order appealed to me, but I realized I wouldn't last five minutes with a vow of silence."

"If you will permit my saying so, Elizabeth, I believe you would find it impossible to keep any of our vows, particularly obedience, longer than five minutes. I'm sorry, that's not fair. You appear to be a very adaptable person, and one who has high expectations of how the world should behave. I think you could keep a vow of poverty very well, if doing so would support a cause in which you believed."

Pepper wasn't sure if that were a compliment. "I wouldn't like being poor."

"No one does. I certainly didn't, but you would manage. As you get older, you may realize you have a lot to thank nuns for. I did."

"You went to Catholic school, too?"

"Yes, but only for my last four years. I came to gratitude later in life."

"Is gratitude why you became a nun?"

"I spent a number of years in the secular world before I opened my heart to my God-given vocation. It was maturity, not gratitude, that brought me to a religious life."

She'd never have a better opening to ask about the sister's background. "What did you do before you entered the convent?"

"Clerked in a department store. I started in a Woolworth's candy counter, and they eventually promoted me into children's clothes and toys."

That sounded innocuous enough. "So you went to a Catholic high school, then worked at Woolworth's, then became a nun?"

The sister stiffened. Her gloved hands tightened around one another. "Why are you so interested in that part of my life?"

Pepper couldn't just admit she was trying to discover if Sister Mary Rachel had any idea how to garrote. If she were going to ask the sister for help, it would be a good idea not to antagonize her. Pepper waived her hand. "Sorry, I have this insatiable curiosity about other people's lives. In the South it's called 'showing an interest.' My mother calls it being just plain nosey."

The sister pursed her lips and looked toward the group of men. "If you will permit me to advise you, Elizabeth, in our current circumstances, nosiness is a bad idea. So are rash actions. William Pocock-Nesbitt may act like a fool, but he is not a man to cross."

So she knew what had happened at breakfast. That didn't surprise Pepper.

"I couldn't agree more, and if I had it to do over again, I'd try very hard to hold back my anger. Sister, I'm dead on my feet, and I've got to sleep. I need to ask you for a favor. Could we go somewhere private to talk?"

"I think a cup of tea in my office would suit us both." She rose, and Pepper helped her gather her bundle of sticks.

From the road, a young man's voice called out. "Hello, the convent."

Everyone stopped, and turned. A dogsled appeared. Two spotted hounds of uncertain parentage, possibly a touch bluetick, pulled the sled in a gangling, most un-sled-dog-like manner. Avivah sat in the sled, bundled in layers of blankets. A young man, muffled in layers of clothing so that only his eyes showed, rode behind. He circled to where Sister Mary Rachel and Pepper stood, and threw up a spray of snow. He touched his fingers to his cap. "Morning, sister."

The sister walked around him. "Toby, where did you get this?"

He unwrapped his scarf and folded up his cap's earflaps, revealing a skinny face with a few acne spots. Pepper recognized him as the same young man who had given her directions at the gas station.

"I built it, from a book they got down to our library. I been studying up on dogsled racing pretty near a year now. Course I ain't got the right dogs yet, but I'm saving up to buy a pair of huskies."

Avivah unwrapped herself and climbed out.

General Bill strode over and demanded, "When is the sheriff coming?"

"He's not. He's knee-deep in a disaster right now."

Toby nodded. "That's God's honest truth. Sorry, sister." He pointed to the dark clouds Pepper had been looking at. "There's two huge low-pressure systems coming together bang over our heads." He hit his fists together for emphasis. "This snow we've already got ain't nothing compared to what's coming. The governor's declared three counties disaster areas. When he called out the National Guard, he said it was on account of we face 'a protracted and unexpectedly severe blizzard.' Nobody's got electricity from north of here to down past Asheville. All up and down these mountains, we already got babies being born in police cruisers, and folks rescued from sure death in snowbound cars. No telling what it will be like by tonight."

Pepper recognized the fire in his eyes. He was part of this great adventure. Decades from now, he'd still tell stories to his grandchildren about what he did this weekend. She'd seen too many young men, a year or two older than Toby, with that fire extinguished. She wanted to tell him to get on his sled, head north, and not stop until he crossed into Canada. He should find himself some old codger who would teach him everything there was to know about dogsled racing, and not let him come home until Vietnam was over.

This thought shocked her. She never imagined she'd want to tell anyone to go to Canada to avoid military service. Here she was, out of the army only two days, and thinking like one of those anti-Vietnam protesters. She glanced at Darby, Benny, and Avivah. Maybe that was the way it should be. Only people who'd been there and seen the war for themselves should protest. At least they would know exactly what they protested against.

Avivah took a badge out of her coat pocket. "Every deputy is already working around the clock. The only way Gary's murder would be investigated before next week was to deputize me to investigate it."

Pepper looked around, but if she hoped to see a facial twitch, some shadow of fear or guilt pass across a person's face, she didn't see it. Everyone just looked tired and confused.

General Bill rubbed his hands together. "Let's get to it then. I imagine you'll want to interview each one of us. That's what detectives do in books." He turned to Sister Mary Rachel. "She'll need an office."

The nun's face looked carefully controlled. Pepper suspected she'd like a go at slapping General Bill, too. "Deputy Rosen is welcome to use my office."

"That's settled then. Who do you want to see first?"

Avivah looked nonplused at the rate with which someone else had taken charge. "I'll let you know in a little while." She led Toby and Sister Mary Rachel a little away. Pepper naturally followed.

"Toby is right about our weather getting much worse. With everything else going on, I'm worried about us being able to keep an eye on Sister Valentina. Do you think sister would go with Toby?"

Darby Baxter had taught Pepper's Medical Evacuation lecture. He said, "When your position is in danger of being overrun, your first chopper out, which may be the only chopper you're going to get out, takes wounded, sick, and weak." A homemade sled and two mismatched dogs weren't the same as a Huey helicopter, but they would do. Getting Sister Valentina to a safe place made a lot of sense.

Sister Mary Rachel looked at Sister Valentina, who was pet-ting the dogs. "I don't know. She's known Toby since he was born. She might."

"She wouldn't be going to no shelter or nothing. We got an empty back bedroom since my grandmother passed. It's a real nice room."

The sister nodded. "I'm sure it is. That's very kind of you. Perhaps, if Helen or Patience went with her, it might work."

He hung his head. "Sorry, sister. With them two dogs not being real sled dogs, I can only take one passenger at a time." He looked up, gauging clouds. "I might can come back, squeeze in a second trip right away."

"Let's see first if she's willing to go at all." They walked over to Sister Valentina. "Sister, this is Toby. We buy eggs and vegetables from his family."

At least she didn't say, you remember Toby, which Sister Valentina probably didn't.

She stuck out her birdlike hand. "How do you do, Toby."

Pepper was startled. She only heard the sister make a keening noise, never speak, and had assumed that muteness was a symptom of her illness.

He pulled off his wool cap and shook her hand. "Sister."

"He would like to give you a ride in his sled. Would you like that?"

"Oh, yes. I like dogs." Eager as a child, she sat herself down. Toby fussed over her, taking care to arrange blankets around her as if he were a senior deck steward on an ocean liner. He asked in a worried tone, "Won't she need more religious clothes and all?"

"If you can get her to your house, come right back for Helen. She will bring clothes."

"Yes, ma'am, I'll be back in two ticks."

"First, try driving her around here a couple of times. See whether she likes it."

"Yes, ma'am."

Toby mounted and called to his dogs. They looked confused, bounced into one another, pulled in opposite directions, then found their stride. Toby guided them in a couple of large circles around, turning up clouds of white snow. Sister Valentina laughed and waved. After making a second circuit, Sister Mary Rachel signaled to him to leave. Toby turned right instead of left and disappeared down the road.

His sled became only a faint swishing sound, then no sound at all. Everyone blew out a collective sigh of relief.

The keening started low, and rose to a crescendo of wailing. At first, Pepper thought a dog had stepped on something under the snow and hurt his paw. Then the sled came back, double-quick, Toby yelling, "I didn't do nothing, sister. I swear I didn't. She just started yelling."

Before they completely stopped, Sister Valentina leapt from the sled. Her tangle of blankets tripped her, and she crawled through the snow, dragging blankets behind her, to Sister Angelus. She clutched at the nun's habit. "Don't make me leave. I'll be good. I promise I will. I'm God's special child."

Sister Angelus, her face red with suffused blood, pulled her skirt free. "You should have left years ago. You are a sick woman, who belongs in a hospital. I was right. You had no business becoming a nun."

Sister Angelus looked to be in her mid-sixties. Sister Valentina looked a few years younger. Pepper suspected whatever had enraged Sister Angelus had its roots decades ago, when the two women were both much younger. A convent might be a place of peace and contemplation, but its closed community also bred long-standing feuds.

Sister Mary Rachel ordered, as gruff as any drill sergeant. "Sister Angelus, you will confine yourself to your room, in prayer and contemplation, until I have time to speak to you!"

Some good that will do, Pepper thought. We're all confined to our rooms.

Sister Angelus pulled herself upright, tucked hands into her sleeves, and gave a little bow. "I hear and obey."

Her face was almost purple and Pepper was afraid she'd have a stroke.

Helen and Patience made a fuss over Sister Valentina, picking her up and brushing snow from her garments. Toby shuffled from one foot to another, his face red. "It wasn't me, sister. I swear it wasn't me."

"No, it wasn't you, Toby. Sister Valentina just doesn't want to leave here."

"No, ma'am, I'd say she rightly doesn't." He looked anxious to get away. "The sheriff might need me soon. Is there anything else I can do for you?"

Pepper felt a hand under her elbow. Darby propelled her toward the sled. "Take her out with you instead."

Pepper freed her arm. "Take your hands off me. I'm not going anywhere."

Darby turned to Avivah, "Captain Rosen, you're in charge now. Order her to leave."

Avivah said, "He's got a point, Pepper. There's no reason for you to stay."

For a moment, Pepper felt relieved. Of everyone here, she was the only one free to leave. She remembered Sam Houston drawing a line in the sand at the Alamo. Leave now or cross this line and volunteer for certain death. Legend said every man in the Alamo crossed it. Of course, in retrospect, it was easier to see that anyone who'd chosen to leave wouldn't have lived, either. And they wouldn't have passed into legend.

"I am not leaving."

As she stormed off, she heard Sister Mary Rachel say, "I don't think anyone is going with you, Toby. Thank you for bringing Captain Rosen back. I'll pray for you and everyone who is working so hard this weekend."

Darby didn't catch up with Pepper until she was halfway upstairs to the dormitory. Pepper whirled to face him. "I paid attention in your Med Evac lecture. First helicopter out is for the wounded, sick, and weak. I'm not wounded, and I'm not sick. That leaves one choice and nothing you can do will convince me that I'm weak."

"Give me a break, Pepper. I was raised in the South. There are some situations where I believe it's my God-given responsibility to protect a woman."

"Why do I need protection?"

"I know you. You can't help meddling in Avivah's investigation and that could be dangerous."

"So you were lying to us in basic training with all that 'pretty lady' talk. We fell for it, you know. You made it sound as if you weren't just referring to a pretty face, but to inner strength. We thought that you trusted us, that you believed army nurses could do anything we set our minds to."

"I did trust you. I do trust you. Army nurses are incredible women. They saved my life twice. You've seen my scars."

"I'm not interested in your scars. Do you think I traded in all that strength you ascribe to Army nurses when I became a civilian? Good-bye captain's bars, hello airhead? Benny was right. In my own mind I should always think of myself as an officer and a gentleman and behave like one. Officers didn't run away on the first dogsled out at the Alamo."

She hoped her oddball humor would calm him down, make him laugh. Instead, he grabbed her and pulled her to him, kissing her mouth hard, smothering her tirade in a flood of memories. When he broke their embrace, he said in a breathless voice, "Just keep your mouth shut about me."

In dim light, Pepper couldn't tell whether the expression on his face was fear or passion. She'd never realized before how, on Darby, those two emotions looked so similar.

CHAPTER 10

Sister Mary Rachel appointed Patience to show Avivah and Pepper to the principal's office. Patience as a guide. Avivah almost laughed at how appropriate that was.

As Patience passed the museum room, she crossed herself. Avivah reached out and wiggled the doorknob. It was still locked. Was it her imagination, or had a faint, unpleasant odor began to waft into the hall?

She was thankful that the sheriff had taken possession of her film and notes. He told her to leave the crime scene undisturbed. She hoped by the time he arrived; they wouldn't be stuffing towels and plastic bags along the door to contain dribbling body fluids.

Patience unlocked an office door, on which gold script proclaimed "Principal." As they entered, Avivah clicked the light switch, and was vaguely surprised when nothing happened. She still took electricity for granted.

Danish modern chairs, a nubby blue couch, and a massive desk almost filled the room. Low shelves held books. An abstract wall hanging, woven out of indigo yarn and decorated with beads and feathers, proved that the sixties arts-and-crafts revival had made at least one foray here. A wooden crucifix, with dried palm fronds stuck behind it, hung over the couch. The room looked so normal that Avivah was disappointed. To hear Pepper tell of her visits to the sister-principal, she'd expected a complete set of thumbscrews and a rack purchased secondhand from the

Spanish Inquisition.

Wind rattled tall window glass. Avivah pushed aside enough heavy drapery to look down into a walled garden. Snow whirled under a dark grey sky. She hoped Toby and his mismatched dogs were safe and warm.

Patience set down her candle. "Will there be anything else?"

"I'd appreciate more candles." Avivah pointed to a big reel-to-reel tape recorder. "Does that work on batteries?"

"I believe it does."

"Ask sister if I may use it, and if so, I'd like every battery and blank tape you can find."

After Patience left, Avivah wrestled the tape recorder around to look for a battery compartment.

Pepper asked, "How can you do that?"

"It's bulky, but it's not heavy."

"I mean, how can you casually rattle that doorknob when you know what . . . who . . . ?"

"Compartmentalization. Like, when you kept working in Qui Nhon when you knew the body shed was full."

"It's a hell of a way to make a living."

Avivah asked absently, "Police work or nursing?"

Pepper sighed. "Both."

"We are what we are."

"I suppose we are. General Bill is a bigot, a racist, a segregationist, a misogynist, and an anti-Semite. He thinks the military is going to hell in a handbasket, and he intends to turn this place into a private artillery range for pure, white males who know how to read."

Like so many of Pepper's summaries, what she said almost, but not quite, made sense. Avivah rested her forehead on the tape recorder's cool surface. "Pepper, neither of us had any sleep last night. Start over, slow down, and fill in enough blanks to make sense. Pretend I'm new here."

As Pepper talked, Avivah first felt angry, then incredulous. A private artillery range had to be illegal. Even a windbag like General Bill could never hope to get away with blowing up half a mountain side.

Patience returned with a basket loaded with candlesticks, fat cream-colored church candles, and a shoe box into which she'd dumped batteries and tape reels. After she'd left, Avivah jammed several candles into candlesticks. "I'll interview you first."

Pepper almost squealed. "Me? Why do I have to be interviewed?"

"Because I need you to act as a witness to other interviews. That means we have to prove you're squeaky clean."

Pepper's face brightened. "You're going to let me help?"

"I don't have much choice, do I?"

"Hot dog!"

Avivah threaded tape. "Try to restrain yourself from such gleeful outbursts on tape." She started the machine, recited her name, date and time, and people present. "State your full name and place of residence."

"Elizabeth Ann Pepperhawk. I currently have no fixed address."

"Why is that?"

"I'm in the process of changing jobs."

"Is there an address for people who would always know where to find you?"

Pepper gave her aunt's name and address in Bat Harbor, Tennessee.

"Were you acquainted with Gary Dormuth?"

"I met him once."

"When was this?"

"Yesterday afternoon, Friday, 1 December 1972, about 1645 hours. I mean four-forty-five."

"Where was this?"

"In a public cloakroom at the Visitation Convent, Crossnore, North Carolina."

She had to give Pepper credit. All that hospital charting she did made her a good subject to interview. She knew how to include details without being asked. "Had you ever met Mr. Dormuth before?"

"No."

"Did you know of him before yesterday?"

"On Sunday, 26 November 1972, Benny Kirkpatrick talked about him during a phone call. He did not mention Gary by name."

"What did Mr. Kirkpatrick say about him?"

Pepper waved at the off button. Avivah shook her head and motioned for Pepper to continue. Tapes with no interruptions stood up better in court.

Pepper made an exasperated face, then said, "That Mr. Dormuth had done a mutual friend a favor. He allowed her to stay at his apartment in New York City last weekend."

"What was Mr. Dormuth doing when you met him?"

"He was going through coat pockets. He took something from a coat and put it in his pants pocket."

Avivah hadn't expected that. "Out of his own coat pocket?"

"I don't know. I had no idea which coat belonged to whom."

"Did you ask him what he was doing?"

"Yes."

"What did he say?"

Pepper looked startled. "Oh, my gosh. The car keys."

"What car keys?"

"He showed me a set of rental car keys. He said it wasn't a good idea to leave them in a public area. If he were killed shortly after I saw him, I'll bet he still has those keys in his pocket." She wrinkled her nose. "You aren't going to take them off his body, are you? That could be . . . messy."

Considering how hard it was snowing, no one would need cars for a while. "Forget about them for now. What happened after he showed them to you?"

"I thanked him for doing my friend a favor. Then he left."

"How long were you and Mr. Dormuth together?"

"Five, maybe ten minutes."

"You said this was *about* four-forty-five on Friday. Could you be more precise about the time?"

"No. I never saw a clock."

"Were you wearing a watch?"

Pepper looked down at her wristwatch. "Not then."

Avivah steadied her voice. "Under what circumstances did you next see Mr. Dormuth?"

"He was lying facedown in the convent's museum. He was dead."

"What time was this?"

"Nearly six o'clock."

"Again, can you be more precise?"

"No."

"Between when Mr. Dormuth left you and when you saw his body, were you ever alone?"

"Only for a minute or so, walking from coatroom to visitors' parlor."

"Who was with you after that?"

"First, Father Lincoln, then five or six people, then I went outside to my van with Mr. Kirkpatrick."

"So almost every minute of your time between when Gary left you and when you saw his body can be verified by other people."

"Yes."

"Do you know the difference between an eyewitness and an expert witness?"

Pepper looked puzzled. "An eyewitness is present at an event;

an expert witness knows a special body of knowledge."

"Would you consider yourself an expert witness about Catholic convents?"

"No, but I attended convent school in Mississippi for twelve years. I know something about them."

"You mentioned twice that you saw no clock. Are clocks common in convents?"

"They tend to be found only in offices."

"Why?"

"Nuns regulate convent life. Clocks are a distraction: we were taught to live in the moment as a praise to God for having given it to us, not wonder how many more minutes we had to endure algebra."

Avivah suppressed a smile. "Have you noticed clocks here in any public area, such as halls or parlors?"

"No."

"Thank you, Miss Pepperhawk. That will be all for now."

Avivah gave the date and time again, and turned off the recorder.

Pepper said, "We have a time problem, don't we?"

"It's either a problem or a blessing. You've just established that Gary died between four-forty-five and six, but that could vary on either end. Unless a person wore a watch, and looked at it often, every suspect we have will be wishy-washy about times. We would spin our wheels asking for precise times, which everyone will guess or make up anyway."

"I never did like those timetable things. We know means. We can assume everyone had opportunity. That leaves concentrating on motive. Does that make our job easier?"

"Motive is never easy." She ran the tape ahead a few inches. "William Pocock-Nesbitt was so all-fired anxious to get things moving. Let's interview him."

When he presented himself, Avivah sat behind the sister's

desk and Pepper, as instructed, melted into a corner. General Bill arranged himself in a vacant chair, crossed his legs, and flicked an imaginary piece of lint from his knee. When he looked at her, Avivah was suddenly glad she had a desk between them. She'd seen that look before: eyes that said Hitler was right, and ovens a good idea. Pepper had been right about anti-Semitism. It was time to pull rank.

"Just so we have this straight, General, I am now a sworn Avery County deputy sheriff, with full authority to investigate Gary Dormuth's death. This is not a holding action until the sheriff arrives. Anything you say can, and will, be held against you in a court of law. You have the right to remain silent and to have a lawyer present. If you cannot afford a lawyer, one will be provided for you. Since we are short of lawyers right now, you may choose to say nothing until one is present. I will record your interview. Miss Pepperhawk is here as a witness to take backup notes and, if need be, to offer testimony as to tape validity. Do you understand your rights?"

General Bill waived his hand in a dismissive gesture. Avivah wasn't sure what he was dismissing. It might be the tape recorder, Pepper's presence, or that two women, one of them Jewish, had taken charge. She stared him down. "I'm afraid a tape recorder can't identify hand gestures. Do you understand your rights?"

"I understand them."

"Do you wish a lawyer present before I interview you?"

"No."

She folded her hands in front of her on the sister's desk. "State your full name and place of residence."

"William Alexander Pocock-Nesbitt. Chicago, Illinois."

"What is your occupation?"

He shuffled uneasily in his chair, looked at his lap, and mumbled something.

"Please speak louder."

He cleared his throat. "I'm midwestern regional sales manager, infant products, Nesbitt Cereal Company. It's a family business," he said apologetically by way of explanation about why a career military officer now peddled pabulum and teething biscuits.

Avivah tried to imagine his office. If half his pictures were artillery pieces, and half sticky-faced babies plopping cereal in their hair, who was more uncomfortable when coming to see him, his old Army buddies or his baby food sales representatives?

"Were you acquainted with Gary Dormuth?"

"Yes. He was my employee; that is, he was an employee of the Saratoga Patriotic Foundation."

"What is your relationship to that foundation?"

"Founder and board chairman."

"Your foundation employed Gary Dormuth to do what?"

"Negotiate a rental agreement with the Sisters of the Visitation of Mary for these buildings and lands."

"When was that?"

"We hired him at our annual general meting, Labor Day weekend, 1971."

Avivah's heart skipped a little beat. On Labor Day, 1971, she'd just landed in Vietnam. She still had almost a month before her world came apart. She made herself focus on the next question. "Did Gary come to you or did you seek him out?"

"We asked him to submit a bid."

"How did that come about?"

"Mr. Dormuth had successfully negotiated purchase of a resort hotel for one of our members. That member recommended him."

"Over the past fifteen months, how often did you meet with

Gary Dormuth in person?"

General Bill counted on his fingers. "Five times."

"Describe, to the best of your recollection, each of those times."

"Immediately after we hired him, he and I spent a week here examining buildings and land. Three months later we met with the Visitation Sisters' lawyers and their mother superior at their motherhouse. In March and September of this year he gave progress reports at our board meetings. The fifth time was this weekend."

So Gary always came to him. Avivah wasn't surprised. "Did you ever phone him?"

"Yes."

"How often?"

"Two, possibly three times a week."

"That often?"

"I like to be kept up-to-date and, from time to time, I offered suggestions."

An obsessed-with-details manager, a meddler, who didn't trust his subordinates. She wondered if his constant suggestions drove Gary crazy. "What was your working relationship with Mr. Dormuth?"

"Cordial. He was a good employee. He worked hard and his reports were easy to understand. He was one hell of a negotiator. I always say this deal would never have happened without him."

"Did you have any relationship with him other than employer-employee?"

"I'm not sure what you mean?"

"Did you like one another? Were you friends? Did you exchange Christmas cards, confide in one another, tell jokes?"

"My wife and I have a very busy social schedule. Our commitments don't leave me time to socialize with my employees."

He hadn't answered her question.

"What about the week you spent here? Did you talk socially then?"

"Not really. As you can imagine, I was quite focused on determining if this would be a suitable property."

"Even so, you must have had some recreational time together, perhaps a walk in the autumn woods or an after-supper brandy?"

"Actually, I stayed with another retired officer, who lives nearby. Gary stayed here. Outside of work time, we hardly saw one another. I'm not sure where you're going with these questions, Deputy."

"Just trying to get a sense of how deeply Mr. Dormuth was in your confidence about *all* your plans."

He made a moue with his mouth, and picked at more imaginary lint. "No doubt you're referring to my plans for our little shooting range. Mr. Dormuth was unaware of that project."

A faint memory from the previous Saturday evening suddenly came into focus in Avivah's head. She'd awoken, confused and muzzy-headed, in Gary's apartment, and wandered into his living room. He was on the phone. He sounded very angry. The only thing she could clearly remember was that he'd said, "This has to be illegal." When he saw her, he said, "I can't talk more right now; I have a guest. I'll call you back." She wondered who he was talking to and if that phone call had anything to do with his death. "Why wasn't he aware?"

"It was none of his business. We hired him to negotiate a deal. What we did after we took possession was our business."

"Were you concerned that he might find out."

"No. It wouldn't have mattered if he did find out. His contract was about to be terminated."

"At your next board meeting?"

"Sooner than that."

"How soon?"

"As soon as possible."

"Why?"

"He'd completed work we hired him to do. I believe in moving on, and not spending money unnecessarily."

"Did you come here this weekend to fire him?"

"Our board came to make a final inspection before taking possession. Finding Gary here was an unexpected serendipity."

"You had no idea he was here?"

"None, but it was convenient that we could finish our business."

"Did you have time to finish that business before he died?"

"No."

"In your military service, did you ever learn a technique called garroting?"

"Yes." He faltered. "At least in theory. A long time ago, when I was first on active duty. Garroting isn't much use to an artillery officer."

"You never used it?"

"Never."

Avivah added an end note to the tape, turned off the recorder, and looked at her watch. There was time to squeeze in another interview before lunch.

General Bill stood. "The Saratoga Patriotic Foundation has very powerful supporters, many of whom still serve on active duty."

Damn it, he said that after she'd stopped the tape. Avivah understood his implication. Push me too hard and you'll find your military career on the skids. She almost laughed. Experts had already worked over her military career. It would take a lot more than General Bill's cronies to top what she'd already endured. It was easy to ignore his threat.

"Ask Dr. Saint-Mathias to join us."

General Bill sneered. "Good luck. I've always found the

earlier you talk to him in the morning, the more lucid he is."

Unfortunately, General Bill was right. Pepper had described Dr. Saint-Mathias as squiffy. He was way past squiffy now. If she interviewed him in this condition, any good lawyer would have it tossed out of court. She didn't bother turning on the tape recorder or reading him his rights.

"I just need a few facts, your name and all. I'll interview you officially first thing tomorrow morning. What is your full name and place of residence?"

"Doctor Yancy Joseph Andreas Saint-Mathias. Baton Rouge, Louisiana."

"What is your occupation?"

"History professor. Louisiana State University."

From her corner, Pepper asked, "Tenured professor?"

Avivah had never heard quite so much venom in two words. Pepper had once explained to her that "southern speak" relied on how the speaker emphasized words. She said that, properly inflected, *the* most cutting social question was, "Who's your mama?"

Dr. Saint-Mathias turned to Pepper. "Soon."

Okay, so he had beaten Pepper for articulated venom, distilling it to one word for her two.

Pepper continued, "I wonder what your tenure committee will say about you supporting a plan to blast prime Appalachian woodlands into toothpicks. I've heard universities are a hotbed of ecological support."

Avivah tried to signal for Pepper to shut up. After General Bill's unrecorded parting shot, she didn't want anything said in this room unless the tape recorder was running. Not having advised Dr. Saint-Mathias of his rights, she couldn't just reach over and turn it on.

"I never knew the details until this morning."

Pepper asked, "But you knew something about it generally?"

"At our September board meeting, I heard Dormuth tell General Bill he'd have to cut expenses to do the fancy things he planned."

Had General Bill lied, or had Dr. Saint-Mathias misunderstood Gary's remark? Avivah stood. "Thank you for coming, doctor. I look forward to talking to you officially, immediately after breakfast tomorrow morning."

After he left, Pepper stretched and yawned. "I'm teetering on exhaustion. Want to take a nap before lunch?"

"That sounds wonderful. Go on. I'll be up, just as soon as I ask Sister Mary Rachel where I can put this tape for safekeeping."

The convent spun dizzily as Pepper peered down three floors, watching Patience, who carried a flashlight and a large bundle of towels, coming up the stairs. Seeing her dowager's hump and how she stopped to rest every few steps, Pepper's first impulse was to rush down to help her. She resisted. This woman had probably carried towels up these stairs before Pepper was born, and would resent any suggestion she could no longer do so.

When she reached the third floor, Patience turned off her flashlight and laid it and her towels on a table. "Are you finished in Sister Mary Rachel's office?"

"For now. We'll need it again after lunch."

Pepper turned toward the dormitory, then hesitated. "Patience, what will happen to you and Helen?"

Patience straightened her spine as far as she could. "Why is that your business?"

"I'm curious. It's a bad habit."

"Helen and I have pensions."

Pepper felt relieved, though she wasn't sure why. "Have you worked here long?"

"On and off since 1922. First as a maid, then I took over managing the convent farm from my husband in 1942."

"When he went into the military?"

Patience compressed her lips and folded her arms over her chest. "No, miss. Not the military."

Clearly, questions about her husband were off limits. "I didn't see farm buildings."

"The farm was closed several years ago. We dismantled the buildings, and sold them for lumber." Animation filled Patience's thin face. "It was a good farm. Dairy and meat cows, pigs, poultry, a large garden, and our own beehives. The sisters understood it was healthy for girls to work hard out-of-doors and raise their own food."

Pepper tried to imagine her classmates—many of whom had only the ambition of making a good marriage—confronted with a milk cow or angry bees. For an instant, she regretted that her school hadn't stressed outdoor work, then a voice in her head ticked off a long list of unpleasant tasks that one had to do when caring for livestock, bees, and a large garden. On second thought, she'd take scholarship over agriculture any day.

"Where will you live?"

"My daughter has made up a little house. It's near here."

"And Helen?"

Patience sniffed, as if Helen had made a decision she wouldn't. "Helen will have a room in the nuns' retirement home."

Convents often made arrangements like that for women who worked for an order all their lives and had no family.

"You'll be all right, then."

"Yes, miss, we'll be all right."

She'd been right. Neither Patience, nor Helen, had any motive for wanting Gary dead. Pepper reached for the towels. "Let me take those for you."

"Thank you, miss. I do have to help with lunch."

As soon as Pepper looked through the dormitory door's glass window, she knew no one would have a nap, not in this room, not any time soon. She dropped the towels, and went running to find Avivah.

CHAPTER 11

A few minutes later, Avivah looked more startled than frightened as she stood, arms akimbo, at the dormitory door. "I'll be damned."

The room sparkled with brilliant white light. Fragile spiky frost grew out of floorboards and over iron bed frames. Etched crystal ferns opaqued tall windows. Where glass panes joined woodwork, ice formed miniature ski slopes. Curtains resembled stiff, gauzy sculptures and wind drove water-oak branches against the glass panes with irritating scratching sounds.

Pepper rubbed her hands over her goose-bump-covered arms. "What is it?"

"Hoarfrost. I've never seen it indoors before. You have to admit it's just plain spectacular."

That was one way to look at it. "It's just plain spooky."

Avivah bent down and pressed her hand to the floor. When she took it away, a perfect imprint, down to skin whorls, remained. "When I was a kid, I thought a meadow covered with hoarfrost was the way into fairy land."

Pepper remembered that malevolent elf who'd whispered in her ear when she arrived. She wasn't looking for fairy land. "Fairy stories have an inherently evil underbelly. People who go into fairy land don't come back. I want out of here."

"What has gotten you so spooked? There's nothing inherently evil about condensation. It's basic physics." She pointed to the large galvanized tubs, which yesterday held gallons of warm water. Now only an ice rime clung to their edges. "The fires pumped all that water into the air, and it condensed as the room cooled."

Pepper trembled. She didn't care about physics. Nothing had gone right since she arrived here. She was tired, cold, hungry, and scared. Most of all, she didn't think she could be brave and resourceful any more. Despite her bravado to Darby, being a civilian felt different from being an officer. She missed the comfort of being surrounded by a whole Army, her Army. She wasn't sure how much longer she could survive if she couldn't stand down, let someone else take her responsibilities, and get some sleep.

Avivah said, "We have to heat the room again. When the hoarfrost melts, we'll mop water and hope our beds dry by tonight."

Stand-down time was nowhere in sight. "It sounds yucky!"

"It probably will be."

Sound cracked like a cannon. Conditioned by ammunition dump explosions in Qui Nhon, Pepper looked toward the windows, expecting to see a bright orange light. Instead, a huge black shadow swayed and fell toward her.

"Incoming," she yelled as she dove under the nearest bed, just as a massive water-oak shattered windows.

Showers of glass shards, snow, and branches pelted down on both sides of the bed, which collapsed on top of her with a resounding *whoomph*. The floor vibrated. Pepper let out a smaller *whoomph* of her own as bed slats hit across her back, knocking air from her and pinning her between the bed and the floor. Room temperature dropped instantly.

As soon as she could breathe, Pepper screamed, "Avivah!"

No answer, only wind and a faint crackle. Two feet away she watched red coals, which the tree had scattered out of a fireplace, melt little hoarfrost circles, just as Avivah's palm had done. Tiny twigs caught fire, sputtered, and went out.

Pepper screamed Avivah's name again into silence.

A nest of small branches burst into flame. Fire crawled outward in a circle. Larger branches smoldered, and varnish on the floorboards stank and bubbled. If the floor ignited, fire would race through this old, dry room. Bitter smoke tendrils snaked toward Pepper. She tried to forget all she knew about death by smoke inhalation.

"Help!" She screamed as loud and as long as she could before smoke choked her.

Oh, my God, I am heartily sorry for having offended Thee, and I detest all my sins because of Thy just punishment, but most of all because they offend Thee, oh, my God. Words came automatically and unbidden. It had been years since she recited the Act of Contrition: a prayer of confession to be said when death was imminent.

The sound of feet pelted upstairs. A cacophony of voices, commands and counter-commands filled the air. Even Thomas and Dr. Saint-Mathias had noisy opinions of what to do next. Civilian life had too many cooks and not enough broth. That line pleased her. She must remember to tell it to Benny she thought, as darkness closed around her.

Something cold trickled around her cheek. Pepper came awake, opened her eyes and saw a rivulet of coal-black water moving toward her. She shut her mouth just in time. Steam hissed, and smoke dissipated.

In a penetrating voice Pepper knew had been cultivated to carry across a playground, Sister Mary Rachel demanded, "Miss Pepperhawk, are you all right? Answer me."

"Yes, sister."

Yes, sister. No, sister. Curtsy to sister. She giggled and pressed her mouth hard into damp floorboards. She was going into shock. She could come apart later. Right now, Avivah needed help. She rousted out her own officer's voice. "Avivah is here somewhere, probably unconscious. Find her first."

The sister said, "Captain Rosen is shaken, but unhurt. We found her in the hall."

Pepper screamed, "I want to talk to her."

"She's not here right now. We took her downstairs."

A likely story. Avivah was dead and they didn't want to tell her.

"I don't believe you. She's dead, isn't she? Tell me the truth. Tell me the goddamn truth." She began to scream those last two sentences, over and over, uncontrollably.

Benny's voice finally penetrated her hysteria. "Pepper, love, listen to me. Avivah really is all right. Thomas has gone to fetch her. Try to calm down, okay? I've got enough of a headache without you screaming your head off."

Her voice raw, Pepper managed, "I told her fairy land was a bad idea."

The babble stopped. Pepper realized how strange that remark sounded. Everyone probably thought she had a head injury. Hell, maybe she did. Coughing and with streaming eyes, she did a quick inventory. Everything worked, nothing hurt. Even the pressure of bed and tree was bearable. She might be trapped, but she hadn't been crushed. She refused to think about what would happen to her if the bed and tree shifted.

She saw a boot; then Avivah's eye peeked at her through branches. "Are you in there?"

"Of course I'm in here. Where did you think I would be? Are you all right?"

"I've got a little cut on my arm where a branch whacked me, but otherwise I'm okay."

Pepper choked up again. "I was so scared. I thought you were dead."

"Well, I'm not, so you just calm down."

Benny added, "And hang tight. We have to find tools before we can free you."

Sister Mary Rachel said, "When we closed, we shipped everything useful to our other orphanages. The only tools we have left are hammers and screwdrivers."

Pepper didn't think hammers and screwdrivers were going to be much use.

Thomas asked, "How did you cut all that wood we carried in?"

Conversation stopped again. When she spoke, Sister Mary Rachel sounded as though she wanted to smack herself in the forehead. "There's a chainsaw and a couple of axes in the woodshed."

General Bill said, "Good boy, Thomas."

Pepper wanted to yell, "He's not a boy. Stop patronizing him." Instead, she said, "Thank you, Tom," with as much warmth and gratitude as she could put into her voice.

It wasn't easy being on the receiving end of people whacking at branches and sawing wood. Every time a piece fell off, Pepper trembled, afraid that the tree would shift and crush her.

Terror could only last so long. After the twentieth scare, with her ears deafened by the chainsaw's constant whine and her body lulled by someone rhythmically whacking with an ax, Pepper's mind drifted. What was that old military adage? *Never stand when you can sit; never sit when you can lie; never stay awake when you can sleep.* Well, she'd asked for stand-down time. It looked like she'd gotten it.

She'd spent her share of nights under her bed in Qui Nhon, sleeping before and after mortar attacks. She'd never actually slept *during* an attack, though she knew people who said that they had. Napping here would be like old times. She sighed and closed her eyes.

By the time they freed her, midday had turned into evening.

Walking wounded. An apt description, but Pepper wasn't sure she'd be doing much walking any time soon. She'd had a sponge bath, washed her hair, downed painkillers and two cups of coffee, but her body still felt as though . . . well, as though a tree had fallen on her.

She was ravenously hungry. As she sat in the warm kitchen, wrapped in blankets, she tried to decide if her hunger was from shock or a result of having missed several meals recently. Convent hospitality had certainly gone down the tubes this weekend.

Around her people in various states of disrepair sat on benches. Some were dirtier than others; everyone smelled like wood smoke and tree sap. Dr. Saint-Mathias' hands trembled. How much of his private alcohol supply was now under the water-oak? Time to break out communion wine, unless they wanted delirium tremors on their hands. She giggled. Tremors on their hands. A joke. Get it? They probably wouldn't, so Pepper didn't share.

Sister Mary Rachel and Darby had been exchanging muted conversation and distressed looks for some time now. The sister clapped her hands for attention. "Mr. Barton is a science teacher, and I'm afraid he has bad news for us."

So science teacher was part of his cover. Pepper paused. Did men graduate from West Point with a degree in something, the same way she'd gotten a degree in nursing? She'd never thought to ask. She'd just assumed that Darby had majored in the military. Maybe he really had majored in science. A science major. It gave her a whole new perspective on him.

He strode to the front of the room. Pepper expected him to assume a position of parade rest, but he simply stood there. Parade rest was what he'd done the first time she'd seen him at basic training, Medical Field Services School, Fort Sam Houston, Texas. She'd been on active duty three days when Darby strode to the center of an auditorium stage, and assumed a position of parade rest with his legs slightly spread and his hands resting in the small of his back. She'd never forgotten how heroic he looked or his first words.

"Good morning, ladies and gentlemen. My name is Major Darby Baxter. I'm a Green Beret. That means I go places I can get hurt. When I'm lying there, bleeding, calling for a Dustoff chopper, it is to my advantage that each of you knows where to send that chopper. So, for the next four weeks I will be your principal instructor for compass and map reading. At the end of that time, each of you will—without reference and without er-ror—successfully complete the map course at Camp Bullis, Texas. My students do not fail because, one day, my life may depend on what you learn."

Pepper wasn't the only nurse who'd fallen in lust with him.

This evening he looked much older than he had in that auditorium. And he looked bone tired.

Darby said, "What was inconvenient twenty-four hours ago, has now become a question of survival. Not only do we have a breech in our outer walls, but . . ."

It wasn't a breech; it was a water-oak. Another joke. Pepper managed to suppress her giggles. She desperately wished someone would feed her.

"The convent's construction, combined with our unusual weather, have produced colder temperatures inside the building than outside. Not that we aren't grateful to be inside, protected against the wind chill, which is no small favor. Saving ourselves from hypothermia will require a concerted effort on everyone's part. We have food and stoves, which greatly increase our chances of survival. Water pipes are frozen, but we will melt snow for water and use honey buckets for waste." He nodded to where Sister Mary Rachel sat. "For any of you who have never used a honey bucket, sister will give you a short lesson."

The sister's comment about not liking living in poverty came back to Pepper. She wondered under what circumstances Sister Mary Rachel learned about honey buckets. Wherever it was, thank God for experts, even honey bucket experts.

"Our biggest concern is fuel. The cut wood supply was limited to begin with, and we used it profligately last night. I did not anticipate our need for fires around the clock for an extended period."

He made squandering wood sound like his personal failure. Give it a rest, Darby. None of them was clairvoyant; no one could have known yesterday what today would be like.

Except she knew Darby too well. He would take not knowing as a personal failure. He'd say something like he failed to consider a wide enough scope of potential alternatives in his calculations. Sometimes he could be a real pain.

"Before anyone suggests using the fallen tree, let me remind you that it is green wood, which burns dirty and increases a potential for chimney fires. We will use it only as a last resort." He turned to Benny. "Mister Kirkpatrick."

Benny stood. He carried a clipboard. "Sister has given us permission to burn anything we can find, but let me remind you to burn only wood, like bed slats, which have no varnish or paint. Our first task is to form into pairs and scout for wood. Stack anything that hasn't been painted or varnished in the hall for collection."

Pepper watched a mime show of looks between the sister and General Bill. He obviously wanted to countermand her offer, but this convent wasn't his to command for another month. This would be Sister Mary Rachel's march through the bedrooms. When Union General William Tecumseh Sherman marched from Atlanta to the sea, he burned everything in his path. The sister had found a similar way to inconvenience General Bill. Instead of an intact convent, ready for occupation, he'd inherit a building with some reassembly required. Pepper loved the delicious irony.

Benny looked at his clipboard. "Teams of two: Helen will look after Sister Valentina instead of collecting wood. Sister Angelus and Patience. General Bill and Dr. Saint-Mathias. Father Ron and Thomas. Avivah and Pepper. Mr. Barton and myself. Sister Mary Rachel, who knows every nook and cranny where we can look, will circulate."

Making logistics look easy was a mark of a professional military leader. Pepper wanted to be just like Benny when she grew up.

Darby took over again, "It's not fair to the sisters or their staff to expect them to cook and clean under these conditions. We will all share those responsibilities. I've drawn up a duty roster that I'll post."

Dr. Saint-Mathias raised his hand. "I don't know how to cook."

Darby fixed him with a cold stare. "Learn. Anyone can heat canned soup and make sandwiches. To cut down on dirty dishes, we will each be issued one plate, one bowl, one cup, one set of silverware. Food is to be served from cooking pots. The last thing we need is dysentery, so we will use field kitchen sanitation: wash, rinse, and bleach. Bill, can you set that up for us?"

General Bill nodded. "After twenty-five years on active duty, I think I still remember how field sanitation works."

He was actually being cooperative and polite. Too bad they didn't have emergencies to which they could send William Pocock-Nesbitt more often. He might be one of those people who worked better under adverse conditions.

Darby nodded. "We may be uncomfortable, but we will survive."

Without reference, and without error. His students did not fail.

"Miss Pepperhawk and Captain Rosen, you're first up on the cooking roster. Please make supper while the rest of us collect wood."

Avivah's face darkened, but Darby held up his hands in a placating gesture. "This has nothing to do with gender. You and Miss Pepperhawk had a difficult experience. You're still in shock. If I had my way, I'd pull you out of the line completely, but we need all hands. Don't worry, you won't show up on our cooking roster again until everyone else has had a turn, though I'm sure the two of you are excellent cooks. It will be our loss not to be favored more often with your culinary skills."

No doubt about it, Darby could be a pain, but he could also be a charmer, especially in an emergency.

Avivah caught up with Benny, just outside the kitchen door. He was watching Darby, who appeared to be giving Pepper a cursory examination. On looks alone, even from a distance, she had to admit they made a fine couple. She and Benny sighed simultaneously.

"Pepper told me about him. Does he always look at her that way?"

"You mean that goopy, soft-eyed look? Sad to see that in a . . . man like Mr. Barton."

Avivah knew he had been about to say "in a Green Beret." "Does she realize how madly in love with her he is?"

"I don't think she has a clue."

Mad. Even as she'd said it, Avivah cringed. Just how far from real madness—the kind that led people to commit murder—was that kind of love? She did not want Pepper hurt, but Darby remained her best suspect in Gary's death. "Will he break her heart?"

Benny pursed his lips. "Almost certainly."

"Even if he's innocent of murder?"

"Especially then. If he's guilty, going to jail will get him out of her hair."

"What can we do to protect her?"

"Not a thing."

Thomas Hackmann joined them. He moved one hand around another, as if washing them. Words came out in a tumble. "I'm sorry, Mr. Kirkpatrick. About last night, I mean. I'm really, really sorry."

Benny went down on his haunches as easily as Vietnamese men, who had a lifetime of practice. When he was lower than Thomas he had to look up at him, giving Thomas a reassuring advantage of being taller and in charge. "It's okay, Tom. You and I both know how fast situations change. Try to put it out of your mind. Go find Father Ron; I know he'll appreciate your help."

"All right. Yes. Thank you."

Benny stood and watched Tom shuffle away. "That's the second time he's apologized. Same gestures, same words. He's stuck, like a record. Poor guy."

"You paired him with Ron intentionally, didn't you?"

"If anyone can put balm on a wounded spirit, it's Ron Lincoln."

Avivah grinned. "Smart man."

Benny leaned against a wall and crossed his arms. Avivah stood beside him, in an identical posture. As if a military choreographer gave a signal, both of them slid down the wall in unison. Avivah thought of that photograph in *Life* magazine of two weary soldiers sitting against a rubble wall. All they needed was cigarettes hanging from their mouths.

Avivah said, "We almost lost Pepper."

Benny reached over and held her hand. His voice didn't

sound too steady. "I could have lost both of you."

"If she'd yelled anything except 'Incoming,' I'd be dead. Sheer instinct. I turned and ran for my bunker, only, for the first time in months, the bunker wasn't there."

Benny pushed back her shirt sleeve, and looked at the white bandage on her arm.

"Did Darby play medic for you, too?"

"Helen did. Four stitches, neat as anything."

"*Helen* sewed you up?"

"She said a vet taught her how to suture when she and Patience ran the convent's farm. Animals were her responsibility, and the vet was tired of coming out here every time a cow cut herself on barbed wire. She had this veterinary first aid kit, with a big blue cross on it. Antiseptic, local anesthetic, sutures."

"In World War I, blue crosses marked veterinary aid stations for horses. Animals even had their own field medics."

As she pulled her sleeve down, Avivah tried to imagine putting a horse on a stretcher. "You are a fount of obscure military trivia."

"Maybe I can go on one of those quiz shows and make loads of money. Might as well get some profit out of the last ten years."

Benny rarely sounded bitter.

"This thing at home still bugging you?"

"Not as much since I went to Ron's retreat. It must have been all that imposed silence and those inspirational lectures he delivered. I did a lot of thinking at the retreat, and a lot of praying. I'm certain of one thing now. I don't want to put my parents through what they are going through; or Lorraine and her boys."

No sense telling him everything would be okay. He was still going back to a small town where not everyone wanted to live next-door to an incipiently crazy ex–Special Forces sergeant.

"It might be better if Lorraine and I pulled up stakes and moved."

"Where? If prejudice against Vietnam veterans happens in Missouri, it happens other places."

He looked at her with a cold expression. "So I don't have to tell anyone I wore a beret, do I?"

That shocked her. Benny was so proud of having been a Green Beret.

His hand moved down his right leg, to the exact spot his beret would have rested in his fatigue pants pocket, as if he were unconsciously trying to reassure himself it was still there. She knew it still was, in his imagination. He said, "I didn't kill Gary. I could have, but didn't."

She wanted to believe him about Gary's death, but she had been a police officer long enough to know that even good friends lied. "Could have as in knew how? Had motive? Had opportunity? All of the above?"

"Knew how."

She didn't have to ask him whether he'd ever garroted anyone for real; the answer was in his voice.

"I probably had opportunity, too, but no motive. Heck, I liked him, and I especially liked what he did for you."

Thomas' story still bothered her. She had to know if Benny had the slightest misconception that Gary had raped her. "Gary and I were lovers by mutual consent."

Benny looked surprised. "Any port in a storm." He ran his hand over his eyes. "I'm sorry. That didn't come out right. I'm glad and sorry for you at the same time. How are you holding up?"

Relief flooded over her. Benny never had any idea that Gary raped her. She was grateful he didn't make a big deal of sympathy. "I'm holding."

"Did Pepper tell you about the blowup at breakfast?"

"Yeah. How did Ron know General Bill's secret?"

"From Gary. After the doctor put you to bed last Saturday, Gary explained it to us. That's what he wanted to talk to Ron about."

"How long had he known?"

"A little over a day. Last Friday morning, some drawings arrived at his office, special delivery. They should have been sent to General Bill, but Gary got them by mistake. They were plans for an artillery range."

"Can a private citizen buy artillery pieces?"

Benny chuckled. "You don't read ads in *Soldier of Fortune* magazine, do you? No, I guess not. Unfortunately, yes, civilians can buy a whole boatload of stuff they should never get their hands on. Plus William Pocock-Nesbitt has a lifetime of military connections. He can get more than most civilians. Eventually, some pissy regulation, like noise abatement, would shut him down, but not before he'd pulverized some very beautiful landscape."

Darby had apparently finished reassuring himself that Pepper would live. He bid her farewell with the slightest hint of a bow. It was easy for Avivah to imagine his ancestors in Confederate grey. Military romance. It happened with every war. Avivah didn't think it was a good idea at all.

She stood up. "I'd better get to the kitchen before Pepper thinks I've abandoned her."

Benny pulled himself into a standing position. "Your investigation has pretty much been knocked into a cocked hat."

"Between trees falling, collecting wood, cooking, and cleaning, I don't know when anyone has much time to be interviewed. I'll manage somehow."

"Whatever you cook, make a lot. Cutting up that tree gave me back my appetite. I could eat a horse."

Avivah discovered that when Pepper cooked, she cooked. She

had a freezer full of ingredients, a hot woodstove, and a head full of southern recipes. Benny was probably going to enjoy smothered round steak, gravy, mashed potatoes, pan-fried biscuits, vegetables, pickled relishes, and vanilla pudding with pineapple more than a horse anyway.

When everyone gathered for supper, pots littered the table. To save wood, Darby asked the nuns and laywomen to eat with them instead of keeping a fire going in their separate dining room. Ron said grace. "Amen" circulated, even muttered by General Bill, who looked embarrassed to be contaminated by popish ritual.

Sister Mary Rachel picked up the pot of mashed potatoes and looked around. Her face paled. "Where are Sister Valentina and Mister Hackmann?"

CHAPTER 12

Pepper's stomach rumbled. She looked longingly at the food before she threw down her napkin. Everyone rose, in unison, except Ron Lincoln, who said, "Sit down. Please."

Polite form, but no less a command. Everyone sat. Ron folded his hands and bowed his head. "Lord, we appeal to You, Who are all powerful and all loving, for fifteen minutes of special protection for Your children, Valentina and Thomas, so that we might nourish ourselves." Pepper had never heard anyone negotiate a supper break with God before. If she'd thought He listened to this kind of informal, almost irreverent prayer, she might talk to Him again.

Ron, having turned their missing duo over to God, helped himself to biscuits, and passed them on. "If we don't take care of ourselves, we won't be any use to them or to each other. Chances are they are both all right, only late for supper."

Helen went to the sideboard. Darby's irritated gaze followed her. "Helen, your assignment was to watch Sister Valentina. How long ago did you lose sight of her?"

Helen stiffened as she collected two extra plates and returned with them to the table. "She likes to walk. I could not stay with her always. My feet, they get tired."

Nonstop pacing was a dementia symptom. Pepper appreciated how exhausting keeping up with Sister Valentina must be. She didn't begrudge Helen for letting her guard slip, but it would have been so much better if she had kept track of the sister.

Sister Mary Rachel said, "Mr. Barton, Helen is, as you would put it, under my command. If there is any disciplinary action needed, I'll take care of it."

Darby blushed, and looked down at his plate. "Yes, sister. Sorry, sister."

By Pepper's wristwatch, it took twelve minutes for everyone to finish eating. God was still on duty for another three minutes.

Sister Mary Rachel stood, "Helen, you remain here. If they are just late, they'll show up soon."

Helen pointed to the two extra plates she'd filled. "I have food for them." She picked up a cooking pot with each hand. "I'll clean."

General Bill, said plaintively, "Clean up and field sanitation is my command."

Pepper felt sorry for him, that he would feel so betrayed to be denied this small chance to contribute.

The tidy pairs Benny set up earlier had dissolved, and everyone looked at each other with uncertainty, as though they were kids choosing sides on a playground. Pepper and Darby grinned at each other. She knew who she would choose for her partner.

Apparently, Benny knew who she'd choose, too. He moved between her and Darby. "Helen and Bill stay here. You are headquarters and rendezvous site. Bill, if either of them returns, come to notify us. Sister Mary Rachel and Patience, please search the nuns' private quarters; Father Ron, chapel and sacristy. Avivah and Mr. Barton, first floor. Dr. Saint-Mathias and myself, second floor. Pepper and Sister Angelus, third floor."

Darn, he'd blocked her being alone with Darby again.

Sister Angelus hurried to her task, and Pepper had to run to catch up with her. Considering the scene they'd witnessed this morning, Pepper couldn't imagine why the sister was in such a hurry to look for Sister Valentina. Guilty conscience, perhaps?

Walking fast was a bad idea. Halfway up the stairs Sister Angelus collapsed to sit on a stair. She gasped; sweat covered her face. Even by candlelight, Pepper could see that her color was terrible. If General Bill wanted to take lessons for how a cardiac patient should look, Sister Angelus would be a good teacher. How chronically ill was the sister? Desperately ill people sometimes resorted to desperate actions, like murder.

Pepper sat beside her. "Do you need water? Medicine? Should I get Sister Mary Rachel?"

The sister waved her hand and panted. "Rest. Stairs after a big meal aren't a good idea." She put her hand to her chest. "I have weak lungs."

With rest, the sister's breathing and color improved. Vaguely, in occasional, muffled sounds, they heard the others searching. Pepper vented her frustration. "I know how hard it is dealing with people who wander, but I wish Helen had kept a better eye on Sister Valentina."

"Helen tries to cover up that her eyesight and hearing have deteriorated. Sister Valentina wanders away, and she doesn't notice it. It's been worse lately."

Pepper couldn't shake the memory of the confrontation she'd seen that morning between Sister Valentina and Sister Angelus. "I'm not trying to pry, but I gather you and Sister Valentina haven't always gotten along?"

Sister Angelus hung her head. "I committed a sin of anger this morning. Sister Mary Rachel counciled me, and I have accepted her council."

Sister Mary Rachel had been right. Obeying military orders was one thing, but Pepper knew she'd never survive a religious vow of obedience. "Do you mind me asking, why isn't Sister Valentina being cared for somewhere else?"

"You saw what happened this morning. She becomes hysterical every time anyone tries to take her from here."

General Bill would take possession in less than a month. "What's going to happen when she must leave?"

The sister stood and firmly grasped the bannister. "Our help is in the name of the Lord, who made heaven and earth."

In other words, Sister Angelus didn't have a clue.

If she were well sedated and taken by ambulance, Sister Valentina might survive a short move, perhaps as far as Asheville. "Where is your motherhouse?"

"Philadelphia."

Roughly six hundred miles. Sister Valentina could never be sedated that long. She said hesitantly, "A long trip for sister."

"God provides."

Pepper found that kind of blind trust irritating. She threw back, "Heaven helps those who help themselves."

Sister Angelus sighed. "We had a plan to sedate her and transport her to our motherhouse by air ambulance. Catholic Charities donated a pilot, a flight nurse, and the use of a plane. It was supposed to happen in January, but with the rental deal being concluded unexpectedly, that plan fell through."

An ambitious plan. Perhaps it would have worked, though Pepper didn't even want to hazard a guess what going to sleep here and waking up in a different environment would do to the sister's already precarious mental state. Throughout their careers, all nuns returned periodically to their motherhouse for conferences, retreats, and vacations. Her only hope was that Sister Valentina retained enough dim memories of visiting there to sustain her.

"I have a lot of friends who were military pilots. After all this is over, maybe I can help you make a new plan."

As angry as Sister Angelus had been toward Sister Valentina this morning, she looked truly grateful. "That's very kind of you. I'll mention your offer to Sister Mary Rachel."

They continued up the stairs to the third floor. The dormitory door was closed. Pepper was startled to see suitcases, some more battered than others, aligned in a row. One, she noted with relief, was her own case. "Who rescued these from the dormitory?"

"I don't know."

Pepper opened the door. Odors of burned wood, old smoke, sawdust, and cut wood tumbled out. Small snow drifts had replaced hoarfrost. Water used to put out the fire had frozen into dirty grey ice. Half the room was a shamble of tree and broken furniture. Beyond the shambles, beds, tables, and a rocking chair stood intact; with only a layer of tree bark, small branches, and detritus covering the beds.

"Tom? Sister Valentina?"

No answer.

This room held no residual terror for Pepper. It was like that popular Vietnam litany Pepper recited to herself during mortar attacks. If you are in Vietnam, you are either in danger or you aren't. If you not in danger, there is no reason to worry. If you are in danger, you are either dead or alive. If you are dead, there is no reason to worry . . . and so on until reaching a conclusive proof that no matter what was happening, worrying wouldn't help. She'd been in danger here, but her friends had saved her. Nothing like friends to temper bad memories. Pepper firmly closed the door.

She and the sister searched empty classrooms, then moved on to small, bleak bedrooms, cells really, with barely enough space for a bed, dresser, and chair. Bed slats and chairs were stacked in the hall to be used as future firewood.

"You really believed in your girls toughing it out, didn't you?"

"Servants slept here."

Pepper was shocked. "Patience and Helen live like this? My

room in Qui Nhon had better decor and more personality."

"You must be careful about putting your own prejudices on experiences. We always hired local girls. Many came from large farm families. For some of them, this was the first time they had a bed to themselves, or a door they could close." She studied Pepper. "Contrary to what you might think, this wasn't one of Dickens' workhouses. We had a vibrant community here and servants shared in that community. Let me show you something."

They walked along the length of the corridor, to a room that was a mirror floor plan of the nursery, minus a wayward water-oak. Closed burgundy drapes gave the room a dark red ambiance, like being inside a pool of blood. Sister Angelus opened several drapes, then stood aside, with her hands hidden in her habit's folds. That gesture grated on Pepper's nerves. She felt a lot better when people kept their hands where she could see them, a holdover from Qui Nhon, where even children's hidden hands might conceal a weapon or a grenade.

Mahogany coffee tables, overstuffed chairs, and floor lamps were arranged into conversation groups. The double fireplaces had been converted to electric heaters. An ancient sewing machine sat in one corner, and a writing desk under a window. Bland paintings, a crucifix, and several glass-fronted curio cabinets decorated the walls. One cabinet held a collection of board games, another miniature dolls. A third contained cut-glass jars filled with keys; antique medicine bottles with cork stoppers; and what looked like found objects: bird's feathers, seashells, Indian arrowheads, and smooth rocks.

"This was the servants' parlor. Bedrooms were off limits during the day to the staff unless our infirmarian ordered someone to bed. They spent off-duty time in this room. Those who had suitors were permitted use of the visitors' parlor on Sunday afternoon."

Pepper knew the sister wanted their kindness toward hired help to favorably impress her, but she couldn't help wondering where servants went when they wanted privacy. Summer wouldn't have been a problem; there was a whole mountainside available for private walks. But what about winter? Where could a servant go if she just had to be alone? That lack of private time was another thing about communal life that would drive her crazy.

Pepper looked out the window. It was dark outside, but easy to see it was still snowing like billy-ho. She hoped Sister Valentina hadn't found another open door leading outside. She'd freeze to death in a matter of minutes.

Pepper pressed her face against cold glass. The snow was bright enough that she could see a walled garden and, from this high up, both sides of the small door, which Sister Valentina had tried to open when Pepper rescued her. She was relieved to see unbroken snow on both sides of that small door, and no nun-sized bundle lying in the snow.

Pepper could trace paths through the garden, and lumpy outlines of what must be benches, large flower urns, and assorted garden decorations. Maybe servants walked in the garden if they wanted privacy. A shape, which looked remarkably like a tombstone, stood where all of the garden paths converged.

Pepper pointed. "Sister, what's that thing?"

Sister Angelus came to stand beside her. "Sister Elizabeth Rose's grave marker." She recited more to herself than to Pepper, "See how the faithful city has become a harlot! She once was full of justice; righteousness used to dwell in her—but now murderers! Isaiah 1:21."

The sister's allusion made no sense. "What?"

"Sister Elizabeth Rose's epitaph. She selected it herself. When she died, the nuns found her tombstone in her recluse house. In her diaries, she described having it carved by a stonemason in

Asheville and delivered secretly to her, years before her death. Her recluse house was over there. Nothing remains of it now. We used her house stones to repair the garden walls."

A recluse house was a tiny building where nuns in contemplative orders lived alone, following a strict code of prayer, self-examination, and silence. "But you're not a contemplative order, are you?"

"No, but in 1909, when she retired from managing this orphanage, Sister Elizabeth Rose applied for a dispensation to withdraw from communal life."

"When did she come here?"

"1860."

Nineteen-oh-nine would have meant Sister Elizabeth Rose spent almost half a century in communal life. She, herself, could never have done one tenth of that without going stark, raving mad. From that epitaph she'd chosen, maybe the sister was mad.

Harlots. Rumors abounded in convent school about what nuns were up to behind closed doors. "Her diaries, did they show she was, um . . . preoccupied with matters of the flesh?"

"The safety of young women left alone on isolated farms preoccupied her, especially during the Civil War."

Pepper remembered the photograph she'd seen as soon as she arrived, a big house and one nun surrounded by girls. Avivah might chide her for not accepting there had been a sexual revolution, but Pepper knew what particular danger unprotected young women faced. Sister Elizabeth Rose was right to be concerned.

"She brought everyone she could here for protection. She convinced some men to ride circuit and check on women, instead of going off to war."

Connections slipped into place. Pepper said, very softly, "Dr. Saint-Mathias' third brother theory is right after all. That's why

Lucas Hackmann never went to war."

"Sister Rose enlisted help from Lucas and his father, Victor, to organize and lead patrols."

"You've never told Dr. Saint-Mathias this, have you?"

Her wicked little smile unnerved Pepper. "He was unkind to me. He accused me to Mother Superior of hiding or destroying the convent deed. Before you ask, I did no such thing. Besides, he makes no bones that he prefers to deal with war from a male perspective. I merely respected that option."

Pepper bet she did. She grinned. "What do Sister Elizabeth Rose's diaries say about the deed?"

"They are silent on the matter." The sister perched stiffly on a chair seat and clasped her hands in her lap. "May I ask you a favor?"

Sweat again formed on the sister's face, and Pepper wondered if she were about to admit to having chest pain. Pepper crouched beside her. "Of course you may."

"There is an empty basement. Years ago, something happened down there to me and Sister Valentina. As her dementia developed, she became fascinated with returning there. We keep it locked to prevent her wandering down there." The sister's breath came in short gasps. "There is very . . . little chance she . . . is down there, but . . ."

Pepper wondered if Sister Angelus were claustrophobic. No, she couldn't be; when Pepper first met her, she'd talked about checking the furnace. What better place for a furnace than a basement? Now, something certainly spooked Sister Angelus. "Let's go find Benny. He'll search the basement for us."

The sister took a deep breath and gathered herself to her full, short height. "I was very rude to Sister Valentina this morning. I have meditated on my sin and penance is required. I must do this for her."

Given both nuns' precarious health, this was not a time for

theoretical discussions on sin and redemption. "I'll come with you."

Sister Angelus patted her hand. "Bless you, my child."

They stopped in the kitchen only long enough to make sure the search was still on. It was.

At the end of a small hall just outside of the kitchen, Sister Angelus paused before a locked door. Her hand shook so badly she couldn't get the key in the lock. Pepper took it from her. "I'll go alone. You stay here."

"God is with me. He protects me. I trust in Him." She clenched her hands tightly in prayer. "I offer this up in penance for my outburst at Sister Valentina this morning, for repose of Hugh Tillich's soul, and in thanksgiving for sparing my life, O Lord."

Was Hugh Tillich Patience's husband? Pepper remembered Patience's story about how she took over the farm from her husband. Just as soon as she could, she intended to find out just why Hugh Tillich had to give up farming, and what he had to do with Sister Angelus.

The sister propped the basement door open with a rubber wedge. Pepper took the sister's hand in hers. The sister's palm was moist.

They descended into a cold, but remarkably clean basement. Pepper raised her candle for a better view. A few black rubber streaks marked the walls, and plaster dents said this had been one place where those servants who slept in tiny bedrooms worked hard. A neat rack of skis and snowshoes lined one side. Further on, chains protruded from the wall at intervals. So there really were chains in convent basements!

Pepper had to concede these chains had held nothing more frightening than bicycles. Several bicycle locks still hung there. Three closed doors led somewhere and a furnace—looking like something that might power Jules Verne's *Nautilus*—loomed ahead of them. The corridor had a faint, unpleasant smell.

"It's not a very big basement."

"It's only a partial basement. You look disappointed."

"I expected cobwebs, dust, Vincent Price. When you go to convent school, you hear rumors about what is in convent basements."

The sister sighed. "We pray daily for God to direct our girls' creativity into more positive channels. Some days, I think He is asleep at the switch." She winked at Pepper. "You won't tell Sister Mary Rachel I said that, will you?"

Pepper laughed. "My lips are sealed."

An ancient hospital gurney, without mattress, stood to one side. It could have come from any Catholic hospital, circa 1930. Pepper wiggled it back and forth. It moved noiselessly on oiled wheels. "What's this for?"

The sister pointed to a large dumbwaiter. "To save our backs. We loaded it with linen or vegetables, and wheeled it to the dumbwaiter. Nuns learn to make do with what's available."

"Like soldiers."

"Probably just like soldiers."

They stopped at the first of three closed doors, which the sister unlocked. Plain, white shelves lined its walls. Someone had attempted to brighten them by sticking down a strawberry-and-leaf pattern Mac-Tac. A few empty canning jars with metal binder rings, but no tops, stood forlornly alone, their metal rings a fuzzy grey. Desiccated, dusty bundles of dried plants hung from the rafters. In one corner, a contraption of huge glass jugs, rubber tubing, more glass pieces, and assorted stoppers filled one table. Pepper recognized it, and it puzzled her. "Of all the things we girls speculated were in convent basements, a still was never one of them."

"For distilled water, not alcohol, but we did keep quiet about it. We called this the preservation room, never its more proper name, still room. Our neighbors, you know."

Alcohol was a touchy subject in the mountains. Some people made it. Some belonged to strict Protestant sects, which believed in total abstinence. "It would never do for even a rumor to get out that nuns ran a still."

"Absolutely not."

"What was preserved here?"

"Food mostly. Waste not, want not."

Pepper looked up at the dried plants. "You made your own medicines, too, didn't you? Another thing local yarb grannies wouldn't have taken kindly. You'd have been their competition."

Yarb grannies were mountain women who practiced a combination of midwifery, herbal medicine, charms, and folklore.

The sister nodded. "Throw in a fear of Papist sorcery, and nothing gets people thinking 'witch' faster than nuns curing sick people. Advertising we made medicines was definitely not a way to keep a low profile."

Pepper noted the middle door was closed, but not locked. This second room smelled like potatoes and onions. Empty bins, faced with metal screening, lined every wall. The sister said, "Cold storage. Fifty girls plus staff went through a lot of food."

They moved to the last room. A plaque beside the closed door read "Laundry." Sister Angelus took a firm grasp of the doorknob. She prayed, "My Lord is my protection and my shield."

Whatever she feared was in this room, but Pepper couldn't imagine what would be frightening about a laundry. The sister opened the door. Odors of stool and urine overpowered Pepper. She gagged and turned away, her eyes watering. When she'd wiped her eyes, she turned back to find Sister Angelus had crumpled into a heap at her feet.

Pepper bent and checked the sister's pulse. She had only fainted. She looked up again at Thomas Hackmann's long, lean body, stretched even longer from the rope wrapped around his neck.

One found, one to go, was all Pepper had time to think before she pitched forward in her own faint.

Sharon Wildwind

to collect evidence the old-fashioned way, with paper and
l.
omemade crime scene kit seemed so clever when she'd
ed Gary. That was before she'd skied out and discovered
rest of the world was preoccupied with its own blizzard
Truth was, no one, except people here, cared yet that
men were dead.
aved two precious flashlights in case anyone had to go
ndles were useless in a blizzard. Desperate situations
esperate measures. The flashlights would be better
s for collecting evidence. As she and Ron stood in
locked basement door, she took one flashlight and
Ron. "Do only what I ask; go only where I tell you

sheen glistened on Ron's forehead. "Are we go-
as down?"
'd rather leave him where he is until the sheriff
not practical. Smells, you know."
ating up the basement stairs were what had
ill that something was amiss. He'd followed
found them, Pepper and Sister Angelus were
t of their faints, but Avivah was still glad
o their rescue.
und belly, and said, regretfully, "It's the
Seminary teaching is comfortable; it saps
haven't looked at death, but it was a long
omething to embarrass myself?"
Avivah thought. It had been almost a
slides in his social justice course. Three
a tree. Before-and-after photographs of
st survivors peering through barbed
those slides the ultimate price for
on for making a personal commit-

Chapter 13

Duty called. Avivah buried her face deeper in her folded arms. Duty had piss-all to recommend itself right now.

At least Pepper was getting a chance to sleep. Despite his almost obsessive desire to conserve fuel, Darby—in his alternate David Barton persona—agreed to a small fire in the nuns' sitting room so that Pepper and a hysterical Sister Angelus could rest in a quiet place. The look on Pepper's face when Avivah tucked her into bed, clearly said that Pepper had never before ventured into a nuns' private sanctum, and she wasn't sure she should be there now, even if it meant she had a chance to lie down. *Hic sunt dracones:* here be dragons.

Avivah had sat beside Pepper until she fell asleep, then returned to the kitchen. Her head ached, and her ski-challenged muscles spasmed. Her eyes felt raw and sandy. From the way her tongue stuck to her mouth, she was dehydrated. She raised her head and stared at Darby, General Bill, Dr. Saint-Mathias, Benny, and Ron. All of them stared back with red eyes and exhausted expressions that mirrored how she felt. If she had any choice, she would tell duty to kiss off, throw her bedding in a quiet corner, and sleep. The problem was, she had no choice.

She poked around in her conscience, and was relieved to find that Thomas' death hadn't left her with additional guilt. More guilt was the last thing she needed right now. Yes, he was dead, and yes, in a righteous world, she would have prevented his death, but she hadn't exactly sat around the past twenty-four

hours reading novels and eating bonbons. T⟩ much one police officer could do. She ha prevent his death, but she intended to see ⟨ she lasted that long; *if* she didn't break d⟨

Memory of her breakdown when ⟨ Gary's body made her cringe. If being gered what she'd come to call "a spe⟨ alone with Thomas' body. Keepin important. She was now not only ⟨ deputy sheriff.

She looked again at the row ⟨ draft one of them to help he⟨ No matter how she shook ⟨ name always came last. A judgment to hell. She ho⟨ ing that Ron couldn't friend or a priest. Bu⟨ was as good a choic⟨

She sat up, feeli⟨ able, I need one ⟨ with me."

Ron started⟨ nodded. Ge⟨ thought he ⟨ himself to⟨ us to kee⟨ want t⟨

Be⟨ to i⟨

ment to justice. His course had led, partly, to her becoming a police officer.

She said, "If you throw up, do it in the hall or laundry tub. You're less likely to contaminate evidence. With water off and pipes frozen, our killer can't have washed up."

Ron made the sign of the cross as Avivah unlocked the basement door. Body waste smells hit them immediately. Oh, yes, they had to move this body soon. They sat, stopping to encase their feet and hands in homemade protective coverings.

Avivah said, "First thing we do is lie down at the laundry room door, and play our lights over the floor. We're looking for evidence before we walk on it."

They lay on cold concrete, sides of their bodies touching like a pair of conjoined Siamese twins. Avivah tried to ignore Thomas' toes hanging a few inches from the floor. After several minutes, she asked, "What do you see."

Ron craned his neck. "Nothing. Not a dust mote or a flake of dirt."

"I agree. Our killer cleaned up so well there aren't even broom marks. That's quite a feat in a dark basement, with no running water."

"Wait a minute," Ron said, as he pushed himself up. He lay down in front of the preservation room, shined his light in, got up, did the same thing in front of cold storage. "Every floor is spotless. What we've got here is Catholic stewardship. 'The Lord has dealt with me according to my righteousness; according to the cleanness of my hands he has rewarded me.' I forget the exact reference, somewhere in Psalms."

That Ron would forget a scripture source showed how upset he was.

"One of the first lessons new priests learn is never interrupt parish housekeepers. We joke that the Second Coming will happen when they can work it into their cleaning schedules. I'll bet you anything that Helen and Patience dust, vacuum, and mop down here at least once a week."

"Bother."

"Why is that a bad thing?"

"It means we have pristine trace evidence, but only if we leave Thomas where he is and lock the basement until help arrives. And we can't do that."

Avivah handed him a pad of paper and a pencil. "Sketch his body, then a diagram of this room. I'll add measurements later. Don't worry about making it artistic, just show relationships. Stick figures are fine."

Ron sat. With a grunt, he crossed his legs tailor-fashion, and balanced the pad on his thigh. Avivah measured the distance between the floor and Thomas' pointed toes.

His elongated feet turned slightly inward. He wore tan moccasins decorated with multicolored glass beads, souvenirs found in any roadside gift shop where Indians lived. On his right moccasin toe, a long, white thread now hung beadless. She looked around the floor. No beads. Either he'd lost the beads a long time ago or he'd been killed somewhere else. He wore white cotton socks. A ruff of worn, frayed threads marked his pants cuffs. Urine and stool had spread down his right leg.

She examined his hands. No defensive wounds. He hadn't fought for his life or tried to claw the rope from around his neck; both were odd. Human instinct was to fight for breath. Chances were he'd been unconscious when he was hanged. He might have been drugged. In this dim light, she wasn't going to waste time looking for puncture marks. If he'd been drugged, by mouth was easier than by needle. More likely, he'd been rendered unconscious first with pressure on his carotid points. Whoever did this had a neck fetish: garroting, strangling, and hanging all involved the neck.

Avivah bent to examine the knot that anchored the far end of the rope. It was crude, fastening rope around a table leg any which way. Done by someone who wasn't skilled at knot craft.

Someone rendered him unconscious, probably not here. There would have been evidence of a scuffle here. Stuff him in the dumbwaiter Pepper had showed her, transfer him to the gurney, wheel it in here and put a rope around his neck. Pull him up and tie a knot. That meant their killer knew the basement, dumbwaiter, and gurney existed, and had a key to the basement door.

She asked Ron, "Did you know about this basement?"

"Not until Friday afternoon when Mr. Baxter and I came down with Sister Angelus to adjust the furnace. I suppose, if I'd thought about it, I could have figured out there must be one."

"Sister Angelus never brought you down here?"

"When I visited, my sister and I spent our time together on walks or sitting in front of a fireplace, catching up on family matters."

"I wonder if anyone showed it to the Saratoga Patriotic Foundation board members when they toured."

"They would have been very remiss not to inspect the furnace. I tell my seminarians to check furnaces and roofs first thing when moving to a new parish. Don't trust your caretaker's word. Both are expensive, likely to go wrong at inconvenient times, and likely to be ignored by your predecessor, who dumped his problems in your lap. At a guess, I'd say everyone here except you, Pepper, and Benny had been down here at some time." Ron tapped his pencil against his pad. "Gary said something or someone was stirring them up."

Avivah measured distance between the laundry table top and Thomas' feet. "Stirring who up?"

"The Saratoga Patriotic Foundation."

"I'd called two murders a little more than stirred up."

"A year ago in September, when he submitted his bid, they

were what Gary described as a jolly group, too ra-ra and flag waving for his tastes, but happy with each other. In July, verbal sniping and odd looks. This September, he was afraid the group might fold before they could pay him."

She snapped her tape measure closed. "Why did he take this job? With how his brother died, I'd have thought he'd stay away from an ex-artillery officer."

"Gary could compartmentalize his life. He was ambitious and boasted he'd be a millionaire by the time he was fifty. He could put aside personal feelings for a lucrative commission."

Avivah started to say, "But maybe not far enough to include a private artillery range," but she never got her words out. This time she felt the flashback start, a smell of rank, tropical vegetation and a feeling of disassociation, as if the whole world stank and everything in her life from now on would be horrible; something she couldn't control. She felt tiny, and vulnerable, and so very, very angry.

She tried to hold onto the table and to reality. She was in Crossnore, North Carolina, in December, not Long Bien in September. She counted to ten, forward and backward. If she had a litter of six puppies, and each puppy weighed two-and-a-quarter pounds, how much worm medicine did she need?

Nothing helped. Blackness rolled over her. She dropped her tape measure. The last thing she said was, "Save evidence."

She awoke curled into a fetal position, with Ron's arms wrapped around her.

He whispered, his voice rich with anger, "I want the person who did this to you."

She took a deep breath, sat up, and felt her dry cheeks. She hadn't broken down in tears. For the first time in months, she had one small victory to celebrate. "No one did anything to me. I did it to myself. That classic sin of hubris. I thought the only way I could understand Vietnam was to go there. Well, I understand it now, and look what good it's done me."

"What happened to you there?"

"You know . . . stuff."

Ron looked at her: patient, solicitous, and unwavering. He would wait forever if he had to.

"No one raped me, if that's what worried you."

Patient.

"And I didn't have to go into combat—God forbid that Americans should send a woman into combat."

Unblinking.

"I had a bit of trouble . . . one night . . . police work." She took a deep breath and hung her head. The words came out one at a time. "I killed an American soldier."

Solicitous. "Go on."

"Three weeks after I got to Vietnam. A stakeout . . . not exactly a stakeout . . . close enough."

Words ran through her head. She sorted them into military and civilian words, desperate for something Ron could understand without her having to explain jargon. "Military police stormed a place. I had their back door. He popped out of an escape route we didn't even know existed. He was as surprised to see me as I was to see him. He tried to shoot me. I had a fraction of a second to make a decision. I fired."

Black night. Fatigue fabric made a swishing sound. Night smells, a mixture of rank grass, standing water, and diesel. Her thought, in that split second before she fired, was that neither of them had any reason to be in this country, this place. How it all felt like a setup.

"He was black. His name was Robert Johnson. He was eighteen, illiterate, and recruited out of inner city Detroit."

All things she'd found out later, because she'd dug for information. Dug in secret, with the sure knowledge that every new fact she discovered made her more dangerous to her commanding officer.

Ron put his hands together, his index fingers touching his lips. It was the pose he always took in class when a student asked a particularly challenging question. Avivah always thought of it as his Jesuit-thinking position. "Do you remember my class about the white man's burden?"

"Sort of. It was a long time ago."

He prompted, "Once you've recognized that your group is in a position to act as an oppressor, and, having made a conscious decision to no longer participate in oppression . . ."

" . . . you can't allow yourself the luxury of feeling guilty for every historical injustice. Guilt over things for which you had no control clouds your ability to act on things that are your personal responsibility. Well, my personal responsibility was that I pulled the trigger."

"Would you feel better if you'd shot a white, Jewish, college graduate?"

"Of course not."

"This isn't about racial discrimination or illiteracy or if eighteen is too young to go to war. You didn't create those issues, and you can't solve them. You have to deal with what happened that night between Avivah Rosen and Robert Johnson."

No, what she had to deal with was what happened for the rest of her year in Vietnam. The part she hadn't told Ron, couldn't tell him, or anyone else, without violating her security oath.

"I don't seem to be doing a good job on that, do I? At least, I've never broken down in front of anyone who matters."

"What am I, chopped liver?"

"I meant another officer. Breaking down every time I see a body wouldn't do my military career any good."

"Avivah, I think you no longer have a military career."

Darby's voice, from the bottom of the basement stairs, said, "I agree."

He carried a shower curtain and a ball of stout cord. "I thought you might need these to improvise a body bag."

Ron asked, his voice angry, "How long have you been there?"

"Long enough."

He didn't have to say it. Avivah knew, from his expression, that Darby had heard her confession. She only thought she'd felt vulnerable before. "Please don't tell Pepper or Benny what you overheard."

"I couldn't, even if I wanted to. They're both civilians now and, I do believe, Captain Rosen, you just came perilously close to violating your security oath. What happens in Vietnam, stays in Vietnam. Father, I know she's not Catholic and this isn't a confessional, but I'd be grateful if you took what you just heard under your confessional seal."

If Avivah weren't so scared, Darby's attempt to coerce a priest on behalf of a Jew would be funny.

"Avivah and I have been friends for a long time. You hardly need to tell me how to behave, Captain Barton? Major Barton? You look a touch young to be a colonel."

"Major."

Avivah put her hands over her mouth. She hadn't blown Darby's cover; he'd partially blown it himself. Apparently, even Special Forces stumbled occasionally.

If Darby was upset, he didn't show it. "I think, Captain Rosen, you'd better have a serious talk with your superior officer as soon as you get back to Fort Dix."

"And if I don't?"

"Ma'am, your fitness as an officer becomes my responsibility only if you're assigned to my command, and that will never happen. I'm a combat officer and, as you said, the American public is not prepared to accept women in a combat role. So, no ma'am, I won't report you to anyone." He nodded at Thomas' body. "And if you're through here, that man deserves to be cut down and treated with respect."

Part of her knew she should continue collecting evidence; more of her was too tired to care. The three of them went into the laundry room. Avivah cut the rope high enough to preserve the knot and a length of rope above it, and lowered Thomas' body to the laundry table. He'd been dead longer than Gary had when they found him. His body was cold, but rigor mortis hadn't set in yet. Darby reached down to close Thomas' eyes, but Avivah stopped his hand. "I don't think you should."

He gently removed her hand from his. "Yes, ma'am, I should." He closed Thomas' eyes. "Whatever else he was, whatever problems he had, our country still saw fit to award Thomas Hackmann a Congressional Medal of Honor. He deserves the most respectful send-off we can give him."

He took something out of his pocket and twirled it in his fingers, then reached for Avivah's hand and laid it in her palm, closing her fingers over warm metal. "Make sure this goes in his coffin."

Avivah held up a gold-colored medallion, about the size of a silver dollar. Its weight confirmed what she'd suspected. It was pure gold. United States citizens could not legally own gold bullion privately, but they could own gold jewelry. Benny told her that, when stationed in Asia, Special Forces often converted gold into medallions: one true ounce of Bangkok gold in each medallion. Insurance, he called it, like sailors once wore gold earrings to ensure they'd have a proper burial if their bodies washed up on land.

She angled it in her flashlight. One side read "When I die, I'll go to heaven because I've spent my time in hell." and on the other side a green beret and "Fifth Special Forces, RVN."

She wondered uneasily how much gold Darby had, and how

he'd come by it. Pepper had been so right to break up with him. He had far too many secrets.

"Oh, I see you're still here."

Everyone jumped and turned toward the door. Sister Valentina stood there, looking as peaceful as if she'd just come from a nap. Darby put his hands on the table and leaned forward, gulping air. Avivah wasn't sure if his posture were frustration or if, like her, he was waiting until his heart restarted after the sister's unexpected appearance. He muttered, through clenched teeth. "I swear that woman walks through walls."

Ron escorted Sister Valentina upstairs, followed by Darby and Avivah carrying Thomas' body. A silent crowd in the kitchen parted like the Red Sea to allow them to pass. When they reached the museum, Avivah reached inside her bra for a door key. She remembered all too well the sight and smell of bloated bodies in Vietnam, and prepared herself for what would be inside. She took a deep breath and held it as she opened the door.

Gary Dormuth's body was gone. Only shards of glass and scattered papers now covered the floor.

.

CHAPTER 14

Once more, everyone searched the convent. No one found a trace of Gary's body. Avivah called an end to their search shortly before ten P.M. "Enough is enough. We're all exhausted. Let's get some sleep and start again tomorrow."

She had some egalitarian idea about casting lots for best sleeping spots, but when Benny assigned the top two spots to her and Pepper, she simply said, "Thank you."

Their tiny pantry was marginally warmer than the kitchen and, since it had a door, private. A single mattress filled the narrow floor. She and Pepper squeezed onto it, back-to-back with their vertebrae meshing, and a mound of blankets over them. *Slumber party* was Avivah's only thought before she fell asleep.

Consciousness returned slowly, drifting nearer and farther away, until she realized that a long time had passed. She scrunched herself over, trying not to wake Pepper, only to discover her bedmate was already awake, lying on her back, with her hands behind her head.

Avivah whispered, "Did you sleep?"

"Like a log."

"What time is it?"

Pepper took her wristwatch from a low pantry shelf. "About four-thirty."

Avivah grunted and turned over. Breakfast wasn't for hours yet. She was balanced on the edge of going back to sleep, when

Pepper asked, "You don't think we ate Gary for supper, do you?"

Sleep fled. Avivah ran her hand over her face. "What?"

"There was this television drama, about a men's club that had a special dinner, only no one knew what their secret main dish was. One member got too curious and . . ."

Avivah remembered that show. "Don't be ridiculous. Even if someone managed without power tools to reduce Gary to round steak, when and where did they do it? We searched this building three times last night. With frozen drains, they couldn't have washed blood away and we would have seen evidence."

"Where do you think he is?"

"Somewhere we don't know to look yet." She turned on her back, mirroring Pepper's position of hands behind her head. "The three common reasons for making off with a body are to bury it, to remove evidence, or for . . . well, less savory purposes."

"You mean like necromancy or Satanic rituals? Don't look surprised, I'm not a complete innocent. I studied abnormal psychology in nursing school."

Avivah was tempted to remark that at times she thought Pepper *was* abnormal psychology, but she held her tongue. "Given this religious atmosphere, a black Mass is barely, tenuously possible. Okay, you're Catholic . . ."

"Lapsed Catholic."

Avivah thought Pepper wasn't as lapsed as she believed herself to be. "Sorry. If you were going to use a body for a religious ritual, where would you hide it?"

After a minute, Pepper said, "This order named itself after Mary's Visitation. Luke described how Mary, pregnant with Jesus, visited her cousin, Saint Elizabeth, who was also pregnant. 'When Elizabeth heard Mary's greeting, the baby leaped in her womb, and Elizabeth was filled with the Holy Spirit.'"

Avivah let out an impatient breath. She'd asked for a body,

not a Bible lesson. "So?"

"If a religious order can obtain a saint's relic, usually hair or bone, they put it in a crypt. Catholic doctrine teaches that Mary was taken into heaven, body and soul, so no relics exist for her, but there just might be something for Saint Elizabeth."

Even after she waded through religious propaganda, Avivah thought Pepper might be on to something. Her stomach tightened. "Is a crypt big enough to hold a body?"

"I don't know. I've only seen one saint's relic: a minuscule bone fragment. It was small enough to fit in a thimble."

"Wouldn't one of the nuns have suggested we look in the crypt?"

Pepper sat up. "They didn't tell us about the basement, did they?" She stared at her watch. "We have to hurry. If Mass is at six, as it was yesterday, someone will be in the chapel soon to get ready."

Resolutely, Avivah pushed her blankets back. She hadn't realized the crypt would be in the chapel, though that did make the most sense. "What if the chapel is locked?"

"Then we have a problem."

Avivah sat on the mattress and put on her boots. Her toes hit Darby's gold coin, which she'd buried deep in her boot for safekeeping. She pulled it out.

Pepper took if from her. "Where did you get this?"

"Darby gave it to me. He wants me to make sure Thomas is buried with it."

Pepper held the coin buried in her palms, fingers extended, like hands in prayer. "He gave it to you? You didn't find it in Thomas' mouth or nailed to the laundry wall?"

"No, he handed it to me."

Pepper's body sagged.

Avivah asked, "Want to tell me what's going on here?"

"Did you ever hear that story in Vietnam about guys dropping the ace of spades on villages the day before they made a bombing run?"

"No."

"Darby explained it to me. It was supposed to scare the bejeezus out of the Vietnamese. Death cards one day, bombs the next. Only, the plan bombed, so to speak. Vietnamese card decks didn't have an ace of spades. The Vietnamese didn't have a clue what the card meant."

"I'm with you so far."

Pepper turned the medallion over and over in her fingers. "Fifth Special Forces are rumored to have left their own special calling card: one of these medallions."

Avivah took it from her and hefted it. "Come on, Pepper. This is gold. Not even Special Forces would leave these scattered around like Crackerjack prizes."

"They didn't leave them everywhere, only on special missions, where they'd taken care of a particularly messy problem, where they wanted the local power guy to know exactly who had done the deed. They'd shove it in the corpse's mouth or nail it to a tree. It was much better than playing cards. Gold and the beret's image spoke an international language."

Avivah put the coin in her boots and laced them. "Do you and Darby always discuss these gruesome topics like other people discuss the weather?"

"Sure. He's been a whole lot more places and done a whole lot more things than I ever will. Listening to him talk is fascinating."

Avivah thought pathological described it better. "Incidentally, he blew part of his own cover last night."

Pepper made a strangled noise. Avivah couldn't tell whether it was glee or horror. "How? To whom?"

Answering how would open up questions Avivah had no intention of answering. Better stick to whom. "To Ron. He admitted he was a major, but not that he was here under an assumed name."

"Oh, that's all right. Ron won't tell anyone. He's a priest."

"Don't go falling into that trap. He's still a suspect." It was a feeble protest, and she knew it. Ron was still at the bottom of her suspect list.

The chapel was open and dark, except for a single candle burning inside a red sanctuary lamp. Both women froze at the door.

Pepper said, "I don't imagine God is happy with me right now. I feel funny going into His house."

"You think you're uncomfortable? I'm a Jew, and I've never been or wanted to be inside a Catholic church in my life."

"It wasn't your fault, you know."

"What wasn't?"

"Christ's crucifixion. Vatican II clearly said that Jews weren't responsible."

"Thank you for that absolution. I'm sure generations of persecuted and murdered Jews are standing up and cheering." She rested her head against the wooden door. "I'm sorry. I know you mean well, but you have no clue how patronizing you sound. You cannot comprehend how literally ill I feel about going in here, and you can't fix my feelings."

"Ron had no business bringing you to a convent."

"He didn't know what else to do with me, only that he had to get me away from New York City and reporters."

"Does this whole convent make you ill?"

"If I thought about it, it might, but the past week I managed to avoid being overwhelmed with Catholicism. I pretended this was just a quiet, empty building."

Pepper sat down on a bench. "What did the four of you do here for a week?"

Avivah sat beside her. "Gary, Ron, and Benny took long walks."

"They didn't invite you along?"

"Not at first. I figured it was one of those guy things. They were three men surrounded by women. It was only natural they'd want to talk guy talk. Of course, that's before I knew about the artillery range."

Pepper cocked her head. "Now what do you think they were doing?"

"Inspecting the grounds to see whether they found anything to substantiate those blueprints Gary had seen; maybe concocting a strategy. Remember phones were working then; they could have called all over the country for all I know."

"So maybe Gary's Saturday night phone call wasn't that important after all."

"It was important; I could tell by his voice that it was."

Pepper leaned back. "I still think it was rotten of them to bring you here, then ignore you."

"They didn't ignore me. I was content to stay in my room and read. We ate together. In the evenings, we talked and played board games. Ron snuck in a bottle of wine one evening. Until two days ago, I felt as if I were on vacation." She looked around. "Not exactly the Catskills, but still a vacation."

"What are the Catskills?"

"An area of New York State north of the city. Lots of Jewish people vacation there."

"What about nighttime? You know, you and Gary? How did you manage it? Did he come to your room or did you go to his?"

She was relieved that Pepper wasn't going to launch into another social hygiene lecture. This was more prurient interest, and the first time she'd seen Pepper express anything except squeamishness about sex. "Both."

Pepper bit her bottom lip. "You and him . . . it wasn't a Jewish thing, was it? I mean because he was Catholic and this was a convent and all?"

Avivah threw back her head and laughed. "Pepper, you and I really must have a talk about men and women being naked together, especially now that I've met *Mr. Barton*. Woman, you need some serious instruction in what Chinese books refer to as courtesan arts." She reached down and took her friend's hand. "Let's get this crypt thing over with; only don't give me a guided tour. I don't need to know what all this religious stuff represents."

Pepper dipped her free hand in what looked like a bronze seashell attached just inside the door. She started to put her damp fingers to her forehead, then wiped her fingers on her shirt. "Old habits die hard."

Avivah's candle provided a small pool of light, as their footsteps made hollow sounds on slate flooring. Avivah kept her eyes straight ahead. She gasped. Unable to speak, she made gagging noises and pointed to the man hanging from a huge crucifix in a dark niche behind the altar.

Pepper squeezed her hand, "It's not Gary. I hate those life-sized Italian crucifixes. Such realistic, unbearable agony, though maybe that's the idea."

Avivah tried to imagine being confronted with a full-sized image of a crucified man every time you came to pray, to seek solace and comfort. Darby's gold medallion said it all. *When I die, I'll go to heaven, because I've spent my time in hell.* It seemed an apt motto for this church and this convent. She wondered that more nuns didn't, like Sister Valentina, sink into their own private madness.

They stopped outside the altar rail.

Avivah whispered, "Where is it?"

"Most likely, in the floor behind that altar or underneath it. If they built the altar over it, we don't have to worry because it would be sealed."

Avivah's courage wavered. "I don't think I can go up there. Do you mind?"

Pepper took a deep breath. "I've gotten this far without a bolt of lightening striking me dead. Maybe it will be okay."

Avivah sat in a pew. Pepper genuflected and bowed, then opened a little railing gate and walked up three steps and around back. She lifted a colored silk cloth and the white, lace-edged cloth under it. "There's a door here."

"Big enough to squeeze in a body?"

"A tight fit, but maybe." Her head disappeared, then popped up again. "I don't smell anything. Of course, I might not, depending on how tight a seal there is." She rattled something. "It's locked."

"Then we're screwed."

"Maybe not. If this is a relic crypt, its keys might be in the sacristy."

Pepper led her behind a screen to a side room. It had a different atmosphere, more like a theater dressing room. Old odors—candles, incense, men—permeated the wood. Cupboards and small drawers completely covered every wall.

Pepper methodically opened drawers. "Every sacristy has a junk drawer; you know, like yours at home with dead rubber bands and lost buttons. Only here it's likely to have broken corkscrews, old Mass leaflets, matches, keys." She opened another drawer and took out a key. "Ah, here we are."

"What do you think you are doing?"

Sister Mary Rachel's voice reverberated in the tiny room. She stood at the sacristy door, a vision of blackness in her cloak. Pepper moved in front of Avivah. "We're looking for a reliquary door key. It's one place we never searched for Mr. Dormuth's body."

The nun grabbed the key from Pepper's hand. "A body could not fit there."

Avivah said, "I need to see that for myself."

The sister glared at her. "Have you been at the altar?"

Centuries of Jewish persecution echoed in that question. Maybe Pepper believed that Vatican II exonerated Jews, but Sister Mary Rachel didn't seem to have gotten that word. Or, maybe, she hadn't wanted to.

Pepper moved closer; to shield her Avivah realized. "She sat outside the altar."

The sister seemed relieved.

Avivah carefully remained far away from the altar as the sister opened the reliquary door. Even from where she stood, it was immediately obvious no body could be hidden there. As Pepper said, the opening was barely big enough for a body, but it rapidly shrank to a space about twelve inches by eight inches, just big enough for the carved wooden box it contained.

Pepper asked, "Whose relic?"

The sister locked the door and pocketed the key. "That is none of your business."

They sat in the sister's freezing office. Pepper sank further into her coat and looked miserable. Next door, a bell had rung to call people to Mass, but Sister Mary Rachel showed no signs of moving. She interlocked her fingers and placed her hands in the exact middle of her desk. If the sister's eyes could have bored holes into Avivah, they would have. "Exactly what did you do while you were in the chapel? Where did you go, and what did you touch?"

Pepper came to her defense. "We walked up the center aisle. Avivah sat in a pew. I made reverence to the altar. I tried to open the reliquary door, but it was locked. We went to look for a key, then you found us."

"That's all?"

"Yes, sister."

Sister Mary Rachel glared again at Avivah. Best to follow Pepper's lead. "Yes, sister."

The sister relaxed a little more, and folded her hands in her lap. Apparently, they hadn't committed an act so heinous that the sister would have to—Avivah had no idea of terminology—disinfect, deconsecrate, or perform an exorcism because a Jew had been inside. One thing was certain. She would never go back into that chapel again.

Avivah started to stand, but Pepper leaned forward. "Are all of you at each other's throats for a special reason, or is this normal convent infighting?"

"It's you outsiders who are at each other's throats. Since you arrived, two men have been murdered."

Pepper shook her head. "This started a long time before we got here. Patience is icy about Helen's choice to go with you to your motherhouse. You're angry with Sister Angelus. Sister Angelus hates Sister Valentina. Sister Valentina seems to have a morbid fascination with getting into both the walled garden and the basement. You all say you are concerned for her safety, but you don't keep a good eye on her."

Sister Mary Rachel started to speak, but it was hard to interrupt Pepper when she was in full throttle, as she was now.

"You've got something in your reliquary I'm sure you aren't supposed to have. My first guess is the missing deed. A reliquary makes a dandy hiding place, but hiding the missing deed makes sense only if it confirms Thomas' claim. If you had proof that he was the rightful owner, why not just burn it and be done with it?"

Sister Mary Rachel stiffened. "Good historians like Sister Angelus don't burn historic documents, no matter what those documents prove."

Avivah kept going back to Gary's phone call. Could Sister Angelus have gotten a phone call without everyone knowing about it? Gary was killed in a museum; by someone he trusted to be there with him. Who better to trust in a museum than a historian?

Pepper sat forward in her chair. "No they don't. Sister, with all due respect, I am in no mood to play any more games. I'm exhausted, and freezing, and more than a little scared. Take your choice: tell us what's in that box or, as soon as Mass finishes, I swear I'll throw away what few religious scruples I still have and do a little breaking and entering."

Sister Mary Rachel looked truly frightened, the first time Avivah had seen her facade crack. "Convents often harbor old secrets."

Pepper wasn't swayed. "After twelve years in convent school, that's not news to me."

The sister's voice became almost pleading. "I give you my word our reliquary has nothing to do with the deaths. Please, both of you, what I tell you must not leave this room." She waited until they both nodded in agreement. "There are bones in the reliquary."

Pepper demanded, "Whose bones?"

"Sister Elizabeth Rose."

Pepper's mouth made a little moue. "Plain old 'sister,' not 'venerable' or 'blessed' or 'saint'?"

"Not yet."

Pepper looked almost gleeful. "Rome will not be happy."

"Probably not." Sister Mary Rachel turned to Avivah. "This must be very confusing to you."

No more than anything else that had happened since Friday. Avivah had become accustomed to feeling perpetually confused.

Pepper said, "There's a long process for declaring a person a saint. By putting Sister Elizabeth Rose's bones in a reliquary, in an altar, Sister Mary Rachel jumped the queue so to speak, which she had no right to do, and which Rome would find more than a little irritating."

The sister said, "I had nothing to do with sequestering her bones. It was done in 1922, three months after she died."

Avivah wondered who had dug up a three-month-dead nun and had, as the sister put it, sequestered her bones. Catholic nuns were stranger and tougher than she'd thought. "But you left them there."

"Me, and several predecessors before me. You might say it's our order's little secret. The Church's power is in the hands of old European priests, who find it impossible to imagine that a North American woman could qualify for sainthood. Prejudice of both gender and geography. In almost five hundred years only three candidates have been successful: Saint Frances Cabrini; Blessed Mother Elizabeth Ann Seton, who—if it pleases God—I will see canonized in my lifetime; and Venerable Rose Philippine Duchesne, whose case has been mired for decades."

Pepper nodded. "Have there been miracles attributed to Sister Elizabeth Rose?"

"Two with enough substance for serious investigation. I told Captain Rosen about one here in 1922. It was after that miracle that my order collected her bones. There was a second miracle, in 1936, at our motherhouse. Unfortunately, Church investigators denied both."

Pepper nodded. "So your order took matters into their own hands."

"Sister Elizabeth Rose was an unusual woman, a saintly woman. That much is obvious from her diaries and from descriptions of people who knew her. Her bones, particularly finger and hand bones, would have deteriorated if left in her coffin. We wanted to preserve them for a future time, when she is canonized."

Even without Catholic indoctrination that made sense to Avivah. Good works flowed through hands and fingers; that would make hand and finger bones especially prized as relics. Avivah asked, "What will happen to them when you leave?"

"I will personally carry them to our motherhouse. We have prepared a resting place there."

Dead end. No matter how much Pepper wanted it to be so, Avivah could see no possible connection between old bones and new murders. She repeated Pepper's question. "Are you at each other's throats?"

A faint bell rang three times. A pause. Three more times. Sister Mary Rachel bowed her head, pressed her closed fist to her chest each time that bell rang, and murmured "The Body of Christ. Amen. The Blood of Christ. Amen."

Avivah looked at Pepper for an explanation, but Pepper had her head bent and her eyes closed as well.

The sister looked up. "I believe Tolstoy said it best. 'All happy families are happy alike, all unhappy families are unhappy in their own way.' Alas; we are no different. House a group of women together, in close proximity for decades, and feuds develop. Sister Angelus has had a particular grievance against Sister Valentina for thirty years. I'm very much afraid that something I did recently might have resurrected an old hatred and given me reasons to fear that Sister Angelus is an ill woman."

"Ill enough to commit murder?"

"That, Deputy Rosen, is a question I have prayed about, unceasingly, for two days."

CHAPTER 15

A small bright spot danced across the sister's desk. Avivah shaded her eyes and looked around for what was reflecting light. "What is that?"

Sister Mary Rachel stood and threw back her drapes. "Sunrise. It's stopped snowing."

They gathered in front of the window. A few wisps of pink-purple clouds banded the rising sun. The pale, clear sky had already deepened into a brilliant blue. Animal tracks—deer, Avivah guessed—crossed otherwise unbroken snow and red cardinals hovered around bird feeders. Under different conditions, it would be beautiful, but as the sun rose, more responsibility pressed on Avivah. Better weather demanded action and resolution, a time to clean up and move on. She wasn't up to this. She was so very tired. All she wanted to do was curl up and let the world move on without her.

The sister asked, "Do you think our killer will attempt to escape?"

An escape wouldn't relieve her of responsibility. She'd owed justice to both Gary and Thomas, and she'd see that debt through to the end. "I don't know. Running admits guilt. The most logical thing to do is sit tight, but killers often aren't logical."

"If he doesn't run, will you be all right?"

Heat rose in Avivah's cheeks. Had Sister Mary Rachel and Ron compared notes about her breakdowns? If he had, she felt betrayed. She'd thought she could trust Ron, but maybe being part of religious communities weighed more than being old friends.

Pepper tipped her head to one side and looked at Avivah. "What's going on?"

Sister Mary Rachel put her fingertips to her mouth. "I'm sorry. I assumed that since you and Miss Pepperhawk were such good friends, you'd talked."

Pepper looked from woman to woman, then waved her hand, as if to dismiss any concerns. Her Mississippi accent deepened. "Oh that. It's old news. Avivah's fine."

Avivah pressed her lips together to keep from yelling at Pepper. If you can't dazzle them with your brilliance, baffle them with your bullshit. That was standard officers' club, beer-soaked advice dispensed to a green officer going before a promotion board. Rather than admit she had no idea what they were talking about, Pepper had gone into southern bullshit mode. Avivah no longer found it an endearing quality. She needed help, not bullshit.

The sister looked disappointed that her gambit, whatever it was, failed. "Would you take a walk with me? I'd like some privacy for what I'm about to tell you." She gathered up her cloak. "We'll have to hurry before everyone gets out of Mass. Otherwise, someone will want to go with us."

Pepper said, "General Bill won't be at Mass. I, for one, would prefer to avoid him."

The sister nodded. "I think that would be best. What I have to say is definitely not for his ears. Meet me by the bird feeders in ten minutes. I must leave a note, or people will conclude we have disappeared, too. I think everyone has done enough building searches."

Avivah and Pepper detoured to the museum. A quick look and sniff said Thomas' body was still there. Gary's body wasn't.

As they stood by the visitors' entrance, putting on gloves and hats, Pepper asked, "What was sister talking about?"

If she tried to stall, Pepper would chew at her like a hangnail, until they were both ragged and bleeding. Best to give a simple explanation. "I seem to be having flashbacks to 'Nam every time I'm with a dead body. Sister found me in the middle of one."

Pepper said, wistfully, "I've never had a flashback, at least I don't think I have. Memories, of course, but never a real flashback."

Avivah pressed her fingers to both sides of her temples, as though pressure could keep her irritation contained. It didn't. Sour-tasting words streamed out. "What do you expect me to do about that? You've got no reason for what you did in 'Nam to haunt you. What could be purer and more noble than tending wounded soldiers? I hate that innocent facade you hide behind. Grow up, Pepper. Take responsibility for the world along with the rest of us." She jammed her cap on her head and left, slamming the front door behind her.

She trudged to the feeders, not knowing or caring what she would say to Pepper when she came storming after her. Only Pepper didn't come after her. A few minutes later, Sister Mary Rachel appeared all in black: ski pants, sweater, and a wool toque. She carried three pairs of snowshoes.

"I left a note saying we had gone for a walk. Isn't Miss Pepperhawk joining us?"

Avivah worked hard to control her voice. "I'm not sure."

The sister busied herself sweeping snow from the seed bin and refilling feeders. "Despite what she said, you haven't told her anything about your problem."

"What I tell anyone and when I tell them is none of your business."

The sister started to say something, then bowed her head.

"I'm sorry. I would say confession was good for your soul, but, at times, confession does more harm than good. I thought I'd learned that the hard way; but it appears I don't really believe it yet."

Pepper came out of the visitors' entrance, a fixed look on her face and defiance in her walk. Avivah knew both. Her *I'll do better* look, her *I promise to grow up* walk. Avivah wondered how long they would last this time.

Sister Mary Rachel showed them how to step into snowshoes and fasten their bindings. She circled the convent toward a well-defined tree break. In about fifteen minutes, they came to an overlook. The view took Avivah's breath away. Miles and miles of Blue Ridge mountains lay on the horizon, gently undulating peaks stacked behind each other, like a torn-paper collage in shades of blue, grey, and white. This was what General Bill wanted to reduce to splintered trees and the smell of cordite.

They took off their snowshoes and stuck them, upright, into a bank. Twisted-branch chairs, mounded with snow, formed a semicircle facing their magnificent view. Brushing them clean took several minutes.

Even through layers of clothes, Avivah's backside felt cold when she sat. The sister's hands made swishing sounds as she smoothed them down her black ski suit. Avivah realized how much Sister Mary Rachel used her big, black cloak as a prop. She could spend minutes arranging it around her, smoothing pleats, distributing fabric. A black ski suit just didn't have the same effect; its tight-fitting contours made the nun look almost-naked and vulnerable. Avivah knew how that felt.

Sister Mary Rachel turned to Pepper. "Contrary to what Mr. Pocock-Nesbitt told you, Gary Dormuth did not have our order by the tits and wouldn't let them go."

That got Avivah's attention. What conversation had she missed? It sounded like a lulu.

The sister continued, "We came to the negotiating table prepared; he came better prepared."

Avivah wanted details. "Give me an example."

"He knew almost to the penny what it would cost to keep these empty buildings heated and in good repair for a year."

Pepper asked, "You mean someone fed him your figures?"

"I mean he did his homework and reached the same conclusion we did. Until a court decided who owned this land, a bad rental deal was better than a vacant building."

Even if they had gotten a raw deal, what connection did that have to Gary's death? "Why was it a bad deal?"

"The rent was less than we preferred."

"That's it? The Saratoga Patriotic Foundation wasn't going to pay enough?"

The sister stiffened. "Sister Angelus and I took a strong moral stand against aligning this convent with war. I do not disparage either of your contributions to this country, but if William Pocock-Nesbitt represents current military thinking, you have my sympathy."

Pepper said, "Thank you, and he doesn't."

Avivah pursed her lips. "How did Gary get around that question of General Bill's, um, obsession?"

The sister smiled. "By staying away. He offered Mr. Pocock-Nesbitt an opportunity to present his foundation's vision to our negotiating team. Mr. Dormuth made it clear that he would leave that meeting completely in the general's hands."

Pepper looked gleeful. "It was a disaster?"

"Before we elected her to her current position, our mother superior taught fifth grade. Her opinion was that Mr. Pocock-Nesbitt would have profited from doing more oral book reports. His presentation was long and unfocused, accompanied by a slide show of images such as the Iwo Jima monument and a Civil War battlefield at dawn, partially shrouded in fog. When

Gary rejoined us, his only comment was, 'That's the man who will be leading the think tank's thinking.' "

Avivah asked, "Implying that nothing useful would come out of the Saratoga Patriotic Foundation, and that you would not be contributing to war by renting your building to that foundation?"

"Implying whatever we cared to decide it implied. One of Mr. Dormuth's strengths was to lay out information in a seemingly impartial fashion and allow people to draw conclusions."

Avivah cocked her head. " 'Seemingly impartial'? "

"He was better than most at concealing his biases."

"Which were?"

"Whatever was good for Gary Dormuth, was good for the matter at hand. He was an ambitious man. He liked money and status and intended to have as much of both as he could."

Avivah cringed. That wasn't a truth she wanted to hear, though she had suspected it from the moment she met Gary. Sleeping together started as a mutually satisfying physical release. Gary found making love here titillating. He'd dropped enough hints that Avivah suspected Gary slept with her because she was unique: a female military police officer, and a Vietnam veteran, and a person who'd made the *New York Times*. All that satisfied his craving for status. Let it go, she told herself. File it with all your other failures.

Pepper reached over and ran her hand along Avivah's shoulders. Her face must have betrayed her.

Pepper asked, "When did you learn about General Bill's artillery range?"

"The morning after Father Ron's party arrived. He told me."

"You had no idea before that of what General Bill intended to do?"

"Not a clue, and I'm sure Mother Superior didn't either, or she never would have signed the rental agreement."

"When you found out, did you notify her?"

"Not right away. Mr. Kirkpatrick suggested they take time to explore our grounds first."

Avivah asked, "For what?"

"What they eventually found. Surveyor's stakes. Someone had conducted a survey on our property without our knowledge."

So that's what Gary, Ron, and Benny had done on their long morning walks.

Avivah had managed to get control of herself. She reached over and squeezed Pepper's hand to thank her for her silent support. "Gary didn't phone you Saturday evening?"

"I was away from Saturday noon until late Sunday morning."

"Were you alone?"

"Patience and I went Christmas shopping at a crafts fair in Boone. Rather than drive back after dark we stayed overnight with Patience's friends, and came back after Mass on Sunday."

That would be easy enough to check. "I gather Sister Angelus didn't go with you?"

"Right now, Sister Angelus would prefer to not go anywhere with me."

"Why is that?"

The sister folded her hands in her lap. "She believes I tried to kill her."

"When?"

"1942."

Thirty years ago. Avivah leaned back against her cold chair. Oh, yes, convent walls contained long-held secrets. She wondered if either nun remembered exact details of what started their feud: perhaps, inadvertent food poisoning, or Sister Mary Rachel leaving a window too far open overnight for Sister Angelus' delicate lungs. "How?"

"By manufacturing chlorine gas."

Pepper and Avivah exchanged one of those "you watch her; I'll go for a butterfly net" glances.

Avivah pursed her lips. "Ma'am, with all due respect, you look as if you would have been ten or twelve in 1942."

"I was fifteen. A pregnant runaway, married to a soldier on his way overseas."

In these Blue Ridge mountains, a married, pregnant, fifteen-year-old girl wasn't that unusual. But, unless she'd had her parents consent, a wedding would require subterfuge and planning. "A priest married you at fifteen?"

"Justice of the peace. I was raised Baptist. I converted to Catholicism as an adult."

"Then why did authorities send you here? Why not just take you back to your parents?"

"No one around here knew me. I wouldn't tell anyone my maiden name or anything about my family. They were a hundred miles away, in east Tennessee, but, they might as well have been on the moon. The sheriff wanted me off his hands, and the nuns were willing to take me."

Avivah considered. "From your tone, I gather it wasn't a satisfactory arrangement?"

"I was their nightmare child, every negative stereotype of a backwoods hellion. Uneducated. Unwashed. I arrived not only pregnant, but with lice, worms, and a vaginal infection. I'd never seen a dentist in my life, and my teeth were black from dipping snuff."

Pepper shuddered. "Dipping snuff is the most disgusting habit I've ever seen."

The sister fixed her with a hard stare. "When you don't have enough to eat, tobacco kills hunger pains."

Pepper looked embarrassed.

Avivah asked, "If your husband was a soldier, couldn't the sheriff contact a military chaplain?"

"To what purpose? The Navy didn't turn troop ships around for one soldier's domestic crisis."

The sister studied Pepper. "No matter what you endured in school, I assure you nuns here treated a pregnant, Baptist girl far worse. I'd never met a nun before, but I'd heard stories: they killed babies and drank their blood; they sold Protestant babies into slavery. I was terrified for my child. I fought the nuns from the moment I arrived. The more I fought; the more they punished me."

Avivah could picture a hungry teenager, with stick-like arms and legs, and a big belly, a cloth tied around her newly shaved head.

"One morning, they sent me to scrub the basement stairs. Sister Valentina went past me, going to the basement, carrying a basket of cleaning supplies. Half an hour later a terrible accident happened. She mixed chemicals, which released chlorine gas. Several women, including Sister Angelus, were working in the laundry room. One woman died, and more would have, except Mr. Tillich, Patience's husband, risked his life to rescue them."

Pepper said, "That's why Patience took over managing the farm."

"Her husband was not physically able to work again. We provided what pension we could, allowed his family to live in our gate house rent free, and gave Patience his job. Sister Angelus' lung problems stem from that gassing. For years she believed that Sister Valentina meant to kill her."

Pepper asked, "Why in the world would Sister Valentina do that?"

The sister attempted to rearrange her clothes again, but it didn't work any better than it had before. "What I've told you so far, I actually witnessed. I found out the rest later, when I became principal here and had access to old records." She looked at Avivah. "The first step to becoming a nun is a novitiate, two years, something like your basic training."

Avivah smiled. "A two-year boot camp. No wonder nuns have a reputation for being tough."

The sister smiled back. "You don't know half of it. Sister Valentina was never a good candidate for the religious life. As part of her novitiate, she attended normal school because we are a teaching order. Within weeks, she had an emotional breakdown and returned here. Sister Angelus was her novitiate advisor. The accident happened three days after she told Sister Valentina she'd failed her novitiate."

Avivah wasn't at all sure she understood this. "Sister Valentina still became a nun? Even after a breakdown and trying to poison a roomful of people?"

"The investigation deemed what happened an accident. Sister Valentina was unstable. She had no family, no money, and no hope of a job. Thirty years ago, the only place to send her was the State Hospital at Morganton. It would not have been a good choice for her." She turned to Pepper. "You are familiar with third orders?"

Pepper said, "They go back to the middle ages. Sometimes they were women who were past marriageable age, and had no one to look out for them. They took modified vows. They often served as go-betweens, dealing with local merchants, caring for livestock, and accompanying nuns on trips."

"Sister Valentina took third-order vows. It satisfied her and allowed her to live here. It did not satisfy Sister Angelus."

Avivah failed at trying to imagine how these three women's lives, filled with suspicion and possibly hatred, wove in and out through thirty years in a closed environment. "When you discovered you had a vocation, why did you return to this order and this convent?"

"When you have a vocation, you don't choose. God guides

you. When I became administrator here, Sister Valentina had been the convent baker for decades. Suspicion about her had long passed away. My relationship with Sister Angelus was always . . ." Her voice faltered. "More problematic. For years, we managed to avoid one another. I was here; she ran our archives in the motherhouse. When this convent closed, I feared sending her here was a mistake, but as Mother Superior reminded me, she *is* the order's historian and we needed to preserve this site's history. I, too, obey."

Now they were finally getting to the crux of the matter. Avivah asked, "Something happened recently?"

"Our order incorporated public revelation and redress."

Pepper looked puzzled. "Third orders I know, but that term stumps me."

"An innovation from Vatican II, more peer counseling than the absolution of confession. You confess a wrong you've done to another community member, and ask that person's forgiveness. Last June, a guilty conscience let me to make a judgment error."

Avivah had a sick feeling. "You really were responsible for the gassing."

Sister Mary Rachel's features melted slowly, like an ice cake placed just close enough to a fire that sharp edges dripped and became rounded. Avivah had seen it before, in a person whose loved one wasn't coming home, even in a police officer who had just too many things thrown at him in too short a time.

The sister bowed her head and, when she looked up, she said, in a flat voice. "No. When it happened, I was in my room, but I did lie to the investigators. They assumed because I was an unschooled child I had no knowledge of chemicals. You learn a lot by trial-and-error on a hard-scrabble farm. I had learned that mixing dregs from household cleaners wasn't a good idea. Fortunately, I was outside when I did it and the gas dissipated.

I knew exactly what the result of mixing those chemicals would be. Anyhow—forgive my pun—I decided it was time to clear the air. At our annual retreat, I publicly confessed to Sister Angelus that I'd lied, and asked her forgiveness."

Avivah pursed her lips. "I gather you didn't get it."

"I only succeeded in awaking old animosities, not only toward myself, but toward Sister Valentina. We three have been together here, in this empty building, for six months. It has been an unsuccessful exercise in Catholic charity."

Avivah asked, "Is there anything in Sister Angelus' background where she could have learned to use a garrote?"

"Sister Angelus spent her life reading history texts. I'm sure she knows many things the average nun doesn't know."

The way the nun had brought them to this lovely and isolated spot to tell them her story bothered Avivah. It smacked of performance art, and Avivah had no idea why Sister Mary Rachel wanted to perform for them. She knew for certain was that she no longer trusted either her or Sister Angelus.

Pepper looked troubled, too. "Pardon me for asking, I know it's your private business, but what happened to your baby?"

"It was a boy and he was, of course, given up for adoption to a Catholic family. In those days, they put birth mothers to sleep for their delivery and never allow them to see their children. They said it made separation easier. Helen snuck him in to me once, so at least I did see him. She did that for all the girls who delivered here. And no, there was neither a birthmark by which I could immediately recognize him, nor did I tuck a family heirloom into his blankets. I would not know my son if he stood in front of me."

Avivah asked, "Your husband?"

Something, perhaps a kaleidoscope of memories, moved over Sister Mary Rachel's face. "B.J. died in Italy."

Avivah was grateful to bend to her task of fastening her

snowshoes. Her fumbling fingers could be attributed to unfamiliar bindings, not to thoughts racing through her head. Depending how far along she was in her pregnancy when she came here, the sister's son would have been born in 1942 or early 1943. Benny had been born in 1942. He loved to tell his story about being born in a truck, in Alaska. He'd even shown her a picture of his mom standing beside an Alaskan road marker, holding a bundled baby. The problem was, all babies looked alike, and there was no way to know whether that baby was actually Benjamin James Kirkpatrick. B.J.: Benjamin James. Could Benny be Sister Mary Rachel's son?

CHAPTER 16

Sister Mary Rachel, Avivah, and Pepper arrived back in the kitchen in the middle of breakfast. Pepper scooted onto a long bench, next to Benny. As soon as she sat down, he bent his head at an odd angle, so she couldn't see him. That wasn't like Benny. She reached over and turned his face toward her.

He sported a fresh black eye. Pepper assumed it was a delayed souvenir of his altercation with Thomas, until she looked across the table and saw Darby's cut lip.

If by some miracle, she and Darby got back together, she'd face a lifetime of trying to keep apart two Green Berets, each of whom thought of himself as her protector. As Avivah would say, Oy vey! She looked back and forth between the two men. "Well?"

Benny and Darby exchanged glances like sheepish teenagers who'd just discovered fists didn't clear the air. Neither spoke. So they *had* fought over her.

Southern wisdom dictated that she should feel pleased to be that popular. Secretly, she *did* feel pleased. No one ever fought over her before, and both men had gotten away with only minor damage. Still, she was still honor-bound to express some displeasure. She reached for a plate of scrambled eggs. "I swear, I don't know what to do with you boys."

After the meal, Avivah sidled up to Benny as he left the table and put her come-along grip on his elbow. Pepper didn't want to miss a minute of whatever was about to happen. She shoveled her last few bites of bacon and eggs into a biscuit, wrapped it in a napkin, and gave Darby a determined look. "Later," she mouthed at him.

Avivah, Pepper, and Benny went to Sister Mary Rachel's office. Pepper finished her breakfast while Avivah threw open drapes. Enough blessed sunlight streamed in that they didn't need candles. Avivah sat behind the sister's desk. Benny sat on the couch, his fingertips gently probing under his eye. "Calm down, Pepper. We sorted things out."

Between bites of breakfast, Pepper said, "For now. Until the next time one of you ticks off the other one." She licked her fingers. "Want to tell us about it?"

"Not especially, but I suspect we're going to sit here until I do."

Both women folded their hands and placed them on the desk. Benny did not capitulate easily, but eventually the silent women outlasted him. "After you two went off to bed last night, Darby and I met to compile a status report and plan for contingencies."

Despite their animosity, Pepper understood how easy it was for them to fall into familiar roles with Darby as the team leader, Benny as an officer's aide-de-camp.

Benny asked, "Pepper, how many people did you tell that you were coming to this convent?"

"None."

"Are you sure?"

"Positive. Remember how it was your last week in the Army? Everyone wanted to know what my plans were. I said I was going to hook up with a couple of old Army buddies, but I never mentioned Crossnore or this convent." She paused. "Wait a minute. I did talk to one of my patients, from Newland, but there couldn't possibly have been any communication between my patient and Darby."

Benny hit the couch arm with his fist. "I knew it. Darby kept pumping me for information about you. Had you found a job? Had you decided where you were going to live? Were you going back to Biloxi?"

Benny might find this alarming, but Pepper didn't. Darby was still interested in her. So much warmth flowed through her that she felt like wiggling in her chair.

Avivah asked, "Is that what started your fight?"

"I told him he was too interested in Pepper for my liking, and, if he didn't back off, that interest would be unhealthy for him."

Pepper groaned. "You questioned his intentions, which, for a southern gentleman, is tantamount to questioning his honor."

Avivah said with disgust. "You two are lucky to be alive."

A trickle of fear passed down Pepper's spine. Avivah had seen what she'd missed. To get off with such light damage, both men had pulled their punches. This wasn't two teenagers in a gym parking lot. It was two professional soldiers. If they went at one another, using everything they'd learned about hand-to-hand combat, there would be one, more likely two, more corpses. With no trace of Scarlett O'Hara in her voice, she said, "Promise me you will never fight Darby again."

Benny leaned over toward Pepper. "I don't like him, and I especially don't like his hanging around you."

Sometimes Benny went too far. Pepper stood and leaned over toward him. "My relationship with Darby Baxter is none of your business, so bow out before I make your eyes match."

A piercing whistle shrieked. They both turned toward Avivah. She took two fingers out of her mouth. "At ease, both of you."

Benny pressed his lips together, but sat down. Pepper eased herself back into her chair, ready to defend herself if need be.

Avivah said, "You two won't solve this without getting Darby in on your discussion. Let's just agree that he has an unusually strong interest in Pepper and let it go at that."

Benny didn't look ready to let go of anything. "Didn't you find it strange that Darby showed up here, on Friday, a couple of hours before Pepper did?"

Pepper countered with, "Maybe he found it strange that I showed up a couple of hours after he did. Either one of us could be the intruder."

"I talked to General Bill and Dr. Saint-Mathias. The general was all bluff, about how Mr. Barton was a prospective board member and had a right to be included in an inspection tour. The professor had a different story. His version was that he, General Bill, and Thomas ran into Darby at the airport car rental counter. Dr. Saint-Mathias thought Darby was as surprised to see them as they were to see him."

Avivah leaned back in her chair. "So they hadn't originally planned to come here together?"

"I think not."

Pepper contributed. "Darby says he's on leave. Maybe he was on vacation, and changed his plans when he ran into the others."

Avivah turned to her. "Does he have anything to bring him here on vacation? Friends? Relatives? Own a cabin around here?"

"I don't think so. We talked a few times about summers I spent with my relatives in Bat Harbor. He didn't mention any mountain connection, and he would have. He liked discovering coincidences we have in common."

Benny pointed his finger at her. "There you see. That's exactly what I'm talking about. He's trying to find out where you'll be, so he can just show up, accidentally like."

Avivah used her captain's voice. "Let it ride." Benny hadn't been a civilian long enough for an automatic response to an officer's order to wear off. He shut his mouth. Avivah continued.

"I need both of your opinions. Was it coincidence that the Saratoga Patriotic Foundation, individually or as a group, showed up here Friday?"

Benny said an adamant, "No."

Pepper agreed. "Not a chance. General Bill came here to fire Gary. He not only knew Gary was here, but he knew that Gary had seen his plans for an artillery range."

Avivah ticked off a timetable on her fingers. "Gary saw the plans a week ago Friday; he called Ron Friday afternoon; we met Saturday; the three of you talked Saturday afternoon while I slept; we flew to North Carolina on Sunday. General Bill and company didn't arrive until five days later. Right so far?"

Benny nodded an agreement.

"So why delay? When and how did General Bill find out what Gary had learned? Did Darby coming here have anything to do with those artillery range plans? If so, when and how did he find out about them?"

Benny blew out an exasperated breath. "The last thing Ron said as we were leaving Gary's apartment on Saturday was to keep this in the family, and not talk to anyone."

"But he did talk to someone. I overheard a phone call Gary made Saturday night. It's driving me crazy trying to figure out whom he called."

Pepper said, "It had to be someone Gary felt was like family, someone he could trust."

Avivah wondered aloud, "Of everyone here, who's the most trustworthy?"

Pepper said without hesitation, "The two of you."

Avivah waved away her comment. "Besides us."

Pepper glanced at Benny. "Until you figured out that Sister Mary Rachel might be Benny's mother, I'd have put her at the top of my list, but now I'm not sure. There's something sharp, and secretive about her."

Benny held up his hands in a T-shape, a referee's signal for time-out. "Wait one minute. What do you mean Sister Mary Rachel might be my mother?"

Pepper jumped in before Avivah could say anything. "She was sent to this convent as a pregnant runaway. About the time you were born, she delivered a little boy, who was given up for adoption. When we find a working phone, will your mother tell us the truth about those photographs you showed me?"

Benny stood up and jammed his hands deep into his jeans pockets. Head bent, his body language coiled and tight, he paced between the desk and coffee table. "Leave my folks out of this, okay? Since I moved back home, all I've brought them is grief and trouble. I don't want to open up old wounds, as well."

Pepper braced herself. Every detail she knew about Benny's parents made them sound like characters in a Frank Capra feel-good movie. She'd always suspected there was a darker side to the Kirkpatrick family.

"You have to swear you'll never tell my parents I told you this. Those photographs are fakes." Benny sat down. "Dad married Mom in Alaska a few months before the Japanese attacked Pearl Harbor. Because Alaska and Japan were so close geographically, Alaskans and Canadians had this hysteria about a northern invasion.

"When Mom got pregnant, Dad wanted to send her and my older half-brother to Missouri to live with Grandma and Grandda Kirkpatrick. Delays happened, and I arrived in a truck on a dirt bush road. Only, the truck wasn't parked in the United States. I was born in Canada, in the Yukon, near Kulane Lake."

Avivah looked puzzled. "Why would that make a difference? Both of your parents were Americans."

"The day after I was born, the Japanese invaded the Aleutian Islands. What had been laissez-faire Alaskan bureaucracy became, overnight, hysterical, nightmare bureaucracy. My father had already spent months trying to adopt my half-brother. My being born in Canada would have added to the confusion. So, a few days after I was born, my folks drove to the other side of the border and took pictures of Mom and me with Alaskan geography and signs."

Pepper felt cheated. "That's it? That's your family's big secret?"

"To this day my parents are embarrassed that they lied to the United States government."

His family *did* belong in a Frank Capra movie. "Are you sure that you are the baby in your mom's arms?"

Blood rising in Benny's cheeks didn't make his black eye look any better. "You think my parents detoured by rent-a-baby before they took photographs, so thirty years later I wouldn't twig to the fact I was really the son of a Catholic nun? Pepper, there are times I think you spent too long in the Mississippi sun without a hat. Put my photograph and one of my Granddda— both age five—side-by-side and we're spitting images of one another."

Avivah said, "Give it up, Pepper. I was wrong. Benny is not Sister Mary Rachel's son. But, I am curious, Benny, if this still bothers your parents so much, how did you find out about it? This isn't exactly a story your parents would write in your baby book."

"My dad told me when I got orders for a second tour in Vietnam. He figured he'd been lucky to get me home in one piece the first time, and he was scared that if I went again, I'd come home in a box. He wanted me to know I had a Canadian connection; that maybe, for all he knew, I was a Canadian citizen. He offered to drive me to Canada and get me across the border."

Pepper thought about wanting Toby and his dogs to run for safety in Canada. She understood a lot of how Mr. Kirkpatrick had felt. "Did you think about going?"

"The two of us drove around so long that night that we used up an entire tank of gas. We said more to one other that night than any other day in my life. In the end, I told him I appreciated his offer more than he'd ever know, but I just couldn't take him up on it."

A different kind of silence filled the room. All three of them carefully avoided looking at one another. Pepper knew all too well there had been days she'd have deserted in a minute, if anyone had made her a similar offer. And days she wouldn't. Finally, Avivah cleared her throat and said, "Who would Gary have trusted enough to phone? Pepper says Sister Mary Rachel." She chose not to mention that Sister Mary Rachel had been unavailable. She wanted to keep this discussion open.

Benny still looked a little flushed, as if he were having trouble getting his focus back. "Sister Angelus. Being Ron's sister, she fits 'keep it in the family'."

Avivah qualified, "Assuming Gary knew they were related."

"Ron told us all about her and this convent, then phoned her from Gary's apartment to make arrangements for us to come here. He left her phone number with Gary."

"Anyone else?"

Pepper thought of another person everyone trusted. She watched the same look spread over first Benny's face, then Avivah's, seconds apart. She said, "Darby Baxter. Overgrown Boy Scout."

Avivah said, "Everyone's friend. A man trained to get people to tell him things they don't even know they are telling him."

Benny added, "West Point graduate, war hero, career soldier, and the one person here who knows enough powerful, active duty officers to put a serious crimp in the general's plans."

Avivah asked. "Did Gary know that you were going to ask Pepper to meet us here?"

Benny leaned back and whacked himself on his forehead with his open palm. "Oh, God, Pepper, I'm sorry. You weren't the leak. I was. I told Gary and Ron all about us at Fort Bragg. Gary must have mentioned your name to Darby."

Pepper wished she could have been there to see Darby's face when her name came up out of the blue. Darby was not a man who liked surprises.

Avivah said, "Now we know why Darby was at the airport: he was on his way here to see Pepper."

Pepper said, "It must have come as quite a shock to General Bill to meet Darby. The general was stuck between a rock and a hard place. Gary is on the short-list to join their board; this was a board-sponsored tour. Thomas might have missed the significance, but Dr. Saint-Mathias is no slouch. He's a weasel type who thrives on bits of information he can use to his advantage. He would have found it worth remembering if General Bill brushed Darby off without an invitation to join them."

Benny added, "I bet General Bill was praying that Darby would turn down his invitation."

Pepper snapped, "General Bill doesn't pray; he issues memos to God."

Avivah stood. "I think it's about time I interviewed Golden Boy. Pepper, I don't want you in on this interview. You're too involved with Darby to make an objective witness."

As much as Pepper hated to admit it, Avivah was right. "I'll make myself scarce."

Benny said, "I don't expect I'd be a very good witness either?"

"After questioning Darby's honor and having a fist fight with him, what do you think?"

Benny opened the office door. "I think that Pepper and I might make ourselves more useful conducting a small interview of our own. Pepper, no matter where you're stationed, who do you always want on your side."

Pepper knew the standard Army answer by heart. "Cooks and supply sergeants."

Benny nodded. "Exactly."

CHAPTER 17

When Avivah went to look for Darby, she found Dr. Saint-Mathias alone in the kitchen. From all appearances and odors, he was stone-cold sober; his suit brushed, his hair and beard groomed. He stood as she entered.

Avivah looked around. "Where is everyone?"

"Sister Mary Rachel took them outside for exercise. I stayed because you promised you'd interview me first thing this morning."

She had promised, and Darby wasn't going anywhere. Or, if he were, she couldn't stop him. She might as well get another interview in her bag.

Fifteen minutes later, in the sister's office, while Avivah threaded tape, Dr. Saint-Mathias moved a chair so he could sit in a pool of warm sunlight. Just like a cat, Avivah thought. This was a man who likes his creature comforts.

She led him through the same preliminaries he'd given her yesterday, then asked, "What is your connection to the Saratoga Patriotic Foundation?"

"I serve on their board."

"Is that a paid position?"

"There's no salary, but my expenses to attend board meetings, and incurred costs, like long-distance phone calls, are reimbursed."

"Do you receive any other money from this foundation?"

"Not now. In the past, I have received research grants."

"While you were on their board?"

"Once."

"Isn't that a conflict of interest?"

"Oh, my, no. Our board has nothing to do with awarding grants. That's done by a separate committee. Applications are absolutely anonymous."

Right. How many professors from Louisiana State University, with an interest in Civil War history, applied for these grants? Figuring out who an applicant was, and that he was a board member who needed to be kept happy, wouldn't be difficult.

"What are these grants for?"

"To support research and publishing, which make American military history accessible to the general public, and to heighten the pride lay readers take in contributions soldiers have made, and continue to make, to the legacy of the United States."

She bet he got that straight out of a SPF pamphlet.

"Has anyone with one of these grants published about Vietnam?"

Dr. Saint-Mathias waved a dismissive hand. "Vietnam isn't history; it is current events. There's no point studying a war until at least seventy-five years after it ends. By that time, who knows whether Vietnam will have any significance at all?"

The first war the U.S. lost? Damned straight it would have significance. She hid her hands below the desk top so he wouldn't see her clenched fists. "You prefer to study a war after everyone who fought in it is dead."

"Exactly."

"No sense in having a bunch of eyewitnesses cluttering up pristine scholarship."

"Precisely my point."

Avivah looked at him closely, but there wasn't the slightest trace that he recognized her sarcasm. She noticed something else. Dr. Saint-Mathias didn't have the appearance of any drunk she'd ever interviewed. He had no broken veins in his nose and cheeks, no unhealthy complexion, no hand tremors, no surreptitious glances toward the door and his next drink. How much of his projected alcoholic haze was real? Why would he pretend to drink heavily if he didn't?

"Who did you meet first, Thomas Hackmann or Gary Dormuth?"

"Thomas."

"When did you meet him?"

"August, 1971. At his home in Lakeland, Florida."

"How did you meet?"

"After I found Ermengarde Hackmann's will, I advertised in several southern papers, something to the effect of, 'Anyone who has family records mentioning Lucas Hackmann, born 1860 or 1861, Crossnore, North Carolina; death date and location unknown, please contact me. I may have something to your advantage.' Thomas' father wrote me."

"What did you find when you visited the Hackmanns?"

"More than I ever hoped: letters, marriage certificates, a family Bible, family trees, everything I needed to prove that Thomas and his father were the only male line descendants of Lucas Hackmann."

"What did you do after you saw their documentation?"

"I phoned General Bill immediately."

"Why?"

"For some time, he had been very focused on finding a permanent home for his foundation. I had been to this convent on research trips, and I suspected he'd jump at a chance to have this setup."

With reimbursed expenses, even his phone call hadn't cost Dr. Saint-Mathias a penny. "What happened then?"

"General Bill came to Lakeland, talked to Thomas and his dad, made a quick trip here, then sent out requests for bids for an agent to open negotiations with the Visitation Order."

"That would be Gary Dormuth?"

"He was the successful bidder."

"When did your organization hire him?"

"A month later, at our annual general meeting in September."

"Between when you went to Florida and this weekend, how often have you seen Thomas Hackmann?"

"Three times, all at our board meetings."

"Did you have any other contact with him?"

"Not with him, but his father and I talked frequently on the phone. He wanted reassurance that we planned to protect Thomas' interests."

"Were you able to give him those reassurances?"

"I hope so. I tried to do so."

"Did you like Thomas?"

"Not especially. Being around him was difficult. I'm not good with sick people."

"Did you ever ask him or his father about Thomas' experiences in Korea, about his Medal of Honor?"

"No, you understand that Korea isn't my period."

Of course it wasn't. It had only happened twenty years earlier, and there were still plenty of veterans alive who might mess up any hair-brained theory Dr. Saint-Mathias concocted.

"Do you have any idea who might want to see Thomas dead?"

"Not a clue. I suspect the foundation, especially General Bill, was more interested in keeping him alive."

You don't kill a goose, not if you want golden eggs that might belong to him.

Dr. Saint-Mathias ran his thumb and forefinger down creases in his trousers. "Under different circumstances, I'd think his death was suicide."

Startled, Avivah realized suicide was physically possible. Thomas could have stood on the laundry table, put a rope around his neck and jumped. But, if he'd done that, there would have been scuff marks on the table. She was sure there hadn't been any scuff marks.

"Why?"

"He attempted suicide twice before."

What had she missed? Had her breakdown caused her to not look carefully enough at evidence? She faltered. "Did he leave a suicide note either time?"

"His father never mentioned that."

"Did he mention what method he'd used?"

"Both times were during unusually cold weather, the kind where they have to light smudge pots to protect orange groves. He took off all his clothes, opened every window in his apartment, went to bed naked, and lay there, waiting to die. His father discovered him both times. He almost succeeded the second time. When they got him to the Veterans' Hospital, he was severely hypothermic. After that, his father insisted that Thomas live with him, so he could keep an eye on him."

As hard as discovering his son naked and freezing must have been on Thomas' father, Avivah felt relieved. Once potential suicides chose a preferred method, they rarely changed it. If Thomas had wanted to commit suicide, he would have taken off his clothes and walked into the blizzard. Pepper had to be right about what happened at Chosin and, when they got out of here, Avivah was very anxious to see Thomas' military records.

Dr. Saint-Mathias moved uneasily in his chair. "Are you through with me?"

Avivah realized she'd been quiet a long time. She pulled herself back from a twenty-year-old war that she couldn't do a thing about. "Not quite. How often did you see Gary Dormuth?"

"When he reported to us at board meetings."

"Did you phone him outside of the board meetings?"

"No. Why would I?"

"Did you like him?"

"For a while."

"For a while?"

Dr. Saint-Mathias pursed his lips, as though he'd sucked a lemon. "About the time Gary came to work for us, things changed. Board members became, well, a little more suspicious of one another. We started sniping at one another. I always suspected that Gary was doing something behind the scenes to stir things up."

She'd assumed that Thomas and Dr. Saint-Mathias were the only board members, yes-men to rubber-stamp General Bill's decisions, but it didn't sound that way. "Are you and Thomas the only board members?"

He pulled back in surprise. "Oh, my, no. There are eight of us."

Trips and reimbursements for eight people, grants, renting a convent, buying artillery pieces. Cost figures began to mount. She was curious about just how much money the Saratoga Patriotic Foundation had, and where it came from. "Tell me about the foundation's financial situation."

"I'm sorry. That's confidential."

"Then tell me what was in last year's annual report. You do send an annual report, don't you?"

Dr. Saint-Mathias looked hurt. "Of course we do. We are completely aboveboard. Last year, we *reported* working capital of just over a hundred-and-fifty-thousand dollars. Of course, General Bill has been especially active recently, raising money to be able to rent this site. The capital may be higher, now."

The way he said "reported" piqued Avivah's interest. She wouldn't be surprised to find hidden pockets, into which General Bill could dip for off-the-record expenses, like artillery pieces. "Your money comes from what sources?"

"The treasurer's description was, 'Supported by donations from individuals and corporations in gratitude for American soldiers' two hundred years of service and sacrifice.'"

Oh, please. Avivah felt as though her eyes were crossing. "Might I recognize any of these corporations?"

He smiled a wicked little smile. "You might."

"Nesbitt Cereal Company?"

"Have you ever eaten military rations?"

"Yes."

"Are they as ghastly as everyone says they are?"

"Some are quite edible."

For a short time. When you were really hungry. But then, they never pretended to be gourmet meals, just high-calorie, concentrated, eat-anywhere food, which kept a soldier alive long enough to get back to a place they served real food.

"I'm delighted to know that. Perhaps you and I could have a further discussion? I'm sure I could sell an article to a woman's magazine, a fluff piece on Army cooking from the female officer's point of view. We could photograph you wearing an apron over your fatigues, holding a weapon in one hand and a large spoon in the other."

That was so insensitive that it rendered Avivah speechless. She gaped at him.

"Oh, yes, I see, not something you can think about right now. You have more serious business on your mind. Well, it was just a thought. Did your ration packs have bread in them? Crackers? Cookies? Oatmeal?"

"Yes."

"Then you've likely eaten Nesbitt Cereal Company products."

"I thought they sold baby cereals?"

"One small part of the company does. Their main production has been to supply grain products for U.S. military contracts since World War I. Let me just say that the Nesbitt brothers—

four of the five have never done military service, you understand—have a deep, abiding connection to the military."

Or to military contracts. And a desire to keep General Bill
busy. Several thousand dollars a year—he probably had other
donors—would have kept him out of his brothers' hair and
might have made a nice company tax write-off.

"If there are eight board members, how come only two of
you are here?"

"General Bill called his inspection on short notice. He
phoned me Wednesday evening. Thomas and I were the only
ones who could get away by Friday."

Avivah zeroed in on this time frame. If Gary found out about
the artillery plans a week ago Friday, it sounded as though it
had taken General Bill a good five days to find out that Gary
knew. How had he found out?

"What reason did General Bill give for this hurriedly arranged inspection tour?"

"Final details. Showing the flag. Creating a presence now
that the rental agreement was signed."

In other words, typical General Bill–speak of wrapping
himself in military terminology and stringing together inanities.
Avivah understood how Thomas' father would encourage him
to come on an inspection tour of property he might own, but
why was Dr. Saint-Mathias here? "That sounds pretty vague to
me. Why did you agree to drop whatever you were doing and
come with him?"

He already reminded her of a cat. Now the way he rearranged
himself in his chair and tucked his hands under the chair
cushion reminded her of a wary cat with all his feet tucked
under his body and his tail wrapped tightly around himself.
"It's almost Christmas break. I had nothing pressing of an
academic nature, and the history department's faculty-student
caroling and Christmas party was last night. I detest both carol-

ing and the forced cheerfulness over eggnog and cookies afterwards."

He hadn't had to tell her that last point. He was toying with her, daring her to hear his under-message. "I gather you sometimes find the Saratoga Patriotic Foundation a great convenience."

He surveyed her through slitted cat-eyes. "Sometimes. I try to be as much of a convenience to them."

"You said you and Thomas were the only ones who could get away. What about Mr. Barton?"

"He isn't a board member yet."

"So why was he invited along?"

"He wasn't, exactly. It was . . . awkward. We met Mr. Barton at a car rental counter in Asheville. General Bill seemed surprised to see him. I gather Mr. Barton had recently told the general he would be out of the country on a teaching exchange for several months."

Darby told Pepper he was on leave. The Army often granted leave just before a long overseas assignment. Was he really on his way out of the country? If he were, he hadn't told Pepper. Yet. Pepper wouldn't, couldn't, keep something like that a secret. Avivah added one more thing to the long list of questions she intended to take up with Darby Baxter when she interviewed him.

"When did he tell General Bill this?"

"I have no idea."

"What did Mr. Barton say he was doing in the airport?"

"He didn't say; he changed the subject."

Avivah suspected this was Darby's typical behavior when he didn't want to answer a question.

"Did General Bill ask Mr. Barton to come with you or did Mr. Barton suggest he accompany you?"

"General Bill asked him."

"What was Mr. Barton's reaction?"

"I think he didn't want to come. He wavered for a moment, then went to a pay phone and called someone, his secretary, I guess. He told them to cancel his afternoon appointments."

It didn't sound as though Darby were on leave at all.

"What happened when your group arrived here? Were you surprised to find Gary Dormuth?"

"I was."

"What about General Bill?"

"He looked as if he'd just stepped in something warm and unpleasant."

"What about Mr. Barton?"

"It wasn't the way he looked at Gary; it was how Gary looked at him. As if he were furious at Mr. Barton for being with us. They had words."

"What kind of words?"

"A whispered conversation. I didn't hear what they said."

"Did General Bill come here to fire Gary?"

"Yes and no. He floated his plan in the car between Asheville and here. Said he'd already talked to the other six board members. They agreed that Gary had fulfilled all of his contract, and that we had no further need of him. I think he never expected to see Gary here."

"Yesterday, you mentioned something happened at your September meeting. Something about blueprints and a conversation you overheard. Tell me about that."

"We broke for coffee Saturday morning. Gary and General Bill went off together. I saw them in a side room, looking over blueprints. Gary pointed to something and said, 'That's going to be very expensive.' General Bill said it was worth it. If they weren't discussing the artillery range, what else could it have been?"

Lots of things: landscaping, private quarters for General Bill, a recreational complex. Avivah could think of several very expensive projects that might fit the heading of grandiose plans. "So you think Gary lied when he said he only found out about the artillery range last week?"

Dr. Saint-Mathias glanced at the tape recorder. "I think that's a possibility."

"He told other people that he'd only found out a week ago. Why would he lie?"

Dr. Saint-Mathias wiggled his flask from his hip pocket. He opened it and put it to his lips. Highlighted by sun streaming through the window, Avivah watched his Adam's apple. He swallowed only a miniscule amount. When he took away his flask, some liquid dribbled out. He used his hand not to rub it away, but to pat it into his beard. The room stank of alcohol. "Don't underestimate William Pocock-Nesbitt. He's not a buffoon. I've found a little protective coloration is a good idea. Maybe Gary Dormuth came to the same conclusion."

CHAPTER 18

Under a cloudless, deep blue sky, Pepper and Benny walked along a newly shoveled path to the garden.

It had to be an old garden. Traditional mountain skills such as building dry-stone walls were now all but dead. A long time ago, an Appalachian stonemason had fitted rocks into one another with such precision that they held together without mortar. Combined with one side of the convent, the walls enclosed a fifty-yard square.

Inside the garden, a circular brick path surrounded Sister Elizabeth Rose's grave. From the circle, four paths radiated diagonally to each corner. General Bill, Darby, and Father Ron had already shoveled the circle clean and were working on the paths. Trailing behind them, Patience, Sister Mary Rachel, and Sister Angelus swept snow, their brooms tidying what shovels left.

Pepper reached out to touch a metal door hinge and jumped as static electricity arced between it and her glove. Cold weather always produced static electricity to zap the unwary. She and Benny walked over to where Helen and Sister Valentina brushed snow from the tombstone. Pepper read the carved inscription.

Sister Elizabeth Rose, OVM
June 18, 1839–November 22, 1921
Committed her life to God's service: June 1, 1857
Arrived in Crossnore: March 27, 1860

Then that weird quote from Isaiah about harlots and murderers.

Sister Elizabeth Rose had been seventeen when she joined the religious life, twenty when she came to Crossnore, and eighty-two when she died. Sixty-two years in one place, doing one thing all her life. Pepper shivered. She, herself, could have been stuck all her life in Biloxi, if she hadn't bucked her parents' wishes and decided that kind of closed future wasn't for her.

Benny asked, "Helen, could Miss Pepperhawk and I talk to you?"

Helen twisted a lock of grey hair that hung down under her hat. She looked worried. "Ya, I suppose." She turned to Sister Valentina. "Find some branches and rocks to decorate for sister."

Sister Valentina wandered off.

"She likes doing that. It will keep her busy."

Considering previous events, Pepper thought it would be a good idea to keep an eye on Sister Valentina while they talked. Helen wasn't proving to be a good guardian.

They walked to a long wood-and-iron bench near the gate. Benny brushed their bench clear, and they sat down. Helen sat up very straight and looked at Benny, waiting for him to begin. Pepper watched Sister Valentina return with a small collection of rocks and pine cones, which she arranged and rearranged in snow over Sister Elizabeth Rose's grave.

Benny said, "This is a very old convent. Have you worked here long?"

Helen smoothed her coat with her gloved hands. "Patience and I come here together in 1922. We come as maids."

Fifty years of service. No wonder Helen had earned a place in the order's retirement home. Pepper asked, "You and Patience have known each other a long time?"

Helen held up two fingers side-by-side, touching one another. "When we were girls, our farms were like this."

Had their families been remnants of that German-American community to which Ermengarde Hackmann had belonged? "Were your farms close to here?"

"Not far. We could ride a horse or wagon here to there, but nuns did not permit. When we come, we must live here."

Pepper thought about those tiny servant's rooms and Sister Mary Rachel's reference to hardscrabble poverty. Was a room of her own, even a small, bare room, an improvement for Helen? "Does your family still live here?"

"Nieces and nephews. They make a house for Patience. They say to me, 'Auntie, come,' but I tell them I go with nuns."

Pepper turned to give Helen her full attention. "You're related to Patience?"

"She is my sister-in-law."

That made Mr. Tillich, the gassed man, her brother. "Were you working here when your brother was gassed?"

For a moment Helen didn't reply. Her gloved hands twisted her coat. Small tears rolled down her cheeks. "Sister Valentina, she is good. It was accident. She did not mean to hurt my brother. I forgive her."

Forgive the sister, maybe, but from Helen's drawn face, it looked as though her brother was something Helen still found hard to discuss. "I am cook; sister is baker. Every morning, four o'clock, just us in kitchen. Everyone else sleeps. We laugh, we cook, we sing, bread bakes, breakfast cooks. I teach her German. We go to Mass together at six o'clock. Is so sad, what happens now to her."

So Helen had progressed from maid to cook. She and Sister Valentina worked together for decades. No wonder Helen grieved about the sister's dementia. Or was she trying to explain that she couldn't love Sister Valentina as she did if she thought the nun intentionally hurt her brother?

Benny asked, "You've known Sister Angelus a long time, too?"

"Ya, but not close. Not like Sister Valentina. Sister Angelus comes many years ago. Is mean to Sister Valentina. Is hurt in accident. They take her away to hospital. She does not come back here to stay for many years. She is not my good friend."

Benny considered for a moment. "What do you think about closing this convent?"

Helen's body slumped. "I do not like it, but Sister Mary Rachel says time has come. I cannot stop time. She promised we would all be together at the motherhouse. She shows me photographs. Rooms are very nice. There is garden. Even Sister Elizabeth Rose goes with us."

Did Helen referred to the box of bones in the reliquary? The box Pepper saw inside the altar hadn't been big enough to contain a full skeleton. Did Sister Mary Rachel plan to disinter what remained of Sister Elizabeth Rose and take that, and her strange tombstone, with them? Pepper hoped that was exactly what Sister Mary Rachel had in mind. She didn't doubt that General Bill would haul that tombstone to a dump the minute he could. He'd probably replace it with a small artillery piece. Thank goodness dry-stone walls were so rough. Otherwise, he'd mount brass plaques to honor the fallen dead.

Pepper had a horrible vision of a bulldozer wrecking these fine old walls and modern bricklayers constructing red brick abominations just so he *could* hang plaques. A secular Way of the Cross, where visitors were encouraged to walk around this garden contemplating great moments in military history.

Benny pointed to General Bill. "Do you like him?"

"I never talk to him. I do not know him."

"Has he been here often?"

"No. He comes only with other men. He never slept here before."

Which seemed to verify General Bill's statement that he had come with Gary, then with his board members. Pepper glanced over at the grave. Sister Valentina wasn't there. Pepper stood up and looked around. "Sister Valentina has wandered off."

Benny looked at Helen. "Should we go look for her?"

"Is all right. She will come back."

Uncertain what to do, Pepper sat down. On the one hand, Helen knew Sister Valentina better than anyone. On the other hand, Helen had lost track of her charge more than once lately. She would give the sister five more minutes, then go look for her.

Benny ran his hand down an imaginary pointed beard. "What about Dr. Saint-Mathias?"

"He comes many times." Helen's gloved hands formed two puppet mouths. She wagged them at one another. "He and Sister Angelus talk, talk, talk. Sometimes they yell, but I think they are not mad at one another."

Heated academic discussion probably sounded like yelling to Helen.

"He asks me about Sister Elizabeth Rose. We walk. I show him everything. Still he asks questions. He walks in woods, alone, around and around, for hours. Sister Mary Rachel does not like it when he is late for supper."

Pepper noticed movement by the door. Sister Valentina returned; carrying something made of dark green plastic. Pepper called, "Sister, what have you got there? Come over here and let me see."

Surprisingly, the sister did as Pepper asked. Smiling, she held out her found treasure, and placed it in Pepper's lap. Pepper put her hands around it. "Thank . . ." She looked down and squealed, "Holy fucking shit!"

Sister Mary Rachel stopped sweeping. "Miss Pepperhawk, I will not have that language in this convent."

Benny was on his feet, one hand pulling Helen upright, the other with a firm grip on Sister Valentina's arm. One secret of being heard across a parade field wasn't to yell, but to project. Benny projected. "No one move."

Discipline, whether military or religious, was still discipline. No one moved.

Pepper didn't dare take her eyes off the small, curved, green plastic box that Sister Valentina had given her. Yellow lettering, "Front to Enemy," pointed straight at her stomach, and a small length of cord, with two prongs hung from behind. She held a Claymore mine, and it was armed. Her heart pounded, and sweat collected beneath her parka and gloved hands. This couldn't be happening. It just couldn't.

Benny pulled the two women out of her line of sight. Pepper didn't dare turn her head to see where they were. Benny's voice projected again. "Pepper is holding an armed land mine. It could explode."

Thanks, Benny. Like she really needed confirmation.

For a moment, there was absolute silence. Sister Mary Rachel's voice began, "Remember, Oh most gracious virgin Mary that never was it known, that anyone who fled to thy protection, asked thy help, or sought thy intercession was left unaided. Inspired with this confidence . . ."

One by one, other voices joined. Pepper had never realized how comforting "The Magnificat," the ultimate invocation to Mary, could sound.

When they finished praying, Benny had more practical instructions. "Helen, take Sister Valentina inside. Don't walk anywhere but on cleared paths. We don't know whether there are more mines buried in the snow. They could kill you and Sister Valentina. Do you understand me?"

A frightened "Ya, ya," then Pepper heard footsteps move toward the door.

Benny commanded, "Once you're inside, stay there."

Pepper remembered how, when she first arrived, she worried that she might be parking on a prized lawn. Right now, she'd love a prized lawn, an award-winning garden, anything but what she might have come within inches of parking on.

She dared to turn her head, a fraction of an inch at a time. Her gaze swept across half a dozen people, all dead still, like a living tableau. Benny unzipped his parka, took it off, and laid it carefully on the path. He took everything out of his pockets and laid them on top of his parka.

"Benny, as long as I don't yank on this cord, it won't explode. Right?"

He carefully worked his belt out of his pants loops. "Partly right. If static electricity arcs across those two metal prongs, it will explode. Don't shuffle your feet. Don't rub your arms on your parka. Don't do anything to build up a static charge."

Pepper remembered how a spark had flown from her glove. That's why Benny was busy getting rid of every piece of metal he wore. She forced herself to take a deep breath. Her voice came out as a dry whisper. "I'm sitting on a metal bench."

"You're sitting on wooden slats, which are an advantage. I might be able to ground myself on the metal uprights. Sister Mary Rachel, is that bench attached to anything?"

"There are four long metal posts, one at each corner, driven in the ground."

Benny actually grinned. That must have been an answer he liked. "Is anyone carrying pure cotton handkerchiefs? It's essential they be a hundred percent cotton: no polyester, no decorations, no monograms."

Both nuns and Father Ron reached in their pockets. If Pepper weren't so terrified, she'd have laughed. Plain, white, cotton handkerchiefs were Christmas-gifts-of-choice for priests and nuns. Pepper had always thought them boring. Never again.

General Bill leaned over and took a handkerchief from Sister Angelus. Stepping slowly and carefully, he collected two more from Sister Mary Rachel, and Father Ron. Every step sounded like a cannon shot. Stop thinking about explosions, Pepper chided herself.

Benny took the handkerchiefs from General Bill. "Everyone lie down. Slowly. That's it. Keep your face down and cover the back of your head with your hands. Whatever happens, don't look up."

He was trying to reassure Father Ron, Patience, and the nuns. Darby and General Bill knew, as she did, that any explosion would go straight through her and pulverize a good bit of rock wall behind her. Caught in a crossfire of metal ball bearings from the Claymore and rock wall fragments, everyone here was likely to be killed or severely injured. Pepper tried to push away images she knew too intimately: chests and bellies ripped open, missing arms and legs.

She kept her eyes on Benny as he moved toward her, turning her head as carefully as if it were perched on oiled glass beads. He squatted beside her. "Ready?"

There was no other choice, but to be ready. "Ready."

He reached out and grabbed an iron bench leg with his bare hand. His eyes narrowed a fraction of an inch. Today, touching bare iron had to be excruciatingly painful.

Nothing exploded. He'd discharged any static electricity he'd picked up. Benny winked his bruised eye at her. "Still with me?"

"Five by five."

I read you five by five was helicopter pilots' talk for "I understood you perfectly."

"Good girl."

He laid a folded handkerchief between two metal prongs, wrapping it around and around the connector.

"Cotton is a piss-poor conductor. Encasing the prongs makes it harder for static electricity to set it off."

Pepper almost relaxed. Static electricity had been her biggest fear. The detonator was a long, nail-like thing, tightly wedged in place. Falling out on its own was unlikely. All she had to do was remain completely still. At least that's what she thought, then she realized all of her weapons knowledge came from happy-hour conversations in the officers' club. She wished now that she'd had more reliable sources.

Benny tied handkerchiefs together to make one long piece of cloth. "Normally I'd just unscrew the detonator and remove it, but I don't want to risk a spark from metal grating on metal, so I'm going to tie it in place. I want you to lift the Claymore enough for me to pass cloth underneath."

Pepper lifted. She didn't know what a Claymore weighed, probably no more than a couple of pounds, but it felt much heavier. Fear added weight.

Benny worked cloth around and under the Claymore until multiple turns held the detonator in place, and kept it from moving even a fraction of an inch. He took the Claymore from Pepper's hands, and walked slowly along swept paths until he found a place to lay it down at the garden's far end.

Pepper looked at her empty hands. Scarlett O'Hara's voice filled her head. She understood Scarlett's rage. As God was her witness, she was going to stop whomever had contaminated this peaceful convent with weapons. Whatever was going on here had become very, very personal.

CHAPTER 19

Benny found more Claymores by a simple expedient: he followed nun-sized footprints from the garden to the empty woodshed, where he discovered a black gym bag with four unarmed mines and four detonators in a separate package.

Either someone had armed the fifth mine as a booby trap or the sister armed it herself. Arming wasn't difficult. Screw a detonator into the socket on top and that was it: an insert-peg-in-hole experiment that a curious nun might try. Avivah thought that if Sister Mary Rachel wanted another miracle to credit to Sister Elizabeth Rose, she had it when Sister Valentina carried an armed mine from the woodshed to the garden without it exploding. The sister really was God's special child.

Afternoon sun had moved to the far side of the building, leaving Sister Mary Rachel's office in shadow. The convent was cold, but not the killing temperature it had been the day before. Avivah, Benny, and Pepper sprawled on the couch in Sister Mary Rachel's office. The room smelled of candle wax, unwashed bodies, excitement, adrenaline; in short, except for the wax, like a cop shop.

Benny hadn't shaved in three days. His black eye and stubble-covered cheeks made him look like an overage juvenile delinquent. He said, "Our biggest safety question is whether five Claymores are the entire cache. My gut feeling is yes."

Pepper groaned. "Gut feeling is not a term I want to explore. I came too close to an intimate acquaintance with my guts."

Benny reached over and, with two fingers, massaged Pepper's neck. "You would never have known what hit you. Neither would I. We were both inside the killing range."

Inside killing range meant instant death, likely disembodiment, that tidy military term for not enough left to scrape up with a spoon. Avivah knew she should be feeling a lot of things such as rage, fear, relief that her friends had been spared, but all she felt was jealousy.

Pepper and Benny had a particular physical closeness from the day they met. It wasn't sexual. Benny would never cheat on Lorraine. It was just that he had always been comfortable around Pepper. Avivah could see it in the way he hugged Pepper, rubbed her neck, patted her on the back. She didn't begrudge Pepper whatever comfort she could find, but there were times she wished she and Benny had the same kind of closeness. With a pang of regret, she shoved jealousy aside and asked, "Why do you think five Claymores is the entire cache?"

Benny said, "Five fit perfectly into the gym bag we found, and that number makes a nice sample size."

"Sample of what?"

"A salesman's sample. Someone is selling military weapons."

Pepper said, "What a world. I can understand guys sneaking home AK-47s to sell. Collectors can shoot them on target ranges, but you're telling me gun nuts buy Claymores? Why? Bookends in their rumpus room? Lamps?"

Benny gave Pepper a pat on her neck and took his hand away. "Vietnam isn't the only war going on in the world. 'Made in America' is a guarantee of high-quality weapons."

Pepper made a face. "Yeah, well, I'm becoming fonder, by the minute, of beating swords into plowshares. Maybe this is one thing at which U.S. manufacturers don't have to excel."

"What, you'd have preferred having a cheesy, third-rate land mine in your lap? Not me. I go American all the way."

Avivah didn't want any more reminders of just how close she'd come, for the second time this weekend, to losing Pepper. This time, she would have lost Benny, too. She ordered, "Stop it! We've got a much more important question to answer. Who brought the land mines here? Do you two agree we can eliminate us, the nuns, Patience, and Helen?"

Both Benny and Pepper agreed that they could. Benny asked, "Father Ron?"

The question didn't surprise Avivah. "He's peripherally involved with Central American civil rights movements—letter writing, fund raising—so he has contacts. But weapons aren't his style, so no, not Ron."

Benny scratched his incipient beard. "Thomas Hackmann?"

Pepper wrinkled her nose, as she did when she puzzled out a tough problem. "I can't imagine him having either contacts or organizational skills to deal weapons."

They'd come down to names Avivah had in mind all along. "That leaves Gary, General Bill, Darby, and Dr. Saint-Mathias."

Benny winced. "Dr. Saint-Mathias in charge of a bag of Claymores is enough to turn my hair white."

Avivah thought about his interview. "Don't let him fool you; his alcoholic professor pose is a ruse."

"How do you know?"

"He as much as told me. He spills more alcohol on himself than he drinks. His clothes are probably saturated with it. He said a little protective coloration was a good idea around General Bill."

"He's got that right. Okay, leave him on the list, but what Pepper said about Thomas goes for the professor, too. Where would he find either sellers or buyers?"

Pepper said, "I agree. Our professor is too enamored of war as a theoretical exercise to want to brush up against any hard realities. It would spoil his academic detachment."

Avivah said, "That leaves Darby and General Bill."

Pepper quickly added, "Don't forget Gary."

Avivah understood why Pepper wanted even a slightly longer list. The larger the list, the less prominent Darby's name would appear.

Benny leaned forward and wearily let his hands fall between his knees. "Try this theory. A week ago Friday, Gary obtained artillery range plans by accident. What if . . . "

Avivah wanted to set the record straight, even if doing so hurt. "Maybe Gary didn't find out either by accident or on Friday. In September, Dr. Saint-Mathias saw Gary and General Bill looking over blueprints and discussing a large expenditure."

"Okay, revised theory. He either found out by accident or pretended to. He also discovered someone had a sideline dealing arms. He collected evidence, and brought it here for safe-keeping."

Avivah had to agree that a convent wasn't the first place she'd look for Claymores. "Our arms merchant found out he knew, arranged a meeting to talk things over, and killed him."

Benny nodded. "After which, he was stuck with five Claymores. He had to keep moving them because we kept searching the convent."

Pepper sat upright; her face paled. She put her hand over her mouth. "Oh, God!"

Was she about to throw up, a delayed reaction to almost being blown apart? Avivah looked around for a container. "What's wrong?"

"What if that bag of Claymores was in the nursery when the tree fell? I remember patients talking about them exploding without a detonator if you hit them hard enough. Five Claymores would have reduced us all to mush."

Benny waved a dismissive hand. "Even if the tree had fallen exactly on the Claymores, chances are they wouldn't have exploded. You need heat and compression. You have to pry the mine open, remove the plastic explosive, set it on fire, and throw a rock at it really hard. We did it to annoy monkeys when we were bored."

Pepper stared at him. "I bet you cooked your rations with plastic explosives. I heard guys say they'd done that, too."

"Burns great."

Avivah felt sympathy with the monkeys. "Can we get back to our Claymores? We have someone moving them around as we search. Once we brought in firewood, he stashed them in the empty woodshed because he knew we wouldn't go back there."

Pepper asked, "Was everyone wandering around the convent Saturday afternoon, while I was under the tree?"

Avivah and Benny looked at one another and nodded. Benny said, "It was chaotic there for a while. Anyone could have made an unobserved trip to the woodshed."

Pepper said, "No one admits to rescuing our suitcases from the nursery, so I'm going on the theory Thomas did that. Maybe he found the Claymores when he went to get the bags, or maybe he saw someone plant them in the woodshed. That's why he died."

For the first time since she discovered Gary's body, the world made sense to Avivah. Like a jigsaw puzzle she'd stared at for hours, only to realize that if she turned a piece here and there, everything fit. "Claymores, here and now, are a better motive for murder than a nebulous, future artillery range. I wish I knew who Gary phoned Saturday night."

Benny asked Pepper, "I gather Gary didn't have a black gym bag with him when you met him in the coatroom?"

She wrinkled her nose again. "I'm sure he didn't. I saw both of his hands, and he didn't pick up a bag before he left."

"He could have already stashed it. Avivah, do you remember if he had a black bag with him at the airport last Sunday?"

"Sorry. I still wasn't tracking very well when we were in the airport."

Pepper wiggled and partially raised her hand, like a child who just thought of a question. "Wait a minute. Since those Cuban skyjackings and that D.B. Cooper thing last year, how could anyone get Claymores on an airplane? Last time I flew home; airport security looked in all my bags."

Benny said, "They check hand-carried luggage, not what goes in cargo holds."

As much as Avivah liked this theory, her cop-sense said they shouldn't get too enamored of it. "Gary sounds like a good bet, but let's consider other possibilities. Who else might have brought the Claymores, and why? General Bill mentioned his good friend in Boone. Maybe he planned to go from firing Gary to meeting a potential buyer at his friend's house?"

Benny nodded. "A little appointment could work for Dr. Saint-Mathias, too."

Pepper sneered, "Who was he going to sell them to, a Civil War reenactment group?"

She had a point. If their arms dealer was selling Civil War muskets instead of mines, Avivah would seriously consider Dr. Saint-Mathias. Whether Pepper liked it or not, they had to discuss the one remaining name on the list. "Dr. Saint-Mathias said Darby phoned someone from the airport to cancel business appointments."

She braced herself for Pepper's denial that Darby could have had anything to do with an arms deal.

Pepper took a deep breath. "What do you want me to say, that Darby is an angel? He's been in the soldiering business a long time. More likely than not, he knows people who would be willing to both sell and buy arms. He knows weapons. I know you think he's your best suspect. There's not a thing I can do to refute that. Bottom line: he's the best suspect."

Benny said, "We've got a more immediate problem than who was selling what to whom. If there are more than five Claymores, is our killer ruthless enough to booby-trap a convent?"

Avivah and Pepper spoke simultaneously. "Yes." "No, not if it's Darby."

Avivah glared at Pepper. There was something rather touching in her dogged determination to stand by him. Touching, but it would be tragic when Pepper finally accepted Darby as a human being and not as a demigod.

Benny brought them back to practical reality. "If there are more Claymores, we are in a shitload of danger. We could search this building twenty-four hours a day, but nothing would prevent him from setting a booby trap ten minutes after a sweep."

To Avivah that sounded like a problem with a simple solution. "All of us—nuns included—stay together until help arrives. We limit ourselves to the kitchen, dining area, room with the honey buckets. No more wandering around, inside or out."

Benny asked, "What about Sister Valentina?"

Avivah had forgotten Sister Valentina. "She would wander. Pepper, can you sedate her?"

"Sister Mary Rachel gave me a list of her medicines. No sedatives. We still have Thomas' sleeping pills, but my prescribing them for her is illegal."

Benny rubbed his head where he'd hit it when Thomas drugged him. "What if we get around that by me or Sister Mary Rachel giving them to her, and not telling you we did it?"

"It's still my responsibility. We have no way of knowing allergies or reactions with other medicines, and she's such a tiny thing, you could overdose her. Bother! I wish you hadn't mentioned sedating her without telling me. Now I have a legal responsibility to lock up the medicines where you can't get to them. I'll give them to Helen. There must be a cupboard with a lock where she can store them."

Benny looked put-upon. "That leaves me with one choice, and I don't like it. I have to give everyone a quick-and-dirty class on how to spot a tripwire, and hope for the best."

Avivah reminded him, "That won't protect Sister Valentina."

Pepper stood. "Sister Valentina is expendable."

Avivah looked up, startled. That was something she'd never expected Pepper to say. Something dark and brooding had replaced Pepper's usual look of open, hopeful innocence. Avivah didn't like what she saw. She wanted to take back all the times she'd said to Pepper that she should grow up. Innocence might be irritating, but Pepper looking this way was downright scary.

"We leave her alone and let her wander. If she blows herself up, I don't intend to be anywhere near her." Pepper thought for a moment. "Do unto others as you want them to do unto you. Everything—blizzard, loss of electricity, fallen tree—gradually squeezed us into smaller and smaller spaces, but until an hour ago, I always had an illusion of safety. Just like in Qui Nhon. As long as I stayed inside American compounds, behind razor wire and guard towers, I could ignore that there were snipers, bombs, and Claymores around me. I never realized before what life was like for the Vietnamese."

Benny stood. He had a sour look on his face. "Welcome to war, Pepper."

He opened the door and almost ran into Darby Baxter, who stood with his fist poised. Darby looked embarrassed. "I was about to knock."

Pepper said, "Sure you were."

Darby stared at her and Avivah knew he had seen the change in her face as well. How long had he been standing there and how much of their conversation had he heard? His listening at doorways was getting to be an irritating habit.

Darby pulled himself up until he was almost standing at attention. "I want to be interviewed. Right now. I swear I'll answer any question you ask."

Why now? Why come pounding on her door at this exact instant? What else had happened, or was about to happen? Avivah couldn't decide if Darby were seeking an alibi or a refuge. She didn't want to give him either.

Benny muttered. "About time, Baxter." Then to Pepper, "Come on. I have a class to teach, and you have to talk to Helen about locking up Tom's medicines."

Pepper didn't move. "I think I'll stay for this interview after all."

Avivah got up and guided both of them out the door as fast as she could. "No you won't."

She intended to pin Darby like a butterfly, and she wasn't about to give Pepper any opportunity to set him free.

CHAPTER 20

As Avivah closed the door, Darby said under his breath. "I'm not a bad person. Why won't she give me a chance?"

Avivah wanted to say, "Because Benny and I just tried to talk her into believing that you are an illegal arms dealer. Because she just started growing up. It's going to be fascinating—but painful—to watch how her growth affects her relationship with you."

Instead of saying that, she turned to her tape recorder, and took extra care to check that it worked. If Dr. Saint-Mathias was a cat, Darby Baxter was an eel. This was one interview she wanted to make sure she taped word-by-word. Finally satisfied, she turned on the machine and explained Darby's rights to him. She took special care to add that they were off-post and, even though they were both active duty officers, the Military Code of Justice didn't apply here. They would play this game by civilian rules. "State your full name, occupation, and address."

He extracted his wallet from a back pocket and flipped it open, displaying a green-and-grey military identification card, just like the one Avivah had. "Darby Randolph Baxter, Colonel, U.S. Army Special Forces."

Avivah had to work at keeping her mouth from falling open. "Colonel, since when?"

"A few days ago."

"When you say colonel, you mean lieutenant-colonel, don't you?"

Lieutenant-colonel was one step above major; colonel was two.

He fixed her with his smoky blue eyes. "No, ma'am. I mean full bird colonel."

She'd never met an officer who had skipped an entire senior rank. Now Darby's involvement in this sordid mess frightened her even more. What had he done, or more likely, who did he know, to have the privilege of advancing in rank that fast? Could he be a front man for arms dealing, with a boss farther up the chain of command than Avivah cared to think about? Things were looking worse and worse for Colonel Darby Baxter. If Avivah's suspicions were true, Pepper's heart would break.

He finished answering her question as if they hadn't just taken a small, and very dangerous, detour. "My home of record is Macon, Georgia."

A home of record was a military equivalent of a post office box drop.

"What's your current military address?"

"I'm on leave between assignments."

"What was your last posting?"

"Fort Benning, Georgia."

"And your next one?"

"I can't divulge that."

No, Pepper didn't know a thing about his new assignment. Even with everything else happening this weekend, if she'd suddenly found out that Darby was about to put himself in harm's way again, she would have let something slip. Which, in itself, was enough of a reason for Darby not to tell her.

He held up his hands. "I know I said I'd answer any question, but I really can't give you that information. If it becomes necessary, I'll give you a phone number in Washington, D.C."

"What good will that do?"

"Depends on your security clearance and your need to know."

What an arrogant, infuriating man!

"Does anyone here know you by a name other than Darby Baxter?"

"Yes. David Barton, science teacher and recruiter for my high school alma mater, Georgia Military Academy."

"Class of . . . ?"

"Fifty-eight. Cadet commander and salutatorian."

Avivah did some quick calculations. He was six or seven years older than Pepper. She couldn't decide if she wanted to hold that against him, too. "Not valedictorian?"

Darby gave a life-happens shrug.

"Who knows your real identity?"

"You, Miss Pepperhawk, and Mr. Kirkpatrick. Father Ron believes David Barton is a major."

He had to say that because she'd been there when Ron guessed his rank. Avivah couldn't decide if Darby were taking pains to appear scrupulously honest or, for once, truly being honest. "Why did you find it necessary to present yourself under a false name?"

"If I used my real name, I was afraid someone would check and find my active duty connections."

"Why would that be a problem?"

He squirmed in his chair. "I'm not here on Army business, but considering General Bill's background, an active duty officer investigating finances of the Saratoga Patriotic Foundation wouldn't thrill him."

"Why are you investigating their finances?"

Darby gave a long *I-guess-the-jig-is-up* sigh. "My grandmother and great-aunt informed me they would take it as a great kindness if I would do that. Let's just say that a gentleman in my family unwittingly contributed more to General Bill's cause than Nana Kate thought proper."

You didn't have to grow up south of the Mason-Dixon line to

know that from ladies of a certain age and blood relation *I'd take it as a great kindness* became a royal command. Fail at your peril. Somewhere in Georgia a grandfather or great-uncle lived on borrowed time.

"Your grandmother and great-aunt will confirm your story?"

Darby sighed again. "Nana Kate and Auntie will confirm any number of my shortcomings, including my failure to salvage family honor. I told the ladies it would be impossible to recover the contribution."

He looked so beaten that Avivah almost felt sorry for him. Between his elderly relatives and Pepper, he'd batted zero lately. A voice in her head warned that he could still be a murderer and an arms dealer. "What did you find out about General Bill's funding?"

"Approximately eighty-five percent comes from Nesbitt Cereals. His brothers consider it an early pension contribution and a tax break. He also has three major fund raisers, two of whom are on his board of governors."

"Is one of them Dr. Saint-Mathias?"

Darby laughed. "Yancy Saint-Mathias is small potatoes, and quite probably won't be on the board this time next year."

How likely would small potatoes be to deal in small arms? Avivah had to agree with Benny and Pepper that the professor was not their best bet.

"Anything unusual about these fund raisers?"

"Cookie-cutter copies of General Bill: that's why they get on so well. Upstanding men in their communities. Prayer breakfasts, hospital fund raisers, fall hunting trips, and a touch of messing in state politics. All ex–senior military officers, all dedicated to truth, justice, and the American way. One possibly has a bedsheet and a can of gasoline under his bed, but nothing proved. And they all know exactly why Bill retired from the military after only twenty-five years service."

"Which was?"

"When he was stationed at Fort Hood, Texas, he liked giving formal dinner parties. Good food, excellent liquor, black maids in black dresses, white aprons, and frilly caps."

A chill passed up Avivah's neck. "These black maids were?"

"Enlisted women, his company clerks."

Her heart beat faster. She knew all too well what kind of influence an officer could exert over women in his command. "Ouch. They didn't report him?"

"He threatened them with damning efficiency reports, including comments that they were lesbians, who flouted their sexual preference during working hours."

A report that was a sure ticket for any woman soldier to a discharge without prejudice. Out of the Army, a bad recommendation, and no possibility, ever, of collecting military benefits. She knew exactly what it felt like. It had almost happened to her. She hoped her voice sounded steadier than she felt. "Did a woman finally get up her courage and report him?"

"No, he invited another general who had just transferred one of his best clerks to Bill's outfit. He recognized who was serving him canapés, and six weeks later William Pocock-Nesbitt was on civvy street, with full benefits and a pension." He cocked his head. "You look a little pale. Are you all right, Captain?"

Avivah got up and pretended to check the tape feed. Her back turned to Darby, she waited out what felt like an interminable pause, while she got her anger and fear under control. "How did you meet General Bill?"

"I phoned him and expressed an interest in his organization."

Her heart rate started going back down. She went back to her chair. "When?"

"August, 1971. I met him in person a month later at the September meeting."

It had been a busy meeting. Thomas became a board

member, and Gary won his contract bid.

"Did you meet Gary Dormuth at that meeting as well?"

"Yes."

"What did you think of him?"

"Intelligent, a good business man. Not really one of them."

"What do you mean by that?"

"He had a job to do, and he intended to do it. He never bought their pseudo-patriotic garbage."

"Did you?"

"I've seen too many men and women offer up more than anyone—even their government—had a right to expect. Empty rhetoric no longer sways me."

It might not, Avivah thought, but she was darn sure Darby, himself, would still use it every chance he had, if he knew it would have an effect on other people.

"Did you kill Gary Dormuth?"

Darby compressed his lips. "My hand never touched the garrote, but I did fail to anticipate consequences of certain tactical moves. So, if we were having a philosophical or ethical discussion, rather than a police investigation, I'd have to say I had a part in his death, and in Thomas Hackmann's."

He might be infuriating, but he did have a clear sense of morals and culpability, and he didn't shy away from responsibility. Avivah began to get an inkling of what Pepper liked about him. If the two of them ever stopped circling one another like wary animals in heat, look out world.

"This *is* a police investigation. Did you kill either of those men?"

"No."

"Did you bring Claymores here?"

"No."

"Do you know who did?"

Darby looked uneasy, embarrassed, as if he missed something

he shouldn't have. "No, and before you ask, before this weekend, I had no idea anyone was dealing in illegal weapon sales."

How embarrassing. The great Darby Randolph Baxter, military officer extraordinary, had missed something important. "Who do you suspect is the dealer?"

He actually blushed. "I don't know. General Bill is my first guess, followed a distant second by Dr. Saint-Mathias."

At least they agreed on something. "Why do you hold yourself philosophically and ethically responsible for these two deaths?"

"Since I joined the Saratoga Patriotic Foundation, I waged a hearts-and-minds campaign on them."

We're here to win peoples' hearts and minds was Special Forces' official line when asked why they were in southeast Asia. What civilians never heard was the second part, which Green Berets said privately. *Even if it means burning their huts to the ground.*

"What did you do?"

"Anything I could to undermine the organization and cause confusion."

So Dr. Saint-Mathias had been only partly right. Someone had been poking a stick in the beehive, but it hadn't been Gary. "What specifically did you do?"

"A few comments to General Bill that Dr. Saint-Mathias never published in military history journals that mattered. Drinks with board members, where I lamented how my GMA commandant strongly suggested I have nothing to do with General Bill. Planting doubts in Gary's head about whether they'd pay him on time. There was more, but that gives you an overview."

"Did you arrange for drawings of a proposed artillery range to go to Gary?"

"Yes."

"How?"

"I riffled General Bill's briefcase and found a letter from a drafting firm. I didn't know anything about plans mentioned in the letter, but I phoned the company and asked them to ship the finished drawings to Gary instead of General Bill. A nuisance factor. All I wanted was to delay things, create a snafu."

Army talk for situation normal, all fouled up. Even if she didn't like him, Avivah had to admire his style. Darby Baxter was one talented shit-disturber. "That was risky."

"A hearts-and-minds campaign is like scattering seeds. 'Other seeds fell among thorns, which grew up with it and choked the plants. Still other seed fell on good soil. It came up and yielded a crop, a hundred times more than was sown.'"

Avivah recognized that was a Bible quote. She ran her hands through her hair. "What is it about this place that has everyone quoting scripture?"

"I don't know. It's like a presence. I guess the blueprint seed did produce a hundred times more than was sown."

Avivah couldn't disagree with that. "After you met General Bill in the Asheville airport, who did you phone?"

He didn't look surprised that she knew about the phone call. "No one. I called Fort Benning's recorded weather line and pretended to have a conversation."

"Why?"

"I had to have a reason for being in Asheville. With General Bill standing right beside me, I couldn't think of a way to warn Gary."

"Warn him?"

"That I'd be arriving with the SPF board."

"Why would that be a problem?"

"More hearts-and-minds. I courted Gary's favor since I met him. It always helps to have a spy on the inside."

"You found out how his brother died and used it, didn't you?"

"You use what works. It paid off. I've known every step of Gary's negotiations the past year. I just couldn't figure a way to derail them."

Avivah guessed the answer to her question before she asked, "Did he phone you Saturday evening?"

"Yes."

"What time?"

"About eighteen hundred hours. We couldn't talk long because he said he had someone with him. He phoned me back early the next morning, after his guest was asleep."

After they made love. She knew it was irrational, but Gary going from their bed to a business phone call seemed the height of insensitivity to her. She understood now what Ron meant about Gary being able to compartmentalize his life. She hung her head. She had become too much like Gary for her liking, pushing parts of her life into watertight compartments, where they touched nothing else, not even her emotions.

"What did you talk about when he phoned you back?"

"I suggested he send the plans back to the drafting company, with a note to be sure to tell General Bill that Gary had seen them by accident."

That accounted for the missing days. Gary probably had a secretary mail or courier the plans back on Monday, after he was in North Carolina. General Bill received them on Wednesday. Wednesday night he called board members. Darby had hit the nail on the head. He did have moral culpability in Gary's death.

"Did you know Pepper was coming to this convent?"

"Yes, Gary mentioned her name. He had no idea I knew her; he just wanted to tell me his plans. Hearing her name, knowing she was coming here, was manna from heaven. It meant I had a chance to say goodbye to her."

"I thought you and Pepper said goodbye in October?"

"That was more yelling goodbye. She ordered me not to see her, write her, phone her. My life changed since October."

It sure had. A double jump in rank and a new assignment. It was too much to hope he'd also taken a hard look at his relationship with Pepper, and decided to drift quietly out of her life.

"When I walked in the door with Bill, Gary looked furious. His expression said he thought I'd played him for a patsy."

"Did you signal him in any way?"

"I managed to whisper to him to meet me after supper, in the chapel, and we'd talk."

"Why the chapel?"

"It was the one place I didn't think General Bill would go."

Darby Randolph Baxter was many things, some of them not to her liking, but she did think he had told her the truth. He hadn't had to be honest about his promotion. He could have said he was a major, and she wouldn't have known otherwise. But, he'd chosen to tell.

She still didn't know why he'd insisted on being interviewed right away, but she strongly suspected it had more to do with Pepper than with the murder investigation. Against her better judgment, she turned off the tape recorder. She could at least do Pepper the courtesy of not having her private business on tape.

"Does Pepper have anything to do with you volunteering to be interviewed?"

"She almost died twice this weekend. She's still in danger. I would do anything, including lay down my life if necessary, to protect her. I want to be part of your team. Let me help with the investigation."

The answer was out of Avivah's mouth before she even considered softening it. "No chance."

"Please." Desperation crystallized in one word.

"I can't. You're still a suspect."

He looked so devastated that she thought he deserved at least a consolation prize. "Do you really want to know why Pepper won't give you a chance?"

A faint hope showed in his eyes. "I would appreciate that more than I can convey."

He sounded so southern, so sincere, that Avivah almost reconsidered his request to join them. Sanity reasserted itself. "You're a brave and capable soldier—everything she admires—so it's easy for her to hero-worship you. You play into that."

"It's not hard. We value the same things."

"That's what scares her. It's pretty frightening to meet your dream come to life. And every time you step out of that dream world and demand real life things of her, she's afraid real life will make the illusions she has about you disappear."

"Pepper was an emergency room nurse in Vietnam. How many illusions can she have left?"

A whole lot less than she had this morning. "Not many, so she's trying to hang onto a few untarnished ones."

"What am I supposed to do?"

"Let her have her cake and eat it too."

"Any idea how to do that?"

"Not one. All I can say is good luck."

"Please don't tell her about my promotion. It would mean a lot to me to tell her myself."

"When were you planning to tell her?"

"When the time was right." He made a helpless gesture. "Don't ask me how I'll know when it's right. I don't know; I just know that I will."

Avivah nodded. "I won't tell her and despite what she told you, my advice is, wherever you're going, write her every chance you get. Long letters. Put some thought into them. Challenge her, make her feel, make her think."

"I won't know her address, and I can't write her care of her parents. She suspects her mother opens her mail."

Avivah found notepaper and a pen in a desk drawer. "This is my address at Fort Dix. Send the letters to me and I'll make sure she gets them."

When she handed him the piece of paper, he took her hand and kissed it, then laid his forehead briefly on the top of her fingers before he let go. Avivah thought, I'm going to regret this. I'm going to regret this big time.

CHAPTER 21

Despite being exhausted, Avivah didn't sleep Sunday night. She and Pepper jostled one another for position on their narrow mattress. Tired of listening to the two of them pretend to be asleep, Avivah said into the darkness, "If it stopped snowing yesterday, when is the sheriff likely to arrive?"

Pepper answered in a petulant voice, "Is this one of those math problems? If one train leaves Washington, D.C., at 6:13 and another leaves Chicago at 9:47, will they meet east or west of Kansas City?"

"I only asked for your opinion."

Pepper flopped on her back and impatiently tried to rearrange blankets. "We're not going to solve these murders, are we?"

Avivah pulled some covers back to her side. "It doesn't look like it."

"I'm sorry. I should have been more help."

"Give it a rest, will you? Your help was fine and, right now, I have no patience left for your southern guilt."

For a long time, the women were uneasily silent. Pepper finally said, "At a guess, I'd say the sheriff will be here later this morning. Murder at a convent will be front-page news."

"No kidding."

"When you add the second murder of a Medal of Honor winner; a missing body; and illegal arms; this whole mess will make national newspapers, *Time,* and *Newsweek.* The sheriff will want to arrive before reporters do."

Avivah mentally added to Pepper's list two female Vietnam veterans—one of them featured in the *New York Times* a week ago.

What happened to her in Vietnam reared its ugly head. She felt sick. She was too exhausted to be interviewed, and she couldn't afford reporters checking her background. If they uncovered what really happened in Long Bien, she'd be lucky to get a dishonorable discharge. A court marshal would be likelier, almost certainly time in a military prison.

Pepper cleared her throat. "So how did Darby's interview go?" The question sounded casual, but it didn't fool Avivah one bit. Pepper was itching to know.

Avivah was surprised she'd held out this long. "Fine."

"Do you still think he's a suspect?"

"Yes, no, and maybe. I don't know what to think of him anymore, but I think he was truthful about not being here on Army business. He got involved with General Bill because his grandmother did not approve of a man in his family contributing to Bill's war chest."

"Nana Kate? Woo, that's scary."

"You know her?"

"I've only heard Darby talk about her. She terrifies him. She's eighty-seven, the *quintessential* southern matriarch. She once baked cookies while holding a would-be burglar at bay. After he was sentenced to thirty days county time, she showed up every morning to pray with him. He still cuts her lawn. She recites family genealogy from memory, glows instead of sweats, and dresses in black every April ninth."

"Why April ninth?"

"Lee surrendered to Grant at Appomattox Courthouse."

"Pepper, you people really have to get over that war."

"Believe me, some of us are trying."

"Gary phoned Darby Saturday evening."

Pepper half sat up and balanced herself on her elbow. "Why?"

"Short version: to give him an update, and to tell him that we—that is, me, Benny, Ron, and himself—were coming here."

"Did my name come up in that phone conversation?"

"Yes."

"That's how Darby knew he'd find me here?"

"Yes."

"And he came here this weekend to see me?"

Avivah clenched her fists. Pepper was as tenacious as a hound digging under a fence. Telling her anything might lead to confessing about Darby's new assignment, but she owed her friend some reassurances. "I think so."

"Then Benny is right. Darby is stalking me. I wish I had a couple of hulking brothers, named Bubba and Junior, who would put God's fear into him."

Pepper had brothers like that, but she didn't realize it. Every letter she wrote to Avivah, while Avivah was in Vietnam, was filled with affection and respect for her patients on Ward Six-A. Avivah bet many of the men returned the feelings. There was, without a doubt, a whole platoon of ex-patients who would do anything Pepper asked. "You want my professional police officer opinion?"

"Yes."

"He's not stalking you. Talk to him, okay? Don't yell at him, or better yet, listen to him."

"Why? What's going on?"

Pepper's questions were getting too close for comfort. "What's going on is that I'm trying to solve a double murder."

"You're not going to tell me about Darby, are you?"

"No."

"Even if I beg?"

"No."

Banter helped. Avivah's terror about facing reporters faded. No matter what, Pepper and Benny would stand beside her. Her stomach relaxed. Friendship was a terrific comfort.

Pepper again sounded petulant. "I'm not giving in gracefully. I want you to note that."

"So noted."

Pepper stopped fidgeting and was silent for a while. "We still have a few hours before the sheriff arrives. Maybe we know more than we think we do. Do you think Gary's death was a spur-of-the-moment killing?"

"It could have been. The picture wire was a pickup weapon, ready to hand. Beserker rage: a moment of extreme passion that leads to murder."

"It has a name?"

"Look it up in any criminology text."

"Why in the museum? Wait a minute, why did you go to look for Gary there?"

"I didn't. When I came downstairs, no one was around. I wandered, looking for anyone. I saw an open door and a light on, so I went in."

Pepper looked at the ceiling light fixture. "I'd forgotten this place has lights. Why do you think Gary went to the museum?"

"To meet someone, to leave something, or to take something."

"The arms dealer, the Claymores, or Ermengarde Hackmann's writing desk."

"Good guesses, but only guesses. Why would he want her writing desk?"

"A desperate last-minute deed search?"

"They signed a rental agreement. Even if a deed turned up, General Bill takes possession until a court sorts out who owns what."

"That leaves meeting someone or leaving something."

"Those are two good guesses."

Pepper asked, "What do you think happened to Gary's body?"

"We've searched this building repeatedly without finding him. There's only one place it can be: outside."

Pepper protested, "There were no tracks at any door."

"Blowing snow might have covered the killer's tracks."

"Why take Gary's body, but leave Thomas where we put him?"

Avivah turned over to face Pepper. "Because there's a clue on Gary's body."

A thin, reedy voice floated up faintly from below them.

"Oh, come, Thou Rod of Jesse, free
Thine own from Satan's tyranny;
From depths of hell Thy people save
And give them victory o'er the grave.
Rejoice! Rejoice! Emmanuel
Shall come to thee, O Israel."

Avivah looked around. "What is that?"

Pepper pulled up a corner of their mattress and laid her ear against a heating grate. "An advent hymn. Bother! Sister Valentina is in the basement. That woman is driving me nuts. I'll go get her."

Avivah rolled again to give Pepper room to move. "I thought you said she was expendable?"

"I can't believe I said that about another human being, much less a nun. It was a weak moment. Talk about a load of guilt if anything happens to her. I won't get any sleep knowing she's down there."

"Has it occurred to you that the basement is an ideal place for a Claymore trap to be set?"

Pepper struggled to get into her coat. "Then go wake Benny. He'll be point man for us."

Point man walked first in a patrol. How nice of Pepper to

volunteer Benny. Avivah got up and found her own coat.

They found the basement door unlocked, but the door closed. Avivah had seen Benny far happier and more cooperative. The weekend had definitely worn on him. With a sigh, he shined his flashlight all around the doorjamb. "Remember pulling out a loose tooth by attaching a string to a doorknob?"

Both women agreed they remembered.

"Doorknobs make great places to attach trip wires. You two stand down the hall."

Avivah wanted to believe they had found all the Claymores. She repeated to herself silently *nothing will explode, nothing will explode*. Benny flung the door open and jumped as far away as he could. Silence. Avivah's heart pounded in her ears.

Benny volunteered. "Let me go first."

She hadn't even asked him to take point. Checking the stairwell, then basement corridor took forever. Avivah couldn't hear the sister singing any more. At least they were at the only entrance into the basement; there was no way she could wander away. They searched laundry, preservation room, storage area, and finally the furnace room, but found nothing new, especially not Sister Valentina.

Pepper stood beneath the furnace. Ducts rose like a giant metal tree above her. "I know I heard her."

Avivah said, "I heard her, too."

Benny looked up to where the ducts disappeared into the ceiling. "Maybe it was referred sound coming through the heating system. She could be anywhere."

Pepper insisted, "No, her singing came up from below. It sounded like it was right under the pantry."

They went back to the foot of the stairs. Benny said, "Stand here until I get back. Don't move."

In a few minutes he returned and measured the floor in paces, first in the corridor, then in the preservation room. He came to a stop just before the far wall of the preservation room. "Your pantry should be just behind that wall." He ran his hand over a wooden table. "Ouch."

"What?"

Benny put his finger to his mouth and spit something out. "Wood splinter. That table edge is uneven." He squatted and looked under the table, extended his arm, and pulled. A section of wall, complete with table and shelves swung open to reveal a dark opening. Sister Valentina started singing again, and a slight, sweet, sickening smell filled Avivah's nose.

The three friends stared at one another openmouthed.

Pepper whispered, more to herself. "The stories were true."

Avivah asked, "What stories?"

"There are always stories in convents about secret tunnels. I never believed them."

Benny pursed his lips. "I think I know where Gary's body went."

Pepper started to walk forward, but Avivah grabbed her arm. "Benny, take point."

He didn't move. "I don't want to take point. I'm tired of taking point." He leaned forward. "Hello in there. We're here and unarmed. Come and get us."

Sister Valentina stopped singing again and there was only silence, until Pepper asked, "Benny, what's gotten into you?"

"This weekend has used up all of my adrenaline. I'm tired and I want to go home. Marching down Main Street with my mom and her cronies, carrying a sign that says 'American Legion for ALL Veterans,' sounds far more sane and sensible than it did a couple of weeks ago. If we have to go in there, I want reinforcements and proper lighting."

Pepper persisted. "And I want to go back to bed. Mounting a search party will take too long. Let me just go in a few feet and call sister's name. Maybe she'll come to me."

"She's a nun, Pepper, not a dog." He sighed again, flipped his flashlight around and handed it to her handle first.

Pepper walked in slowly. "Sister Valentina? Are you all right?"

As Pepper walked through the space beyond the door, Avivah saw more old wooden bins lining the walls. The place reeked faintly of apples. "Since this opens into the preservation room, my guess is they used this cold cellar to store fruit until they could turn it into jelly."

Benny complained, "This place is turning me into jelly. I don't suppose you asked for a gun when the sheriff deputized you?"

"No."

"I swear this is the last trip I'm taking without sufficient personal firepower."

As Pepper rounded a corner to the left, her light became only a diffused glow. "I found her. It's okay. She's alone and the passage ends here. You were overreacting, Benny. Both of you have to come see this."

Benny let the door swing shut behind them. He and Avivah felt their way through the storage area. Dirt floor gave way to an old-fashioned wide-plank floor, and the low ceiling opened up into a living room–sized, candlelit area.

Except that the room was underground and windowless, it looked like a parlor from an abandoned Victorian house. An overstuffed horsehair sofa sat against one wall. A matching chair and a reading lamp with a beaded lampshade occupied a corner. Old dolls and small toys filled a glass-fronted corner cabinet. Piles of junk lay on shelves of a built-in bookcase. A framed drawing of the Blessed Virgin, surrounded by five or six children, hung over the bookcase.

Avivah never liked Dickens' *Great Expectations*, especially the table set for a wedding feast that never happened. This room reminded her of that story, and she didn't like reality any better than she had literature.

Pepper shined the flashlight over all the floor. "No body, but from that smell it was here. Someone moved it again."

In the center of the room, Sister Valentina sat at an old table, whose dark finish had crazed into a bumpy surface. She wore her nun's cloak, a white nightdress, and what appeared to Avivah to be faded red long johns. A wool nightcap covered her short grey hair.

Benny said, "Sister probably followed whomever came to get the body, and it was easier to just let her stay here while they moved it. Our murderer is likely to come back for her soon. We need to leave, now!"

With great attention to detail, the sister sorted old school exams, pages from a child's coloring book, and printed leaflets, layering papers carefully into a slant-top wooden box. Ermengarde Hackmann's writing desk. Sister Valentina looked up at Avivah and said, "Hello. I'm glad to see you."

She fooled us all, Avivah thought. There's not a thing wrong with her. Then she looked more closely at the sister's vacant eyes, and wondered to whom she thought she just said hello.

Benny asked, "What is this place?"

Pepper said, "My guess is the cellar of the original house, an equivalent of a priest's hole. Sister Elizabeth Rose and her girls needed a safe hideout if roaming bands of not-so-nice men appeared. Down a secret staircase, bar the door behind them, and no one would know they were here." She ran her finger over the arm of the sofa. "Except for that lingering unpleasant smell, the air is surprisingly fresh down here. The furniture hasn't mildewed and the candles burn brightly. With great ventilation like this, sister and her charges could survive even if the house burned down over their heads."

Avivah pointed to a lightbulb dangling on a cord, which ran

across the ceiling and down the wall to a round Bakelite switch by the door. "People used this room long after 1865. It's been retrofitted for electricity, and those toys in the cabinet look like they're from the nineteen-twenties."

Benny asked, "So why didn't someone mention this room when we were looking for Thomas's body?"

Avivah suggested, "Maybe they didn't know about it?"

Pepper shook her head. "Sister Angelus had to know. She knows the orphanage's entire history, and she's read Sister Elizabeth Rose's diaries."

"Then I have to conclude that Sister Angelus had reasons of her own for not wanting us to know this room existed."

Pepper said, "Wait a minute. I think she did know. When everyone was looking for Thomas and Sister Valentina, Sister Angelus was scared spitless to come down here. She said it was something she owed to Sister Valentina. I think she was getting up her courage to bring me in here. Then we found Thomas's body."

Avivah squatted down beside Sister Valentina, who was now taking out all of the papers she'd just put into the box. She reached for one of the sister's papers, but the nun pulled it away.

"Mine."

Pepper squatted down on the sister's other side, "Yours and very nice it is. Can we just look? We won't touch it."

Avivah took Benny's flashlight from Pepper and shined light over the box. Black ovals, difficult to see against the dark wood, covered part of the box. Straightening up, she said. "Finger-prints."

She took an old spelling quiz, twisted it into a screw, and, by inserting it into the neck of a heavy cut-crystal and silver ink bottle, picked it up. Dried black ink covered one side.

Sister Valentina tried to grab for it, too. "Mine."

Avivah hastily found a larger piece of paper, wrapped the bottle, and handed it to the sister. It disappeared under her cloak. Seemingly satisfied, she went back to sorting.

Pepper said, "I'll bet they displayed this desk as if Ermengarde just stepped away. A partially finished letter on top, a pen, and an open bottle of ink, with a clear plastic seal over top. I saw that once in a museum. It gives the illusion of an open bottle."

Avivah agreed. "When someone tried to steal it, the plastic seal came off and ink went everywhere. Perfect, inked fingerprints all over Gary's clothes and body. I didn't see his glasses when I went to document evidence, and I assumed they were under his body. It's equally likely they were covered with fingerprints, too, and the killer took them away."

"I didn't see any fingerprints when I tried to take his pulse."

"He lay on his stomach. We never turned him over. His shirt front could be littered."

Avivah took a printed leaflet from the sister's pile. When she saw the diagram of a Claymore and, underneath, instruction in Spanish, her heart broke.

She knew only one person here who had ties to both South American antigovernment movements and to Sister Angelus. Pepper called this a priest's hole. How could Sister Angelus resist showing her brother a priest's hole? She said flatly. "I was wrong about Ron. It looks as though he *is* supplying arms to South American causes."

As Benny took the paper from her hand, a section of wall opened noiselessly, framing the man standing there. He took a pistol from his pocket. Dr. Saint-Mathias said, "Oh, dear, sister. I see we have visitors. How very, very unfortunate."

CHAPTER 22

Sister Valentina said, "Hello. I'm glad to see you."

No one else is, Pepper thought, as she looked around for a weapon. The heavy inkwell would have been perfect, but it was now buried deep inside the sister's cloak.

Dr. Saint-Mathias pointed his gun at Sister Valentina's head. "Deputy Rosen, put your flashlight on the floor."

Avivah squatted and laid the flashlight on the wooden floor.

"Kick it away."

She kicked the light into a corner.

Dr. Saint-Mathias retrieved a length of chain and a lock from tangled items on the bookshelf. Pepper remembered seeing more chain like it in the basement where the bicycles had been stored.

"I've seen in movies what Green Berets can do with their feet. I don't consider Hollywood a reliable historical source, but why take chances? Lie down, Mr. Kirkpatrick, with your feet against that wall and your hands behind your head."

Benny mumbled, "I told you we should have left."

"Miss Pepperhawk, I'm sure you had a bicycle. Wrap this around Mr. Kirkpatrick's ankles in a figure eight; pretend you are securing your bike to a rack."

After wrapping it securely around both of Benny's ankles, she had trouble making ends come together. "It's too short."

"Pull hard."

"No."

Benny looked up at her. "Do what he says."

Benny closed his eyes as metal bit into his ankles above his boots.

"Get him on his feet."

That wasn't easy. Benny swayed and toppled in a heap. He cursed and reached down to try to keep the chain from biting into his flesh, but to no avail.

Hot tears streamed down Pepper's face as she helped him up again. "I'm sorry, Benny, I'm so sorry."

He balanced himself as he took minute steps, like a Chinese woman with bound feet. "It's cool, Pepper."

Dr. Saint-Mathias pointed toward the open wall panel. "Mr. Kirkpatrick first, then Deputy Rosen. Finally Miss Pepperhawk and I will be, as you military types say, 'tail-end Charlie.' Sister, are you coming?" He added, almost as an apology, "I discovered almost immediately that it was less trouble to let her do exactly what she wanted."

Sister Valentina got up and joined them.

One-by-one they walked into a stone passage. One thing about adrenaline: senses grew keener. Sandwiched between Sister Valentina and Dr. Saint-Mathias, Pepper could almost count every stone in the walls. Everyone's breath made little white puffs. Benny had to brace himself frequently to keep from falling. Following behind him seemed to take hours. A rank smell made the slow trip more unpleasant.

To her left, Pepper saw a suspicious bundle. Garbage bags and duct tape neatly packaged Gary's body. What had Sister Angelus said about that old hospital gurney parked beside the dumbwaiter? It saves our backs. Nuns learn to make do with what's available.

Someone had indeed made do with what was available.

Pepper's mind raced through a dozen improbable ways for escape, but all that stuck in her head was a bit of forgotten convent lore. Every convent had stories about tunnels, about how nuns use them to meet their priest-lovers and, later, as a place to bury their illegitimate babies. Older girls used stories like that to frighten new girls.

Being pregnant, and terrified of Catholic nuns, Sister Mary Rachel would have believed those stories. She had to know this tunnel existed. Why hadn't she told them about it after Gary's body disappeared? She turned to face Dr. Saint-Mathias. "Who showed you this tunnel?"

"I found it on my own."

"Someone gave you a clue."

"Sister Angelus, Sister Mary Rachel, Helen, Patience, each had a little story to tell. That's what research is, fitting together small stories. When Sister Valentina inadvertently produced chlorine gas, Patience's husband used this tunnel to rescue everyone. After that, with Mr. Tillich incapacitated, and no other man around, safety became a issue. They didn't want a tunnel men could use as a back door, so they sealed it and, I dare say, they think it's still sealed."

Avivah asked, "How did Gary discover you were selling arms?"

Dr. Saint-Mathias said, "As far as I know, he didn't. I'm not your killer, just a simple businessman. It was disconcerting and a bit smelly to discover his body down here. I wish whoever put it here had showed more consideration. They might as well have hung a 'Going Out of Business' sign around my neck. By the time the sheriff gets finished down here, I would have been finished, too."

Pepper believed him. Only a self-absorbed jerk like Dr. Saint-Mathias would see a body as a lack of consideration for his illegal arms deals. She couldn't resist a dig, and pulled out her southern vowels because she knew they sounded more sarcastic. "Just like General Bill could have shown more consideration when he asked you to leave his board? Though, oh my, perhaps he hasn't asked you yet, but he will."

Dr. Saint-Mathias matched her southern accent, only when he did it, it sounded like a smirk. "Of course, Bill, I completely agree that's it's time for new blood on the board. You're right, Mr. Barton is *so* qualified. Could I, perhaps, offer my services as your librarian here? No salary, but an expense-paid trip here once a month? That would be very generous, Bill. I accept with pleasure."

A nice pirouette, turning dross into gold. He would be here on a regular schedule. All he had to do was take one of those long walks Helen complained made him late for supper. He'd hold a brief woodland meeting, exchange goods, and go back to Baton Rouge richer than he arrived. He wouldn't even have had to pay travel expenses. "How did you find customers, advertise in *Soldier of Fortune*?"

Benny rested for a moment against a wall. Pain filled his voice. "*SOF* readers are too conservative. Spanish instructions. Castro in power thirteen years. Long enough for Cuban refugees to build investment capital."

Benny's pain didn't break Pepper's heart, but it at least bent it. He'd always come through for her. Now it was her turn to do something for him. She wished she had a plan.

"Very good, Mr. Kirkpatrick. People forget how many Cuban refugees relocated in Louisiana, as well as in Florida."

Selling Claymores to Cuban refugees couldn't be that profitable. Either they were his first customers, or he was a tiny fish in a miniscule pond. Pepper decided that was the image she needed. He was a tiny university professor, who looked at least ten years older than herself. He probably didn't even work out. One good thing about moving: a few weeks of packing boxes and washing walls had built muscle. She had youth and strength on her side; all she had to do was cultivate a killer instinct and wait for a moment she could overpower him.

She certainly had a model for killer instinct. Come on, Darby, teach me your stuff. It wasn't as if she were praying to Darby, more channeling him, remembering every scrap of time she'd seen his killer instinct peek through that good-ole-boy ambiance he choose to show to the rest of the world. When the time came she was going to be ready.

The tunnel ended in a stone wall.

"Put your shoulder to the wall and push, Mr. Kirkpatrick."

Benny pushed and a section of the wall swung open. Benny fell, and had to drag himself out of the way so no one stepped on him.

Faint orange bulbs lit a stone room.

Avivah sounded more incensed than frightened. "You have a generator!"

"A small one. As the convent turned into an iceberg, I was tempted to confess having it. At least we could have kept the furnace going. I hope you don't mind that I opted for profit over comfort."

Once they were all inside, Dr. Saint-Mathias inserted a combination lock through a hasp and spun several tumblers. Tidy: no key to misplace, and only he could open that door. He'd probably chosen an obscure Civil War date.

Fear pricked at Pepper's scalp. Every time a door locked, escape opportunities decreased. Pepper made herself breathe slowly. That wasn't the way to think. That wasn't the way Darby would think. He would focus on what was left. Every time a door closed, the battle moved into a smaller space. Smaller spaces were easier to defend.

They were in a space the size of a bedroom. Metal hooks hung from ancient beams, and wall pegs—now empty—could have been intended to hold any number of things. A wooden ladder led to two flat doors set in the ceiling. Another combina-

e doors.

place had an odor of farm work that Pep-
aunt once showed her an under-barn,
rock. Expensive to build, but once built,
co... and a luxury for the farmer, who entered
the tunnel in his cellar and emerged through a door in the floor
of his barn. They must be directly under where the barn stood
when this was a working farm. Someone thought nuns deserved
such luxury.

The gasoline-powered generator chugged in one corner, and
a second gym bag—this one navy blue—stood open on a rock
ledge. Pepper saw more Claymores inside it. What had been a
trickle of fear became a torrent. She hadn't even been much
afraid of Dr. Saint-Mathias' gun. She didn't think he could
cultivate a killer's instinct if he had to. A Claymore didn't have
to cultivate an instinct. It was a ready-made killer.

She could almost hear Darby whispering in her ear. Use fear.
Channel it. Shut up, she told him. She couldn't channel
anything when she was about to pee in her pants.

"We will allow sister to wander. She becomes so unmanage-
able when she's forced to sit still. The rest of you sit down, with
your backs to one another, in the middle of the floor."

Benny, who was still on the floor, dragged himself a few feet
to the center of the space. His blood-caked socks looked black.
Avivah and Pepper joined him. The stone floor was freezing, but
Pepper could almost find comfort in their two warm backs.

Dr. Saint-Mathias picked up a Claymore and positioned it on
a shelf. "Front toward Enemy" pointed directly at Pepper's
chest. She tried to tell herself looking at those letters was getting old, but feeble humor wasn't helping. "If you already had
Claymores here, why bring more?"

"Habit, though I admit not a good idea for this particular
trip. But then, I didn't come expecting murders and a blizzard."

265

Coldness had replaced pain in Benny's voice. "H[...]
seen, close-up, what a Claymore does to a human being? I h[...]

"Seen from a sufficient number of years away, war is merely
an interesting intellectual exercise. I regret you will not have
time to develop that perspective. Empty your pockets."

They turned out keys, bandannas, lipsticks, and coins.
"Deputy Rosen, tie everything up in the bandanna, if you please.
Then slide it toward me."

He picked the bandanna up and put it on a high shelf. Time
was running out. Desperately, Pepper looked around for a
weapon, but didn't see anything, only dust pattern outlining
shapes. Until recently, more gym bags filled with Claymores
had been stored here.

"Where is the rest of your stock?"

"Arrangements were made."

His smugness got the better of Pepper. She screeched, "You
had no telephone, no car, and we've been snowbound for two
days. What arrangements could possibly have been made?"

Dr. Saint-Mathias bent over her. "Something that involved
me not getting much sleep this weekend."

He was off-balance and angry. He'd just admitted he'd gone
without sleep. Take him down now! Pepper lunged for his legs.

Benny yelled, "No!"

She felt him lunge, too, but hampered by the chain, he came
up short of his target. There was a crunch as Dr. Saint-Mathias
brought his pistol down hard on Benny's right hand. Benny
screamed and curled up in a fetal position. Pepper ended up on
her back, winded, covered in sweat, looking into a very nasty
gun barrel. "You are becoming increasingly tiresome, Miss Pepperhawk. I don't appreciate tiresome."

Pepper rolled over and crawled to Benny. When he finally let
her see his hand, she knew immediately that one, maybe two, of
his fingers was broken. She removed her overshirt, and tore a

wide strip of cloth, which she used to bandage all his fingers together, using uninjured fingers as splints. He whimpered. She cradled his head in her lap. It was all she could do.

Pepper looked at Avivah, who hadn't moved, hadn't tried to help at all. Avivah's eyes seemed unfocused. She didn't look like she was in this room at all. Some professional cop! A deep hole opened in Pepper's heart. Benny was down, and, other than asking a couple of questions, Avivah hadn't really been any help at all since Dr. Saint-Mathias captured them. Whatever happened now, rescue was completely up to her. There was a good chance none of them was going to get out of this alive. She might as well go out in a blaze of glory. Darby would.

From a wall peg, Dr. Saint-Mathias took what looked like raw materials for a spider web. He laid a detonator close to the Claymore and strung four wires radiating out, waist-high, in four different directions. Two wires crossed just over their heads, and Pepper and Avivah had to bob down so as not to get their hair tangled in them.

Dr. Saint-Mathias went up the ladder and opened the outside doors. Pepper saw a rim of faint grey daylight through the trees. It must be close to dawn. She desperately hoped no one else was already up and looking for them, but she knew there was little chance that everyone was still asleep. Ron said Mass before dawn. By now, everyone should be looking for them.

After putting the lock in his pocket, Dr. Saint-Mathias came back down the ladder and turned off the generator. The faint orange glow faded, replaced by grey dawn shadows. There was still enough light to see him carefully screw the detonator into place. "I do hope this is right. Unlike Mr. Kirkpatrick, I have no practical experience." He pointed to Sister Valentina, who was busy examining something in a corner. "Stay as still as you like. She, eventually, will wander into a wire."

He backed away carefully, picked up his gym bag, and scurried up the ladder. When he closed the door from the outside, the room plunged into total darkness. Pepper heard the combination lock being reapplied on the outside of the door. Sister Valentina began keening.

Benny whispered, "Lie down." There was no trace of whimpering now.

His head moved off of Pepper's lap. Sounds told her that Benny was dragging himself toward the Claymore. "Fucking civilians. Never put all trip wires at the same height." There were a few minutes of unidentifiable noise, then he said, "Okay, I have my hand holding the wires in place. I don't think I can keep it from going off if sister comes barreling into a trip wire and with one good hand, I can't disarm it. Pepper, crawl over to me."

Sister Valentina's voice wandered. So far it sounded as though all she was doing was bumping into walls, but one slight turn and they would all be dead.

"Damn it, Pepper, where are you?"

"Right here."

"Keep crawling. Reach ahead of you, keep your hand close to the floor, and sweep your hand until you find my body."

Her hand landed on his jeans. "Good girl. Trace up my body, until you find my left hand."

She put her hand over his.

"Feel that round thing with ridges?"

"Yes."

"It unscrews counterclockwise."

"What about static electricity? You didn't want to unscrew the one in the garden."

"It's warmer in here and we don't have any other choice. Do it!"

Pepper moved around until she cradled the front of the Claymore against her stomach. At least, if it went off, her body would absorb most of the shock. She and Benny would be dead, but Avivah and Sister Valentina might survive. She put her thumb and index finger around the detonator and gave it an experimental turn. It moved surprisingly easy. Metal turned on metal. One turn, two turns, and as something fell into her hand, the sister cried out. Wires jerked through Pepper's palms. She threw herself on the Claymore.

Nothing exploded.

Benny said, "Pepper, reach down and get my Zippo lighter out of my right boot."

She found his cold metal lighter, opened it, smelled lighter fluid, and lit it. Sister Valentina lay prone, tangled in wires. Avivah was already scrambling toward the generator. She turned it on. It whined and, slowly, lights came on. Avivah went to untangle the sister from her wire cobweb.

Pepper closed the lighter and tucked it in her pocket. "How did your lighter get in your boot?"

"The best moment for diversion is when something first goes down. While you chained my ankles, I slipped my lighter into my hand; when I tripped as I got up, I shoved it into my boot." He leaned back. "Smoke and mirrors, Pepper, that's all Special Forces is, smoke and mirrors."

Yeah, but what smoke and mirrors.

"All right, ladies, let's blow this popsicle stand. Pepper, I've pretty much shot my bolt. You're going to have to do this. Pry off the back, and take out the C-4."

Pepper eyed the Claymore suspiciously, but she did what Benny said. The back popped off surprisingly easy. She looked down into a cavity filled with what looked like white modeling clay.

"Take out that white stuff."

It felt like modeling clay, too.

"Break off a good-sized chunk and roll it until it's a thick rope. No, sister, don't try to help her. We'll do arts-and-crafts with you another day." Avivah came and persuaded Sister Valentina to move to a safe distance.

"Good job. Press it along one side of the door."

Pepper got the idea. "We're going to set it on fire with your lighter, then throw something at it, like you used to do to annoy monkeys?"

Benny picked up the mass of tangled wires. "No Pepper, today we have a simple trip wire. We're going to make it go boom the easy way. I'll hold on to one end. You string the wire and bury the detonator in the C-4."

In a few minutes, Benny said. "Everybody take cover. Avivah, sit on sister if you have to. This is one time she absolutely can't wander."

Benny pulled, just like he'd pull on a string attached to a loose tooth. It required no effort at all. In the fraction of a second before the explosion, Pepper realized just how easy it would have been, on both occasions, for the Claymore pointed at her to explode. She couldn't stop shaking.

The explosion brought down tons of dust; daylight showed through the blown door. Everyone coughed.

Something fell at Pepper's feet. She squealed and jumped. Once she'd batted away enough dust, she saw it was a thick, oilcloth-wrapped square. Unwrapping it took a few seconds because there were so many layers. It was an old, leather-bound book. In the dim daylight she read the first page:

Sister Elizabeth Rose, OVM

May 1 to November 30, 1865

May God have mercy on my soul.

Chapter 23

Benny shivered, a little at first, then growing until his whole body shook. He mumbled, "I hate it when this happens."

Five minutes, Avivah thought, as she unzipped her jacket so she could wrap it around him. She couldn't have been in the flashback any longer than that. One minute she had been sitting down, her back to Benny and Pepper; the next thing she knew Benny was lying on the floor whimpering in pain, with his head in Pepper's lap. Whatever had happened, she hadn't been there at the critical moment, and Benny and Pepper could have died because she wasn't. She couldn't pretend any longer that she was okay. She needed help.

Pepper stood with her hands on her hips, body tense, looking around. "He should drink something hot. Find a container. Fill it with snow. We can burn C-4 to heat it."

What was this fascination Pepper had developed for setting C-4 on fire? This might be an emergency, but she'd gotten far too bossy for Avivah's taste.

Benny pushed away Avivah's coat. He patted the ground beside him, and said, through chattering teeth. "Keep your coat. Come here. You too, Pepper. I need both of you."

Pepper sat on his right side; Avivah, on his left. Avivah held him. Except for long hugs he'd given her when she left for Vietnam and when she returned, she'd never been this close to him before. She reveled in the closeness. Through unwashed body odors and burned-out adrenaline, she smelled essence of

Benny. Her friend. She understood how animals could recognize one another by smell.

Sister Valentina padded over to the group. She lay down, her head on Benny's thigh. Her cloak spread itself over his shackled legs like a black ginkgo leaf. She looked up at them with vacant eyes. Benny reached down and touched her cheek. "Yeah, you, too, sister."

After a few minutes, he stopped shaking.

Pepper started to get up. "I'll go for help."

Benny's uninjured hand fluttered in a little *stay* movement. "Not yet. Our idiot professor might be watching. He wouldn't want to leave until he knew we'd blown ourselves up. I'm betting he can't tell the difference between a little C-4 blowing the doors and a full-fledged Claymore ripping us apart. Let's give him time to make his next stupid mistake. Besides, I don't think we're that far from the convent. If anyone heard an explosion, they'll come to investigate."

He hugged both women, taking care to protect his injured right hand. His voice sounded husky. "God, I've missed both of you. I can't tell you how many times in the past few months I wished we were back at Fort Bragg together. I never thought going back to Missouri would be so lonesome."

The three of them had been together only two months at Fort Bragg: between when Pepper reported in and Avivah left for Vietnam. Avivah remembered them as two golden months, filled with friendship, danger, and, eventually, fun. She said, "I made a mistake going to Vietnam. If I hadn't been so stupid, we'd have had a whole year together."

Benny patted her hand. "You would have spent every day of that year wondering what you'd missed by not going. You were ready. It was time."

Avivah pulled her arm away and hugged her chest. "When I arrived in Long Bien, my military police commander refused to allow me to report for duty. He ordered me to remain in transient quarters. To him I was a package—military police officer, female, one each—and he refused delivery. I sat on my ass in quarters for twenty-seven days."

Benny nodded. "Then all hell broke loose."

Had Benny kept track of her? What if he already knew what she'd tried so hard to hide? She studied his face. There was no secret knowledge reflected there, no pity or anger. He'd just been a soldier long enough to know that, after a while, no matter where you were in Vietnam, all hell broke loose.

Words rolled out. She didn't try to stop them. "He showed up in my quarters one morning at 0200 hours, and threw a flak jacket, helmet, and sidearm at me. He said he needed me on duty. I reminded him that I wasn't part of the brigade because I'd never signed in. He told me that he'd backdated his records. According to his duty log, I'd been under his command since the day I arrived. If I knew what was good for me, I'd come along without asking questions."

Pepper pursed her lips. "Who was this bastard?"

"I won't tell you his name."

"I still remember how to make MARS calls to Vietnam. I can find out in twenty-four hours." Pepper made it sound as though finding out the officer's name was a challenge she would enjoy.

"So can I." Benny made it sound like a threat.

She jumped to her feet and began pacing. "I know either of you can find out. Why the hell do you think I haven't told you any of this?"

Sister Valentina whimpered and pulled herself tighter into a little ball. Benny reached down to stroke her head. "Stop yelling, you're scaring sister. It's all right, sister, just close your eyes."

Avivah rested her forehead against the cold rock wall and hugged herself so tightly that she had trouble breathing.

"Promise me you won't ever try to find out who he is. Both of you. Ever. For the rest of your lives."

"Give me one good reason to promise that." Pepper sounded defiant. She probably thought this was still a game.

Avivah spun around. "You've been so all-fired anxious to hear what happened to me in 'Nam. This is the price and it's not negotiable."

Benny's gaze was bone-chillingly cold. "My price—not negotiable—is a straight story from you. No holdout, no half truths. Otherwise, Pepper, me, and a few ex-berets I know go after this mystery man and get his version, by whatever means works. We're all civilians now. That loyalty oath we signed only applied to what we learned on active duty. I guarantee you, if we go after your story, the gloves will be off."

Benny had never come close to threatening her before and the fire in his voice left no room for doubt. She wavered. "There are parts I can't tell you because of national security." God, she sounded like Darby.

Benny's gaze didn't budge. "Then tell us everything right up to those parts."

Avivah sat down across the room from them. Telling her story would be impossible if they were trying to be warm and cuddly. She took a deep breath. "He drove me to a remote part of an American compound. It looked deserted. There was tall grass and empty quonset huts all around us. He ordered me to shoot anyone who came at me."

Pepper considered for a minute. "Did you consider that a lawful order?"

Soldiers weren't required to obey unlawful orders, though regulations were vague on what constituted an unlawful order. It surprised Avivah that Pepper, not Benny asked that question. Maybe hanging around Darby had sensitized Pepper to finer points of being a combat officer.

"Hell no. Despite what he said, I knew I'd never officially reported, never been oriented, and sure as hell not briefed on what was going down. By then I was desperate just to be accepted. I thought it might be a snipe hunt, a way to scare the new woman. See what she was made of or send her running to personnel asking for a transfer."

Benny asked, "How long did it take you to find out it was no snipe hunt?"

"About an hour and a half. It was a storm-the-front-door operation, and I had their back door. Only no one really believed there was a back door. I'd been set to guard what wasn't supposed to exist, just so he could show he'd gone by the book by posting a rear sentry. The guy popped out of a hole in the ground, and fired at me. He missed and I took him down. Robert Johnson, private first class, eighteen. He had thirty-six days to go in-country."

Benny said, very gently, "We've all seen friendly fire deaths."

Heat rose in Avivah's face. "Seen, not been responsible for, unless there's something you've held back on me, Mister Sergeant First Class Ex–Special Forces Kirkpatrick."

She and Benny glared at one another. She'd never imagined there could be a gulf this wide between them, but something she couldn't name had just changed in their relationship. He reached down to stroke Sister Valentina's head once more, as if the gesture comforted himself. "No, not been responsible for."

Pepper said, "You acted the way a police officer was supposed to act in a raid."

Benny's voice sounded wary. "This wasn't an ordinary police takedown. 'He came up out of a hole in the ground.' A tunnel, not the back door of a building. Some weird shit went down that night."

Avivah took a deep breath in an effort to stop trembling. "This is as far as I can tell you about that night. We stop here."

Pepper asked, "Could you tell us if we were still on active duty?"

"Not even then. If I blow this, I will end up in Leavenworth."

Fort Leavenworth was a military prison. Hard time. End of her career. Stripped of all rank, all benefits, all hope of ever being a police officer again, with her own rap sheet for murder.

Benny was quiet for a long time. "Slide on by what happened. Take us out the other side. What happened after that night?"

Gratitude gradually replaced fear. Benny wasn't going to press her for what she couldn't tell him. "I lied to military investigations about deaths of U.S. soldiers in Vietnam."

Benny cocked his head, "Investigations, plural?"

"Three."

Benny hit the dirt floor with his left fist. "Lady, you are in deep shit. The Army doesn't mount three separate investigations for something small. Was this bastard, who you won't name, aware that you'd lied?"

"Yes."

"Before or after you lied?"

"Both."

Pepper asked, "Did he order you to lie?"

"He never gave me a direct order."

Pepper wouldn't leave it alone. "An indirect order? Innuendo? Threat?"

"He showed me an efficiency report, which said I was promiscuous and that my promiscuity compromised brigade order and conduct. If he filed that report, I'd not only be on a plane home, but headed for a discharge without prejudice."

From the anger in Benny's eyes, Avivah knew she'd made the right decision to withhold her commander's name. Otherwise, right now, he'd be dead meat.

Benny said, "There had to be other military police officers

privy to what happened that night."

"The others all transferred out within a couple of weeks. My commander didn't trust women. He told me that often enough. He wanted to keep me where he could keep his eye on me. Until he rotated home, he was scared to let me out of his sight. I had to work only shifts he worked, which meant straight days. I couldn't go anywhere, even to the officers' club, post exchange, or off-compound, without his permission. He'd show up wherever I was, as though he were following me."

Pepper looked as if she sucked on a sour lemon. "How long before rumors got around?"

"You mean the rumors that I was his mistress and his personal property? Not long."

Benny asked, "Before he rotated home, did he give you an Officer's Efficiency Report?"

"Yes."

"There are ways of protesting a bad OER."

Drained and exhausted, Avivah leaned back against the wall. "Yeah, but no way to protest to a good report. After months of threatening to give me an efficiency rating that would destroy me, he gave me a wonderful report and a Bronze Star for valor."

Pepper pulled her eyebrows together. Her thinking face. "You weren't wearing a valor decoration when we met you in San Francisco. I would have noticed."

"I took it off. He got me coming and going. Who's going to listen to complaints about a great report and a medal for valor? Uniform regulations say I must wear the damn thing and, every time I do, I feel dirty and dishonest. A woman officer, a Vietnam veteran, with a 'V' on her Bronze Star. Do you have any idea how curious that makes other officers? Every fucking person I meet wants to know my story and I can't say a thing. He even mailed a copy of the citation to my mother. It was all I could do to convince her not to call local papers and make a big splash.

Can you see me telling any part of this story to a reporter?"

Benny said, "That's why you freaked in New York when the reporter tried to interview you about Central Park."

Her breath came in sharp gasps. "I cannot, now or ever, talk to a reporter. I can not have the press checking my background."

Benny said, "It's going to come out eventually, Avivah. How many guys were involved the night you can't talk about?"

"Five."

"Five men cannot keep a secret. Someone, somewhere will blow this story."

"It won't be me."

Pepper looked confused. "I don't know what we're talking about. Blow what story? That Avivah got a medal? We all got medals."

Benny said patiently, "That Avivah got a medal for being involved in something that, in all likelihood, will blow Lieutenant Calley and My Lai off the front pages."

Two years earlier, Lieutenant William Calley had been court-martialed and sentenced to life imprisonment for premeditated murder of Vietnamese civilians. Some Americans had never gotten over the rancor and bitter taste that their red-white-and-blue boys could be that kind of killer. It was part of what fueled the hatred Benny felt from his neighbors.

Benny added, "Something that fucking commander of hers knew she lied about, condoned the lies, and gave her a medal for doing. Oh, he screwed you coming and going all right, and there's not a damn thing you can do about it."

"You're right, Benny. Right this minute, some other guy who was there, is sitting stoned or drunk on his ass, building up a head of steam to go public. When he does, I'm going to be in deep, deep trouble. I figure I've got, at most, a few months before it leaks. You know what hurts most? I never made a friend the whole time I was in Vietnam. Guys either avoided me because they thought I was the commander's private property, or they figured if he had a piece of my ass they could, too. War is one of the greatest bonding experiences human beings experience, and I never made a single fucking friend the whole time I was there. That's what hurts the most."

The *whoop, whoop, whoop* of a police siren broke the early morning stillness, an electronic equivalent of the Appalachian custom called "helloing the house." Sister Valentina jerked awake and sat up, looking confused.

Pepper looked pale and shaken. "I'd say the sheriff just arrived. I wonder how far behind him the reporters are?"

CHAPTER 24

When no rescue appeared, Avivah and Pepper argued about who would go for help. Pepper wanted to scout for reporters. Avivah insisted Benny needed Pepper to stay with him in case he went into shock again. Benny settled the argument by thinking of a number between one and ten. Avivah went for help.

She brought back two middle-aged men, who wore ragged ski pants and red nylon jackets with swirling silver letters: *Newland Volunteer Fire and Rescue Squad.* They carried a bolt cutter, a first aid kit in a dented fishing tackle box, and a surplus Army stretcher. Pepper's heart gave a little tug when she saw the latter. She'd lost count of how many times she'd hosed blood from identical stretchers in Qui Nhon.

One, then another, familiar face popped up around the blown doors, peering down, until they made a circle of faces. Sister Mary Rachel, Darby, Father Ron, General Bill, Helen, and Patience. Father and the two nuns crossed themselves, no doubt relieved to see everyone alive.

Pepper half-expected Sister Valentina to say, "Hello, I'm glad to see you." But the sister had retreated into her own darkness again. She wandered, touching walls, as if she expected to find a way out.

A third stranger elbowed an opening through the little crowd and climbed down the ladder. He wore an Avery County sheriff's uniform. When he reached the ground, he nodded to Avivah and gave a little tug on the brim of his hat. "Captain

Rosen. Good to see you again, ma'am."

Pepper bet Avivah was the first woman deputy in the Avery County sheriff's office. She doubted the sheriff tipped his hat to male deputies. She stood. "You must be the sheriff."

"Acting sheriff. Sheriff Daniels picked a hell of a time to be away on vacation." He held out his hand, which Pepper shook. "Rabon Walker. Most people call me Rab."

She liked him immediately. He had a laid-back, good-old-boy demeanor, but there was nothing slow about the expression in Rab Walker's eyes. "Elizabeth Pepperhawk. Most people call me Pepper."

Avivah said, "You need to issue a be-on-the-lookout request for Dr. Yancy Saint-Mathias of Baton Rouge, Louisiana. He probably had a car stashed near here, make and model unknown. He has a handgun and an unknown number of Claymores."

Rab looked confused. "Claymores? Like those things they use in Vietnam?"

"I'll explain later."

"Is Dr. Saint-Mathias our killer?"

"He says not, but I'd give you fifty-fifty odds that he is. Just say he's armed and dangerous, and wanted for questioning about events at the Visitation Convent."

As she herded Sister Valentina toward the ladder, Pepper thought Dr. Saint-Mathias was mostly a danger to himself. If the professor didn't like war up-close and personal, she wondered how he'd respond to an armed police officer. She'd maneuvered Sister Valentina to the bottom of the ladder, placed her hands on the rungs, and said, "Go on, climb."

For all her problems, the sister was surprisingly agile.

Pepper called up to Sister Mary Rachel. "There's a small generator down here. It's big enough to run your furnace pump."

The sister looked dubious. "Maybe. If our oil isn't frozen solid."

One of the rescue squad—"Bud," according to the name embroidered over his right front pocket—said, "Sister, as soon as we get our man here fixed up, we'll haul that generator for you."

Pepper looked dubiously at Bud and his partner, "Junior." She wasn't sure she wanted to turn her precious Benny over to them. "I'll help you. I'm a nurse."

Benny waived away her offer. "Let's give these guys a chance to use those first aid classes they sat through."

She was grateful that he wanted to spare her being there when they peeled the chain from his macerated ankles. Truth to tell, it wasn't something she wanted to watch.

Junior said, "He's right, miss. We spend a lot of drafty Thursday nights sitting through classes down to the fire hall, just for something like this. We'll fix him up, then take him to the hospital when we take . . . the others."

He meant Gary's and Thomas' bodies. It wouldn't be the first time Benny rode out with body bags, but a little bit of Pepper's heart hoped it would be the last. She also hoped he would be able to sit in the cab instead of riding on a stretcher. Being in close proximity to those bodies wasn't going to be pleasant.

She gave Benny a quick hug and left him with his dignity intact, so Bud and Junior could do what had to be done. Tucking Sister Elizabeth Rose's diary safely in her coat, she climbed out of the under basement. Avivah and Rab followed her up the ladder.

It was a gorgeous morning, bluer and warmer than yesterday. Rivulets from melting ice dripped from branches, making a lovely plinking noise in the wet pine needles. A small path, big enough to accommodate one man tramping snow, wandered down the mountain through heavy woods. Tracking Dr. Saint-

Mathias should be a cinch.

Benny had been right, this under barn was only a hundred yards behind the convent. Why hadn't anyone come when they blew the doors? Had everyone been distraught after discovering five people had disappeared without a trace? Or, had a sturdy Victorian building and snow-filled woods muffled noise?

In retrospect, Pepper realized leaving a note would have been prudent. At the time, "Going downstairs to get Sister Valentina—be back in five minutes" hadn't occurred to any of them.

Avivah turned to Sister Mary Rachel. "Sister Valentina has important evidence in her cloak pocket. Can you persuade her to give it up?"

Sister Mary Rachel looked a little perplexed. "I'll try. Sister, let me see what you have in your pocket."

With gentle persuasion, Sister Valentina yielded possession of her newspaper-wrapped inkwell, which Avivah handed to Rab. Everyone crowded around.

He unwrapped it enough to see what it was, then rewrapped it. "I suppose there's an explanation?"

Avivah jiggled from foot to foot. "It's full of fingerprints, and I think Gary's clothing is, too. I'll tell you about it inside, where we can warm up and get some coffee."

Helen adjusted Sister Valentina's cloak more firmly around her. "She is cold. We must take her to get warm."

Father Ron said, "Sister, I'll check the furnace oil for you."

General Bill offered to go along and help him.

Those two men were very anxious to get to the basement. Pepper called after the little procession, "Rab, send a deputy to the basement with them. There's a secret tunnel down there."

The sheriff said to Avivah, "Is that also part of the long explanation?"

"You haven't heard anything yet."

Bolt cutters snapped, and Pepper heard a cry from Benny.

She walked a few feet away and put her arms around a birch tree, just to have something solid to hang onto. The bark was refreshingly rough against her hands. Darby came to her, and rubbed his cheek against hers to block out any sound except skin rubbing against skin.

A fire she'd never felt before began deep inside of her and rose, like a flame, pushing aside every thought until only her body consumed her. She could have him. All she had to do was say yes.

She turned to face him and pulled his mouth down to her. His cheeks were cold and smooth. She kissed him; her tongue probed his mouth, exploring and darting. The back side of his teeth felt incredibly smooth under her tongue. He'd taken time to brush his teeth. It seemed such a thoughtful thing to do under the circumstances.

Sister Mary Rachel cleared her throat.

As Pepper broke away, Darby whispered in her ear. "I wish I'd known a long time ago that Claymores had this effect on you."

Pepper looked past him. Sister Mary Rachel had a knowing smile on her face. Sister Angelus looked appalled.

He gave her a final squeeze and let go. Red-faced and breathless, Pepper covered her newfound sexual ardor by handing Sister Elizabeth Rose's journal to Sister Angelus. She opened it and both nuns read the inscription. Their mouths dropped.

Pepper said to Sister Angelus, "You said sister's diaries were silent concerning the missing deed."

At least the sister had enough decency to look chagrined. She also looked like a child who had a year's worth of birthday and Christmas presents handed to her all at once. "When Sister Elizabeth Rose's diaries came to our motherhouse after she died, this volume was missing. Sister opened her next journal with an apology for having been absent so long from her pen.

We assumed, in the months after the Civil War ended, she was too exhausted and emotionally overwhelmed to keep a journal."

Darby had suddenly acquired a look that Pepper found disconcerting. Anyone else, she would have described as desperate. He reached for the diary, but stopped himself with his fingertips a fraction of an inch away from the book, as if he were afraid to touch it . "Please, sister, may I look at that book? I have to. I just have to . . . Under your supervision, of course."

Sister Angelus gathered oilcloth folds around the precious book. "Not until I have it safe inside. You will wash your hands and wear gloves."

As she struggled through partially tramped snow toward the convent, Pepper couldn't figure out what could be so blasted important to Darby about a hundred-and-seven year-old diary.

Once inside the convent, she started to follow Darby and Sister Angelus down the hall, but changed her mind. Except when she'd been pinned under the tree, she hadn't been alone since Friday. What she desperately needed right now was a few moments of privacy. She climbed to the third floor, found the niche housing the Sacred Heart statue, and wedged herself in at its foot. She felt safe there, with the statue against her back and an open view spread out before her.

Everything below was foreshortened. Avivah and Rab stood talking next to the sheriff's car. Parked next to it was a battered 1957 Chevy pickup. Bud or Junior probably had it up on blocks in his barn. No doubt, Rab pressed the old truck into service, as he'd done with Toby and his ersatz dog team. She hoped Toby and the dogs were finally somewhere warm.

Pepper sighed and leaned back against the statue. Rab would take over now. She and Avivah had held until relieved. Just like that order given to a British airborne commander before D-day. Take a bridge over the River Orne, and hold until relieved, which they did until Peter Lawford, President Kennedy's brother-in-law, showed up, accompanied by a bagpiper playing "Blue Bonnets over the Border."

Those details didn't quite make sense, but Pepper was too tired to care. No doubt, she'd combined memories of Darby's military history rambles and watching *The Longest Day*. Or maybe Darby had delivered the ramble while they watched *The Longest Day*. What mattered was that she and Avivah had lived through this weekend.

Certainly they'd taken casualties. Gary. Thomas. Benny. Avivah was walking wounded. If Rab had ordered Avivah to solve the murder, they hadn't achieved their mission objective, but if he'd only ordered her to investigate, they were, as she said in Vietnam, "Number one, G.I."

The words flowing through her head embarrassed her. How had Miss Elizabeth Pepperhawk, a nice, middle-class, southern girl, who wouldn't say boo to anyone, come to think in such military jargon? Nice ladies didn't . . . didn't what? Something her mother had said a long time ago.

She was four, taking a Sunday afternoon ride with her parents. They passed what seemed to her an unending lawn of perfect grass, flowers, and white buildings, surrounded by a green wrought iron fence. It would be years before she knew it was the Biloxi Veterans' Administration Hospital. At age four, the only other place she'd seen with a fence like that was the New Orleans zoo.

She'd asked, "Is that a zoo?"

Her father laughed, as though she'd said something terribly funny. "I guess you could say that."

Her mother slapped him on the arm. "Don't tease her like that. Honey, that's where they take care of sick soldiers." She'd added, more to herself than to Pepper, "Nice ladies don't go there."

Her mother had been wrong.

She tallied dates on her fingers. That Sunday must have happened the year after Thomas earned his Medal of Honor.

Pepper realized, with a shock, that she was a veteran now and herself entitled to benefits. She had only the vaguest idea what they were. What had she heard her patients talk about? Medical care for service-connected injuries or illnesses. That didn't apply to her, because unlike Benny, she had no service-connected injury. Money for education? Something about a house loan?

With a VA loan, she could buy a house. The thought shocked and scared her. She'd never known an unmarried woman who owned her own house. She had no idea how much a mortgage payment might be. Could she afford it on a nurses' salary? Did being a veteran mean a VA Hospital had to give her job preference? She wished she'd at least looked at that packet.

There was a veterans' hospital in Asheville; she'd discharged many of her patients there from Fort Bragg. A job in Asheville with the Veterans' Administration, and a house. It was better than no plans at all, which were what she had when she came here. Beggars couldn't be choosy, she thought as she watched Bud and Junior emerge from the woods, each carrying one end of Benny's stretcher. Pepper automatically evaluated their technique with a practiced eye. Not bad. Maybe it had been okay to leave Benny in their care.

The pantry was the only place Pepper could think of where Benny could have privacy and a nap. She helped him stretch out on their mattress. Thick bandages covered his ankles, and a plastic bag packed with snow served as an ice bag for his splinted right hand. Confined with him, behind a closed door, Pepper realized how much Benny smelled. She went to find a basin of water and some towels.

She looked down at the water. When Thomas brought Benny in unconscious, taking care of him had been an emergency.

Bathing him was different. There were some intimacies she had no desire to share with Benny. "I haven't been this nervous about giving someone a bath since my first week in nursing school."

Benny ran his hand protectively over his chest, where his shirt hid the burn scars he rarely showed anyone, even Pepper. "Tell you what. What I really want to do is brush my teeth. Help me do that and wash my face, and we'll call it quits."

It was as much patient-nurse relationship as either of them could stand. Pepper put the glass and toothbrush on a pantry shelf. "Is it pure and noble to tend wounded soldiers?"

"What brought that on?"

"A crack Avivah made."

"Oh hell, Pepper, I don't know. I never thought about it. Nurses were there for me when I needed them. Probably. Probably not. Take your choice."

It wasn't an answer that satisfied her.

Benny held up his splinted hand. "You and I have unfinished business. Finish this sentence: never let your iron head . . ."

It was a common Army phrase. Pepper felt herself blushing. "Overrule your eggshell ass."

"When you jumped Dr. Saint-Mathias, you came too damned close to getting us all killed."

"Are you saying you had a plan, and I wrecked it?"

"I was still working out a plan, when you forced the issue."

"What were you going to do with your cigarette lighter?"

"That was one of the things I was still working out. Probably try to set Saint-Mathias' clothes on fire. All that alcohol he rubbed on himself would have made his clothes vulnerable. Fire is a weapon. It was the only one I had, so it was the one I would use."

"In spite of knowing what it felt like to be burned?"

Benny's fingertips brushed his scars lightly. "Darby has done the worst possible thing he could to you. He gave you an inkling of a beret's attitude without making sure you had enough physical or mental toughness to survive. You need some serious training."

"I thought you didn't think women belonged in combat."

"They don't. I haven't changed my mind about that, and we're not talking about combat. We're talking about you not getting your partner killed in a tight situation. Until I recover from this weekend, promise me two things. First, if a bad guy is holding you and a Green Beret hostage, you'll let the Green Beret decide when it's time to do the takedown."

"I don't plan on being held hostage with a Green Beret, or anyone else, any time soon."

"Promise me, okay? I can't bear the thought of turning you loose to wreak havoc on any of my former team members you might meet in civilian life. I like most of those guys."

"All right, I promise. What's the second thing?"

"Get in shape. Build muscle and stamina. I can only teach you so much. The rest will be up to you."

"All that packing and cleaning *did* build muscles."

"No, all it did was give your body an illusion that muscles might be a possibility. If you'd had real muscle, and knew how to use it, you would have lain Dr. Saint-Mathias out cold."

Pepper looked down at her lap. "And you wouldn't be hurt."

The blankets moved as Benny tentatively wiggled his toes. "There's no permanent damage. Let's just think of this as a training exercise. People get hurt all the time in training exercises."

If he could let go of blaming her, Pepper decided she could let go of blaming herself. "How much muscle?"

"Start with *some,* then we'll see."

There was a knock and, without waiting for an answer, Father Ron opened the door and looked in.

Benny said, "Hi, padre, visiting the sick?"

Lights came on. Accustomed to only candlelight for three days, Pepper felt her pupils slam shut. Benny, who had been looking straight at the ceiling bulb, groaned and threw his uninjured hand over his eyes. A puff of cold, dusty air came up through the floor vent. Apparently, the furnace had started, too. In the harsh light, Ron's face looked absolutely white.

"Father, you better sit down."

Benny scooted over as much as he could, and Ron sat. Father said, "We have a problem."

As if the whole weekend hadn't been one problem after another.

"Saturday, when you paired me to work with Thomas, I knew he had something on his mind. We talked and, eventually, Thomas asked questions about confession and forgiveness. I thought he still felt guilty about what had happened Friday night. I offered to hear his confession, but he said he confessed a long time ago."

Father Ron reached in a pocket of his cassock and took out two sheets of paper. He handed the first one to Pepper. "I just found this in my suitcase, folded inside my spare cassock."

She read out loud. "Father, please do this for me. Thank you. I never understood about reparation before. Tom."

He handed her the second piece of paper.

December 2, 1972
Visitation Convent
Crossnore, North Carolina

My name is Thomas Hackmann and I live in Lakeland, Florida. This is my last will. There is another will in my father's safety deposit box at our United Service Bank in Lakeland. Tear that one up, and use this one instead.

I don't know the proper words that lawyers use to write

a will, so I hope using just English is all right.

On December 3, 1950, in South Korea, I was responsible for the death of my immediate superior, Captain Ernest C. Kraft, of Topeka, Kansas.

Captain Kraft had three children. They are grown now, and I don't know where they are. To make reparation to them for what I did to their father, please find them. I want any money coming to me from sale or rental of this convent to go to them. If no one can find them, or they are dead, I want my money to go to a scholarship for children whose father died or was listed as missing in action at Chosin Reservoir.

Thomas Darby Hackmann

Pepper's head reeled. She handed the will to Benny.

His response echoed her own. "Oh, shit."

Ron's voice was flat. "I think Thomas killed Gary and then committed suicide."

Avivah had called Gary's death beserker rage. Pepper wondered if Captain Kraft had looked anything like Gary and if he had died by being garroted. There had been a lot of cooking smells that night. While she doubted anyone was cooking fish and broccoli at Chosin, odors produced very individual responses. Had cold, snow, and a triggering smell, coming on the twentieth anniversary of what he did at Chosin, unhinged Thomas?

Benny asked, "How did Thomas know about the tunnel? He would have had to in order to hide Gary's body there."

Oh, drat. As far as they knew, Thomas had only been to the convent once before, when the SPF board came as a group. Pepper said, "He had an accomplice. Someone who moved the body and perhaps cleared away any evidence that Thomas hanged himself."

As soon as she spoke, Pepper wished she'd kept her mouth shut. All remaining color drained from Ron's face. He whispered, "I hadn't thought of that."

Five people likely knew about the tunnel: Dr. Saint-Mathias, Helen, Patience, Sister Mary Rachel, and Sister Angelus. Dr. Saint-Mathias was unlikely to be Thomas' coconspirator. It didn't fit with his self-serving attitude. Helen, Patience, and Sister Mary Rachel had no reason to help him, but Sister Angelus did. She was furious with Sister Mary Rachel. Just as taking the beds apart for firewood inconvenienced General Bill, so hiding Gary's body and the ink-stained writing desk had made life more difficult for Sister Mary Rachel. How ironic that the basement, the site of Sister Angelus' original injury, could now be used for revenge.

Covering up Thomas' suicide, or even worse helping him commit suicide, was a far more serious matter. In the eyes of the Church, assisting a suicide in any way was a mortal sin. Father Ron must have just realized that his sister could be capable not only of breaking the law, but of committing a sin that would condemn her soul to hell.

Pepper took the papers and grasped Ron's hand firmly. She wasn't about to let him go to his sister right now. "We have to show this to Avivah right away."

She held the pages close to her chest. Sister Angelus' culpability wasn't the only thing these papers implied. Avivah was sure to spot what Pepper hoped both men had missed: Thomas Darby Hackmann and Darby Randolph Baxter shared a name. Darby wasn't that common a southern name. It often ran in families. There was some relationship between Darby and Thomas, and she intended to find out what.

A tentative voice came from the kitchen. "Hello? Anyone here?"

Pepper opened the pantry door. Kitchen lights shined on a

tall man in his early thirties. His stringy, black hair badly needed cutting. Or maybe it had been badly cut. His eyes were red and watery. A bent paperclip held his thick glasses together at one temple. He wore a pair of brown, polyester pants, so old they pilled, and a faded shirt. Even from several feet away, she could tell he smelled worse than Benny did. What had he been doing, wallowing in a pig's sty?

She asked, "Can I help you?"

He looked down at a pad of paper in his right hand. "I'm looking for Acting Sheriff Walker or Deputy Rosen."

"And you are?"

"Saul Eisenberg. *Watagua Democrat,* Boone, North Carolina."

He was probably a stringer, a reporter wannabe, paid a few dollars for each story about Rotary Club meetings or elementary school Christmas pageants. No doubt, he'd been drafted, like Toby and his dogs, or Avivah being made a deputy sheriff. Pepper concluded Saul Eisenberg couldn't find a real story if he tripped over it. He didn't look like a reporter who would have the faintest idea about digging into Avivah's background. Still. "You definitely want Acting Sheriff Walker. He's in charge. Deputy Rosen won't be of any help to you."

Thank you, Lord. Avivah's luck had finally changed.

CHAPTER 25

When the phone in Sister Mary Rachel's office rang, Avivah gave a little shriek. She hated herself for being so jumpy. She should have expected phone service soon after the lights came on. She desperately hoped it wasn't a reporter.

Rab answered. "Visitation Convent, Sheriff Walker."

There was a loud knock. Rab turned his back to the office door and put his finger in his ear. "I'm listening."

Listening, not talking. That didn't sound like a reporter. Relieved, Avivah got up and opened the door. Pepper and Father Ron looked so frightened that "Who died now?" slipped out before she stopped to think.

Pepper said, "No one" with an air that made Avivah almost wish someone had died. Whatever they had come to talk about wasn't good. Ron sat on the couch.

Pepper pulled Avivah into the hall. She whispered, "A reporter named Saul Eisenberg, from the *Watauga Democrat,* just arrived."

Avivah's heart thumped. She forced herself to breathe slowly. She could handle this; she had to handle it.

Pepper rubbed her hand over Avivah's back and made soothing noises. "It's okay. You got lucky. He's a stringer for a little mountain newspaper in Boone. It's not like he's David Brinkley or anyone important. Besides, I think he might be Jewish."

"You think? With a name like Saul Eisenberg?"

"He's a ditz. He looks as if he can't remember his last haircut or square meal. He probably lives with his mother, but I doubt she picks his clothes. Believe me, this guy is no threat. Dazzle him with your *mazel tov* and he won't know what hit him."

"*Mazel tov?*"

"I'm probably not pronouncing it right. Attitude. Up close and personal."

Despite her fear, Avivah laughed. "I think you mean *chutzpah. Mazel tov* means good luck or congratulations."

Pepper put both hands on Avivah's shoulders. "Then *mazel tov*, you've ended up with a reporter you can wrap around your little finger."

Avivah wasn't convinced. "Where is he?"

"Eating. He's one of those string-bean types who looks as though he's never full. I told him Sheriff Walker was who he needed to talk to, and that he was in conference. Then I pointed him toward the stove, and told him to cook whatever appealed to him. He looked as if he'd found Nirvana."

Rab came to the door "Am I interrupting?"

"Pepper just wanted to tell me a reporter showed up. Saul Eisenberg. *Watauga Democrat.* Do you know him?"

"I read the *Democrat,* but I never heard of him."

Pepper gave her a *see, what did I tell you look,* then scooted in, and sat down beside Ron. She took his hand. Oh, great, now Pepper was holding hands with a Jesuit priest.

Rab looked at his notebook. "A state police officer—who, incidentally, was a marine in Vietnam—stopped your boy just this side of Blowing Rock. They had a safety check set up to advise travelers and make sure people had chains."

Pepper asked, "Did he have Claymores with him?"

"Twenty-four of them, under a blanket in his trunk. He claimed he never saw them before, had no idea what they were. He suggested the farmer he paid to store his car must have put them there."

Pepper looked disgusted. "How stupid does he think we are? We can shred his story in a minute."

Avivah reminded her, "There was an explosion. He thinks we're dead or in no shape to make statements."

"I think Louisiana State University better start looking for a new history professor, don't you?"

Rab said, "I'd say that's a good possibility."

Avivah and Rab looked at Pepper and Ron. They looked back, then they looked at one another, as if encouraging each other to say something first. Finally, Avivah asked, "Is there something we can do for you?"

Pepper gave Ron's hand a squeeze. "We have to tell them."

He nodded.

Please don't let them tell her they'd fallen in love. Avivah didn't think she could handle that today, though an imaginary headline gave her a moment of malicious pleasure. "Ex-Army Nurse in Love Nest with Priest" might push her off tabloid front pages. Not that, even on her worst day, she'd wish that kind of publicity for either Pepper or Ron. Then there was Darby. He already acted eternally grateful because she'd agreed to receive letters for Pepper. She had no desire to explain Pepper and a priest to him.

Ron took papers from his pocket and handed them to Rab. Avivah read them over Rab's shoulder. It wasn't really a suicide note, but it came close enough she bet it could be admitted as evidence in court. Thomas Hackmann hadn't been murdered. He'd committed suicide. She asked, "Where did you get this?"

Ron said, "I thought I might clean up a little and change clothes. It was folded in my spare cassock, at the bottom of my suitcase."

Rab asked, "Any of you familiar with Mr. Hackmann's handwriting?"

Everyone shook his or her head.

"First thing I'll have to do is get this handwriting verified. That shouldn't be hard. Let's assume for now it's genuine. Where does that leave us?"

Rab and Avivah listened while Pepper explained her theory about Korea and flashbacks. When she finished, he said, "So you're telling me that something that happened twenty-two years ago led Hackmann to commit a murder now?"

Avivah asked, "You ever do military service?"

"Peacetime Navy."

"Any of your shipmates ever think they were back in World War II or Korea?"

He looked uneasy. "Sometimes, especially at night. You want me to believe, after over twenty years, these flashbacks were still strong enough to make Hackmann believe he was back at Chosin Reservoir?"

Avivah rubbed her hands over her arms. Just contemplating enduring twenty years of flashbacks confirmed Pepper's suicide theory for her. If her flashbacks kept happening, she wasn't going to be alive in twenty years. Thomas might have looked like an invalid, but he'd been one tough man. In the end, memories killed him.

Pepper had more theory. "I think Thomas passed the museum and saw Gary, maybe bent over looking at Ermengarde Hackmann's writing desk, or even trying to steal it. Something—a sight, a smell; there were cooking odors that night—triggered a flashback. He was in Korea; Captain Kraft was doing something that would get him and his buddies killed. He responded as he had in Korea."

Rab fiddled with paper clips from the sister's desk, stringing them into a long chain. "Then he used going for help as a way to escape, only when Avivah sent Mr. Kirkpatrick with him, he drugs the guy, but instead of escaping, he carries him back here. That makes no sense."

Avivah thought about that chaotic Friday night. "General Bill was pushing him to be a hero. By the time Benny and Thomas went for help, Thomas might not have remembered killing Gary. He might have honestly thought he was going for help."

"So when Mr. Kirkpatrick passed out, why didn't Hackmann keep going?"

Pepper said, "More history repeating itself. When you check Thomas' Medal of Honor citation, I think you'll find that he carried Captain Kraft's body back rather than leave it to be defiled by the Chinese."

"So, we fast-forward to Saturday afternoon. Hackmann remembers what he did and talks to father. Guilt takes over. He writes his will and commits suicide."

Ron looked sick. "I've gone over and over everything Thomas and I said. Yes, I thought he was depressed. Gary dying that way, plus everything else we'd endured in the previous twenty-four hours depressed me, too. None of us were thinking clearly by that time. Yes, I thought he felt guilty about something, but there was no one thing he said or did that pointed to him being suicidal."

Avivah realized what was wrong with this theory. "Suicide doesn't wash. He could have strung a rope, put it around his neck, and stepped off the laundry room table, but there were no footprints, no marks. Who cleaned up after him?"

Ron's voice sounded choked. "My sister."

Avivah felt empty, as if all hope had just drained out of her body. She would have done almost anything to spare Ron the pain of his sister being an accessory to murder and suicide. She said to Rab, "Sister Angelus is father's oldest sister."

Ron continued, "As a young woman, she was injured in an accident at this convent. That accident has been on her mind a lot lately."

Rab rubbed his hand over his chin. "Is she having flashbacks, too?"

Ron faltered, "I don't know." He turned to Pepper. "Can civilians have flashbacks, too?"

She considered. "I don't know. Maybe."

Father Ron asked Rab, "Does Bryn Mawr mean anything to you?"

"No."

Avivah said, "It's an old, very prestigious woman's university near Philadelphia."

"Angelina fit in well there. She was brilliant, first as a student, later as a teacher and researcher, but she wasn't happy. The students she taught often came from privileged families. Angelina came to believe God gave her a vocation to teach with less fortunate girls. Her accident took away her chance to do that."

Pepper said, "After she was injured, she wasn't strong enough to teach?"

Ron looked sad. "No. More important, she wasn't the scholar she had been. She was still very, very good, way above average, but no longer brilliant. Instead of an international reputation and possibly, one day, presidency of a woman's college, she became the historian for a minor religious order. She has spent her life contending with the hierarchy of the planet's most male-dominated, tradition-bound organization."

Brought to that fate, Sister Angelus believed, by a poor, uneducated mountain girl, just the kind of girl that the sister had imagined herself helping. A girl who was now her superior. Rab asked, "How long ago did this accident happen?"

Avivah understood Sister Angelus' bitterness now. "Thirty years ago, but a few months ago, Sister Mary Rachel, with nothing but good intentions, made Sister Angelus think about that event."

Ron said, "She's been so angry for months that I've been

afraid for her health. I think she either witnessed Gary's murder, or arrived shortly after it happened. Thomas was a lost and confused soul. When she was younger, my sister felt great compassion for the lost and confused. She might have moved Gary's body to help him, so fingerprints on Gary's clothes wouldn't implicate him."

It hurt for Avivah to bring a little perspective, but good perspective was good police work. "Or she might have done it just to cause problems for Sister Mary Rachel."

Ron didn't disagree.

Rab said, "Lugging a body around would be pretty risky."

It would have helped if he'd spent that crazy Saturday with them. Avivah said, "Not as much as you imagine. There was a lot of time on Saturday when we were all busy, searching for firewood, or freeing Pepper. It probably wouldn't have taken more than half an hour to move Gary's body. I doubt a person's absence for thirty minutes would have been noticed."

Pepper added, "She knew about the dumbwaiter, tunnel, and gurney. She'd spent a lot of time with Dr. Saint-Mathias recently. He wasn't as smart as he liked to believe. He might have dropped hints that he'd found and opened the tunnel, or she might have seen him going into the under barn on one of his *walks*. I'm sorry, Ron, but there's a good chance sister led me to the basement so I would discover Thomas' body."

"But Miss Rosen said you both fainted when you found the body."

"Fainting is easy to fake. Since I fainted a moment later, I didn't have a chance to examine her thoroughly. When I came around, she was already sitting up."

Avivah changed her mind about the ultra cleanliness of the basement. Obsessive cleaning staff wasn't responsible. "She cleaned the laundry room after Thomas died. It's possible he left not only his will in Ron's luggage, but a suicide note as well. Sister might have removed it."

Ron looked uncertain. "I don't think he'd leave a note. Suicide is a sin, and a suicide victim can't be buried in consecrated ground. Thomas and I talked a lot about his father. He loved his father, who is a devout Catholic. Leaving only a will leaves the suicide question open."

Avivah thought of a more prosaic reason. "Sister probably also had to tidy up evidence of moving Gary's body and it would have looked strange to clean everywhere else and leave the laundry untidy."

Rab stood. "Where will I find Sister Angelus?"

CHAPTER 26

The convent looked so normal it seemed bizarre. It was warm enough that, for the first time in four days, everyone wore only indoor clothing. With lights on and drapes open, Sister Mary Rachel's office had a tired appearance.

The sister herself stood in the corridor outside her office door, glaring at Rab, who had his arm across the door opening.

"As Sister Angelus' superior, and a representative of our Mother Superior, I must be present when you interview her."

"When you show me you are a member of the North Carolina Bar Association, you may act as sister's legal council. Otherwise, no." He shut and locked the door.

Sister Angelus, her face pale, sat in a chair. "Thank you. I've had about all of that woman I can take."

Pepper sat in a corner, ready to work the now-plugged-in tape recorder and take notes. She remembered her own aching need for privacy that morning. "You know, if you wedge yourself in that alcove on the third floor, with the statue; no one bothers you."

Sister Angelus gave her a wan smile. "I'll add that to my list of hidey-holes."

Pepper was glad when Rab joined Avivah on the couch, instead of taking the more formal chair behind Sister Mary Rachel's desk. She had a feeling Sister Angelus would need all their encouragement to get through this interview.

Rab said, "Miss Pepperhawk, please start the tape."

Pepper did, and Rab recited time, date, and people present, then advised Sister Angelus of her rights, finishing with, "Do you understand your rights."

The sister sounded old and tired. "I do."

"Do you wish to have a lawyer present?"

Sister Angelus looked at her hands. "No, not right now."

Rab said, "Please state your full name."

"My given name was Angelina Theresa Lincoln. My religious name is Sister Mary Angelus."

Rab established that the sister had lived at Crossnore for over a year and that, before this weekend, had met Thomas Hackmann only once, when SPF board members came to tour in March. She'd had no other contact with him.

"When he arrived last Friday, were you surprised to see him?"

"Yes. We had no idea that Mr. Pocock-Nesbitt and the other gentlemen were coming."

"Their unexpected arrival created problems for you?"

"To save money, we've kept most of this empty building barely above freezing and heated only a few rooms comfortably. To accommodate our extra guests, I had to prepare additional rooms."

"Late Friday afternoon, you went to the visitors' parlor to tell people gathered there about sleeping arrangements."

"I did."

"Where were you immediately before that?"

"Lying down in my room."

"Why?"

"Dust in the unoccupied rooms made me short of breath."

Pepper thought that could account for her breathlessness when she arrived in the visitors' parlor.

"Were you alone in your room?"

"I was."

"What did you do after telling people about their rooms?"

"Father Lincoln and Mr. Barton accompanied me to the basement. After we checked the furnace, I finished preparing guest rooms, took a few minutes to say my evening prayers, and went to set the table for supper."

"Was anyone with you?"

"Not between the time when we left the basement, and when I went to the dining room."

"How long were you alone?"

"Probably forty-five minutes."

"Did you go to the museum during that time?"

The sister looked nervous, not scared. "No."

"Did you see Thomas Hackmann during that time?"

"No."

"Did you see Gary Dormuth, either alive or dead, during that time?"

"No."

"Any time on Friday night or Saturday, did you move Mr. Dormuth's body?"

Sister Angelus shuddered. "I did not."

"You knew a tunnel existed?"

"Yes, but I believed it to be sealed."

"Did you know Dr. Saint-Mathias had reopened that tunnel?"

"No, but I'm not surprised that he had done so."

"Did you talk with Thomas Hackmann any time on Friday or Saturday?"

"Only social conversation."

"Did he give you reason to believe he was depressed?"

"No."

"Did he seem suicidal to you?"

"He seemed distracted."

"Did you assist Thomas Hackmann to commit suicide by hanging?"

Sister Angelus gasped and crossed herself. "Absolutely not. That poor man."

"Did you find Thomas Hackmann already dead in the basement?"

"Yes, Miss Pepperhawk and I discovered his body."

"When you took Miss Pepperhawk to the basement did you already know Thomas Hackmann was dead?"

"No."

"Did you take Miss Pepperhawk there so she could discover his body?"

"No."

"Miss Pepperhawk has told us that you seemed agitated when you suggested going to the basement. Is that true?"

"I suppose I was agitated."

"Why was that?"

"I had a horrible experience there years ago."

"Yet you went down there, almost casually, to check the furnace on Friday."

"Lights and heat were on then. Father Ron and Mr. Barton were with me. Mr. Dormuth was still alive. I felt safer then."

"Did you see any suicide note Thomas might have written?"

"No."

"Did you clean any part of the basement on Saturday."

"I don't clean. I told you; I must avoid dust."

This wasn't how Pepper had expected this interview to go. Sister Angelus answered each question immediately, her voice never wavering. Pepper didn't think the sister was a whiz at lying. She began to doubt their conclusion that Sister Angelus had acted as an accomplice. For Ron's sake, she was glad. That still left them with too many unsolved mysteries.

Avivah asked, "Why didn't you tell us a tunnel existed after Gary's body disappeared?"

Pepper recognized Avivah's tone. She was slipping into bad

cop mode. Would Rab pick up that he should play the good cop?

"Sister Mary Rachel and I discussed telling you. She said she'd check the tunnel's enterance. When no one said anything about the tunnel, I assumed she'd found it still sealed and knew the body couldn't be there."

Avivah's expression hardened. "Was a tunnel mentioned in Sister Elizabeth Rose's diaries?"

"Several times. There are quite detailed passages of the sister and her girls hiding there on three separate occasions."

Avivah remained hard. "I find it difficult to believe that, as the order's historian, you've never seen that tunnel."

For the first time, Sister Angelus looked uneasy. "I wasn't historian the first time I came here, nor had I yet read Sister Elizabeth Rose's diaries. I was unconscious when Mr. Tillich carried me to safety and, by the time I recovered my health and was made historian, the tunnel had been sealed."

Avivah cranked up bad cop a notch. "You expect me to believe, in thirty years, you never asked permission to unseal it, just for one little peek? Especially after the convent closed, and you knew you'd never be able to come back here?"

"I did petition. Last year. I wanted to photograph it. Sister Mary Rachel turned down my request. She said there was nothing there."

Pepper kept waiting for Rab to jump in as good cop, but Rab folded his arms over his chest and kept quiet. Pepper realized there was a way for three to play good cop–bad cop. You added a silent cop to form a triangle. Or maybe, Rab figured if he didn't understand what was going on, it was best to keep silent. Pepper had never believed in that. Forgive me for doing this to the sister, she prayed. She tried to sound amazed. "Then you've never seen the toys."

Sister Angelus looked perplexed. "What toys?"

"There's a wonderful little sitting room down there. It looks just like a Victorian parlor. Sofas, chairs, a table, and a little cabinet full of Victorian dolls and toys. I can't even imagine how much perfectly preserved Victorian toys might be worth."

Sister Angelus, the historian, was almost salivating. She looked at Rab. "Sheriff, do you think, after poor Mr. Dormth's body has been removed, that I might have a look? For the historical record, of course."

Pepper knew one thing now. Sister Angelus had never been in the tunnel. It wasn't she who hid Gary's body.

Avivah said, "You're wrong, Pepper. Those toys are just cheap things from the nineteen-twenties. I bet older girls took younger ones down there to play house."

Sister Angelus had an animated look; her body suddenly filled with energy. "No, no they would never have done that. I've seen the notice, which sister-principal posted in 1942 after sealing the tunnel. She was very specific about penalties for any girl who was caught in the tunnel. There was a book for each year of disciplinary measures handed out. I helped a student research those books. There are no disciplinary records of any girl being in the tunnel." She sounded frustrated. "This would be so much easier if Sister Valentina were still lucid."

Pepper couldn't figure out a connection. "Because she did her novitiate here?"

"Because she was one of our girls. She would remember if there had been any stories about the tunnel."

Avivah asked, "How old was she when she came to you?"

"Only a few days old. She was a foundling, left on our doorstep."

Avivah sat forward. "Do you know the exact date she was abandoned here?"

"February 14, 1922. That's why she took Valentina as her name, after Saint Valentine."

Avivah asked, "Was she the baby with pneumonia? The one Sister Elizabeth Rose healed?"

"Yes. That's why she loves tending sister's grave. The nuns told her she was part of a miracle."

Pepper counted backward nine months. A baby born in February would have been conceived the previous June. The baby's mother would have gone through the last months of her pregnancy in winter, when it would have been easier to hide her growing stomach under layers of winter clothes.

Helen's voice came back to Pepper. "We could ride a horse or a wagon from here to there."

Helen said she and Patience lived on adjoining farms, not far from here. Two good Catholic girls who were friends. Who else would one of them have gone to if she found herself pregnant? Where else, except to this Catholic convent, would they have brought an unwanted newborn? Then both girls came here as maids, one of them to watch her daughter grow up. That tunnel room resembled a parlor, where a mother might sit and read, while her child played. Mother and daughter, playing house. The only question was, who was Valentina's mother, Patience or Helen?

Helen made sure Sister Mary Rachel saw her son before he was whisked away for adoption. The sister said Helen did that for every mother who delivered at the convent. Patience was going to live with her children. Helen was desperate to go with Sister Valentina to the motherhouse.

General Bill said it over and over; if it weren't for Gary Dormuth, the rental deal would never have gone through. The nuns' plans for taking Sister Valentina to their motherhouse had fallen through because Gary pushed through the rental deal on a fast timetable. He had trapped Sister Valentina here without a way out, and made it likely that she would be taken to a nearby nursing home, not to the motherhouse. Gary had taken away the one thing Helen loved.

Pepper remembered Avivah's cut arm. Helen took care of farm animals. "Sister, when there was a farm here, did Helen have anything to do with butchering?"

"Yes, certainly. I know she killed chickens. I believe she helped the hired butcher each fall as well."

A woman with a strong enough stomach to butcher animals would have had a strong enough stomach to use a garrote. Helen might be an older woman, but she had strong hands and forearms. Institutional cooking required lifting and stirring. Pepper stood, her heart pounding wildly in her chest. "Where is Helen right now?"

Sister Angelus also stood. She looked frightened. "I don't know."

They mounted another search. Benny sat this one out, but Rab, Bud, Junior, and even Saul Eisenberg joined in.

They found both of them in the damaged nursery. Helen had pulled a rocking chair into a little space where branches of fallen water-oak formed a natural clearing. Sister Valentina still wore her long white nightgown. Her head was on Helen's lap; her grey hair made a smooth corona around her head. It looked as though Helen had died brushing Sister Valentina's hair. On a table beside them was the open veterinary first aid kit and Thomas' empty medicine bottles. Gelatin capsules from one of the medicines littered the table. The other three medicines had been pills. A pestle sat in a mortar, which held a white residue. There were also an empty syringe and a small Bunsen burner, with a spoon attachment. Pepper had seen one like it in a medi-cal museum. Doctors used it to dissolve powdered medication in water, so the medicine could be injected.

Pepper gripped the top of an iron bed frame. She whispered, "I told Helen everything about how dangerous those medicines would be for Sister Valentina. I killed them. I killed them both."

Avivah took Pepper into her arms. Both women held on to one another for support.

Chapter 27

Sun dropped toward the mountain ridge. In an hour, it would be dark.

Benny and Avivah sat in Bud's truck, waiting for their driver. Pepper had managed, at least temporarily, to control her hysteria and guilt. Later, when she was alone and away from here, she planned to get roaring drunk for a long time. She rested her arms on the window frame, glad that a tarp covered the four body bags in the truck bed.

Avivah said, "I think Helen let Sister Valentina play with the writing desk as a child. You saw how possessive of it sister was. Gary probably either came upon sister taking it from the museum case and tried to stop her, or they found him trying to borrow it to see whether the deed was inside. They struggled, ink spilled, and sister's fingerprints ended up all over his clothes."

Benny added, "Gary might have yelled at sister, or even slapped her, and Helen took him out. Four lives over a piece of furniture."

Pepper said, "It was over a lot more than a piece of furniture. Sister Valentina had been Helen's only life. I suspect she and Patience took the jobs here so she could be close to her baby. Gary had taken away the one thing she had left, going with sister to the motherhouse. A nursing home in Asheville might have accepted sister as a patient, but they would never have allowed Helen to live with her. Helen knew they were going to be separated."

Avivah ran her finger over the window ledge. "Anyone thinking what I'm thinking about that chemical accident thirty years ago?"

Benny asked, "What are you thinking?"

"I want Rab to ask Sister Mary Rachel, Sister Angelus, and Patience a lot more questions about that day, especially if Helen was anywhere near the basement when the accident happened. The timing is just too coincidental."

Pepper said, "You mean because it happened three days after Sister Angelus told Sister Valentina that she would have to leave the convent?"

"Exactly. Helen might have been protecting her, or seeking revenge, even then. She got what she wanted. Sister Valentina was able to stay at this convent."

Benny asked, "You think Helen mixed the chemicals instead of Sister Valentina?"

"Maybe mixed them herself, maybe told Sister Valentina what to do. I guess that's one mystery that won't ever be solved."

Pepper hoped for two unsolved mysteries. She didn't want a forensic examination to be able to tell whether Thomas' death was murder or suicide. "Ron said there was enough doubt whether Helen had killed Thomas or not. In the absence of a suicide note, he will argue for burying Thomas in consecrated ground, with full Catholic ritual. From my experience, Jesuits can be very persuasive arguing a cause."

Avivah handed Pepper the gold coin. "Give this to Ron. He was there when Darby asked me to make sure it went in Thomas' coffin. He'll make sure it happens."

Pepper knew Avivah had managed to avoid Mr. Eisenberg all afternoon. "You coming back here after Benny is admitted to the hospital?"

"No. Rab will take my statement at his office."

Benny said, "Besides, she has to phone Lorraine and explain how come I'm coming home in worse shape from a Catholic men's retreat than I did from a shooting war."

"You're making a mistake not talking to Mr. Eisenberg."

Avivah wouldn't look at her. "It won't be my first mistake, or my last."

Bud came from the convent and opened the truck door. "Say your goodbyes now. I want to get off this mountain before dark. Headlights on this thing aren't all I'd like them to be."

Oh, great, Pepper thought. This truck going off the mountain would be the perfect end to a perfect weekend. She reached in her pocket and handed Benny's lighter back to him.

"Thanks." He put the lighter in his pocket and brought out a set of keys, which he stared at, as if he couldn't remember what they were. He handed them to Pepper. "Good thing I didn't go off with these. Ron will need them to return our rental car."

Pepper looked at the keys, which had a different company logo than the ones Gary had shown her. "I thought Gary had your rental keys."

"No, I've had them since we arrived."

Pepper jiggled the keys. "Then whose keys did Gary have?"

"There are only two rental cars here, ours and General Bill's."

In unison, the three of them turned to look at the tarp covering the bodies.

Avivah said, "Gary was furious about General Bill showing up here. Misplacing the keys to inconvenience the general is something he would have done. It looks like General Bill's rental keys are in Gary's pocket."

Benny asked, "Anyone care to retrieve them?"

No one did.

Bud started the engine and shifted into gear. "That's it, folks, we're leaving."

Pepper watched the truck amble down the road. She cupped her hands around her mouth and yelled. "I'm moving to Asheville. Come and visit me."

Benny stuck his head out the open window. "Send us your new address."

Avivah's head crowded out Benny. He ducked down. "I told Darby he could write to you care of me. I'll forward his letters to you, once I know where to send them."

"Yes. Okay."

Pepper stood and waved until the truck disappeared. She walked around the convent and followed the path to the little clearing Sister Mary Rachel had shown them. Darby stood and waited, like a gentleman, until she was seated.

"Benny and Avivah just left with Bud. Where is everyone else?"

"Father Ron is holding a prayer meeting cum grief-counseling session with Sister Mary Rachel, Sister Angelus, and Patience."

"Rab allowed them to get together like that? Isn't he afraid they'll collaborate on a story?"

"He and Junior are sitting in. Might do a couple of good old Baptist boys some good to hear Catholic praying."

"Where is General Bill?"

"Explaining to that Eisenberg fellow how he barely knew Dr. Saint-Mathias and had no idea he was dealing in illegal arms."

"I feel sorry for him."

"General Bill?"

"Yeah. He arrived with a perfectly good plan: fire Gary, keep his plans for an artillery range secret, and move in here in three weeks. Now he's lost control of money he hoped to get from Thomas, he's got a board member up on charges for illegal arms sales, the convent he's rented is in shambles, and I suspect he won't be able to find his rental car keys."

Darby put his arm around her. "No plan survives contact

with the enemy."

She snuggled against him. "Carl von Clausewitz, 1780 to 1830."

He kissed the top of her head. "Very good."

The sun dipped lower. Miles of cloud banks came alive with purple and gold streaks. "You and Thomas were related, weren't you?"

"Half-first cousins, once removed."

Pepper wrinkled her brow, and gave up trying to figure out intergenerational relationships.

"Lucas Hackmann married twice. His only child from his first marriage is my grandmother, Nana Kate. His only son from his second marriage is Thomas' father."

"Does that mean you inherit the convent?"

"Ermengarde Hackmann's will specifies direct male descent. I descend through female connections."

Darby took an old, cracked leather folder from his jacket pocket. He held it so Pepper could see a photograph of a young man, in a Confederate officer's uniform, standing in front of a white tent. In firelight or on a mist-covered field it would be easy to see that this man and Darby were related.

Pepper asked, "Who was he?"

"Darby Randolph Mahoney. My great-great-grandfather."

"You're named after him!"

"I am."

He turned the photo holder around. The companion photograph was of a tall, young woman, in a black dress, with her blond hair tied up in severe braids over her ears. Her eyes held the same expression of fatigue and satisfaction Pepper had seen too often in her bathroom mirror in Qui Nhon. Pepper noticed the same tent as in the previous photo.

"This is his wife, Suzanne Hackmann Mahoney."

Pepper was stunned. "They were Lucas Hackmann's mother and father!"

"To be precise, Lucas Darby Hackmann's mother and father."

"Wait a minute, you're related to Lucas through both your grandmother and your great-great grandfather?"

"Not exactly, but I am related to Darby and to the woman he would have married if he hadn't gone for a soldier and met Suzanne." He grinned. "Under different circumstances, I could have been my own cousin."

Pepper's head hurt. Only in the South, she thought. "How long have you known this?"

"Since Dr. Saint-Mathias first advertised. That's when Nana Kate told me her secret. She was adopted from this convent. When Lucas' first wife died, he brought his infant daughter to the nuns who raised him. She wanted me to find out what Dr. Saint-Mathias was really up to."

"What happened when you found out?"

"When I gave her a report on General Bill and the Saratoga Patriotic Foundation, she was horrified. 'Stop that man before he brings dishonor on my father's name.' Of course, for full effect, I'd pound with a heavy oak cane between every word. I barely escaped with ten toes intact."

Pepper took the photo case from him. "Where were these photographs taken?"

"Somewhere with the Army of Northern Virginia. When Dr. Saint-Mathias was carrying on about Lucas Hackmann never going to war, did it once occur to you that his sister might have gone instead?"

Pepper felt incredibly embarrassed. "Never."

Darby shook his head. "Tut, tut, tut. And you being an Army nurse and all."

"It's just I never . . . I mean women didn't . . . I mean I have read about women who did, but . . . "

"But you never imagined that Suzanne Hackmann was one of those women."

"Was it that old story of dressing up like a boy?"

"No, it was much more clever. At the beginning of the war—long before she met Darby—she posed as a married woman, traveling with her servant, to join her husband. When she finally found what became the Army of Northern Virginia, she stayed with them."

"She was a camp follower?"

"That's what most people called them. For almost four years she endured the same hardships as the men. She foraged for food, cooked it, washed and mended clothes, nursed the sick and wounded."

"And was likely a prostitute."

"Darby Mahoney didn't think that. His entries about her in his journals—there were many—refer to her, with utmost respect, as his friend."

"So a southern gentleman never tells, even in his diary?"

"If they were lovers, they were either lucky or careful. She didn't get pregnant until after they were married. Why does she have to be his mistress? Weren't you ever just good friends with guys in Qui Nhon?"

It was all Pepper could do to keep from blurting out about Avivah not having made any friends. "I was lucky. I had many friends."

"When she got pregnant, Darby convinced her to come back here. When she reached home, she found her father and brother dead, her mother embittered. Darby died a few weeks after they married. I never knew, until today, if Suzanne received word that he had died before she did."

"Did she?"

"Not according to Sister Elizabeth Rose's diary, but sister

wrote that Suzanne never lost hope that he would come for her."

"Then she died in childbirth. How sad."

"She didn't die in childbirth, Pepper. Ermengarde Hackmann smothered her, and would have smothered the child, too, if Sister Elizabeth Rose hadn't arrived and intervened."

What he told her took her breath away. "What?"

"Ermengarde Hackmann saw her daughter as a disease-ridden prostitute who'd spent four years with soldiers, and as the person responsible for her own son's death."

"What did Suzanne have to do with her brother's death?"

Darby took a piece of paper out of his pocket. He squinted at it in fading light. "Sister Angelus promised to send me a copy of sister's entire diary, but I copied down this one entry."

September 9, 1865. I visited Horace Teague, and I don't know now if I am happy or sad that it was as Ermengarde Hackmann described to me. Teague and his companions didn't pick a fight with Lucas Hackmann over his refusal to serve. They had been with the Army of Northern Virginia and knew Suzanne Hackmann. When they told him his sister was alive, and what she had become, Lucas became enraged. He pulled a knife, and the proprietor threw them out. It was not Teague who waylaid Lucas going home, but the other way around. Lucas tried to kill them to protect his sister's honor. Teague fought to defend himself and Lucas Hackmann died.

Darby took the photo holder back from Pepper, placed the paper inside, and carefully returned it to his pocket. "That's why Sister Elizabeth Rose burned the convent's deed instead of registering it. She considered the gift of the convent blood money, a bribe to keep quiet about knowing that Ermengarde Hackmann killed her own daughter because Suzanne was a woman had gone to war."

The sun reached the mountain ridge. There were only a few more minutes of daylight left.

Pepper asked, "Is tending wounded soldiers noble and pure?"

Darby considered. "I'll try to answer that question, if you answer one for me. What were the rumors about me at Medical Field Service School? I tried to get a handle on them, but they always shifted, like sand."

"It was just idle talk."

"How would you like idle talk behind your back?"

"I wouldn't . . . One version was that nurses saved your life, and you wanted to repay them. One was that you'd screwed up so badly in Vietnam that you were sent to Fort Sam to learn a little humility. Most days, opinions ran about three-to-one if you'd actually been court-martialed."

Darkness gathered behind his eyes.

Pepper's heart raced. "Oh, my God, you were court-martialed, weren't you?"

"I was a hotshot major—first one from my West Point class to make the promotion list for lieutenant colonel—and I thought rules didn't apply to me. I did something stupid. Fortunately, before I caused irreparable damage, I ended up bleeding all over a helicopter. Next thing I knew an Army nurse bent over me. I looked in her eyes and said, 'I'm dying, aren't I?'"

He chuckled. "She said, 'If you stop thrashing around on this stretcher and cooperate, I'll see what I can do.' Neither of us believed I had a chance, but I figured what the hell, I was on my way out anyway, so why not do what she said? She helped me beat the odds. Six months later, I was on the carpet, at Fort Bragg, in front of a livid Special Forces general."

Details flooded her. A dirty hand in hers. How odors of hot, crushed grass and blood complimented one another. The odd crystal color of one patient's eyes. How the whole world could squeeze down to two people, engulfed in a cocoon of tradition, patriotism, honor, and courage. Pepper admitted to herself that to have been a part of such a bindingly humbling experience took her breath away. She understood now why Darby would never give up the military for anyone, even her.

"Special Forces generals are a lot like parents of teenagers. As soon as they know you haven't killed yourself, they plan to ground you for life. I traded two years teaching at Medical Field Service School to keep my beret."

"Do you know her name?"

"The nurse in that emergency room? No."

"You never tried to find her?"

"What for? For a couple of hours on December 15, 1968, we were as intimate as two people can be with their clothes on . . . well, she had *her* clothes on. That's what I want to remember. Why? Do you think I should get in touch with her?"

"She might like to know you made it." In her heart she knew Darby was right to leave those two hours untouched.

He took a square, blue-velvet box out of his pants pocket. Pepper put her hand over it. "Please don't."

"It's not what you think." He opened it. The setting sun sparkled on a golden eagle, insignia of a full colonel.

Pepper managed, "What? You're just going to skip lieutenant colonel and go straight to full bird?"

"I've got an assignment where the Army thinks an eagle's clout would help. It's a brevet appointment, temporary only, but who knows, if I behave myself, they might let me keep it."

"When were you promoted?"

"Eight days ago. My general pinned one shoulder. You know the tradition about the other shoulder?"

"The most important woman in your life pins your new rank there."

He fell back into his heavy Georgia accent. "I'd be mighty

grateful, pretty lady, if you'd finish up that ceremony."

She looked across at the seemingly unending layers of mountains. "Here?"

"Right here, right now."

"It would be my honor, sir."

Darby stood and hit a brace: head erect, eyes straight ahead, back stiff, arms at his side with his thumbs precisely aligned with his pants seam. Counting Georgia Military Academy and West Point; he'd been standing at attention half his life. No matter how much Pepper wished otherwise she couldn't ask him to walk away from what he'd worked so hard to achieve. She pinned the eagle carefully on his left shoulder, then stepped back and gave him her best military salute, which he returned.

"Congratulations, Colonel Baxter. Well deserved. If you dishonor this insignia, you'll have me to answer to."

He took her in his arms and kissed her with the same fervor she'd kissed him earlier that morning. Now that there were no nuns to censure them, Pepper returned his kiss with even more fervor. He moaned. "You drive me crazy. Why now, when I'll be gone for months?"

Pepper thought of Gary and Avivah. There were still all those empty bedrooms "We still have tonight."

"No we don't. I'm already a day late for my assignment. At least with the phone working, I reported in, so I won't be charged with being AWOL, but I really, really have to leave, just as soon as Junior can use the sheriff's car to drive me to pick up a rental car."

"Where are you going?"

He pursed his lips, and Pepper sighed. "I figured it would be like that. Avivah told me you two made arrangements. Write to me. If you feel like it, write to her. She can use all the friends she can get."

"Want to tell me what's going on with her?"

"I can't. Not now, not ever."

His eyes grew dark and smokey. "Whatever it is, it's not going to be easy for her."

"It's not going to be easy for any of us. Benny doesn't want to live in the same town as his parents any more. I don't know what that's going to do to his relationship with Lorraine. I have no idea how to be a civilian again, only that I have to try. Avivah is burdened with a shitload of stuff that's going to come crashing down around her one day soon. All any of us have going for us is to keep moving and hope for the best."

The sun set. Darby said into the darkness. "Amen, pretty lady. Amen."

ABOUT THE AUTHOR

Sharon Wildwind was born and raised in Louisiana. She served in the U.S. Army Nurse Corps from 1968 to 1972 and was stationed in Vietnam in 1970–1971.

In the first ten days after she left the Army she moved across North Carolina, interviewed for a job, drove to Louisiana, got married, and drove back to North Carolina, arriving late one night. She started her new job at 6:45 the next morning. She doesn't recommend this to anyone.

Sharon is now a Certified Gerontological Nurse. She is married to a military historian.

First Murder in Advent is the second in a planned five-book series, which features her three veterans as heroes and detectives. For them, adjusting to civilian life is murder.

She is currently at work on the third book in the series.